A. A. Dhand was raised in Bradford and spent his youth observing the city from behind the counter of a small convenience store. After qualifying as a pharmacist, he worked in London and travelled extensively before returning to Bradford to start his own business and begin writing. The history, diversity and darkness of the city have inspired his Harry Virdee novels.

For more information on A. A. Dhand, see his website at aadhand.com

'Outstanding – relentless, multi-layered suspense and real human drama make this a crime debut to relish'
Lee Child

'A tense slice of neo-noir that has won Dhand comparisons to both BBC drama *Luther* and HBO's *The Wire*'
Observer

'A sombre, gritty race through the unsettling underbelly of the city . . . compelling and unflinching'
Yorkshire Post

'This up-to-the-minute debut is a scorching story of a city divided . . . Written with pace and precision, it gives us a character destined for television but also announces the arrival of a formidable crime writer'
Daily Mail

www.penguin.co.uk

STREETS OF DARKNESS

A. A. Dhand

CORGI BOOKS

TRANSWORLD PUBLISHERS
61–63 Uxbridge Road, London W5 5SA
www.penguin.co.uk

Transworld is part of the Penguin Random House group of companies
whose addresses can be found at global.penguinrandomhouse.com

Penguin
Random House
UK

First published in Great Britain in 2016 by Bantam Press
an imprint of Transworld Publishers
Corgi edition published 2017

A CIP catalogue record for this book
is available from the British Library.

ISBN
9780552172783

Typeset in 11.25/14.75pt Aldus by Falcon Oast Graphic Art Ltd.
Printed and bound by Clays Ltd, Bungay, Suffolk.

Penguin Random House is committed to a sustainable
future for our business, our readers and our planet. This book is made from
Forest Stewardship Council® certified paper.

MIX
Paper from
responsible sources
FSC® C018179

1 3 5 7 9 10 8 6 4 2

For my family

ONE

BLOOD.

Arterial spray haemorrhaged across Harry's face.

He wondered if his karma was tainted.

When you accept a new life into the world, it will be without consequence as long as your karma is clean.

Perhaps it was because Saima was overdue. Or perhaps being suspended from duty meant he had more time to relive a past which refused to stay buried.

It was something the damn peer-saab had said to Saima the day before which was needling Harry. She had invited the holy man, an Islamic preacher who claimed he could predict the future, to their house to make sure her pregnancy was without issue.

Saima loved that shit.

Harry looked at his hands. He could still see the blood. You got away with murder, he thought, remembering the last scream of his victim.

The air was heavy with moisture, a result of three days of torrential downpours. The sun wouldn't cast its rays across Bradford – not unusual for October – but even in summer, it shied away, ensuring the bleakness that had strangled the city for over a decade remained firmly in place.

He ran harder through Lister Park, keeping off the grass which glistened with overnight dew. It was only five thirty but Harry hadn't been able to sleep.

How could you be so reckless?

When he couldn't sleep, he ran, trying to tire his body into relenting. Harry preferred running in darkness: the park trapping shadows between the branches of hundreds of ageing oak trees. Saima thought it was dangerous. But Harry was six-three, ninety kilos of mostly muscle and spent his Sundays bulldozing rugby players as a second-row forward.

Harry slowed in front of the castellated gatehouse at the north-east corner of the park and arrived at the Norman Arch exit. It had a medieval-looking gate. He placed his hands on it and rested his head against the iron. From the other side it might have appeared he was in jail. The image was fitting. Detective Inspector Harry Virdee suspended from work – IPCC investigation.

What a fucking joke.

His temperament was the problem. Always had been. Harry was tired of playing nice.

Especially in this city.

Especially with the choices he'd made.

Remember the blood, Harry? It's always about the blood.

He turned around and faced the hill which led up to the boating lake. He took a moment, glanced at the statue of Sir Titus Salt on his left and wondered what Bradford's most famous son would have made of the city now. In the 1800s, Titus had built the largest wool empire in Europe and made Bradford one of the richest cities in the world. Salt had created the entire suburb of Saltaire and built a village for his employees, complete with one of the most advanced wool mills ever seen.

Those times were gone. Bradford was a relic, its glory days past, suffocated by mass unemployment caused by the collapse of the textile industries. Salt's only legacy was a few books in the library and the dirty-white statue Harry was staring at. It had been moved from the entrance of the Town Hall to this corner of the park.

A forgotten legacy for a forgotten city.

Harry hit the incline hard, sprinting past Salt's statue. Grimacing against the pain, he blew out hot, stale air and tried not to close his eyes. He focused on the one memory which sat most uncomfortably in his mind. He recalled the wide-eyed horror of his victim and the flash of steel as Harry had hammered a pair of scissors into the man's neck.

The final image of his victim's eyes rolling lifelessly away before his body folded to the floor got Harry across the finish line.

Tonight Lister Park would be the setting for the start of

the largest Asian Mela in England. The three-day event was returning after an absence of several years. Last year it had been in City Park in the town centre as a celebration of the new Centenary Square. There had been a live, televised stage show of *Bollywood Carmen*. It had been one of the largest-scale events to be held in the city.

This year Bradford Council had decided to return the event to Lister Park. They had good reason; today was also the Islamic festival of Eid and the turnout was going to be a record-breaker. Five thousand at least.

Harry was bringing Saima in the evening for some low-quality Asian food and to enjoy the bazaar-like atmosphere. She loved everything Asian.

Like Harry, Saima was trapped in a nightmarish world where she had crossed a religious divide by marrying outside of her faith. But whereas Harry had never been religious, Saima clung desperately to her Muslim identity. They had both been cast out by their families, an experience which was still raw. Harry was from an orthodox Sikh family and Saima from a strict Muslim household.

What had started as a taboo affair had evolved ultimately into a choice: their families or each other? Most days Harry reminded Saima that history was full of couples who had persevered, even when those close by disintegrated. She said she blamed him, his persistence in asking her out after a stint in A & E. Harry had split his head open during a scuffle with an assailant. Saima had stitched the wound and eventually agreed to dinner.

A few soft dates had turned into endless nights in bed,

and finally an obsessive relationship had resulted in a marriage which cost them their families. Sikhs and Muslims were not supposed to mix. Harry routinely teased Saima that her bedside manner, whilst she had stitched his wound, was to blame. The pause which had held his eyes, the alluring scent of her skin, and the way she'd whispered seductively in his ear.

Harry trailed his feet against the gravel as he approached the exit, feeling the burn in his thighs subsiding. Saima didn't know Harry had been suspended. She was a week overdue with their first child and he didn't want to burden her. She would be tormented by worry about the consequences of Harry losing his job – money, stability and, moreover, what it meant for their future. It was on his mind too; Harry's head was bursting with questions he didn't have answers to. He realized how his file would read.

And this time?

This time, the IPCC would burn him.

He was a civilian, Harry. You nearly killed a civilian.

'Fuck,' he whispered.

A goddamn civilian.

Bastard deserved it. Sometimes the law didn't cut it. Son of a bitch is lucky I didn't . . .

The blood.

There it was again: surfacing in his mind like a clandestine tumour.

Harry clenched his fist and pressed it against his temple. His knuckle was sharp against the skin.

There's nothing you can do.

It wasn't true. There was one man who could have helped: Harry's father.

I'm not asking him. I'll die before I return there.

The Norman Arch took him out of the park on to Keighley Road, opposite Bradford Grammar, the most prestigious school in the city. It was a place Harry hoped his child might go to one day. But it would be impossible if he didn't have a job. Saima was an A & E sister and, even if she went back to work full-time, they wouldn't be able to afford an extravagance like private education. It was something Harry had experienced, and something he wanted to offer his own child.

He unlocked his ageing BMW – the black paint was smeared in dirt so thick, it almost looked grey – but he didn't get in. The sight of a skulk of foxes running across the road into the grounds of the grammar school caught his attention. It wasn't especially uncommon at this early hour. The sun was yet to break and the roads were deserted. Commuter rush hour was at least two hours away. But there was something in the frenzied way they were moving – like a hunt.

Harry locked his car. He hadn't much else to do except make another bullshit excuse to Saima about why he wasn't at work. He crossed the road and climbed the shallow wall, into the enormous school grounds. Straight ahead was the main building.

The grass was treacherous to walk on. It hadn't been cut recently and was ankle high. His feet felt as though they were skating. It wasn't long before icy saturation worked through his trainers, soaked his socks and assaulted his toes.

Harry had tracked the foxes to a wide, triple-fronted sandstone building when the security lights came on. For a moment he stopped breathing.

The foxes were on their back legs, scrabbling up a wall, straining to get their teeth into a dangling pair of feet.

Harry let out his breath slowly. He clapped his hands together loudly and the animals ran, without turning to look at him.

Harry took tentative steps to his left so he was in front of the body. He focused on the wall.

The naked corpse of an older male was suspended, crudely crucified, three feet above the ground. There were rods through his outstretched wrists and his feet were not positioned traditionally but spread wide like da Vinci's Vitruvian Man.

Harry moved closer, mindful not to disturb the scene. He glanced behind and then to all four corners and was satisfied he was alone.

He crouched down and stared up at the face of the man. There wasn't enough light, so he took out his iPhone and turned on the torch. He held it high and, for a moment, couldn't quite believe his eyes.

There were words scrawled in blood on the wall next to the body: *Christ died for our sins; he died for his.*

But that wasn't the real cause of Harry's panic. The man's identity was unmistakable. The most powerful

Asian man in the city was staring lifelessly at him. There was a swastika brutally carved in the middle of his chest, blood still glistening.

Harry got to his feet and hurriedly dialled the third number in his recent call history.

Bradford, so often on the precipice, was suddenly primed to fall.

TWO

NINETY MINUTES SINCE HARRY had discovered the body and Bradford Grammar was heaving with members of HMET, the Homicide and Major Enquiry Team. On any other day he'd be with them. Not today though: today he was an outcast. A witness at best.

His close colleagues were courteous, some engaging in banter. But others, the more senior members? They knew. They knew he was done. He wouldn't be returning to work.

He had been a boss they all looked up to, but a boss who, this time, had bent the rules so far they had boomeranged and returned to hit him on the arse.

It was half past seven when his own boss, Detective Superintendent George Simpson, arrived at the melee. He made his way past the SOCOs, detectives, forensics and uniforms to the hastily erected tent in front of the body. Harry hung back, away from the drama, spinning

15

his mobile phone incessantly in his hands. It was excruciating not to be involved, not to be the senior investigating officer and organizing the scene. He was on the other side now and it felt like hostile territory. Awkward smiles, a few nods his way and plenty of questions from those who didn't know why he had been suspended. As they were discreetly updated, their mouths dropped open and they glanced clumsily his way.

Harry Virdee: story of the week.

But most of HMET were focused on the crime scene, because this was no ordinary murder.

Simpson spent half an hour checking details and liaising with officers before slowly making his way over to Harry, gait more laboured than usual, the cold stoking his arthritis.

George Simpson: five days from retirement with the mother of all crises on his hands. He looked forlorn and tired – more tired than Harry had ever witnessed. Simpson didn't just want retirement, he needed it. Bradford would do that to you.

He was cautious with his approach; the grass had already put three SOCOs on their backsides. Simpson's gold Rolex glimmered in the morning gloom as he drew nearer. 'Harry.'

'Sir.'

'Can't keep you out of mischief, can we?'

Harry shrugged.

'What are you doing out here at six thirty?'

It wasn't an accusation. Just interest.

'Running,' replied Harry. 'Couldn't sleep. Not much else to do.'

Simpson nodded. It was awkward. The last conversation they'd shared had been heated, the suspension a foregone conclusion, the barrage of abuse he'd thrown at Harry warranted.

'You want to reinstate me? Help you clear this mess up?'

Simpson patted him on the shoulder. 'Let's walk a little, Harry. Away from here.'

They moved from the overloaded crime scene, back towards Lister Park. The sun had started its laboured ascent but the park was still sombre. The exterior of the Norman Arch had an obscenely yellow banner advertising the Mela, starting at eight o'clock that evening with a concert featuring 'Techno-Singh'. Pretty tacky and not really to Harry's taste, but the Mela would end on Sunday with a superb headline act: Feroz Khan, the world-renowned ghazal singer. He was a favourite of Harry's father, who would most certainly be attending. For that reason, much as he would have enjoyed it, Harry would be giving it a miss.

Their last meeting had drawn blood and Harry didn't want a repeat.

'There,' said Simpson, pointing past the statue of Sir Titus Salt. 'Up there.'

They headed up the hill where Harry had finished his run. Now they were hidden from Bradford Grammar,

Harry gently took hold of Simpson's arm and supported him up the steep incline. His boss was in the early stages of Parkinson's disease and Harry was one of only three senior officers who knew. Simpson didn't protest and they walked in an eerie silence past the boating lake towards Cartwright Hall into the Mughal Gardens.

'Like a different world, isn't it?' said Simpson, pointing at the flowers.

The garden had been designed to reflect the Asian cultural heritage of Bradford. Mughal architecture was a synergy between Islamic and Hindu designs and reflected the diverse ethnic mix of the city. A million pounds had been granted by the Heritage Lottery fund and the result was breathtaking.

There were beds of pink, red and yellow geraniums with a border of ferns protecting them. The flowers were guarded by a bronze statue of the Greek goddess of hunting, Diana. There was a natural tranquillity to the Mughal Gardens, usually complemented by the soft trickle of water from an adjacent fountain, which today had iced over.

'Agreed,' replied Harry. 'I'm always amazed this place hasn't been vandalized.'

'Always the cynic,' replied Simpson.

They were standing in the archway of Cartwright Hall, in front of the flowers. Harry pointed back towards Bradford Grammar. 'Try telling that to Shakeel Ahmed.'

Simpson fell silent. Harry knew he was plagued by the violence in the city. Bradford was in the grip of an endemic drug problem which the police couldn't contain. It was now one of the most drug-fuelled cities in England with homicides on the rise.

'I'm not seeing things. Right? It was him?'

Simpson nodded. He scanned the entrance of the listed building and motioned for Harry to move away from the CCTV cameras, into the gardens, towards the water.

They walked past the statue of Diana and followed the path descending to a paved area. The fountain was dormant and the pond frozen.

'You want to tell me what this is about?' asked Harry.

Simpson pointed to a bench. An hour before, Harry had been sweating in the park but now the bitter chill was slicing through his clothing. They took a seat and Simpson turned towards Harry, his face tired and weary. 'Gotham City's on edge, Harry.'

'Jesus – not you as well?'

'It's true,' answered Simpson. 'I can't deny the comparisons any more.'

'That article was a joke. The only similarity between Gotham and Bradford is that we have a city full of dark knights and more than our fair share of jokers.'

Simpson grunted at the soft attempt at humour. 'PC as ever,' he replied. 'How I wish that were true.'

'You want to tell me how a guy who won the Bradford West by-election last night ended up crucified on that wall?'

Simpson took another cautious look around. But they were alone and well concealed from prying eyes.

'Ahmed was reported missing just after midnight. He left the victory party early; tired, we assume, from celebrating. When his son arrived at his father's residence he found signs of a break-in. Front door was smashed. Signs of a struggle in the kitchen.' He paused and then added: 'Blood.'

Shakeel Ahmed might not have been the new Titus Salt but he was a hugely influential businessman who had tried to reverse Bradford's decline. In the city's heyday the population had dramatically increased, with hundreds of textile mills providing thousands of jobs. That industry was now dead. The factories were closed. The city's fortunes had taken an unprecedented fall and unemployment was at a record high. Thousands of immigrants, welcomed into Bradford to work in the sixties, had found themselves without prospects when the trade collapsed, unable to educate themselves or find alternative jobs. Bradford crumbled into a bleakness from which it couldn't recover.

Ahmed was a first-generation immigrant who had left the textile mills and started a small takeaway. Now, it was a chain of eleven restaurants. 'Ahmed's' routinely won Bradford's 'Indian restaurant of the year', which was no mean feat – there were hundreds of them in the city. Ahmed had also been given an MBE in 2008 for services to Yorkshire. He had built three mosques, owned several charitable foundations and had recently funded a new wing at Bradford Royal Infirmary.

'How long before Forensics get any data? Have we ruled out the son?'

Simpson ran a wrinkled hand through grey hair and sighed. His watch sparkled again before disappearing beneath his raincoat.

'You already know who it is, don't you?' said Harry, leaning closer to his boss.

'Yes,' he replied.

There was something troubling Simpson. He was hesitating, grimacing at the question he knew was coming next.

'Who?'

'Before I answer, Harry, I need something from you,' replied Simpson.

'I'm listening.' Harry's breath formed a white mist in the air.

'I need your assistance.'

'Can you help me with next week?' replied Harry, almost too eagerly.

Simpson shook his head. 'What happened is on you, Harry, and you alone. There isn't a damn thing I can do.' He paused and then added, 'There is, however, something you can do to "help" your case.'

'I'm all ears.'

'I need you to operate off the books on this one. You're in enough trouble as it is, so I'll understand if you refuse.'

'I'm not sure what you're—'

'You will.' Simpson held out his hand to silence Harry. 'In all the years I've known you, I've never asked you how you solved so many cases. Nobody has your success rate.'

Harry felt an unease prickling through his body. Simpson's tone was tinged with ambiguity.

'But I also know . . .' He paused, poking Harry gently in the chest and waiting until he met his gaze. '. . . that no one achieves those kinds of results without *help*.'

'Meaning?' Harry blurted out before he could stop. He didn't want to pursue this conversation.

'Meaning that I've always taken a back seat when it came to exploring where or how you got your information. You seem to have every convict in Bradford in your pocket and I don't know how you've managed it. Truth be told, I never much cared because as long as the cases were brought to a satisfactory conclusion, my job was done.'

'I keep my ear to the ground,' said Harry. 'That's all.'

'No, Harry. We all do that. Hell, I've got detectives with twenty years more experience and far more brains who can't deliver what you do.'

'They don't work hard enough.'

Simpson shook his head. 'That's not fair, Harry. They work hard. But no one works like you. No one needs to. You punish yourself. It's the perpetual need to prove something. Look, we're getting off the point here.'

A couple of blackbirds hopped on to the fountain. They lowered their beaks cautiously to the surface.

'Hardeep—'

'Harry,' he corrected. 'I'm not in trouble. Why don't you just cut to the chase, sir? What *is it* that you want?'

'I need your help. Off the books. You know the streets

better than anyone. I need you to find Shakeel Ahmed's killer.'

'And that is who exactly?'

'First I need your word this won't go—'

'Jesus,' said Harry impatiently. 'As if you even have to say it?'

'I do. Right now, I need to hear it. Because when I tell you what I know – you'll understand. I need to contain this for as long as I can. So I need your utmost discretion.'

'You have it,' replied Harry. 'In spite of my current predicament, you still have my loyalty. So, who am I tracking?'

'I'm asking you because you seem to enjoy working outside the constraints of the law which the rest of us abide by. And today I'm asking you to do whatever it takes to find me Lucas Dwight.'

Harry stared at Simpson, momentarily lost for words. The blackbirds stopped pecking at the ice and fixed their jet-black eyes on the men.

'What?' whispered Harry, as if saying the name out loud might trigger a curse.

'His DNA was found at Shakeel Ahmed's house. We got a match a few hours ago,' said Simpson.

'He's – he's . . . in jail?'

'No,' replied Simpson solemnly, 'he's not. He was released four days ago.'

THREE

LUCAS DWIGHT WAS ALONE in the one place no one could bother him. In the fourteen years he had been in prison, some things had changed dramatically. He couldn't buy two pints of milk with a quid. He couldn't even spend his last nugget on a lottery ticket. Two quid for a flutter?

But some things hadn't changed. Bradford was still a shit-hole. In fact, it was the same shit-hole it had been when he'd been jailed. The centre might have had a posh new shopping centre but it was still a ghost town. Even the charity shops had closed down; seemed even philanthropy had deserted Bradford.

Lucas was standing in the middle of the gymnasium floor. The boxing gym had closed in 1991 and was the only thing Lucas owned that he hadn't lost yet. It had been passed on to him by his grandfather, a well-respected boxer back in the forties. The building was derelict, like all of its neighbours. It was smack in the centre of

Bradford, engulfed between huge construction boards.

He wasn't sure quite why he'd hung on to it.

Perhaps because it represented the happiest times in his life – being taught by the man who had raised him. Lucas had boxed his first professional fight in the ring. Third-round knockout. He could still remember the adrenaline rush of that first victory.

There were twenty punch-bags ghosting around the gymnasium. They comforted Lucas, like old friends. He corrected his stance in front of one and raised his back foot so he was on his toes. Lucas whipped a brutish right hook into the bag. The sound lifted his spirits and echoed around the gym.

Great shot that, young Lucas – near damn exploded that nigger's liver!

Lucas swallowed a lump in his throat. He'd spent years honing that liver punch, and won six out of his first ten fights with the devastating blow, bringing his opponents to their knees and counting to ten with the referee.

Good times.

His grandfather had died in this very ring. He had been sparring with Lucas when he'd suddenly dropped his hands. His face had become clammy and pale. So terribly pale. Lucas hadn't thrown the punch. He'd known instantly something was wrong. His grandfather had collapsed and died from a massive heart attack.

Lucas brought the punch-bag close to his face and held it there. Lost in memories, inhaling the smell of sweat and leather.

25

He let the bag go and walked towards a cracked mirror behind him, staring at his reflection with jaundiced eyes. Lucas was woefully thin but, whilst he might not have packed the same power, he still had the speed and precision of a boxer.

'Double-jab, dip, uppercut,' he whispered and began to shadow-box, ducking and weaving from his reflection, trying to warm up and repel the bitter cold. He was pleased at the speed with which he was able to move. His punches retained the fluidity of a professional.

At one time, he had been the most dangerous man in Bradford; he'd been the leader of the BNP. He had bathed in more blood than water.

But no more.

Fourteen years in a hell-hole prison changed a person.

Lucas stopped boxing and took a quick nervous glance around the deserted floor, then raised his shirt. He focused on a freshly etched tattoo, the outline still crusted with blood, and ran his hand across it. He couldn't quite believe he had done it. Nobody would ever understand – but he didn't need them to. It was a sign of change and, as such, it comforted Lucas.

He leaned forward and spread his hands on the mirror, resting his face against it. 'I'm sorry, Granddad,' he whispered and walked away, back towards the boxing ring. 'Try to understand.'

He climbed on to the canvas and from his pocket removed the white powder he'd spent his money on. Fourteen years might have passed, but his usual dealer was still in business and had given him a freebie. A welcome-home gift.

Prison had changed Lucas. But not his addiction. The perpetual need for a hit.

The methadone programme Lucas was enrolled on wasn't working. Shit, thirty millilitres a day was for amateurs. His doctor had said she would increase his dose steadily according to his need. Lucas couldn't wait.

Twenty minutes later, Lucas was ready. He needed to make his stash last five days, just until his benefits cleared. The last pound in his pocket would buy a loaf of cheap bread. Thankfully the taps in the gym still provided water, so for now Lucas had his five-day plan organized. Not that his plans ever carried through. Yesterday he'd been so high he couldn't even remember what he'd done. Or where he'd been. He'd smoked a week's worth of marijuana in a single day.

This time he was going to make the drugs last. He'd got the heroin that afternoon and was relieved he hadn't used yet. His dealer had been desperate for Lucas to shoot up with him, got aggressive when he'd refused. But Lucas liked to get high alone, to forget in solitude. His days of communal shoot-ups were over. Besides, he had to make this last. Lucas was going to inject a fraction of what he was used to, just enough to take the edge off so he would fall asleep in the middle of the boxing ring. It would make another day pass and bring his benefits that bit closer.

Lucas prepared the syringe and slid the needle into a

pulsing vein in his arm. Then he lay down and looked at the wooden beams running across the roof. Dust flickered across the lights like the fall of snowflakes.

The euphoria never materialized.

Something was wrong.

When his airways seized, he knew – he just bloody knew.

This wasn't what he'd ordered.

Whatever Lucas had injected had rendered him barely able to move. He managed to roll on to his side so if he vomited, he wouldn't choke.

As the world started to fade and convulsions racked his body, Lucas saw images of his grandfather's body hitting the canvas. He heard the false echoes of someone screaming and saw his grandfather's eyes widen in pain before they fixed for ever.

FOUR

'LUCAS DWIGHT – *THE* Lucas Dwight?' Harry asked. 'You're shitting me?'

Simpson tensed the muscles on the side of his face and nodded. 'Same guy. Same problems.'

'Jesus wept, sir.'

'You see where I'm sitting now?'

'Are you sure?' Harry was struggling to believe the revelation.

'Not the kind of development I wouldn't have checked. The blood found at Shakeel Ahmed's house has been run twice. It's Lucas Dwight's.'

Harry got off the bench and made his way over to the fountain. The blackbirds flew away as he approached. He placed a hand on the ice and left it to turn numb. Then he ran it across his face. *Lucas Dwight.*

The man had nearly burned the city to the ground. A crazy fascist who was as deadly with his mind as with his fists. Harry had arrested him fourteen years earlier, after the Bradford riots. He still had mental scars from what it had taken to apprehend him.

'It doesn't make sense,' replied Harry quietly. He didn't turn to face his boss and put his hand back on the ice. 'How did he even get to Ahmed's front door? How could he get that close? Hasn't Ahmed got security gates? CCTV? An intercom?'

'No. Surprisingly, Ahmed lived in relative modesty. He was a man of the people. Being hidden away in a mansion didn't suit his image.'

'So there was no security at his house?'

'Gates. Easy enough to get over. No CCTV.'

Harry shook his head. 'Lucas fucking Dwight,' he whispered.

'Can you see his play?'

Harry stared around the park, then back towards the crime scene and nodded. 'We've got the biggest Asian festival in England tonight. It's Eid, and Bradford just elected its first Muslim MP. The ex-leader of the BNP just crucified Bradford's favourite son, so all in all, I'd say . . .' Harry turned to his boss. 'That we've got a big fucking problem on our hands.'

'Agreed,' Simpson said. 'Five days from retirement and this shit hits the fan. I won't leave this city in a mess, Harry. I won't let all the hard work I've done be pissed away by some vicious prick like Lucas Dwight.'

He swore so infrequently that Harry was momentarily surprised.

'As you'd expect I've got every officer at my disposal on this. And I mean *every* officer. But,' Simpson added, staring at Harry, 'I don't have my best.'

Harry sighed. 'There's not much I can do from where I am.'

'You're wrong. It's because of where you are that you can be of most use.'

'I don't follow.'

'You need me to spell it out?'

'Actually, this time, sir, I do. I need you to tell me exactly what you're thinking.'

Simpson let out a sigh which expressed a burden Harry was familiar with. The pressure of Bradford. Of carrying expectation and the fear of falling short.

'You were not designed to be in law enforcement,' Simpson said abruptly. It caught Harry off guard.

'I'm sorry?'

'I'm going to speak candidly, Harry, because to be honest, with less than a week of my tenure left, I don't have the luxury of sugar coating.'

'Speak freely, sir.'

'I've known you, what . . . eleven years? I knew immediately you had an edge. Something drives you, Harry. Something you've never spoken to me about. Perhaps I'm reaching here, but I'd say you got into this job off the back of some memory which bothers you.'

A flash of scissors. The scream. The blood.

Harry turned away. Simpson was staring at him with an intensity which made him uncomfortable.

'You're always reining in your temper, Harry. I can see it. Testing the boundaries of what is necessary force and what is excessive, and I'm not just talking physically. We all get frustrated by the constraints of the job – the rules, the politics; the times when we know the perp did it and we can't carry it forward—'

'Actually, I think you should get to the point, sir.' Harry kept his eyes focused across the park, back towards Mughal Gardens.

'Blunt trauma?'

'Sure.'

'I think you enjoyed what you did last week. I think when you put that son of a bitch down, no matter what happens on Monday, deep down, you think you're right.'

Harry didn't reply.

'Your file is a glowing tribute to a detective who has closed more cases than anyone else but who has also had more investigations about his conduct. And . . . I think you've had help. I think . . .' He walked in front of Harry so the detective was forced to look at his boss, and pointed to the fountain. '. . . that the difference between right and wrong as far as you're concerned is about as thin as that sheet of ice.'

They held each other's gaze. 'I want you to do whatever you need to do. If you have to break the law, then break the bloody law. Only this time, you'll have *my* support.'

It was, by far, the most astonishing thing Simpson could have said. He only ever played by the rules.

'I'm not sure I heard that right,' Harry replied quietly.

'You heard it just fine.'

'I don't break—'

'Don't try me, Harry. It insults my intelligence and' – he pushed his index finger into Harry's chest for emphasis – 'we both know it's bullshit.'

Harry let out a slow, heavy breath. 'I want my job back. On Monday, I want them to give me one last chance. Can you make that happen?'

'No. But what I can do is highlight in the strongest terms possible that you single-handedly brought me Lucas Dwight. That you saved Bradford from probable meltdown. And in this city, *that* is more valuable than all the rules put together.'

'What's the evidence against me?'

'CCTV footage. At the back of the restaurant.'

'Clear?'

'Borderline. But the rest of your file doesn't read well.'

'Self-defence?'

Simpson frowned. 'No one's going to believe that.'

Harry smiled and looked away. 'Destroy the footage.'

'Couldn't, even if I wanted to.'

'You seem to think that to help you I might have to break a few more rules. So – not that I am saying I have any idea what you're talking about – how does this help me exactly?'

'You need to think like a politician. Just for once, remove that "hard justice" hat you wear so proudly and think about the media. If you manage to bring me Lucas

Dwight, you've solved the brutal murder of Bradford's most-loved son. A high-flying politician. MBE. Community warhorse. You will be in the spotlight. Those IPCC bastards will think a lot harder before signing off your P45. They will look for anything which might put a different spin on what happened. And like I said, the footage is borderline.'

'What does your gut say?'

'You bring me Lucas Dwight, you walk.'

'No offence, sir, but you know who you're looking for. After all the earache I've had from you, why this request to work off-line? What's different this time?'

'Me,' said Simpson coldly. 'Bradford has worn me down. We're losing the fight. And with Lucas Dwight as the perp, we've got a disaster on the horizon. *My horizon.* I won't have my final act smeared in the city's blood. There is only one person, in my experience, who can manipulate these streets better than Lucas Dwight.' He fixed Harry with another stare. 'And I need his help. I won't retire with the city taken back a decade; to the carnage of two thousand and one.'

'It hasn't changed in a decade, sir.' Harry crossed his arms defensively. 'Earlier, when you said I'm not designed to be in law enforcement, what did you mean?'

'I meant exactly that.'

'This isn't really the ideal way to get me on board, sir. Telling me I'm not fit for purpose.'

'That's not what I said.'

'What did you mean?'

'People get into this job for all sorts of reasons. Make the world a better place? Stability? Maybe money? And then there are those who do it to compensate.' Simpson put a hand on Harry's shoulder. 'I'm only saying this because in five days' time I won't be here to say it to you. And you need to change, Harry. You need to start figuring out some way to deal with . . . your situation. You're about to become a father, which means you need to calm down. You asked me what I meant before. I meant that being a detective doesn't suit you because when things don't go your way, you dish out your own justice. And that's not how this world works.'

'Until now?' Harry removed Simpson's hand from his shoulder.

'Yes. Until now.'

'What do I have in terms of assistance?'

'Me. You need something, you pick up the phone. No red tape. These . . . these . . . avenues you have, the ones which get you information before anyone else, I need you to tap them. And quickly. Very quickly.'

'How long before the media get Lucas's name?'

Simpson shrugged. 'I don't know. Maybe noon? I'm going to have to use them to get all eyes looking for him.' He brushed water from his raincoat. 'I've taken up enough of your time, Harry. I'm not asking as your boss. I'm asking as a friend who wants to retire peacefully.' He turned away towards the Mughal Gardens. 'And,' he added, 'what do you really have to lose?'

'Let me help you—'

'I can manage.' Simpson raised his hand defiantly before walking away.

Lucas Dwight.

The name was echoing through Harry's mind.

Simpson had him. He was a crafty old man. He knew Harry couldn't let something like this go. He'd planted the seed and knew what would grow. Much like Simpson, Harry loved the city. Bradford may have become a relic of its former glory days but it was still home. He had spent his years cleaning up the streets, one arsehole at a time. He wasn't about to let the ex-leader of the BNP wreak havoc. Fourteen years in jail clearly hadn't rehabilitated Lucas Dwight.

Harry pulled out his iPhone and accessed his favourites menu, hitting the top entry. Mixed emotions as the phone rang. Hesitation. A little anxiety.

'Harry?' came the rough male voice.

'We need to meet. Right now.'

FIVE

THE FIRST THING HARRY saw when he opened his front door was a pair of old slippers resting on top of a small table. It was a familiar sight. They were the only thing Harry's mother had given him before he left her house for ever.

He wasn't superstitious, but every morning for three decades Harry had touched his mother's feet before leaving the house and again on his return. It was a sign of respect within his community. His former community. His former life.

Harry touched the slippers and then ran his hand through his hair, a symbolic act of respect, acknowledging these were slippers which had walked many hard paths and made difficult sacrifices.

Above them, on the wall, was an Islamic painting on which the word 'Welcome' was transcribed in Arabic, the first sign of many in this house of two worlds colliding.

Harry's house in Manningham, on Oak Lane, was only a few hundred yards from Lister Park. The area should have been the heartbeat of the city. Instead it was a flat-line, and no amount of resuscitation could get it breathing again.

Manningham hadn't been Harry's first choice but Bradford Royal Infirmary, Saima's place of work, was close by and Harry's post at HMET only a few miles away. A century before, it had been the richest part of Bradford, with textile mills and wool merchants' houses. It was historically an exclusive Jewish area.

Now, Manningham was notorious as the setting for two race riots, in 1995 and again in 2001. They called it 'the Asian ghetto'. It resulted in cheap house prices but, even so, generously sized Victorian homes often accommodated several generations of the same family. It was a traditional arrangement: elderly parents living with their children.

Not in Harry and Saima's case. They were alone. Through necessity more than desire. The melodrama from their inter-faith marriage knew no boundaries. After trying to appease hostile families, Harry and Saima had made their choice: each other. They had chosen exile.

Harry's Sikh upbringing had taught him about reincarnation and his mother had often preached that if he lived a good life now, in his next one he would return as something better. That was fine with Harry. He often joked that he wanted to return as somebody white. Life seemed a little easier on that side of the fence. He could make his peace with the Tooth Fairy, the Easter Bunny and Santa. Navigating the minefield of Asian religious politics was damn near impossible.

Harry slipped off his running shoes and made his way into the living room. It was half past eight and he thought Saima might have been awake but the room was undisturbed. He made his way into the kitchen where he found evidence of an early-morning raid. There were left-overs from fried eggs, toast, beans and hash browns on a plate. A kitchen knife was stained red from the slicing of strawberries, and the only milk carton was empty. Harry shook his head. His pregnant wife seemed to be consuming everything in the house these days. She was going to give birth to a record-breaker.

Harry made his way upstairs. On the landing he stripped off sweaty running clothes and threw them in the laundry basket. In the bathroom, he took a quick shower and then made his way into the bedroom, a towel wrapped tightly around his waist. Saima's body was hidden under the duvet.

Today was Eid, the most important day in the Islamic calendar, and they should have been making plans. It meant little to Harry but Saima would have been expecting a day out, maybe a meal on Leeds Road before ending their day at the Mela. In order to change those plans, Harry was going to have to tell her something credible.

The only thing he had was the truth. That he was suspended.

And the reason why.

He made his way to her side of the bed and sat down next to her. Sunlight was creeping through a gap between the curtains, throwing a solitary ray across the bed.

Saima stirred and stared at him with oval-shaped green eyes. They had first caught his attention six years ago. Eyes you couldn't ignore. There was a scar on the side of her face from ear to jaw. It was a permanent reminder of the darker times when she had abandoned her family to be with him. Saima often curled her hair down the side of her face to hide it or masked it with make-up. Harry placed his hand on it and let his finger run down the ridges. Saima moved her head discreetly. Purposefully.

'Hey,' he said.

'Zara,' she replied, yawning.

'Veto,' he said. 'My child isn't a fashion shop.'

She frowned. 'Jaan, we are never going to name this baby if you keep vetoing everything.'

Jaan: that was what she called him. It meant 'life' in Urdu. Saima had picked it up after they'd been to see a cheesy Bollywood movie on their second date. Harry sometimes wished he'd taken her to watch *Rocky* or *Rambo*. He might have acquired a manlier nickname.

'Zara doesn't work for me,' he said and gently kissed her forehead. 'You getting up?'

Saima shrugged. 'She's awake,' she said, throwing off the duvet to reveal her enormous belly. 'Flipping cartwheels.'

'Gymnast?'

'More like a protest at my early-morning feast.'

'You must have got up just after I left.'

She nodded. 'Yasmin?'

'I'm not naming my child after a contraceptive pill.'

'Rafeena?'

'That's got an "eena" in it.'

'Jaan, come on, it's—'

'Against the rules. If you put "eenas" on the table then I'm having "deeps".'

They had made a pact not to give their child an authentic Asian name but rather to try and find one that somehow fitted both worlds as well as this new world they'd created together. Names ending in 'eena' were traditionally Islamic and ones ending in 'deep' were Sikh.

'Sukhdeep? Ramandeep? Jasdeep?'

Saima quickly retracted Rafeena. 'Well played,' she said, unable to hide the contempt in her voice. 'I still like Ruby. There is nothing wrong—'

'Not naming my daughter after a stripper.'

'How come you don't have any suggestions?'

'I do. I still like Gemima.'

'With a "J"?' she said. It put an Islamic slant on it.

'No, with a "G".'

'I hate you.'

'Come on.' Harry offered her his hand. 'Let's get you both out of bed.'

'Where are we going today?' she said hopefully. 'And where's my Eid present?'

He pulled her body upright and she shuffled her legs comically to the side of the bed, placing swollen feet on the carpet. Saima put her hands on Harry's body; his skin was still wet from the shower. She slid her hands around the Maori tattoo wrapped around his right arm and wolf-whistled, which she couldn't really do. It came out as a forced rush of air.

'It's a good job you never tried that one when we met.' Harry helped her to her feet, standing in front of her in only his towel.

'Muslim girls aren't allowed to whistle,' she said.

'So don't.'

'Look at our situation. I think finally conquering a whistle is the icing on the cake.'

'Soft lips,' he replied. 'Like this.' Harry looked her up and down suggestively and whistled before sliding his hand down her back and pulling her closer to his body. Saima moved her hands to his chest and winked at him; again, something she couldn't do. Harry shook his head. 'Jesus, it's a good job you're hot. Can't whistle. Can't wink.'

'Hey, I totally can.'

'You wink with one eye, not two.'

She frowned. Tried again. And failed.

'Come on,' said Harry, 'let's go downstairs. We need to talk.'

She was immediately on the defensive. 'About what?'

'We'll start with the fact that you finished all the milk,' he replied and left the room, whistling as he went.

*

Downstairs in the living room, Saima brought him a cup of Indian tea with fennel and cardamom seeds still floating on the surface. She placed it on a coaster on the coffee table and took a seat opposite him, perching on the edge of the couch.

Harry took a sip of tea and frowned.

'Carnation milk,' she said, finally finding a comfortable position on the sofa.

'What exactly did you eat this morning?'

'Everything. I had to.'

'Why?'

'You forgot as well. Nearly jinxed the whole day.'

Harry was lost. 'Eh?'

'What is today?'

'Eid,' Harry replied confidently. He had a gift for her in the car.

'Yes. But it's also something else. First full moon of winter? What happens today?'

'I don't know. Werewolves come out?'

She rolled her eyes. 'It's the twenty-third of October? Ring a bell?'

'Stop talking in riddles.'

'Today is Karva Chauth.'

'Oh.' Harry sighed again. 'You're pregnant, so you don't need to—'

'Yes. I do. What if something happens to you? I don't want that on my conscience.'

'If you are due to give birth, you are exempt. This is an

43

Indian tradition not a Pakistani one. You're not familiar with the regulations. In fact, I recall quite vividly that clause four hundred and fifty-seven, paragraph twelve, sub-section C states that all pregnant women are exempt from the lunacy of starvation in the hope it might grant their husbands a long life.'

Another roll of her eyes. She shook her head and placed her hands on her stomach, rubbing it protectively. 'Don't be so dismissive. For centuries Asian women have been fasting for the longevity of their husbands.'

'And for centuries', Harry said, picking the cardamom seeds from the tea, 'men have still died on days like today.'

'Don't be so morbid. Anyway, I can't fast on Eid – it's forbidden. So I'm having water. Maybe a piece of fruit later on. A fusion-fast.'

'I don't think Junior will approve.' Harry pointed to her stomach. 'Twelve hours without food?'

'Eleven actually. The moon is visible at five tonight. And I've already eaten a day's worth of calories before sunrise. I'll be fine.'

'What about our Eid plans?' Harry was relieved at the chance to cancel their arrangements. He glanced at the clock on top of the mantelpiece. It was just after nine. He needed to be on his way.

'We can still go out. We need to buy a baby monitor.'

Harry nodded slowly, trying to find the words. She needed to know. The ticking clock at the back of his mind was getting louder, bringing the pressure to the surface.

'Saima, there's something I need to tell you,' Harry

mumbled without looking at her. He placed his tea back on the table and took a deep breath. 'You're not going to like it.'

'What is it?' Saima raised her voice just enough to show him she was alarmed.

His neck felt weighted to the floor, as though there was a brick tied around it. Harry took a moment before finally looking at his wife. 'Last week, on Thursday night . . . I lied to you.'

SIX

COLIN REED HAD GIVEN the dealer two very clear instructions: *Make sure he shoots up with you. Make sure he dies.*

Without a body, Reed couldn't be sure. The doubt was getting to him. And today, of all days, wasn't the time to fail.

He wasn't a man who left things to chance. This was a fast-moving operation. The city was vulnerable. He didn't have time to dwell on a missing body. Once the Asian communities found out about Ahmed's death, they would be outraged.

It was time to channel that energy. Keep it raw. Make sure the city vented its anger.

Reed was en route to Baildon Moor. Usually it took twenty minutes but the impenetrable fog and constant drizzle stretched it to forty. He headed north towards Baildon Top. Two hundred and eighty metres to the summit. On a clear summer's day, it gave a view right across the city. Reed knew it well. He walked the moors regularly: respite from the pressures of his job. It could be stressful being one of the most dangerous men in Bradford.

As the ascent became steeper, fog clung to the windscreen of the Range Rover. Unable to see anything, Reed stopped the car, removed the satnav from the glovebox, punched in the postcode and waited for a GPS signal. It took nearly two minutes to show him that he was still just over a mile from the turn-off. He put the car in gear and crawled up the winding hill, wary of waterlogged trenches by the side of the road.

The unearthly fog and total isolation of the moors comforted Reed. He'd always preferred doing business this way. His partner was the front man; his role was different, behind the scenes.

Isolated. Largely invisible.

He slowed down and peered to his left where the satnav instructed him to go. He took the turn and was swallowed into a hazy void. Branches from overgrown bushes tapped on the windows. Prying, pointing fingers – trying to claw their way into the car. Despite himself, Reed felt a touch of claustrophobia.

A few tense minutes later, he arrived at a small clearing. An abandoned Portakabin blocked the track. The windows were smashed and the door was missing.

As an unfathomable ghost descended on the land, he hoped he wouldn't be kept waiting.

Reed reached into the glovebox again and removed a green tie. The first two words of Nelson's semaphore signal were etched on to it: *England Expects*. To the unsuspecting eye, it was just a tie. But to those who knew, it was an identifier: a symbol of the Trafalgar Club, the sister party of the BNP.

Reed knotted the tie carefully around his twenty-one-inch neck. Suddenly there were headlights behind, cutting through the fog. They flashed twice.

Reed lifted a black holdall from the passenger seat, unlocked the car and got out. He headed towards the grey Jaguar with blacked-out windows. His size-thirteen boots sank effortlessly into the mud.

Inside the Jag sat Martin Davis, the leader of the BNP. Reed got in the passenger side. The suspension creaked. They acknowledged each other with a solid military handshake.

The interior of the Jaguar contrasted with the gloom outside: expensive white leather and a warm orange glow from the dash.

Even this early, Davis looked alert, as though he'd been awake for hours. He had a tanned complexion, was wearing an expensive Hugo Boss suit and his shoulder-length dark hair was slicked back, tucked neatly behind his ears.

'Covert meeting this early? This better be important,' Davis said.

'Important?' Reed replied. 'When is it not?'

'We should consider an alternative meeting point – this place gives me the creeps.'

'I value my anonymity.'

Davis lit a cigarette. He lowered his window to release the fumes.

'Keep it closed.' Reed pinched the cigarette from Davis's mouth, stubbing it out in the ashtray on the centre console. 'Can never be too careful of prying ears.'

Davis was used to Reed's obsessive secrecy. He didn't protest.

It had stopped raining but there was an intermittent drip of water on the roof from the trees overhead.

'There's something wrong with this place,' Davis said. 'Don't know if it's the fog or what happened in the sixties with those kids.'

'The Moors murders were on Saddleworth. We're fifty miles from there.'

'What's with the SOS? Don't you know I just blew an election?'

'I know. Why do you think I'm here?'

'Nothing I could do about it. Twenty-five per cent of Bradford is Muslim. Shakeel Ahmed played the Asian vote – and from what I hear threw a million quid at it.' Davis shook his head. 'Can't compete with that in *this* city.'

'You clearly haven't heard yet so let me enlighten you. Shakeel Ahmed was murdered. Early this morning.'

Davis searched Reed's face for signs of a joke. 'Murdered?'

Reed nodded. 'From what I hear it was your mate Lucas Dwight who did him. Crucified him to the side of Bradford Grammar.'

Davis's mouth dropped open. 'Lucas? He's in prison.'

'Nope. Released four days ago.'

'How do you know all this?'

'This is my city. I keep my ear close to the ground.'

'Crap,' Davis said. 'This is going to piss all over my campaign message. We're not the same party Lucas left.'

'I know that but Lucas doesn't. Hell, he's been holed up for years. Maybe he just wants to go back inside. You get used to prison life.' Reed spoke almost ruefully, like a man who knew that struggle.

'Lucas fucking Dwight?' Davis whispered. 'You know,' he said, grabbing his cigarette from the ashtray, 'I was this close to taking Bradford West. This close.' He held his finger and thumb together in the air. 'My campaign was tight and you know what? I had some solid policies. *Solid.* Just as we're turning the corner – becoming serious contenders – this son of a bitch Lucas turns up.' He placed the stubbed-out cigarette back in its packet.

Davis had significantly improved the BNP. Over the past three years, violence, aggression and hate had given way to policy, reform and substance. Davis had used his Oxford degree in politics to overhaul the decaying party. Membership had increased five-fold. The party accounts showed them to be the fourth wealthiest political organization after the big three.

The north was becoming something of a BNP stronghold with huge gains in Newcastle, Oldham and Sheffield. The recession helped; when the chips were down, patriots always turned on the foreigners.

'I can't disagree – terrible timing. But it must be pointed out,' Reed said, 'we have . . . an opportunity here.'

'Figured you would say as much. Always the way with you.'

'Hey, I don't need that attitude. You want to know what's in this bag?' Reed asked, ruffling the holdall. 'Quarter of a mil.'

That got Davis's attention. It was the largest amount Reed had ever offered. 'Jesus. Two hundred and fifty? How do you expect me to cover that?'

'Put it the same place you ditched the rest.'

'What are you asking this time?'

'I can give you Bradford,' replied Reed. 'And I mean guarantee it.'

'There are no guarantees in politics.'

'There are in my world.'

'I'm listening.'

'There's going to be another by-election. If you want to win it, you need to do exactly as I say – exactly.'

'When have I not?' Davis nodded towards the bag. 'That kind of gift will get almost anything done.'

'That's what I'm hoping. What I want from you – what I *need* from you' – Reed emphasized his words – 'is to organize a BNP march through the city tonight. Eight p.m.'

'A march? They're going to be associating Lucas Dwight with us; nobody's going to want to do that.'

'I know. That's exactly the point.'

'I'm not following.'

'The Bradford Mela starts tonight, right?'

Davis nodded.

'You'll have over five thousand Asians in Lister Park. Give it an hour and they'll become restless. As usual, there'll be some trouble, some arrests. Same shit as every year. Only this year, there needs to be mayhem.'

'If we start trouble in Bradford, there'll be—'

'We', Reed snapped, 'are not starting anything. You hear me? This needs to be a one hundred per cent peaceful march. No engagement.'

'Talk straight, Colin.'

'By this evening, Bradford is going to be shaking from Ahmed's . . . demise, for want of a better word. You put your guys in Bradford – in the park – and the Asians will react. You know how this city works. We need the smallest of sparks. The petrol's already there. There'll be cameras in the park. Media. You tell your boys that they stand down – they do not *start* anything. But once they are provoked, well . . .'

Davis cottoned on. 'Let the Asians ignite the violence and it'll be like two thousand and one all over again?'

'Bingo. They'll burn the city. And once it starts, tell your boys to get out. The mob – the Asians – will do as they always have: torch Bradford, and who do you think the seventy-per-cent-white population will lean towards at the next by-election? You keep your shit clean and do exactly as I say and we both win.'

'What's in this for you?'

'Like you, it will serve me just fine to see the city burn. *And I mean burn.*'

'No, it's more than that.'

'This is "not to know".' Reed ruffled the bag again. 'And, Martin, there's another two fifty if you get this right.'

'In the two years we've known each other, you've never offered me this much. I need something to go on here. What the fuck is this?'

'Let's just say I represent some powerful businessmen and it's in *their* interest for this to happen. Shit, Martin, what am I really asking here? Just to organize a peaceful protest to clearly demonstrate you had *nothing* to do with Shakeel Ahmed's disappearance. That you condemn it. You're being the good guy – offering Bradford solidarity. And you're telling the truth.'

'You and I both know that's not what you're asking.'

'A knee-jerk response is what I'm counting on.'

Davis wasn't sure. But half a million quid was a retirement fund he couldn't ignore.

'You get what you need and so do I.' Reed put his hand reassuringly on Davis's shoulder. 'Shakeel Ahmed shouldn't have won yesterday. He manipulated the system and got an ethnic vote. That shit's not right. Fair policy – fine, but a protest vote? Come on.'

Davis nodded. 'It's a risky play, this, Colin.'

'Nobody ever won a battle by playing safe. We're just using the history of this city. Is it our fault they love to watch the place burn?'

'You're dead right,' Davis said, warming to the idea. He could gain the first MP seat in Westminster for his party and create history.

'Your boys wait for provocation,' Reed repeated. 'Then they get out.'

'They will. We'll make this a spectacle of Asian fury against its own city.'

Reed handed over the bag. 'Another two fifty afterwards.'

'These . . . businessmen you represent,' said Davis. 'When will I meet them? I'd like to show my gratitude.'

'They're aware.' Reed brushed him off. 'The indigenous people of this country appreciate the work you do, Martin. You've turned the party around.'

Davis swelled with pride, pleased his hard work was being noticed.

'Eight p.m.,' Reed said. 'Let the Mela get warmed up and then release them. You've still got a lot of supporters in the city from yesterday. Organize this covertly, Martin. Don't let the police get wind of the march. We clear?'

Davis nodded. 'We're clear.'

'I need to know, for certain, if you can manage this?'

'Yes. If I need you, where can I contact you?'

'You've got my mobile. It'll be active until midnight. After that, we shouldn't need to meet for some time.'

'It's frustrating that this relationship only goes one way.'

Reed shook the bag again. 'That's what this is for.'

Back in his car, Colin Reed waited for Davis to pull away before calling his boss. He removed the Trafalgar Club tie, lowered his window and threw it outside where it landed in the mud. He wouldn't be needing it any more.

The phone rang six times before a male voice answered.

'Secure line?'

'Yes,' Reed replied.

'We good?'

'He bought it.' Reed smiled. 'The stupid son of a bitch bought it.'

SEVEN

HARRY AND SAIMA WERE sitting on their couch. They appeared close but Harry's confession had just put a huge distance between them.

'You did what?' Saima asked incredulously, shuffling forwards so she was perched on the edge of the sofa, elbows on her knees, hands underneath her chin. She couldn't bring herself to look at him.

'I put Pardeep Singh in hospital.'

'Why? When? How?'

'I saw him leaving the restaurant just after we did. When I told you I went back for my wallet, I confronted him and . . . things got out of hand.'

'What did you do, Jaan?'

Harry got off the couch. He lifted his cup from the table, carried it to the bay window and looked out on to Oak Lane. A few elderly men were on their way to the Jamia Masjid mosque for morning prayers, walking arm in arm.

Harry sipped his tea.

'Jaan? Talk to me.'

Last Thursday evening, Harry and Saima had been having a meal at Akbar's Café, one of Bradford's popular restaurants. Pardeep Singh, a friend of Harry's father, had also been there. He was an orthodox Sikh and a senior member of the gurdwara committee. He found Harry's choices in life abhorrent.

Pardeep had spent most of the evening sneering at Harry from across the restaurant, whispering and gesturing to his wife, who didn't even try and conceal her delight at the scandal. Harry ignored it at first. But when they were still at it half an hour later, he had gone over to their table and the conversation had become so heated that the manager had asked them both to either walk away or leave. Harry had returned to his table – to finish a ruined evening with Saima. Later, on his way out of the restaurant, Pardeep had made a point of passing Harry's table and muttering something about Saima's pregnancy. Saima had put her hand firmly on Harry's arm and told him not to react.

He hadn't. Not then.

But the red mist which blighted his life had seized control and, once outside, Harry had lied to Saima about forgetting his wallet and taken the opportunity to confront Pardeep in the car park.

A shove had turned into a punch, then a scuffle, then a full-blown fistfight, Harry stopping only when Pardeep's wife had put herself between both men. By that time, Pardeep's jaw was hanging off his face.

There were cameras in the car park. Harry hadn't noticed them.

An assault charge had been filed and in light of Harry's previous misdemeanours, his boss had had no option but to suspend him. Harry told all this to Saima without facing her. Not because he was ashamed but because she would see that he wasn't and that would hurt her the most.

She remained quiet.

Harry then told her what had happened that morning at the park. About Shakeel Ahmed's body and Simpson's offer.

Finally, she replied. 'You lied to me?'

They never lied to each other. Never. It was the rule.

Through everything they had overcome, they had always told each other the truth.

'I didn't want to upset you,' he said. 'Not so close to giving birth. I was hoping the hearing on Monday wouldn't be so bad. But from what Simpson said, I'm looking at a P45. Maybe worse.'

'So why tell me now?'

Harry heard Saima get off the couch. 'Because I need to leave. I have one chance to fix this. I need to find Lucas Dwight in the next ten hours.'

'You really think you can?'

'I don't know. I've got to try.'

'Jaan, look at me.'

Harry placed his empty cup on the window ledge and turned to face her.

'We chose this life,' she said. 'We knew it would be hard and in this city somebody is always going to disapprove, somebody who knows the hurt and dishonour we've caused.' Saima walked over to where Harry was standing. He crossed his arms defensively on his chest. 'You worry me,' she continued. 'Not because you defend me – but because you don't know when to leave it alone.'

'I won't have some snooty-nosed bast—'

She glared at him and Harry suppressed the profanity.

'Snooty-nosed idiot judge me,' he said. 'The guy's daughter ran away because he beat her and he judges *my* choices?'

'Exactly. He has *no right* to judge us – so why bother with him?'

'He insulted my wife.'

'And a hundred people might do so, but sticks and stones, Jaan.'

He nodded. 'I know, but I *can't* turn the other cheek like you, Saima. Somebody makes me angry and I *can't* back down. I don't need to back down. If you're going to try it with me, then you better expect to defend yourself. That's who I am – that's who you married.'

'You can't? You *can't*?' She pushed a finger firmly into his chest, her face flushing a deep red. 'You *will* and you *must*,' she replied. 'You think when our child arrives, we won't have more problems? You think she's not going to wonder why she has no grandparents or cousins? You don't think *she* will be judged? What will you do then?

Beat up everyone who upsets her? You're going to be a father,' she said, raising her voice, 'and that comes first and foremost. Not your willingness to dish out some sort of justice.'

Harry uncrossed his arms and held out his hands defensively. 'OK, OK. Just take a moment. Don't get upset.'

'Maybe that's what *you* should have done last week.'

'Perhaps.' Harry corrected himself before she gave him another lecture: 'I mean, yes, I should have.'

'Right. Let's sort out this mess. Pardeep is on the gurdwara committee with your father. You need to call him and tell him to get Pardeep to retract the—'

'Over my dead body am I calling him,' Harry said, raising his voice. 'No,' he continued when Saima started to object. 'There is more chance of Lucas Dwight knocking on my front door than of me asking my father for a damn favour.'

She didn't fight him. She knew he would never have gone along with it.

'So you need to find this Lucas Dwight. Can you?'

Harry shrugged. 'I can try.'

'Is he dangerous?'

Harry thought back to 2001 when he had apprehended Lucas. A bloody affair. It had taken five officers to get him in cuffs. 'No more than any other criminal,' he lied.

'So you're leaving me here, alone on Eid and Karva Chauth, to pursue this? Is that right?'

'Yes. I need to do this.' He put one hand on her bump. Then the other. 'You understand?'

She nodded. Hesitantly. 'I have one condition.'

'Go on.'

'I'm fasting for you today. *For us*. I know you don't believe in these things, but I do. And it's important to me. If you could make it back in time? Tell me you'll at least try?'

'I can't promise, Saima. What time?'

'Before the moon comes out. I want to complete the tradition, the right way, so no bad luck is cast upon us.'

'Bad luck?' Harry stopped himself from touching the scar on the side of her face. 'I think we've had a generation's worth.'

'That may be so, but it's really important. I won't be able to get it out of my mind. So you can go and tear this city apart looking for this guy, but make it back in time for me to do this.' Saima was massaging her tummy, staring pleadingly at Harry.

'OK. I can do that,' he said.

'You need to give me your kasam.'

Kasam. A sacred Indian promise which literally meant you would die before breaking your word.

'Saima, you know I don't like doing that. It's unnecessary.'

'It's the only way I can be sure you'll return. That you won't break your promise. If you don't, I won't let you leave.'

Harry sighed. Although he was pragmatic and didn't engage in Asian melodrama, the same couldn't be said for his wife.

'OK. I give you my kasam.'

'And we're doing Karva Chauth the right way. You know what that means?'

He nodded hesitantly and looked away. She held his face gently and turned it back towards her. 'Agreed?'

'OK,' he replied, trying not to snap, and removed her hands. 'I need to go, Saima. I need to meet with someone, get this thing started.'

Harry walked away but before he reached the door, she asked him the one question he didn't want.

'Who are you meeting?'

Harry hesitated by the living-room door.

'Who are you meeting?' she repeated and pushed past Harry, blocking the doorway. 'Who?'

Harry stared at her blankly. 'Ronnie. I'm meeting Ronnie.'

She couldn't not react. 'Why Ronnie? Why do you always need to meet Ronnie?'

'Look, Saima, Ronnie is the only person who—'

She held up her hand, clenched her jaw and turned around but not before letting Harry see she was hurt. Then she walked out of the room and slammed the door.

EIGHT

HARRY HATED LEAVING SAIMA the way he had. She would never understand his relationship with Ronnie. She saw him as a threat – a reminder of the old world.

Harry put the emotion to one side as he approached Fulneck, a private school opened originally by Christian refugees in the eighteenth century, fleeing persecution from Catholics in Czechoslovakia. They had travelled to Germany, before arriving in England and settling on the Leeds–Bradford border. The school was set in the middle of a community which housed mostly elderly residents. It was where Harry and Ronnie had been privately educated. Ronnie was now chair of the Old Boys' Association and seemed to spend much of his time helping out.

Harry drove slowly through the stone-pillared entrances. Half-term meant the usual congestion that gridlocked the road snaking through the enormous grounds was absent. There were small cottages on his right, some with rose-baskets hanging by the windows. Others had milk bottles outside their doors, still waiting to be collected. It had the feel of a sleepy community from a forgotten fairy-tale.

Harry left the car under a tree and walked towards the fields where Ronnie would be waiting. He loved the nostalgic atmosphere of the area: the cobblestone path leading into the school, the church steeple halfway down and the whole route lined with overbearing oak trees. There was an air of peacefulness.

Simpler times.

Simpler because they hadn't been corrupted by the absurdity of life, by the complexity of having brown skin in a western land.

He made his way up a steep path to the rugby pitches. Up ahead was a pavilion where Harry could make out the faint silhouette of his brother.

Harry walked slowly across the frozen grass, seeing images of himself as a teenager snatching tries on each pitch he walked across.

'Looking a little heavy these days, little brother,' said Ronnie, sticking out his hand.

'Ninety kilos, same as always.' Harry jabbed his fingers into his older brother's stomach before shaking his hand. The two men embraced, each patting the other firmly on the back. 'You're getting fat,' said Harry.

'It's called the takeaway life. Two eleven-year-olds and a teenager do that to you.'

'They also stop you from shaving?'

Ronnie rubbed his chin. 'No worse than yours.'

'My stubble adds character. Yours just makes you look older. Aren't you forty next month?'

'Forget forty. Sometimes I feel fifty chasing Raj and Kiran around these pitches.'

'She plays rugby?'

'She likes to copy her twin brother.' Ronnie shrugged. 'Hey, whatever burns them out. I get tired running after them.'

Harry looked around the fields. 'You never were too quick on your feet.'

Ronnie tapped his head. 'I was quick enough up here not to let my feet be a problem. It's about which ball you decide to deliver and which you decide to charge that separates the men from the boys.'

Harry smiled. 'You said the same thing to me twenty years ago – passing it on to Raj?'

Ronnie nodded. 'Good advice never goes out of fashion.'

'What about Tara?'

Ronnie shook his head. 'Her temper becomes more like yours every day. I'm glad the twins don't have her attitude. Yet.' He shot Harry a knowing smile. 'She wants to move out now – change the world. Got a damn answer for everything. Sound familiar?'

Harry grinned and checked his phone to make sure Saima hadn't texted. He hoped she wasn't dwelling on his meeting with Ronnie.

'What are you doing here on a Friday morning? It's half-term.'

'Kids go stir-crazy. We've got a friendly against Crawshaw – just keeps them busy. You know?'

Harry nodded.

'Plus, like you, this is the place I find most peace,' Ronnie said. 'Good times.'

'The best. How's . . .' Harry stumbled over his words. '. . . the family?'

Ronnie sighed. 'The same.' He paused and added, 'OK.'

'Mum?'

Ronnie shrugged. 'Fine,' he said abruptly, clearly not wanting to say more.

'I'm just asking, Ronnie. You don't have to freak out.'

'You know how Mum is. The same. Good days and bad. You're about to become a father. Put your focus there.'

'It's human nature to care.'

'What can I do for you?' asked Ronnie. 'I take it this isn't social.'

'You rushed?'

'No, but the kids will be here shortly and, to be honest, it's not worth the headache with Mundeep for them to go home excited at having seen Uncle Harry.'

'I'm still their—'

'Not going there,' Ronnie snapped. 'Not the time or the place. You know the score – let's just leave it alone. I need you gone before they get here, Hardeep. OK?'

Mundeep, Ronnie's wife, had taken up his parents' position, or his father's at least, and banned Harry from seeing his nephew and nieces for fear that his choices might influence their judgement, lead them to think it was acceptable to cross the religious divide and marry a Muslim.

'It's bullshit,' Harry whispered, but loud enough for it to irritate Ronnie.

'Sit down, Hardeep.'

'It's Harry.'

'OK, Harry, sit down. Let me give you an insight into my life – last night in particular.'

'Listen—'

'Sit,' Ronnie snapped again, pointing at the steps they were standing on. 'Fucking humour me.'

Harry took a seat.

'So Dad is telling Raj a bedtime story last night,' Ronnie said, perching on the step opposite Harry.

'Bedtime story?'

Ronnie acknowledged the improbability. 'I know. Broken English and everything.'

'He's eleven, bit old for a bedtime—'

'Just listen. You know the story of the three little pigs and the big bad wolf?'

'Of course.'

'That isn't the version Dad told Raj. He told him the tale of the three little Sikhs and the big bad Muslim.'

'What?'

'Yeah, the big bad Muslim chases the three little Sikhs around each of their houses, saying he is going to huff and puff and blow them down unless they convert to

Islam. In the end, the three little Sikhs trap the Muslim in the chimney and burn him to death.'

'Jesus, Ronnie.' Harry shook his head and looked away.

'It wasn't as bad as him telling Kiran about Rupinder,' said Ronnie.

'Who?'

'Rupinder – rather than Rapunzel – is the Sikh princess trapped in the tower by a Muslim king. Being orthodox Sikh, she grows her hair until it's long enough for the Sikh prince to climb up it, into the tower and slay the evil Muslim king.'

'For fuck's sake,' Harry said, putting his hand up. 'Enough already. You let him tell this shit?'

'You know how Dad is. I just leave it the hell alone. But my point is, when someone will go to those lengths to ensure his grandkids do not repeat what his son did, you are never going to win. It's over, Harry. Done with. Leave it the fuck alone and get on with making your own family and your own future.'

Harry hadn't meant to get into this but it was still too raw for him to admit defeat. His mother still loved him. He knew it. He could *feel* it. But his father had witnessed the partition of India and the brutality which had resulted from it. The deaths of five million people. The shocking images of trains full of dead bodies being shipped across newly forged borders. Of women being converted to new religions or being raped so they were ruined and cast aside by their families. Harry's father had repeated the horror stories to Harry on a weekly basis and made him swear that he would never, ever marry outside of his Sikh faith and especially not a Muslim girl. Promises Harry had made. Promises he had meant to keep, until a chance encounter with a beautiful A & E sister had wrecked his world.

Until a single date had destroyed the years of propaganda.

'Prison taught me a lot of things,' continued Ronnie. 'Five years in the slammer makes you realize all types of people are good and bad. But Mundeep, Mum, Dad, the kids, they don't know that world. They know the world as they see it, so whilst I will always give you my time, brother, it's all you can have. My time. Nothing more. You in trouble?'

Ronnie said it as though it was fact, rather than a question. His eyes narrowed, searching Harry's face for deceit.

Harry shook his head. He missed Ronnie. The guy had an IQ of 198 and could have done anything with his life if he hadn't gone to jail. The reason he had been imprisoned bound the brothers together: a dark secret nobody knew.

'Need your help,' whispered Harry, trying to shake what they had spoken about from his mind. It seemed wrong to bring painful memories here. These fields were a shrine to the good old days. Rugby wins and fumbling with girls behind the pavilion. Misery had no place. 'Lucas Dwight. He's out. Causing trouble. Need to find him.'

Ronnie hesitated and raised an eyebrow. '*The* Lucas

Dwight?' he said. 'BNP guy?'

'The same.'

'What's he done?'

'Classified.'

'Seriously?' Ronnie asked. 'The stuff I could sink you with and you're playing me the "classified" card?'

'Just messing with you.' Harry smiled. 'Implicated in a racist murder. Kind of critical.'

'Shakeel Ahmed?'

'How the fuck did you know?'

'Radio,' Ronnie replied. 'Breaking news.'

'Jesus. I thought you had somehow pulled it from my brain. Always quick off the mark – too bloody quick. You could have worked for NASA or something like that.'

'Nah, I've got sixteen corner shops, four cash-and-carries, two takeaways and a crematorium. Who needs NASA, bruv?'

'Couldn't lend us a few quid, could you? Got myself suspended.'

Ronnie didn't act surprised. As though he already knew. As though it was a routine revelation.

'What was it this time?' asked Ronnie. He glanced cautiously at the bottom of the field, waiting for his kids to show.

'Something of nothing,' Harry said unconvincingly.

'What happened?'

Harry gave him the highlights.

'You daft fuck,' Ronnie said. 'How bad is it?'

'Broke his jaw.'

'Who was it?'

'Pardeep.'

'The arsehole whose daughter bolted because he forced her into a marriage to some freshie from India?'

'Same guy.'

'You think he's worth losing your career over?'

'Listen, I get it.' Harry held up his hands. 'I've had it in the arse from Saima already. It wasn't worth it. I lost my cool – it happens. If someone had a go at Mundeep, would you take it?'

'No. I wouldn't. I'd think it through – get it right.'

'That's the difference between you and me.' Harry tried not to raise his voice. 'I don't have your brains in my locker.'

Ronnie went over and put a hand on Harry's shoulder. 'Listen, from an older brother who has *always* looked out for you, the choices you've made are going to hurt for ever. You have to find a better way to control your anger. Hasn't the past taught you that?' Ronnie's voice trailed away and they both stood in silence, remembering their terrible secret.

Flashes of blood. A pair of scissors.

'Look,' said Harry. 'Thanks for listening – as always – but seriously, get those street voices who buy your black-market booze and fags to start talking. You've got reach in this city and finding Lucas Dwight might be the only way I can save my damn job. Sixteen corner shops is a lot of "chatter". This is serious, Ronnie. You know how this city might react. We've got thousands of Asians at the Mela tonight and the BNP supporters are still here from yesterday's elections. This goes toxic, it's going to be bad for your businesses. I let you sell enough contraband to call this in as a priority.'

The brothers had an understanding. Harry would alert Ronnie if the authorities suspected his underground cartel. In return, Ronnie filtered information about crime to Harry. That's why his results were so good.

Harry pointed in the distance. 'Kids are coming. I better be going. Ask around, will you? You'll hear about it before I do. Pick up the phone?'

Ronnie nodded. 'I'll find out what I can.' They shared an embrace. When they were growing up, Ronnie had been more like a father, watching Harry's back, helping him with his studies and covering for him when Harry was out with yet another girl. His older brother was the one solid thing in his life. Ronnie could have maintained the same position as the rest of his family. He had chosen not to and Harry was immensely grateful.

Saima didn't understand their relationship. She didn't trust Ronnie and she couldn't forgive him for keeping Harry at arm's length especially when, prior to his relationship with Saima, Harry had been inseparable from Ronnie's kids.

Cool Uncle Harry who could lift all three of them at the same time and carry them on his shoulders without tiring.

Saima wasn't aware that the real bond between the

brothers was far darker than she could have imagined. That wasn't a lie, just a sin of omission on Harry's part.

'I'll call you, kid,' Ronnie said. 'If I hear anything.'

Harry walked away, raising his hand, without looking at the approaching children.

NINE

BASHIR IQBAL'S TAXI WAS off duty. Not because his shift was over, but because he'd paid Clare, his usual prostitute, thirty quid for oral sex. It was Friday morning but in Bradford, the kerb-crawlers worked by day as well as night. It was a sign of how desperate the city's fortunes had become.

Bashir had popped a Viagra, but it wasn't working. So he thought about the only thing guaranteed to make his blood surge to where he needed it.

Murder. The one he had yet to commit. The one he had been waiting forty years to carry out.

Casually, Bashir lit another cigarette and tried to enjoy the blow job. The gori was his usual girl.

'Gori – what does that mean?' she'd asked him once.

'White girl,' he'd replied, without clarifying whether it was derogatory or not.

Bashir had specific tastes and Clare was the only one

who indulged him. He wasn't horny. He was fifty-nine years old and hadn't been horny for years. He was angry – and if he didn't get a release, he was apt to lose control.

The darkness he'd buried for so long finally seemed destined to be unearthed.

Shakeel was dead.

And with his death came an opportunity.

Bashir had been waiting patiently for decades. Shakeel had always stopped him from committing the one murder he coveted so badly, in case it compromised his role within the business.

Now, the time was close. In fact, tonight would provide the perfect opportunity.

Bashir grabbed the hooker's head and forced her to quicken her rhythm. She resisted momentarily.

The taxi was parked in a dark alleyway off Thornton Lane, the red-light district of Bradford, close to Manningham. Bashir's car was parked facing the dead end, hidden in the shadows of two decaying factories, both eight storeys high. Bashir glanced in the rear-view mirror every few minutes to ensure they wouldn't be disturbed.

It was unlikely. Bashir had been parking here for years without incident. A lone taxi with its lights off wasn't unusual on Thornton Lane. Bradford's Asian taxi drivers were the working girls' most regular clients.

Bashir removed a cut-throat razor from the pocket in the driver's side door. His erection became firmer and his breathing quickened. Clare put a hand firmly on his thigh and tensed her body. Dirty fingernails. Chipped pink nail polish.

Bashir opened the razor and admired the sharpness of the blade. It looked unused, which was far from accurate. He slid the blade slowly down Clare's back, lightly caressing her skin. He arrived at her buttocks and pushed the blade softly into her wrinkling skin.

Clare squeezed his leg and released a muted anxious gasp.

Fear.

That he'd go too far.

Bashir grabbed the back of her head. He bunched her hair in his fist and forced her into an aggressive rhythm.

Then, slowly, with deliberate malice, Bashir cut her, slicing the skin where the fold in her thigh met her buttock. Bashir made a wound next to many others. As a sudden burst of blood tarnished the silvery blade, Bashir climaxed powerfully.

Finished with her fifteen-minute punt, Clare slipped a dressing over the wound, collected her bag from the back seat and left the vehicle silently.

No words were exchanged during their encounters. Bashir would pull up by the kerb and she'd get into his taxi, knowing exactly what he needed and how much she would be paid. There was always a little extra for his specific tastes.

Bashir zipped up his trousers, struggling to close them over his bulging stomach. His back felt damp against the seat, but it wasn't sweat. Bashir was bleeding.

He was *always* bleeding, but that was another story.

He carefully removed a strand of Clare's dirty blonde hair from the passenger seat and watched her limp across the road, awaiting her next punt.

Clare was forty-five and overweight. Her stomach escaped her mid-cut top and her thighs were covered in cellulite. Her best feature was her desperation. It was in her eyes. She was either a drug addict or an alcoholic. Bashir didn't care which. He had known immediately that an extra twenty quid would break her resolve and buy him the freedom he required.

He pulled the Toyota Corolla from the side street and turned the taxi radio back on. He could hear the animated sirens of police cars around him, more than usual. It was all to do with Shakeel's murder. But the police wouldn't get justice. That would be taken care of in-house.

Few people realized which circles Shakeel had really moved in. He'd been a great advocate for Bradford, building three mosques and setting up several charitable foundations. Ahmed was a shining pillar of the community. But even pillars started off as rough pieces of stone. Shakeel hadn't reached such an esteemed position without getting his hands dirty. And Bashir knew, more than anyone, that bad deeds eventually caught up with you.

Karma was a bitch.

The radio crackled. It was Rachel, his dispatch co-ordinator. 'Bashir, where the hell are you? Pick up your damn radio! Over.'

Rachel irritated him. She was a middle-aged former

alcoholic. Her struggle to kick the habit had turned her into a bad-tempered bitch.

Bashir switched off the radio. He was taking a few hours off.

He didn't drive taxis for money but to get away from his miserable wife, whose mind was broken by depression. If she spoke five words a day, Bashir was lucky. She was a statue, frozen by a dark past she couldn't forgive Bashir for. It was all Bashir ever thought about.

And now, with Shakeel's death, Bashir was free. The leash was broken.

Bashir was going to right a wrong he'd suffered for forty years. Nobody but Shakeel knew about Bashir's need to draw blood. They were friends from decades before; both had grown up in the same region of Pakistan. In the seventies they had moved to Bradford, but whilst Shakeel had been driven to earn money and forge a legacy, Bashir hadn't the same hunger. He was driven by a darker force. Shakeel had seen that Bashir would be of more use in the shadows. Until the day came when all things would be put right.

Now? That day had arrived. Bashir had learned many things from Shakeel. He had watched as Shakeel masterfully manipulated Bradford. Tonight was Bashir's chance to put that knowledge to use.

He drove slowly through Thornton, past the derelict buildings which stood squalid and decaying. The alleys and abandoned yards provided ample cover for the whores to make their money.

It was Friday, which meant afternoon prayers at the mosques. Bashir wasn't religious – he hadn't even bought his wife an Eid gift – but he tried to make Friday prayers. It kept his community from whispering.

There were many like him. Mostly taxi drivers who drank at night, smoked marijuana in the day and didn't give a damn about anything else. The guys Bashir worked with used their taxis as cover, all of them members of a club which supported an underground world nobody spoke about.

Since today was Eid, attendance at the mosque was mandatory – to Bashir's dismay, because he didn't like making conversation at the best of times. But there would be special prayers today to mourn for Shakeel and if he didn't attend, it would be noticed. If Bashir's wife hadn't been such a wreck, she might have done this for him, kept his name high within the community. Bashir had often thought about ending her life. But he couldn't.

She fed his bitterness.

People within his community mocked Bashir. He had no children, a tiny maisonette in Thornbury and little money. Shakeel had offered him plenty; but Bashir had no need for it. No appetite to be rich. There was only one thing which kept him alive.

The image of slicing his cut-throat razor across a carotid artery and watching a life ebb away.

Bashir wasn't going to Friday prayers.

Not today.

Because within the melodrama and outrage of what

had happened to Shakeel, something had dawned on Bashir.

Opportunity.

Bashir was supposed to be attending the Bradford Mela tonight, with the rest of his colleagues, but he wouldn't be there. His focus would be elsewhere.

The lights were on in the enormous detached Victorian house. Bashir knew it well; he'd watched it for years. He knew it was fifteen steps from the gate to the front door. Once inside, it was forty-two steps from there to the back door and thirty steps to the conservatory. He thought about the locks. The front and back doors were robust. The lower windows were out – too small for Bashir to squeeze through – but the conservatory was vulnerable. The crowbar slotted nicely between the doors.

Bashir thought about what was happening in Bradford. It had the feel of instability. Exactly what he needed.

Bashir clenched the steering wheel and gritted his teeth. *'Benchauds,'* he whispered, cursing in Urdu. The time was near. He closed his eyes and breathed deeply, allowing his rage to build.

Bashir opened his eyes and looked towards the darkening clouds.

Six hours before sunset. Tonight was the night.

Bashir was comforted with the knowledge that soon a story forty years in the making would finally end.

They would scream. And that was fine.

It was the soundtrack of his dreams.

TEN

HOLME WOOD WAS KNOWN as the white Bronx of Bradford, the largest council estate in the city, infested with crime. Simpson had sent Harry the last known location for Lucas: temporary council housing before they relocated him. The place was a shit-hole where drug addicts released from prison with nowhere else to go ended up.

Harry was fidgeting nervously with the gearstick. Holme Wood brought back memories of his youth. His father's corner shop was on the outskirts of the estate. Harry and Ronnie had done paper rounds for years and Harry would always remember one specific incident: it was etched on his memory. They had entered one of the tower blocks and were heading for the fifth floor but never got past the third. The discovery of a dead junkie, sprawled on the floor with a needle still in his arm, had forced Ronnie to pull them out. The guy had clearly been robbed; his wallet was lying across his chest and his pockets had been turned out.

Only in Holme Wood.

Harry entered the north of the estate. To his left were neglected fields, with several malnourished horses roaming next to an abandoned gypsy cart.

Harry had learned to judge an estate by the appearance of the local corner shop. Shutters across the windows when it was closed were the norm. Metal grilles across them when it was open suggested a high-crime area. And no windows because they were bricked up meant the area should be avoided at all costs. Holme Wood's shop fell into the third category.

But the local store was also the best place to gain local information. Anything a corner shopkeeper didn't know wasn't worth knowing.

JJ SINGH CONVENIENCE STORE.

Harry knew the owner. He had gone to the Sikh gurdwara for Saturday prayers with Mr Singh's daughter, Gurpreet, who, unlike Harry, had followed convention and married a well-respected Sikh pharmacist.

Harry was a rabid dog in his community: talked about; pointed at; mocked for dating a Muslim. For getting caught in her web and never wanting to break free.

Harry needed to start somewhere and Singh was the best person to ask. He would be nosy, perhaps throw in a few barbs about Harry's life choices but without ever being openly offensive. The moment Harry left, he would surely discuss Harry's brazen attitude with his wife, who would modify it, magnify it and spread it around the temple where Harry's mother would eventually get an exaggerated version.

Fuck, he hated Asian gossips. Asian gossips were the worst kind. They played a sort of brutal Chinese whispers.

Harry left his car and approached the decaying store. The pointing in the brickwork had eroded, giving the building a lopsided appearance. The blue off-licence sign was cracked, exposing wiring beneath. Exterior CCTV cameras tracked his movements as he approached the front door.

It was closed.

There was a hastily written note on the front door: 'Gone Cash & Carry. Back one hour.'

The note wasn't timed, so Harry had no idea when the hour expired. He had a wry smile on his face as he got back to his car. Tacky notes taped to the front door. Just like old times.

Harry drove down the road to where Lucas had been staying. The hostel looked more like a prison, a whole row of terraced houses which had been merged into bedsits. There were bars across ground-floor windows, and power cables dangling perilously by the side of the building. A live-in warden called Bernard was supposed to help the residents with paperwork and liaise with the council about moving them into more permanent accommodation.

Harry spoke with him and was told HMET detectives

had already visited. By all accounts detectives were parked close by, watching the hostel. Harry hadn't noticed any of his colleagues and assumed they'd pissed off somewhere for a coffee. He was their usual gaffer and without him at the helm, they were sure to slack off. He knew what they were like.

Bernard repeated what he had already told other detectives. That Lucas hadn't returned the previous night and that he had filled out an incident report. Harry dismissed the report; he wasn't interested in Bernard's procedures.

Harry was led to Lucas's room on the second floor. The smell of marijuana was patently obvious in the corridor. The warden left Harry inside and told him to return the master key before he left.

Lucas's room was bleak. Dismal light filtering through dirty windows made it feel gloomy and magnified the isolation.

Harry switched the light on and took a slow walk around the room. Stained magnolia walls, a single bed, a wardrobe with a missing door, and a tiny sink in the corner. The mirror above it was cracked. The wardrobe was bare, as were the bedside cabinets. Harry got on his knees and checked under the bed.

He stripped the bedding but found nothing. His team were trained well. They would have lifted anything useful. Harry had hoped to gauge something by visiting but there was nothing.

There was a sudden knock on the door. Harry covered the ground in three strides and opened it.

'Oh,' the scrawny-looking teenager said. 'Ma bad. Fort you was Lucas. Heard you movin' 'round.'

Harry shook his head. 'I'm Detective Inspector Virdee.' He give the kid a once-over. The smell of marijuana hit Harry like a slap. 'You smoking weed in here, kid?'

The ginger-haired boy's mouth dropped open and he tried his best attempt at innocence. 'Nah, not me. I ain't touched it.'

Harry raised his hand. 'I'm not bothered if you have. You know Lucas?'

The kid shook his head. 'Nah. I was just, ya know, wantin' to chill an' dat.'

Harry pulled the kid into the room and closed the door, startling the youngster.

'Hey!'

'Relax. I just want a few details and I don't want the whole building to hear. Sit down.' Harry pointed to the bed.

'Listen, like . . . I gotta chip, yeah, cos—'

'Sit. Quicker we talk, quicker you can "chip".'

Reluctantly the kid sat down.

'When was the last time you saw Lucas?'

'Yesterday. Nah, I didn't see him yesterday,' the boy corrected, waving his finger in the air as if plucking the answers from an imaginary calendar. 'It were day before. Wait, what day is it today?'

Harry sighed. 'Friday.'

'Yeah, so like, Wednesday. I fink.'

'You speak with him?'

'Sorta.'

'Sorta?'

'Yeah. He was teachin' me 'bout boxin' and fings.'

'Boxing?'

'Yeah, man. Lucas is like, pow, man!' The boy mimicked an uppercut.

'Right. He tell you where he was going?'

The kid shook his head. 'Dem ova guys already been askin' me dat.'

Harry nodded. 'So you don't know where he went, or any friends or connections he might have had?'

'Nah.' The boy tapped his feet on the floor. 'I just came in to tell him dat I dig his lyrics an' dat.'

'Lyrics?'

The kid nodded. He stuffed his hand in his pocket and handed Harry a crumpled piece of paper. 'Check dem lyrics out, man. I been sayin' dem to the ovas and shit.'

Harry took the paper.

'Life is like a boxin' ring. Don't get trapped in the corners. Take the centre and don't ever wait for the bell to save you . . .'

Harry was surprised at the philosophical tone and read it several times. 'Lucas wrote this?'

The boy nodded. 'Lucas is fly wiv boxin' an' shit.'

'I'm going to keep this.' Harry read it again before putting it in his pocket.

'"From ma hands to your lips."'

'What?'

'It's dis lyric on dis track I been bouncin' to.'

Harry grilled the boy for a few more minutes and then let him go. He scanned the room once more and left, tossing the key to Bernard on his way out.

Harry was driving out of the estate, mulling over Lucas's note, when he saw Mr Singh unloading his Volvo in front of his store. His grey beard was flapping in the wind and the bright orange turban on his head was in stark contrast to the dreary gloom of Holme Wood. Harry pulled over. He got out and made his way quickly towards Singh, who had dropped a crate of Lucozade and was hurriedly scooping up the bottles.

'Here.' Harry crouched to help. 'Let me.'

Singh looked at him suspiciously, afraid at first, and then registered who he was. 'Hardeep?'

He nodded. 'Long time, uncle.' Everyone was an 'uncle' in the Asian community, friend or foe. It was respectful to address them that way.

'I no see you long time!' Singh accepted Harry's help.

'My timing's impeccable,' Harry replied. 'I used to hate doing this at Dad's shop.'

It took a few minutes to unload the car. Harry was lifting five crates of bottles at a time, ignoring Singh's protests that he would hurt his back. With the car emptied, Harry accepted a cold drink and took a seat behind the shop counter.

Like home, he thought.

The interior was dimly lit. Several of the fluorescent tubes on the ceiling had fused. There was an old fourteen-inch television hanging above the counter, playing a Bollywood movie. Singh took a seat behind the till, next to Harry. His turban almost touched the bottom of the TV and his tracksuit was ripped in several places.

'How's the family?' Harry asked, getting the niceties out of the way.

'Oh, they be doing fine.' Singh smiled. 'Gurpreet is having children now and your auntie, she is not well so we are sending her to India for holiday. We are looking to sell the shop.'

'Really?' Harry asked, feigning interest.

'For two years but no one is wanting shop in Holme Wood.'

'No, I don't suppose they are.'

'How are you, beta?'

Beta.

For a moment it took Harry's breath away.

Son. That's what he had called Harry and for the briefest of moments he sounded just like his father.

Harry composed himself quickly.

'Oh, I'm fine, you know, working hard.' Harry took his time looking around the store before meeting Singh's gaze again.

'You . . . you are in hard position,' Singh replied, acknowledging what Harry's relationship with Saima had cost. 'I am seeing your mum and dad sometimes . . .'

'I'm actually here on business,' Harry said, as officially as he could, leading the conversation away from the minefield.

Thankfully, Singh didn't push it. 'Oh?'

Harry nodded and began talking in Punjabi. It made eliciting information from Singh easier. He asked if he knew who Lucas Dwight was. Singh knew; he read the local newspaper every day. Whilst Lucas's release this week hadn't been front-page news, it had made the insides.

'Have you seen him?' Harry asked.

Unexpectedly, Singh nodded.

'Did he come in here?'

'Yes.'

'When did you serve him?'

'Yesterday. About lunchtime.'

'Did you speak with him?'

'Not exactly. He wanted credit.'

'What did he want?'

'Cigarette papers, a Coke and a magazine. I refused credit so he put them back.'

'How long was he in here?'

'Maybe five, ten minutes?'

'Why so long?'

'Reading the bloody magazine.' Singh shook his head. 'I told him, this isn't a library!'

'Which magazine?' Harry hoped it wasn't one of the adult ones on the top shelf. Singh stepped away from the counter to the magazine rack to his left. He handed Harry a copy of *Boxing News*.

Harry leafed through the pages. 'He was reading this?'

Singh nodded.

'Did he say anything else?'

'He asked me which bus goes into town. I told him, the six thirty.'

Harry stepped away, still flicking through the magazine. There was a page missing. Torn out. Harry picked up another copy and flicked to page sixty-seven. He speed-read the article and then whispered, 'Well, I'll be damned.' He put his hand in his pocket and pulled out a five-pound note. 'Here,' he said, giving it to Singh. 'I'll take this.'

'Oh no.' Singh switched back to English, pushing Harry's hand away. 'You take. Please. You help me unload car. I give you magazine and drink.'

Harry smiled. 'Thanks, uncle. Anything else you can tell me about Lucas?'

'Is he doing something bad already?'

Harry shook his head. Clearly the news about Lucas being implicated in Shakeel Ahmed's disappearance hadn't gone viral. Harry wondered what today's edition of the *Telegraph & Argus* would say. Singh would know by the end of the day exactly why he was here.

'No. I just need to follow up on a few things. Do these cameras work?' Harry pointed to several dotted around the ceiling.

Singh laughed. 'Lights not working. Sometimes fridge not working. Many things not working in my shop, but cameras', he said, pointing to them, 'always working.'

'Figures,' Harry said. 'Holme Wood won't ever change.'

Singh shook his head. 'People no bother me. Not any more. Too many drugs in this area now. Kids are coming in my shop with bundles of twenty-pound notes. I charge them one pound for can of Coke – they are throwing five pounds at me and saying keep change. So much drugs money is in their hands.'

Harry nodded. 'I know.'

'Police – they never doing anything,' Singh protested. 'They come, they arrest and peoples are back here within few weeks. I don't understand.'

Everyone said it. The tag of 'Gotham City' had drawn media attention, with the local papers running articles about lawlessness in Bradford. It didn't make for attractive reading but the newspapers weren't far wrong. The police were losing the war on drugs. Heroin was flooding into the city on a scale they hadn't seen before and all they could get a hold on were the low-level dealers, not the major players.

'Thanks, uncle,' said Harry. 'It was nice seeing you.'

Singh opened his mouth to say something else and then reconsidered. 'Good luck, Hardeep.' Harry wondered momentarily what he was referring to.

Back in the car, he opened the magazine at the page Lucas had removed. 'Always the minor details,' he said, and turned the key.

ELEVEN

BRADFORD HAD BECOME THE cesspit of Yorkshire, cowering next to the thriving rival cities of Leeds and Harrogate. You could buy a three-bedroom house in the centre for sixty grand. That wouldn't even get you a shed in Leeds.

For over a decade, Bradford town centre had decayed and regeneration had dwindled. False promises, a crippling recession and poor planning had ruined the city. It had become known locally as 'the hole in the ground', with half-arsed projects that came to nothing and derelict buildings with no plans for how to redevelop them. Now, finally, 'the hole in the ground' was a soon-to-open brash new shopping centre. Harry thought it was unlikely to succeed. Bradford was more suited to pound shops than designer stores.

Harry parked down a cobbled street just off Upper Piccadilly, opposite the Russian Restaurant. The place had closed down a year earlier after suffering two arson attacks in the same week. The owner had subsequently relocated to Shipley; not smart by any means but most areas were better than the centre. Dereliction was the norm here. Huge Victorian buildings from the industrial era were covered in black soot. They stood abandoned and ashamed.

It felt like foreign territory for Harry to be working alone, but when he thought about it he realized he was fooling himself. He had always preferred working this way. Rules and regulations were the death of progress.

Upper Piccadilly was the portal which connected the old world with the new at the heart of the city centre. It gave access to the antiquated John Street market and also led down into Centenary Square, which was the new home for bars, restaurants and even an art gallery.

Harry turned off the engine. A lazy drizzle started to mist on his windscreen. He looked at the article in his hand: 'Boxing in Yorkshire – a profile of Arthur Dwight's academy'.

Back in the eighties when Yorkshire boxing was booming Lucas's grandfather had been a trainer. Harry was unaware of the gym but he figured with Lucas coming back and removing the page from the magazine, it was a fair bet he might be holed up there. According to the magazine, Arthur Dwight had died in the nineties and the gym had closed.

Harry got out of his car and took an umbrella from the boot. He threw on his raincoat.

The immediate area was deserted and Harry had no idea where the boxing gym was. He spied Mamma Mia, Bradford's oldest Italian restaurant and certainly the best pizza in Yorkshire. The article mentioned the restaurant, how the owner used to give leftover pizzas to the boxers, much to the annoyance of Arthur Dwight. His boxers were always sluggish after a twelve-inch Margherita.

Like the rest of the city, time had stood still for Mamma Mia. Its eighties décor was somehow part of the charm. He checked the time. It was just before twelve and the staff inside were preparing tables.

Harry tapped on the door and one of the waiters shook his head and pointed at his watch. Harry knocked incessantly until the waiter approached, shaking his head in annoyance and tapping his wrist.

'Is eleven forty. We open in twenty minutes,' he said in a strong Italian accent.

Harry showed him his badge, retracted his umbrella and stepped inside without waiting for an invite.

'Detective Inspector Virdee. Is your boss in, Franc?' The waiter's name badge was faded and Harry corrected himself on closer inspection. 'Sorry. Franco.'

'The boss? Matteo?' replied the waiter.

'Yes.'

'*Problema?*'

Harry shook his head. 'I need his help.'

Franco invited Harry to sit down but he refused. The waiter muttered something in Italian to a dark-haired girl who looked no older than fifteen. She disappeared through a swinging door. Harry remained by the window, looking across the street, wondering where the gym might be.

Harry had visited Upper Piccadilly many times and was certain he had never seen a boxing academy. The eighteenth-century building opposite housed the Piccadilly Project; a programme to help recovering alcoholics. Harry knew it well; Ronnie had attended meetings there after being released from prison.

'Mr Virdee?' a voice to his left asked. Harry turned to see a young man approaching, hand outstretched.

'You're the owner?'

'My father,' Matteo replied in a broad Yorkshire accent. 'I've been running this place for three years.'

'You're a little young to be the boss,' Harry said, shaking his hand, a good solid handshake which Harry thought told you a lot about a man.

'I'm actually thirty-five.'

'Jesus. Same as me but I look like I've got ten years on you. Secret?'

'Italian olive oil. The good stuff. How can I help you, Mr Virdee?'

'Call me Harry,' he replied. 'And I'm not sure you can. I'm looking for a boxing academy that used to be around here. Maybe thirty years ago? Your father might remember. I think he knew the owner.'

'Boxing academy?' Matteo shook his head. 'That's news to me. I can phone him – ask if he knows anything?'

'Would you mind? I might be searching for hours.'

Matteo nodded and told Harry he would be back in a few minutes.

A couple of waitresses were spreading red cloths across the tables. One of them offered Harry a coffee. He declined. Pizza, he would have considered – he'd missed breakfast.

Matteo returned, looking pleased. 'He knew even before I finished asking, but is sure it closed down decades ago.'

Harry nodded. 'I'm sure. I just need to know where it is.'

Matteo led Harry to the front door. The rain had turned to hail, thudding across the windows. 'You see that street there?'

'Behind the Piccadilly Project?' Harry asked, raising his voice to overcome the drumming of the hailstones.

Matteo nodded. 'Exactly. Go down there and . . . my father cannot remember which side of the road it is on – he thinks left – but there are some steps leading down below street level. That is where the gym used to be.'

Harry thanked him, stepped out into the sheets of hail and raised his umbrella.

The side street was consumed by shadows from the towering buildings on either side. There were no street-lights and it felt like a sinister step into the unknown. The street was a dead end and looked utterly bereft of life. Harry approached the gloom cautiously, half expecting to bump into Lucas Dwight coming the other way. He made his way down one side, angling the umbrella to protect his face from the hail. The left side of the street revealed nothing so Harry crossed over. The sweep of the right side also proved fruitless.

Harry cursed the weather and started again. He put the umbrella away, allowing hailstones to hammer into his face so he could get a detailed look at the street.

Halfway down, he stopped. There was a tiny break between two buildings and a flight of narrow stairs leading into a darkness that was absolute. Harry held the umbrella like a weapon in his right hand. He descended the steps carefully.

This was the place.

A pair of metal boxing gloves was welded on to a steel gate which protected a large wooden door. There was a thick iron padlock and whilst Harry was dismayed at first, on closer inspection he found it wasn't locked. Harry removed it, feeling his heartbeat quicken. He kept the lock in his hand. It made as good a weapon as any.

Harry tried to open the gate.

It didn't move.

The hinges had fallen away, lowering the gate on to the concrete. Harry pulled at it and it screeched in protest. The sound was deafening. He stopped immediately. He might as well have announced his arrival with a loudspeaker. He looked at the door behind the gate. It was slightly ajar.

Harry put the umbrella and padlock to one side and grabbed the steel gate with both hands. He bent his legs and lifted it, groaning quietly. Damn thing must have been twice his body weight. He opened it enough so he could access the door, which mercifully opened without protest.

The smell of damp was rancid and overpowering.

The rubber soles of his shoes slipped on the concrete. Harry paused, removed his mobile phone and turned on the torch. He picked up the padlock but left the umbrella propping the door open. Harry took several apprehensive steps inside, met only by blackness.

His phone had only 10 per cent battery left. Harry dismissed the on-screen warning and continued inside. The passageway was narrow – wide enough for only one person. Harry kept his left hand on the wall, using it to pull his body further into the darkness, being careful not to drop the padlock and signal his arrival. The light from his phone only illuminated a few feet.

At the end of the passageway were two doors. The one on the right had a toilet sign on it, the other a pair of bronzed boxing gloves, identical to the ones outside. Harry covered the torch on his phone. He heard his breathing, heavy and short.

A voice was telling him to back off and call this in. He knew it well, the voice of reason, something he had repressed for years. This was just how he did things.

Harry turned the handle and pushed, but the door didn't give. He put his body against it and gave it a shove. It rattled open and Harry immediately tensed, prepared for an attack. Sweat trickled down his face, in spite of the bitter cold. He couldn't see a thing. He shuffled inside, keeping his hand firmly over the torch, trying to remain invisible. Harry had been holding his breath and now let it out. Slowly.

He splayed his fingers and shone some light on the side of the wall. It took him a few seconds to find a light switch. He pulled the cord and waited.

One fluorescent tube after another powered up in sequence, the room lighting up a few feet at a time.

There was a large boxing ring in the centre and punch-bags hanging from the ceiling to all four sides. To his right, the entire wall was mirrored, which meant he could see if anyone snuck up behind. It was comforting and Harry stepped boldly into the gymnasium.

He repressed a sneeze as large amounts of dust swirled around his face. The smell of damp was nauseating and Harry could taste the acidity of sweat on his tongue. The air was saturated with it.

There were only two obvious places to hide. Either behind the ring or under it. Anywhere else and Harry would have noticed. He walked towards the ring and then slowly around it, keeping his distance. The base was secured to the floor with huge steel bolts.

Lucas wasn't here.

Harry walked towards the mirror. When he reached it, he looked at his reflection, only for a few seconds.

Here he was again. Alone. Running around Gotham, looking for salvation. Putting himself in dangerous and unnecessary situations.

And for what purpose?

So he could prove that all the things his family and the community said about him weren't true? That he wasn't a failure?

Harry dropped his head and stared at the floor.

This isn't about proving anything. I need to save my job so I can provide.

That wasn't true.

No, Harry. It's about that night. About making right what you did. Paying your debts.

It's about the blood.

It was always about the blood. Spraying across his face whilst his victim choked on it. The sound of that final blood-gargle before the silence took over.

There was a sudden noise from behind. Harry turned and fell to a crouch, backing up against the mirror.

Lucas Dwight was standing in the doorway, staring at him. He looked so different to the last time they had met. Fourteen years was a long time. Like Bradford, Lucas had decayed. He was lighter – almost anorexic-looking – and so pale. *So terribly pale.*

'I know you,' Lucas said. The fluorescence from the tubes caught the blade in his hand and it flickered momentarily. He walked slowly towards Harry, almost a prowl.

'You're under arrest, Lucas.'

'I'm getting déjà vu here.' There was no emotion on Lucas's face. Just a cold blank emptiness.

Harry gripped the steel padlock. He was calculating whether to throw it and charge or to save it for closer combat.

'Arrest for what?' said Lucas. 'Being homeless?'

'Murder.'

Lucas cocked his head to one side and pointed accusingly at Harry. 'I haven't murdered anyone.'

'There is a nice way and a not-so-nice way to do this.' Harry edged closer. 'But you already know that.'

Lucas raised the knife and pointed the blade towards Harry. 'You want to tell me what this is about? Because someone tried to kill *me* and now you're here saying *I'm* under arrest?'

'You'll get your chance to tell your story. But if it kicks off now, then it's resisting arrest.'

'I'm going to resist all right. I intend to find out who is stitching me up – even if I have to go through you to do it.'

'You don't want to take me on, Lucas. Look at you – you're barely forty kilos in those rags. You look sick. Do the smart thing. Put down the knife and get on your knees.'

'This is *my* gym,' Lucas snapped, 'and I'm undefeated here. Now get lost, Detective Virdee. This isn't two thousand and one. The rules have changed.'

'I'm here to bring you in, Lucas. Same as always.'

'No, this is different.' Lucas was becoming more and more agitated. 'This time, I'm in the right and you . . .' He waved the blade at Harry. '. . . are in the wrong.'

Lucas flipped the knife in his hands a couple of times whilst staring at Harry. Then he closed the switchblade and put it in his pocket. 'You don't use a weapon in a boxing gym. You use these.' He clenched his fists. 'I'm not going to disrespect my grandfather by using a knife in here. It's not how we do things.'

Harry looked carefully at him. Taking in every detail. *Wilting. Pale. Sick.*

Slowly, Harry put the padlock on the floor. 'You're forcing my hand?'

'You're forcing your own.'

'I'm leaving this place with you, Lucas.' Harry removed his coat. 'It's up to you to decide in how many pieces.'

TWELVE

FOR ZAIN AHMED, HIS father's death had come as something of a relief. For years he had thought about taking the old man's life so he could finally assume control of the family empire.

But the fact his father had been brutally murdered by someone else *did* bother Zain. In fact it bothered him more than he could have anticipated. Because in their line of work, allowing such an act to go unanswered made them look impotent.

Zain needed to find the culprit and send a message: a clear signal the new boss wasn't soft. That he wasn't nearly as useless as his father had suggested.

Shakeel Ahmed's flagship restaurant on Great Horton Road was silent. They had closed all eleven restaurants as a sign of respect. It was unnerving: usually there would have been staff charging around the premises in preparation for the 5 p.m. opening, but today there was just Zain, sitting at his father's desk, with his feet on it, twirling his father's golden fountain pen through his fingers. The pen his father had used to sign his first restaurant lease and all subsequent deals.

A pen with a razor-sharp tip: Zain had once seen his father stab it into somebody's eye and then simply wipe off the blood on a piece of blotting paper. Zain stared at the pen and thought he might use it the same way when he apprehended his father's killer – a fitting start to his own reign. He felt his father would have approved – something Zain had seldom experienced.

Zain switched his attention to the CCTV monitors. The man he had summoned for today's work had arrived. He watched him open the back door of the restaurant and waited the few minutes it took him to make his way through the enormous kitchen to the rear office. The man knocked on the door, paused, and then entered without waiting for a reply.

Bashir Iqbal wasn't surprised to see Zain Ahmed sitting comfortably in his father's chair. But he was irked at the disrespectful way Zain had his feet on the mahogany desk.

The two men acknowledged each other with a nod. Zain made no effort to get up and Bashir felt no need to extend his condolences.

'Do you know where that desk came from?' Bashir asked in Urdu, sitting down. The leather chair creaked at the size of his frame.

'Pakistan,' Zain replied and continued to rotate the pen in his hand like a helicopter blade.

'Islamabad, to be precise. Majlis-e-Shoora, the Pakistan parliament. President Jinnah signed the creation of our country on that desk.'

'Would you like me to remove my feet from it?'

'No. It is not for me to give you orders, Zain. I am simply pointing out its history.'

The two men stared at each other for a few seconds.

'Do you know what I would like, Bashirji?' Zain asked, adding the 'ji' to his name as a sign of respect for an elder. There was another, covert reason: Zain knew Bashir's real role within the company. He needed to get the old man on-side.

'Enlighten me.'

'I would like to get hold of the man who killed my father and pin him to this desk. Then I would like to use this pen, my father's pen, his favourite pen, to stab out his eyes.'

Zain searched Bashir's face for approval but there was none. There was no reaction at all.

'Do you think that would be a final fitting act for this table?'

Bashir took a moment, sizing up whether Zain was serious or just grandstanding in his new role. 'I think you shouldn't spill foul blood on that table,' he replied.

Zain smiled and removed his feet from it. He moved his chair closer to the desk. 'Do you know who killed my father, Bashirji?'

'No.'

'I do. Well, I know how to find out. But I'm going to require your help. *Your* expertise.'

Bashir shrugged his shoulders. 'I'm just a driver. You need a lift?'

Zain smiled. He picked up the pen again. More rotation through his fingers. 'I don't think so. I know exactly who you are. And what you used to do for my father.'

Bashir didn't reply. He was like a statue in the chair, trying to analyse Zain and see if the kid was serious. He knew Shakeel had little faith in the boy. Privately educated. Wrapped in cotton wool. Cleanly shaven, Jacuzzi baths and designer clothing.

'I'm just old man,' Bashir replied, switching from Urdu to broken English, something he did to appear simple and far from threatening.

Zain leaned forward and pointed the pen at him. 'Are you telling me that you don't wish to find out who killed my father? Your closest friend?'

Bashir remained silent. He didn't like Zain. He was a boy in a man's chair.

'May I be honest?' Zain asked.

Bashir nodded.

'I know your story. I know why you are here. My father told me – only a few months ago, as it happens. He told me that if I ever needed to trust somebody, then it should be you. I think he was afraid that getting into politics might make him a target for, well, something like what has happened. He told me about many things, even . . . even about Ruksa.'

Now Bashir's demeanour did change. His face tensed and he stood up, towering over Zain, who shrank into his chair. Bashir's expression twisted into a snarl and he leaned forward, placing both hands on the desk.

'What?' he asked, real malice in his voice. There was an anger which Zain had never seen before and didn't know how to handle.

'Look—'

Zain didn't finish. Bashir yanked his delicate frame out of the chair, grabbing his neck with both hands. Zain tried to scream but his voice was strangled in his throat. Bashir dragged him across the desk, sending its contents flying across the floor.

'In thirty years, not even your father spoke her name.' Bashir had reverted to Urdu. He pulled Zain closer to his face. 'If you know who I am and what I do, then realize this, Zain,' he said, spitting on his face, 'when somebody's tongue becomes offensive to me, I bite it from their mouth. When somebody's eyes look at me with ill intent, I remove them.'

Bashir's face had darkened like a fruit turned rotten. Zain was desperately trying to talk. Bashir kept him close for a few more life-threatening seconds and then threw him angrily back into the chair.

Bashir retook his seat. 'What is it that you want?' he asked peaceably, yet still smouldering that Zain knew secrets he had no business knowing.

'I want revenge.'

'No, really. What is it that *you* want?' Bashir was

tiring of Zain's infantile posturing. Too much chatter. He was also massaging his neck and looked like he might start crying. The altercation had caused wounds on Bashir's back to open. He could feel the stickiness of blood soiling his clothes.

Zain stopped massaging his throat. 'I . . . I . . . want—'

'Respect? Power? For Allah's sake, just tell me once, clearly, what little Zain Ahmed wants?'

'I want to be feared!' Zain shouted and slammed his hand on the table, hard enough that Bashir almost felt the sting. 'I want people to respect me, like they did my father. I want to keep this organization powerful and make sure that I build, not dismantle.'

'And why should I help you do that?'

Zain took a moment and tried to compose himself. He was blinking excessively and his hands were shaking. 'My father has some items which belong to you? Some land in Pakistan he promised you, and some money. Call this your final act?'

'Those items are mine. Already mine. Owed to me.'

'Yes, but I need you to carry out one more job – and for God's sake, I am asking you to avenge the man who was your closest friend. Don't you want that?'

'I don't know who killed him. And yes, I would like revenge for your father, but I have other things on my mind.'

'I know.' Zain paused and then held up both hands respectfully. 'He told me. What you plan to do. He told me the only reason you hadn't done it yet was because of him. Now he's not here, I know the time must be soon.'

Sooner than you think, thought Bashir.

'Please,' Zain said. 'My father would want you to help. Why else would he have told me these . . . these . . . secrets? He said you were the only person I would be able to trust if anything happened to him and that I should call on your services.'

'So tell me, Zain, what do you want me to do?'

'I might not be street dirty, but I'm not stupid. I know who can tell us what happened to my father.'

'Go on.'

'I want you to bring me Martin Davis, the BNP leader.'

Bashir laughed. 'Stupid fool,' he spat and looked away.

'There is talk that Lucas Dwight, the ex-leader of the BNP, did this to my father and he is now in hiding. Martin Davis is in Bradford, at the Midland Hotel. We have "friends" there. Watching.'

Bashir was surprised, almost impressed that Zain was making a play.

'All you have to do is bring him to me and he will know where Lucas Dwight is and what happened. He is the only man to gain from my father's murder.'

'No,' replied Bashir. 'There is one more who has gained greatly from his death.'

Bashir and Zain shared an awkward silence.

'I would never have done this,' Zain said eventually.

'I know. You don't have it within you.'

Zain ignored the jibe. Just what he was and was not capable of would soon become clear. 'I want the leader of the BNP. What I do once I have him is *my* concern.'

'And then?'

'Then you are free. You can go and seek out those you want, then disappear to Pakistan, back to the land you are owed. I will make it happen – just like my father promised. You have my kasam.'

Kasam: a sacred promise.

'You want to engineer a reputation so your father's business does not crumble?'

'Yes.'

'And you want revenge?'

'Yes.'

'It is not an easy thing what you are asking. To take this man.'

'Like I said, we have people in play at the Midland Hotel,' Zain replied. 'They are just waiting for you. But time is tight. Can I count on you?'

'I leave after this. Your father was holding a lot of money in an account in Pakistan for me. And there are land registry papers he has which need assigning to me. I want them immediately.'

'No. I will release the land to you now; the money when I have Martin Davis here.' Zain took a folder from the desk, opened it and pushed the papers towards Bashir.

'Do we have a deal?'

'I need to be on a plane first thing tomorrow morning.'

'Tomorrow morning?'

'Yes.'

'But what about . . . your plans?'

Bashir thought about the house. About the blood. About a recurrent nightmare which had plagued him for decades. 'I will bring you Martin Davis. I will get him to talk because you won't know how. Then tonight – I will finish my business.' Bashir stood up to leave. He turned his back on Zain and then paused. 'I need only one ticket for tomorrow. You will make sure my wife is taken care of here. Give me your kasam on that as well.'

'You have it.'

'Say it.'

'You have my kasam. I will take care of your wife.'

Bashir made his way towards the door, opened it and again paused. He didn't like that Zain knew his secrets. Especially about Ruksa. He turned around and walked back to the desk. 'Just so you know – if you cross me on this—'

'I gave you my kasam.'

'I need to be clear,' said Bashir. He pushed his hand under his shirt, and when he removed it, it was covered in blood. Bashir grabbed Zain's hand, who tried to pull away but gave up once he felt the iron strength in Bashir's grip.

'Now we have understanding,' said Bashir and smeared his blood across Zain's palm. 'Now we are bound.'

THIRTEEN

'JUST TURN AROUND AND walk away,' Lucas said. 'I'm not your man. Someone is setting me up.'

Harry was within striking distance. The two men sized each other up, neither willing to engage first.

'Doesn't work that way,' Harry replied. 'I'm bringing you in, like it or not.'

'At least *tell* me what I'm supposed to have done, who I'm supposed to have murdered? Does it sound like I know what you're talking about?'

Lucas had changed. Gone was the anger burning behind his eyes. He looked calm, arrogant in his dismissal of Harry. He was painfully thin. The wrinkles on his face made him look much older than Harry even though he was a year younger. His clothes were filthy and he looked more like a homeless tramp than a feared fugitive.

'We can talk it through down the station,' Harry replied. 'Now drop your hands and turn around.'

'Someone tried to kill me. And now you show up? Coincidental, isn't it? Doesn't it seem like a set-up to you? Are you that naïve, detective? Because I don't think you are.' Lucas wasn't shouting but there was an edge to his voice and a spark of the old anger in his eyes.

'I'm not going to ask you again,' Harry said. 'You are under arrest.'

'Don't.' Lucas put out his hand and altered his stance as Harry stepped forward. 'It will end badly for you. You're top-heavy and too slow. I'll see your shot coming. I'll land three before you regroup.'

Lucas's physical demise may have mirrored Bradford's, but the belief he wouldn't be beaten was also learned from the same streets.

'Listen to me. Back the fuck off.'

His attitude puzzled Harry. The old Lucas Dwight would have jumped at the chance for a private tussle with Harry, but Lucas was reluctant.

Frightened. He's frightened. You're twice his size, fit, healthy. He's bluffing. Isn't he?

'I'm not the same man I used to be,' continued Lucas. 'Fourteen years in prison is a long time not to change.'

'Whether you are or not, you're under arrest. If you are innocent, you'll get your chance in court.'

'No. A dealer tried to kill me. Gave me a spiked heroin batch. I want to know why, especially now you're here trying to detain me. I don't trust the law.'

Harry lunged at Lucas, tired of his bullshit. He threw the first punch, missed and then absorbed what felt like a

113

knife wound to his lower abdomen. The energy drained from Harry's legs. It felt as though his feet had opened up and were leaking his life force across the gymnasium floor; his lungs felt compressed and he crumpled to the floor, gasping desperately.

Lucas stepped out of the way. 'Liver punch,' he said matter-of-factly. 'Impossible to get up from in two minutes, never mind ten seconds.' Lucas listened for the first desperate wheeze from Harry, then sat down on the floor, cross-legged.

'It'll take a minute.' Lucas raised his hand, urging Harry to calm down. 'Relax, you're not dying. It just feels like that.'

The pain crippling Harry's side was intense. With one single body blow, he had been reduced to a wreck. Instead of taking Lucas's advice, Harry was getting angrier. He tried to get up but there was no power in his legs.

'Don't listen, do you?' Lucas said calmly. 'You, my friend, are going nowhere.'

Several minutes had passed without either man moving. Harry's liver felt as if it had ruptured and Lucas continued to stare at him, waiting for Harry to decide whether he wanted another crack.

'I'm man enough to admit when I'm beaten,' said Harry.

'I'm glad we—'

'And that time hasn't arrived.' Harry struggled on to his side.

Lucas shook his head. 'You've got some anger inside you, haven't you?'

'I'm not leaving this place without you. You're a racist nutcase whose blood was found at Shakeel Ahmed's residence this morning. Care to explain that?' he whispered while massaging some feeling back into his side.

'Shakeel Ahmed? The guy running for Bradford West?'

'So you know him?'

'Of him. This place is covered in posters and flyers of the guy's campaign. I'm not blind, detective. He's dead?'

Harry nodded.

'I'm sorry to hear that but it's of no interest to me.'

'I would hypothesize that, with your background, hating the man who beat the BNP *is* of interest to you.'

'No. The guy you think I am left a long time ago.'

'Yet you're still fighting with the police.'

'Hey, you came at me, brother.'

Brother? Did Lucas Dwight just call him brother?

'You're resisting arrest.' Harry felt the pain subside a little. He was gradually trying to get to his feet, gritting his teeth at the throb in his side.

'It's convenient, don't you think?'

'What?' Harry was on his knees now, squarely in front of Lucas.

'That four days after I'm released, I supposedly murder this guy and leave my DNA for you to find?'

'You were careless. A junkie on a killing spree. You're not exactly Einstein.'

'A few hours ago I was lying in the middle of that ring.' Lucas pointed at it. 'Seconds away from dying.'

'You seem fine now.'

'It was luck. If I'd taken the proper hit, I'd be dead.'

'I'm not buying it. I took you down in two thousand and one, remember? What was it you were on? A Paki-bashing spree? Isn't that what you called it?'

'Like I said, that man's been dead a long time,' Lucas said uncomfortably. 'If a decade in jail doesn't redefine you, something is wrong. Wouldn't you agree?'

Harry struggled to his feet. The pain in his liver was sharp but his legs felt sturdier. One thing was for certain, he wasn't about to out-box Lucas Dwight. 'That was a great punch.'

'Took me five years in that ring to perfect it.' Lucas got to his feet and resumed the same stance. 'Dip the left shoulder, fake an uppercut and hammer a liver punch into the side. Impossible to recover from.'

Harry nodded. 'No argument there.'

'You can leave now, detective, I'm not coming with you.'

'When I get outside, I'm calling this in.'

'I won't be here when they arrive. Don't waste their time.'

Harry glanced at the padlock on the floor. There was only one way out. If he sealed the outer door, Lucas was trapped.

'Don't bother. Next I'll drop you with a kidney punch. You won't get up for a week. Do I even sound or look like the man you put away?'

'You're a racist, drug-abusing prick who probably got so high last night, you can't even remember what you did. Come on, where were you last night before you supposedly overdosed in here?'

For the first time, Lucas was unsure. 'I . . . I can't remember. I—'

'No alibi. Previous history of violence towards ethnics and a strong affiliation with the BNP. I'd say that's—'

'I'm *not* the same man!' Lucas shouted. 'Can't you see that? Fourteen years ago, I'd have spread your teeth across this place. Do I even sound the same as that guy? Is this how I used to speak? Can you not see I've educated myself in prison? That tap I gave you was to put you down so I could make you see reason.'

'You can't reason with me. There is *nothing* to convince me you are not involved in Shakeel Ahmed's murder. *Nothing*. Just because you've read a few books and done some courses in prison, that doesn't change who you are. Inside.'

Lucas dropped his eyes to the floor. 'And if I were to prove I've changed? Would you entertain the possibility?'

'What could you conceivably do to show me you're different?'

'Answer my question!' Lucas snapped, raising his voice and pointing at Harry. 'If I showed you how wrong you are, would you entertain it?'

Harry nodded. 'Yes. I would. But I'm talking adopt-an-ethnic kind of shit.'

'Do you believe based solely on our conversation so far that I am a different man to the one you put away fourteen years ago?'

Harry mulled over the question. 'It is possible.'

'And do you also believe that, based on our current situation, if I wanted to hurt you – I mean *really hurt* you, whether it's using this knife or just my fists – that I could? That leaving this gymnasium is in my control?'

Harry wasn't about to confess he was a beaten man. He'd underestimated Lucas, that was for sure. 'I wouldn't say it's completely within your control. You'll still have to get past me.'

Lucas shook his head and gave Harry a patronizing stare. 'Really? You were down for what? Four minutes? I could have beaten you. Stabbed you. Walked away.'

'Fine,' Harry replied tiredly. 'You had your chance.'

'You've still got one hand on your liver.'

'What exactly do you want, Lucas?'

'Are you carrying cuffs?'

Harry nodded.

'I want you to secure yourself to that ring-post and give me the key.'

'Do I look fucking stupid?'

'Far from it. You've got your detective hat on and all the clues are pointing towards me.'

'And the point in doing what you ask?'

'So I can show you something.'

'Feel free.'

'No. I don't trust you not to take advantage.'

'I don't follow.'

'You will. Cuff yourself and hand me the key. As you do so I will put the knife in your hands. An even exchange?'

Harry considered his options.

'You're not even slightly curious? I'm going to hand you the knife.'

'Surrender it first.'

'And you'll do as I say?'

Harry didn't reply.

'Didn't think so.'

'Call it a gesture of good faith. I'll consider your request a hell of a lot more seriously.'

Both men measured each other suspiciously. Then, apparently making a decision about Harry, Lucas put the switchblade on the floor and kicked it towards him. 'There.'

Harry remained steadfast.

'I'm asking you to give me one opportunity.' Lucas's patience was starting to fracture. 'You can't even do that? I'm unarmed. I could have killed you fifteen minutes ago.'

There was a fundamental difference to the man Harry had arrested fourteen years before. And Lucas was right. If he had wanted to hurt Harry, the chance had been there.

'OK.' Harry covered his hand with his sleeve and lifted

the knife from the floor. He put it in his pocket. Then he removed the cuffs and walked over to the ring-post. Harry secured his wrist to it and threw the key on the floor, by Lucas's feet.

'Show me they're fastened.'

Harry tensed the handcuffs and Lucas nodded.

'Your move.'

'Thank you.' Lucas didn't pick up the key but left it on the floor, five feet away from Harry. He walked away to a sink in the corner of the room where he washed his hands, face, then removed his shoes and washed his feet.

He made his way back towards Harry and picked up an exercise mat from the floor. Lucas placed it carefully a few feet away from Harry but within clear line of sight and got on his knees. He then did the one thing which proved without question *he had changed*. Harry stood open-mouthed and astonished as Lucas Dwight, ex-leader of the BNP, put his hands behind his head and started praying towards Mecca.

FOURTEEN

'*ASH-HADU AN LA ILAHA illa Allah. Wa ash-hadu ana Muham-madun rasul Allah.*'

It was the most bizarre thing Harry had ever witnessed. The words, even the rhythm, were authentic. Lucas was reciting an Islamic prayer. Harry had witnessed Saima worshipping many times and recognized every gesture.

Lucas Dwight had converted to Islam?

It sounded too far-fetched.

Harry slipped his hand underneath his shirt and massaged the area around his liver. The dull ache was still pulsing. He glanced to his right at the mirrors. His reflection was whispering.

You were brought up hating Muslims, yet you married one.

Harry looked away. But the voice continued.

You're a hypocrite if you believe Lucas is incapable of

change. He doesn't look the same. Doesn't sound the same.

Harry touched his pocket where the switchblade was.

Weapon surrendered. On his knees. *Praying.*

Saima's voice was in Harry's head.

People change, Jaan. Promise we won't ever judge on what we've been taught, but on what we see. What we feel.

What we see?

What we feel?

Saima had a way of getting inside his head. Always at the right time.

Harry remained silent, watching Lucas as he raised his body and then bowed it in prayer.

A few minutes later Lucas was done. He remained on his knees, back towards Harry, staring into the darkness.

The silence became awkward.

'Can't find the words?' Lucas said eventually.

Harry was leaning on the side of the boxing ring. He no longer felt vulnerable secured to the post.

'You've converted to Islam? Is that what you're telling me?'

'Hard to believe?'

'Yes. It is.'

'Seemed the only way to prove I've changed. You seemed so sure I was incapable.'

'I put you away, remember? I've seen first-hand what you're about.'

'So you've never met anyone who changed your perceptions of life? Never met anyone who ripped apart the bullshit you'd been fed?' Lucas might as well have stood Saima in front of them with Harry's parents burning in the background.

Harry didn't reply – because Lucas had him. They had fought the same struggle.

'Go on.' Harry had thought finding Lucas might be the end of Ahmed's investigation. An easy 'in' back to his job. Clearly not the case.

'Like I said, prison changes a man.' Lucas seemed content on his knees, talking into the emptiness of the gymnasium.

'It's not like it was your first time inside.'

'It was my first sentence of so many years.'

There was a brief pause.

'I'm listening,' Harry said.

'For the first couple of years I was reckless. Fights, angry, bitterness. One day I was cornered by a Polish gang. Outnumbered. I took a heavy beating, had my face caved in – probably would have died – but someone intervened. Big guy. Called Abdullah. He ran the boxing academy. He got the Poles to back off and looked out for me. I didn't appreciate it, but no matter how much shit I gave him, he remained . . . I don't know . . . calm.' Lucas turned around and pointed at Harry, who was still massaging his side. Lucas grinned. 'I can hit you in the ribs so the pain evens out.'

Harry shook his head. 'Keep on with your story.'

Lucas got up from the prayer mat. 'There was something different about Abdullah. He knew what I was about, yet he never tried to change me. I got myself in a couple more scraps and he bailed me out. Think he was trying to change my perceptions. Instead of hating me, he showed me something I've never experienced.'

'Compassion?'

Lucas nodded. 'We became friends. Not quickly. And it wasn't easy. I didn't trust him. Takes a long time to figure things out. He didn't brainwash me. Didn't preach. He showed me how to channel my anger. Provided a little structure. Truth is, he calmed me down. Don't get me wrong, there's still a lot wrong with the policies of this country. But I don't blanket hate any more. I'll get to know you and then judge.'

'When did you convert to Islam?'

'Few years ago. I'm not going to advertise it, because I've learned two things in prison: that religion and politics should never be discussed.'

'Give me a break,' Harry whispered, scratching the stubble on his face. He closed his eyes and sighed heavily.

Lucas raised his shirt and pointed to a newly inked tattoo. 'Can you read the inscription?'

'No.'

'It says "change" in Arabic. The language of the Koran. I've evolved, detective, the same as this city has.'

'I'd call it regression.' Harry didn't explain whether he meant the city or Lucas's choices. He removed a spare key to the handcuffs from his pocket and unlocked them.

'Figures,' said Lucas. 'You can't arrest me. Someone is playing a game I don't like, which involves me taking the fall for things I didn't do.' He said it calmly and with utter conviction. 'If you take me in, I'll be the scapegoat. It's too easy not to look for the truth when you've got me gift-wrapped.'

'I can't let you walk.' Harry put away the cuffs. 'Even if you might be telling the truth.'

'We have a problem then. Because I don't want to damage your kidney as well.'

'There is another option.' Harry felt a tinge of apprehension. It was more than that. It was the voice of reason, which, as usual, he was ignoring.

'I'm listening.'

'What's your plan if I don't arrest you? Clearly you have one.'

Lucas nodded. 'The dealer, Daniel Levy, who supplied me last night. I'm going to find him. Ask who gave the order to put me down.'

'How do you know it wasn't a duff batch? Christ, the city is rife with it.'

Lucas inched towards Harry. 'Because this guy tracked *me* down and gave me a freebie. Out of the goodness of his heart,' he said sarcastically. 'I didn't ask questions. Figured he wanted a favour down the line. But now I realize he *needed* to give me that bag. Pressed me into shooting up with him. Got angry when I didn't. Weird shit. Didn't think anything of it at the time. Odd, wouldn't you say?'

Harry agreed. 'Odd enough to ask questions.'

'We're on the streets. You ask questions, you get lies. You want the truth? You put something on the line.'

'Such as?'

'His life.'

'So you're a religious man but not a pacifist?'

'An eye for an eye. That's my world. Someone takes a shot at you? That gives you right of reply. No more. No less.'

'I don't care what he's pulled. You're not taking another man's life. We can, however, make sure he talks.'

'We?'

Harry nodded.

'You think I'm going to trust you? I've changed but I'm not stupid. What do you have to gain by helping me?'

Harry hesitated. Lucas was quickly on to it.

'What are you not telling me?'

'I need this as badly as you do.'

'For a promotion?' Lucas mocked.

'No. I need a bit of redemption too.'

'Come again?'

'I'm . . . not on the books at the moment.'

'They fired you?'

'Suspended. Pending an investigation.'

'You're shitting me.'

'No. I'm not.'

'Why should I believe you? Even if it's true, what would I gain?'

'Next week, I'm in front of a board that's going to tear my arse out. And I've got sweet FA to counter what I did. Maybe I find Shakeel Ahmed's killer and maybe they look favourably on me.'

'That's a lot of maybes. What did you do?'

'Broke somebody's jaw.'

Lucas whistled. 'I'm not really feeling the trust part of our relationship growing.'

'I was defending my wife.'

'That does shed a different light on it. But I still don't believe you.'

'OK. Let me prove it.' Harry removed his mobile phone from his pocket and started to dial.

'Easy now.' Lucas closed the gap between them. His breath was stale on Harry's face. Lucas put his hand across the phone.

'You dial then.' Harry handed him the iPhone.

'Don't know how to. Don't get posh phones like this in prison. Who are we calling?'

'May I? I'm going to call my boss. Reiterate that helping out today might save my job. Put you in the loop. You hold the phone. I say something you don't like – you hang up.'

'Even if you are telling the truth, I don't need you. You're extra baggage.'

'Think it through. I've got everything at my disposal. Contacts, connections, data. Whoever killed Shakeel Ahmed framed you easily. You're going to need me.'

Lucas mulled over Harry's offer. Then he handed him

the phone. 'Put it on speaker. You stray from the script and I'm going to unleash holy hell on you. And this time, you won't get up. Clear?'

'Crystal.'

Harry dialled Simpson and let Lucas listen to the conversation. It was brief but Simpson confirmed that finding Lucas and closing the investigation was Harry's only chance.

'Satisfied?'

Lucas nodded.

'I can't let you leave this gym unless you're with me,' Harry said. 'I'll buy into the fact you've changed. Enough to give you a chance. You have your name to clear and I have a job and a city to save.'

'Real-life goddamn hero, aren't you?'

'Listen,' Harry snapped, 'you're not getting a better offer all fucking year. You've got a senior detective offering to help you. Off the books. Why don't you think this through?'

Lucas raised his hands and backed off. Into the shadows. Cracking his knuckles. 'The guy I need to find – the dealer.' Lucas's voice echoed around the gym. 'I know where he'll be once it's dark.'

'When we find him, there are rules involved. I don't have a problem with a shakedown but you cross the line and I'll slap the cuffs on.'

'Sounds fair.' Lucas turned his back towards Harry. 'Meet me back here at five.'

'I can't leave you. I don't trust you not to disappear.'

'I'm a man who believes in people's word.'

'You've got a long way to go to earn my trust.'

'That goes both ways.'

'Surrender to me,' said Harry. 'We'll . . . how do I put it, hang out. Hell, I'll even feed you. God knows you look like you need it.'

'I have your word that you won't double-cross me?'

'Yes.'

Lucas considered it for a moment. 'Fine.' He turned around to face Harry. 'In that case, we have a deal.'

'Your blood was found at Ahmed's house,' said Harry. 'You can't fabricate DNA.'

'My blood?'

'Yes. How did it get there?'

'I've no idea.' Lucas's eyes narrowed. 'Let's take this one step at a time?'

'We'll find this dealer, and if he's not involved, then I take you down the nick?'

'He *is* involved. And I'm not going anywhere with you except to meet Daniel Levy. If he's not there . . . we can talk about that when and if. No games. No fucking about. Agreed?'

Harry gave it some thought. He was agreeing to a deal with the devil. And no matter the outcome, he was going to lose. 'Shake on it?'

Lucas made his way over and accepted Harry's out-stretched hand. 'Sure,' he said, shaking it firmly.

'Wouldn't have thought such a skeletal-looking bugger could drop me so easily.'

'I doubt we'll have to go there again, partner,' Lucas replied with just enough bite.

'Partner? I suppose. But, Lucas, we're doing this on my terms. Don't cross the line.'

'Let's just track Daniel Levy. Then we'll see just exactly where the line is.'

FIFTEEN

DETECTIVE SUPERINTENDENT GEORGE SIMPSON was at Trafalgar House, Divisional Headquarters and temporary home of the Homicide and Major Enquiry Team. There was a frantic rush of detectives outside his office. The door was closed and the blinds were drawn.

Just five minutes of peace.

An incident room had been set up and every detective at his disposal was on the Shakeel Ahmed murder case.

Of all the cases to hit his desk five days before retirement, why this one?

Lucas Dwight's name was out. It was inevitable. Public-sector pay was at an all-time low and morale was always boosted by a few quid from savvy journalists. Leaks happened. Once upon a time, George Simpson had been in the same boat. But as seniority replaced ambition, it was easy to forget those struggles.

Lucas Dwight.

He picked up a crystal glass. Nothing but water inside, even though he had a bottle of Dalmore in his top drawer.

Not today.

Maybe tonight.

Definitely tonight.

His hand was shaking. Others wouldn't have seen the tremor, such was its slightness. But for Simpson, Parkinson's was now a friend who would take him to the grave. He took a sip of water and put the glass back on his desk.

He swivelled in his leather chair to face the window behind. It gave a view across the town centre.

Gotham City.

Ever since that article had gone viral, there was graffiti all across the city, embedding the name across communities.

Gotham – where hope didn't exist.

Where fictitious heroes were needed to save the city.

Bradford was perhaps as close to Gotham as it got. The article had wounded Simpson, because for all his candour and hard work, he was losing the battle. Drugs had flooded the city over the past decade on a scale never seen before. Government cutbacks were crippling, and uniformed presence on the streets was minimal.

Bradford didn't stand a bloody chance.

It was becoming more polarized. The Asian communities were closing rank and mistrust was now traded like currency.

Shakeel Ahmed's death, a racist assault on the city, would go down badly – unless they nailed Lucas Dwight quickly. Demonstrated the very definition of swift justice.

George Simpson didn't want his legacy to be a ruined city. He glanced to his right. The calendar on the wall had a large black circle around today's date: 'Friday 23 October. Bradford Mela. Eid.'

Simpson sighed and the unease in his chest made the Parkinson's seem like a children's ride at the fair.

Need to settle this quickly.

Need to find the bastard.

There was a knock at the door and then it opened.

Simpson didn't turn around.

There was only one person who would enter without permission.

'George?' she said and closed the door.

'Hmm,' he replied. He was looking out of the window at darkening clouds and the first falls of hail.

'Have you taken your medication?'

'Mavis,' he replied without turning to face her, 'I'm not a child.'

He felt her close, at his shoulder.

'I'm worried about you,' she said. 'You might be the chief in this place, but right now, you're just my husband and I'm worried.'

'Don't be,' he said. 'Whatever will be, will be.'

She placed a hand on his arm. 'Why don't you pass this on to someone—'

'Because there is no one else,' he snapped. 'I didn't get here by choosing the soft options. We'll sort this.'

He glanced again at the calendar. He had hundreds of officers covering the Mela. The planning had been going on for months and all of Bradford's Asian community leaders had been emphasizing the importance of a peaceful event. So why did he feel so uneasy? Why wouldn't the ache in his chest go away?

'Your medicine,' Mavis whispered again. 'Just tell me you've taken it.'

Simpson crossed his body with his left hand and put it over hers. 'See,' he said. 'Not shaking.'

He was purposefully avoiding her questions. Whether his doctor reassured him or not, the pills dulled his mind. 'I'm going to be home late, Mavis.'

She stepped closer, so her body was touching his. 'I know.'

'I need to be there tonight,' he said. 'At the Mela. They need to see me. I'll be on stage for the opening, with all the bigwigs.'

In light of that morning's revelations, Mavis Simpson desperately wanted her husband not to attend. She was under no illusions what might happen. How quickly racial anarchy could erupt in the city.

Simpson desperately wanted to stand down. He didn't have the strength for such pickled politics. He had been mentally winding down for the past month. Delegating more and more to Detective Inspector Harry Virdee, a man who, prior to the previous week, had a chance to one day become the first Asian detective superintendent in Bradford.

Not because he was the best candidate. Far from it. He was reckless and unable to follow protocol. But because his face fit. Because, whilst Harry thought his marriage to his Muslim wife might be the breaking of him, powers higher up than Simpson saw it as an opportunity to showcase diversity. Install a man near the top who embraced both sides of Bradford.

Now, that was in ruins. Virdee was history. Unless he delivered Lucas Dwight. But that in itself was just about as likely as Virdee surviving the following week's hearing.

'George?'

'Hmm,' he said, turning to face her at last.

'Where did you go off to?' Mavis was five years younger than Simpson. Her eyes were creased with wrinkles but they held a natural wisdom which Simpson loved.

'Just . . . thinking,' he said.

Another concerned stare.

'Hey,' he reassured her, 'your husband has weathered far worse storms.'

She nodded and kept her hand on his arm. 'They're waiting for you. In the media room. Are you sure you're up to this?'

'I have to be,' he said and moved away from her, towards the desk. 'Mavis . . . give me five minutes, please.'

She nodded and squeezed his arm once more before easing out of the room.

His wife worked as a clerical assistant within the department. Not because they needed the money but because if she didn't, she might never see her husband. He had a work ethic that meant you didn't come home when the shift finished but when the work was done, which in this job made for an erratic home life. They had no children, which was a good thing. Simpson wouldn't have wanted them to suffer the same way his wife did.

George Simpson didn't have an unparalleled work ethic because he was driven.

He had another reason. One which he would take to the grave.

Simpson sat at his desk and opened the bottom drawer. He checked his door was closed and then removed a bible. He turned to a much-thumbed page, Psalm 32, and read a highlighted passage.

'Blessed is he whose transgression is forgiven, whose sin is covered. Blessed is the man unto whom the Lord imputeth not iniquity, and in whose spirit there is no guile.'

He repeated the passage several times. Although he had it memorized, reading it from the page felt more meaningful.

He knew it was a false promise.

Simpson put away the bible and made his way over to a mirror at the far side of the office. He checked his appearance and took several deep breaths.

It was time.

He was about to leave when his mobile rang. It was an unknown number.

'George Simpson,' he said, answering on the fifth ring.

'Alone?' the male voice asked.

Simpson's heart sank.

Why now?

'It's not a good day.'

'You're wrong,' Colin Reed replied. 'It's a perfect day. In fact, it's exactly the day I've been waiting for.'

SIXTEEN

HARRY AND LUCAS LEFT the gym, keeping their heads down, away from the hailstones which had started again. The wintry darkness refused to release its grip on the city.

'No, get in the back,' Harry said when they reached the car. 'I can't risk anyone seeing you.'

The hoodie was pulled low on Lucas's face. He opened the rear door and got in.

Harry started the engine and turned on the heaters. He asked Lucas for his mobile phone.

'Do I look like I own one?'

Harry shrugged. 'That's a no?'

'I've got one damn quid left in my pocket. Don't need a phone. No one to call.'

'You'll appreciate our relationship is low on trust?'

'Tonight, when I'm proven right,' said Lucas, 'we'll correct that.'

'I don't trust anything but facts. You better hope for your sake this dealer is complicit.' Harry turned off the heaters. They were too slow. He leaned forward and smeared his hands across the windscreen, wiping the condensation clear.

'When we establish I was supplied with poison you'll know I'm being set up. Right?'

'Right.'

'There's just one problem you have to help me with.'

'Go on.' Harry grunted at his inability to clear the windscreen, which was starting to mist over again.

'I have a methadone script at Rimmingtons Pharmacy. Don't suppose I can get there without being apprehended. I can do without my HIV meds for a few days but not my methadone.'

'You're HIV positive?' said Harry.

'Yes. Change anything?' There was a defensive edge to Lucas's voice.

'No. The pharmacy is out. Obvious place to stake out.'

'Unless you call them off?'

'Not going to happen.' Harry knew he couldn't even if he wanted to.

'In that case I need to score.' Lucas wiped perspiration from his brow. 'I'm already struggling. In about two hours I'll be willing to sell my grandmother for a hit.'

'Jesus.' Harry shook his head.

'Hey!' Lucas glared at Harry with jaundiced eyes. 'I'm being upfront with you. Leave your judgemental shit out of this. I'm an addict. I need a hit. It's out of my control.'

'I'm not helping you score heroin.'

'Heroin won't help either of us. What I need is methadone.'

Harry looked at Lucas in the rear-view mirror. 'And how exactly do we do that?'

'I know where I'll be able to get some, but I need some money . . .'

Harry sighed. 'How much?'

'Fifty mils.'

'No – I meant how much money?'

'A fiver. Eight quid tops.'

Harry pulled out his iPhone and selected his news app. He checked the headlines and was dismayed to see Lucas's name.

'Crap,' he whispered. 'It's out,' he said to Lucas. 'You're the most wanted man in Bradford right now.' Harry handed his phone across his shoulder. 'See?'

Lucas took it and scanned the article. Harry searched his face for any signs of weakness. Lucas returned the phone. 'Makes scoring a little harder. *You'll* have to do it.'

Harry tucked away the phone. He put the car in gear and pulled out of the side street and away from Upper Piccadilly. 'I had a feeling you were going to say that, but you can score your own shit. With that hoodie no one's going to see you.'

Lucas instructed Harry to head towards Lumb Lane, another of the city's red-light areas.

It was adjacent to the Jamiyat Tabligh mosque, one of the grandest in the city. It had been constructed with a size-able donation from Shakeel Ahmed amid ferocious objections from local residents.

Bradford didn't need *another* mosque.

There were already eighty-five within the city, mostly concentrated at the centre. Ahmed's wealth had ensured the council passed the plans.

Lumb Lane was in stark contrast to the grandeur of the mosque, which towered regally over it, its grey dome blending with the colour of the skies.

Factories which had thrived only decades before now stood fallow and humiliated, with broken windows and yellow stonework soiled in black soot.

'Over there.' Lucas pointed towards an enormous aban-doned factory.

'There's no one there,' Harry said, taking the right turn.

'I know how to score in my own city.'

'You've been locked up for fourteen years. Things have changed.'

'Look around. Does it look like change to you? *Nothing* has moved on. You think a fancy new shopping centre makes any difference? This city couldn't win the lottery if it had all the tickets.' Lucas turned away and looked out of the window.

'OK, where now?' Harry asked. They were in a deserted cobbled street. The terraced houses on his right looked as forsaken as the factory on his left. A seedy red bed-sheet spread across one of the windows caught his eye. Might as well have stuck a sign on it saying 'Knocking Shop'.

'Go to the end. Turn the car around and then stop outside the factory. So the door's facing the driver's side.'

Harry followed Lucas's instructions.

'You got the money? Need it exact – you're not getting any change.'

Harry handed Lucas five pounds.

'I might need—'

'Negotiate.'

'They see you like that, they're going to smell a cop a mile away.'

'Relax,' Harry said, 'I could be a dealer. Brown skin. BMW. In this city, you're halfway there.'

'Your words not mine. But that's not the issue. Your teeth are.'

'What?' said Harry.

'If I was spotting you, it's the first thing I would clock. Dealer or user, your teeth give you away. If you use, you expect to have a fucked-up mouth,' said Lucas bluntly. 'Not a set of pearly whites.'

Harry glanced in the rear-view mirror. Lucas gave him a grin that would have frightened the devil.

'Keep your window wound up and face the other way – like you're ignoring whoever approaches.'

Harry did so.

'Good.' Lucas wound down his window. A crisp iciness filtered into the car.

'We just wait?' Harry asked.

'They're watching,' Lucas said. 'Don't worry about that.'

After several minutes, Harry turned on the floor heaters. The temperature in the car was plummeting rapidly. Harry kept his focus on Lucas, who was keenly searching the shadows inside the open doorway for signs of a score. He was chewing his lip nervously. Harry didn't have to look to his right to know someone was approaching. He saw the reaction in Lucas's face, the smile of anticipation.

'Help you, baby?' came the voice. Harry turned his head slightly from Lucas to the driver's side mirror. He saw a mini-skirt that struggled to contain cellulite and red stilettos which were badly scuffed. Blonde hair was masking dark roots and the smell of stale smoke wafted into the car.

'Go back in there and get me some methadone,' said Lucas arrogantly.

'I give you more than that, baby.'

'Fifty mils. You can blow me later.'

'Later? Ain't no such fing as later, baby.'

'I haven't got all day,' Lucas snapped. 'You want paying or shall I go down Thornton Road?'

She whistled, turned around and disappeared, telling him she would be back.

'Smooth,' Harry said. 'Real James Bond.'

Lucas didn't reply. His gaze was back on the doorway, drawn magnetically to where she had disappeared.

She returned with a small plastic medicine bottle

concealed in her left hand. 'Fifteen quid,' she said, and slipped her open palm through the window.

'Bitch, do I look fresh to you?' Lucas waved the five-pound note at her. 'Take it or leave it. Thornton's got plenty more.'

'You want that puke-shit, you piss off to Thornton. This is legit. Ten or leave it.'

Lucas beckoned towards Harry. 'Start the car. Bitch is deluded.'

Harry started the car and put it in gear.

'Fucker!' she spat. 'Gimme the money.'

Lucas handed her the note and she gave him the methadone before storming off, cursing under her breath. Lucas opened the brown plastic bottle and drank its contents in one go.

Immediately, he lunged for the door, attacking the handle. It startled Harry who quickly undid his seatbelt.

'Open it! Open it now!' Lucas screamed.

'What the hell—'

'She did me! Open the damn door!'

Lucas leaned back and kicked the door. His need for a hit seemed to have suddenly overwhelmed him. Harry released the child lock and Lucas sprinted out of the car.

'Fuck sake,' said Harry, turning off the engine and getting out of the car in pursuit.

Inside the factory, Lucas was ten metres ahead of Harry. The whore was standing next to three scrawny-looking men, one of whom had a pathetic little knife and was brandishing it wildly at Lucas.

'Hey, hey – put it away,' Harry said to the guy with the knife.

'You ripped me off, bitch,' Lucas spat. 'I'm going to skull-fuck you unless you make it right. You hear me, Blondie?'

'Come on,' said the man with the blade. He had an accent. Eastern European. Probably Polish. The city was flooded with them. Harry put his hand on Lucas's shoulder. 'Calm the fuck down,' he whispered, 'we can't get into shit like this.'

'Bitch robbed me.' Lucas pointed at her. 'I want my methadone or I'm putting all you fuckers down.'

The man with the blade continued striking air with it, clumsily waving it around. He was far from intimidating. The other two were quiet, making up the numbers. They were liable to disappear if anything kicked off.

Lucas suddenly snapped out a lightning left jab and struck the guy with the blade in the nose. There was a crack of bone and the man stumbled backwards, tripping over his feet and falling comically to the floor. The others weren't as cowardly as Harry had envisaged. They leapt on Lucas. The first one threw himself to the floor and grabbed Lucas's legs. The other pounced on his chest and knocked him down. They looked like three tramps having a tussle.

Harry folded his arms and observed bemusedly as the three of them rolled on the floor. The hooker didn't know whether to run or stay.

'You move,' Harry said, pointing at her, 'I'll put you off the street for a week.'

Harry grabbed the man who was on top of Lucas and lifted him off the ground, throwing him nonchalantly across the floor. Lucas had the other contained in a choke-hold.

'Let him go,' Harry said. 'Jesus, you want to kill the bum for a fiver?'

Lucas struggled for a few more seconds and then pushed him away. He got to his feet and clicked his fingers at the girl. 'Meth,' he said. 'Now.'

At the gym, Lucas had been almost too controlled. He had dealt with Harry coolly, with a resolve Harry didn't think he had. But now, the need for a hit showed who he really was. A desperate drug addict. Lucas's cheeks were flushed and sweat was pouring down his face.

The hooker didn't move and shook her head.

'Really?' Lucas asked. 'You're going to make me come and get it?' He reached out and grabbed her by the throat. 'Where is it?' he hissed.

Harry shuffled towards them, ready to pull Lucas away if he took it any further.

'In my pussy!' she spat.

'Don't think I won't go there.'

'You be my fucking guest.'

Lucas shoved his hand down her skirt. Her expression never changed as Lucas invaded her privacy and took out a small plastic bottle. He shoved her away and she fell to the ground. Lucas removed the top of the medicine bottle and poured a little on to his finger. He tasted it and then drank the contents, throwing the empty container at her.

Harry grimaced. 'We good?'

'Yes.' Lucas spat on the floor towards the hooker.

Outside Harry was dismayed to see both driver and passenger doors open. 'Argh, shit.'

Lucas remained stone-faced.

'We just fell for the oldest trick in the book,' Harry said. 'Ran after the small loot while they ransacked us.'

'Anything in there?'

Harry nodded. 'My wallet,' he said, pointing at the open glovebox.

'Much in it?'

'Maybe forty quid. Cards. Licence. Usual stuff.'

'Let's go back in and get it.'

Harry shook his head. 'Look around this street. Curtains twitching on every house. We're in addict central. Eyes everywhere. Put the hoodie back over your head and get in the car. We need to leave.'

'What's the plan?' asked Lucas when they were back on the road.

'What time can we get to this dealer?'

'The little runt opens his business at sixish.'

'Business?'

'He'll be at Undercliffe Cemetery when it gets dark. That's his spot.'

'To deal?'

'Deal. Sleep. Both. Some guys keep to a routine. That way when you want to score, you know where to go looking.'

'That's a lottery expecting him to be there. I don't like the odds.'

'He'll be there.'

'Why are you so sure?' Harry glanced at the rear-view mirror and saw Lucas taking in how the landscape had changed over the fourteen years he'd been inside.

'He told me he'd be there in case I needed to score again.'

Harry was mulling over his options. 'There's only one place I can really keep you safe. Every pair of eyes in Bradford will be looking for you.'

Lucas was perceptive for a junkie. 'Your place?'

Harry nodded. 'But my wife is about to give birth and I can't be worrying her.'

'She know who I am?'

'Yes. But taking you there is asking a lot.'

'Because I'm HIV positive?'

'Because you're the most wanted criminal in Bradford.'

'Ex-criminal.' Lucas leaned forward so his breath was warm on Harry's ear. 'Why don't you just drop me back at the gym?'

'If I found you there, others can.'

'I can keep myself hidden on these streets. I ran them for long enough. I got friends.'

'No, you don't. That was a long time ago. Trust is something you can't afford. I'm not risking the streets swallowing you up. Don't forget, you're my investment.'

'Odd way to look at it. It's not a risk taking me into

your home. Give me a quiet corner, maybe a little food and I'll be silent.'

Harry thought of Saima. He'd have to tell her the truth.

No lies in our house, Jaan. Not ever.

'I'll take you to mine on one condition.'

'Go on.'

'You're going there in cuffs. I don't fuck about in my home. My wife's overdue and my tolerance for bullshit is zero.'

Lucas sprawled his body across the back seat. 'This is next-level crazy. Years ago, you put me in cuffs and sent me down. Now you're putting me in cuffs to take me home?'

'Exactly. Agreed?'

Lucas nodded and closed his eyes. 'I'll trust you. Know why?'

'Because it will keep you safe.'

'No. I'll trust you because if you double-crossed me at your place, you'd spend the rest of your life looking over your shoulder.'

Harry looked at him in the mirror again. They held each other's stare for a beat before Harry looked away. He removed the handcuffs from his pocket and passed them over his shoulder.

SEVENTEEN

GEORGE SIMPSON WAS ON his way to meet the informant he knew only as Colin. He'd finished the media briefing and released Lucas Dwight's name to the public.

Lucas was now the most hunted man in Yorkshire.

Meeting Colin wasn't difficult from a time perspective. The journey was a ten-minute walk from Trafalgar House and he'd excused himself for an hour following the briefing. Getting there unnoticed, however, was challenging.

Colin usually had information which Simpson needed to hear. And today he was in the mood to listen. Simpson couldn't walk out of the headquarters unnoticed so he was forced to drive. He pulled out of Trafalgar House and headed towards the Bradford Hotel, a quarter-mile away, bang in the centre of the city. Up until recently it had been a Hilton, but their patience at Bradford's inability to regenerate had finally run out.

Simpson paused at the traffic lights outside the hotel's

multi-storey car park. City Hall was to the left and a sudden rare block of sunshine escaped darkening clouds, lighting up the side of the mammoth Victorian building. Statues of former Kings and Queens of England were placed high on the exterior, polluted by hundreds of years of industrial soot. Simpson's eyes were drawn to the only statue who wasn't royalty: Oliver Cromwell. A fitting political figure to guard over Bradford, he thought. A man constantly defeating the odds to survive, usually after heavy bloodshed.

Simpson parked his Audi in the hotel car park and laboured towards Sunbridgewells. It was only around the corner but it took some effort. Simpson was convinced that he didn't need his Parkinson's medications, but he couldn't deny that everyday activities like a simple walk were taking more and more effort.

On the street, Simpson took another moment and observed the calmness of Centenary Square, Bradford's fightback against decay. It contained a four-thousand-square-metre mirror pool with more than a hundred fountains, including the tallest in the UK. Watching over it was the City Hall clock tower, rising 220 feet above ground level and inspired by the Palazzo Vecchio in Florence. It was the old world watching over the new and, for the briefest of moments, Simpson found hope for Bradford.

Sunbridgewells was a development of underground tunnels located under Sunbridge Road. A private investor was throwing a million pounds at the project to turn the ancient Victorian tunnel systems into quirky sub-terranean markets. Yet further attempts at change. Innovation.

Simpson approached the ancient wooden doors. Finding them ajar, he slipped inside and turned on his torch. Light bounced off exposed brickwork covered in white chalk.

The tunnels were spread over a huge area and Simpson had read that, to date, three hundred tonnes of dirt had been excavated in preparation for the underground plaza to be built. It was an ambitious project, but it seemed there were those in the city who believed that 'Gotham' could be rehabilitated.

'Over here,' a voice said.

Simpson pointed the torch to his far right and saw the broad outline of Colin.

'Of all the places we could have met,' Simpson said.

'Discretion. You won't get any better.'

'I believe discretion is what *you* insist on.'

'Come. This way.' Reed turned on an industrial torch which was fixed to the ground. Extremely bright rays of light bounced off the shallow ceiling, hitting rows of steel beams running horizontally from one side of the tunnel to the other. There was construction equipment on the floor and evidence of a crew somewhere at work: bags, tools and boots.

Reed took Simpson gently by the arm and led him further underground, helping him to avoid ditches in the ground. There were more lamps highlighting the route, more evidence of construction. They walked down a narrow set of steps. Simpson didn't touch the handrail. The iron had rusted long ago and sharp fractured metal looked ready to pierce skin.

They arrived at a wide section of tunnel. Paving slabs on the ground had been recently washed and the smell of damp wasn't as overpowering. Reed spoke nostalgically of the tunnels. Of memories of the sixties when there had been bars and shops within them. The ancient network of passageways had hosted niche gigs by artists like the Beatles and even Jimi Hendrix. A world nobody knew about. A time long forgotten when Bradford was steeped in success.

'There.' Reed pointed to an entrance halfway down the track. He let go of Simpson's arm now they were in a safe passage and led him to the barren room. Simpson stepped through a doorless opening, into a room no more than six feet square.

'Used to be a prison cell, this,' said Reed. 'Courthouse used to be above.'

'Fascinating,' Simpson replied irritably, 'and when I've got time for a history lesson you can give me the grand tour. For now, let's get to it. What is it that you know?'

Reed towered over Simpson, who was no slouch at six foot. The room seemed to close in around him and for the briefest of moments Simpson felt threatened.

'I want to feed you some information that will be of interest. That's the nature of our relationship,' Reed said.

'We don't have a relationship.' The tunnels were arctic and Simpson was trying to stop his teeth from chattering. 'Relationships are two-way streets, which this is not.'

'What are you so antsy about?' Reed asked. 'I've got a pressing matter which couldn't wait. I know what's on your radar.'

'I dislike meeting this way. It makes me uncomfortable. Like I have things to hide, which I do not.'

'But I do,' Reed replied. 'In my line of work discretion is key so I can't be seen to be your pet. I offload information and let you take care of the dirty work. Or have the cases I've handed you over the past three years not been welcome?'

Simpson didn't answer. Colin Reed had forced his way into Simpson's life by offering information about a large ring of paedophiles. Simpson had ignored him initially but underground vigilante gangs had ratcheted the pressure to such a level that, in desperation, Simpson had listened to Reed. His scepticism had been short-lived. Reed was legit and had since proven to be a powerful if elusive ally. He claimed helping Simpson clean up Bradford was in his business interests.

'I'm a source. A snitch. Call it what you want,' said Reed. 'And that means I get to keep my anonymity. You don't like that – it's fine. You don't have to deal with me much longer. What is it? A week left?'

'What's the information you want to share?' Simpson pulled his coat tighter around his body. The chill was unrelenting.

'Have you arrested Lucas Dwight?'

'I just gave a press conference half an hour ago,' Simpson said, unable to hide the contempt in his voice. 'You think he's going to fall out of my arse in that time?'

'So you're telling me he's not been arrested. He's not in custody?'

'I just answered that.'

Reed sighed. 'He's already been found. Lucas Dwight is currently running around Bradford with one of your detectives. Virdee. Hardeep Virdee, I believe.'

Simpson shook his head. 'Not possible. I have an understanding with Harry.'

'He's suspended, from what I hear.'

The fact that Reed seemed to know everything that happened in the city needled Simpson. Reed was the most connected source he'd ever encountered.

'I'd love to know which of my guys is on your payroll.'

'The better question is, which one is not.'

'So why always come to me then?'

'I like dealing with the boss. That way I know there are no crossed wires.'

'Virdee doesn't have Lucas Dwight,' Simpson said. 'He's about to lose his job. He couldn't afford not to bring him in.'

'I'm with you. Which begs the question, why hasn't he?'

'Because he doesn't have him. What makes you so sure?'

'Somebody told me.'

'Who?'

'A drug addict.'

'A drug addict?' Simpson sneered.

'Yes. Virdee and Dwight scored some methadone about an hour ago off Lumb Lane. While they were busy, one of the addicts broke into their car and stole Inspector Virdee's wallet.' Reed put his hand in his pocket and handed a brown leather case to Simpson. 'How else would I have got this?'

Simpson opened it up and pulled out the credit cards: 'Hardeep S. Virdee'.

'How did your addict know to contact you? With this?'

'Because I have a bounty on Lucas Dwight's head. It's in my interest he's apprehended.'

'How so?'

'The people I represent have business interests in this city.' Reed nodded at the tunnel systems they were in. 'They're afraid this case might create instability in Bradford.' He paused and added, 'And we all know what *that* looks like.'

Everything sounded inconceivable. But Simpson couldn't argue with the fact that he was holding Virdee's wallet. 'I'll look into it.' He slipped the wallet into his pocket.

'Good,' replied Reed. 'There's one more thing, though.'

'Go on.'

'I need a favour in return this time.'

'*You* want a favour?'

Reed nodded. 'Just this time and since it's our last rendezvous, I think it's time to cash in.'

'Cash in?' Simpson replied, unhappy with the inference. 'We don't have a financial relationship, Colin.'

'It's delicate, this situation. I'm hoping that in light of everything I've told you over the past three years and the good work we've done together, you'll trust me.'

'What is it you want?' Simpson asked, tiring of the cloak-and-dagger act. The cold was starting to bite and his joints were beginning to seize.

'When you apprehend Lucas, I need you to hand him over to me.'

'What? Are you crazy?'

'Not indefinitely. I just need to ask him a few questions.'

'Last time I checked you weren't on my payroll.'

'After everything I've given—'

'It was never a reciprocal arrangement. Never.'

'That's true, and if this wasn't vitally important, I wouldn't ask. But it is. There's a right way and a wrong way to do this and I'm trying to be . . . well, nice.' Reed let the statement hang in the air for a moment and fixed Simpson with a venomous stare.

'Is that . . . Are you threatening me?' Simpson said.

'Yes,' Reed replied brazenly. 'I am, because I really have no choice if you won't give me five minutes with Lucas.'

Simpson withdrew his hands from his pockets and folded his arms defensively. The cold had vanished and an adrenaline heat started to permeate his body. 'Do you know who you are threatening? I could arrest you right now.'

'But you won't, because if you do . . . let's just say that people might become aware of several large payments made to your wife's bank account by a subsidiary I represent, which . . . on closer inspection might prove to be not so . . . clean.'

'What? I have no idea what you are talking about.'

'Three years ago, you were contacted by a solicitor who told you that a distant relative of your wife had died and left instructions in her will to deposit fifteen thousand pounds a year into your wife's account for four years, which, by my reckoning, ends next July.'

Simpson felt his face flush. He opened his mouth to speak but couldn't find any words.

'Insurance,' Reed continued. 'Don't worry – it's not blood money. Just some pounds the taxman didn't get. From what I gather, it's given you a nice little conservatory.'

'What the hell *are* you?' Simpson asked. 'A snitch or a spy? Have you been playing me all these years? Drip-feeding me snippets—'

'They weren't snippets. They were career-making cases,' Reed said fiercely. 'Listen, George. My interest is to protect my clients. And sometimes that means I've got to turn black and white into grey. Work between the lines. All I'm asking you for is a few minutes alone with Lucas Dwight. And you *will* do this for me or, to be frank, you'll see a side of me you'd rather not. And I don't want to play that game with you. I respect what you've done for this city.'

'You're a treacherous piece of work.'

'I'm a friend. But the line between friend and foe is five minutes with Lucas Dwight. Go see Inspector Virdee. Pick up Lucas and bring him back here. To me. You take a little walk, I ask my questions, you take him in. Everybody goes home happy.'

'How did I not see that money was tainted?' Simpson asked, more of himself than of Reed.

'Because when you offer people a windfall, they usually take it without digging too deeply. It's human nature. Don't be too hard on yourself. And, like I said, it's unaccounted-for tax money. There are worse things it could be.'

Simpson was seething. Five days from retirement and he had a murder, a restless city and now a blackmail attempt. 'It's not going to happen. You drag me wherever you want. I'm clean. Always have been.'

There was a pause of a few seconds; then Reed stepped closer, so Simpson could feel his breath on his face. 'Let me put this another way . . .' Reed dropped his voice. 'I'm a man who walks a path between you and a side of Bradford even you don't know exists. The people I work for know I'm here. They know what I know. And after they leak details of the "improper" payments, life is likely to become very difficult for you.'

'I don't take kindly to threats.'

'Of course you don't. You didn't get where you are by

caving at the first sign of trouble. But . . .' Reed put his hand in his pocket and pulled out a Polaroid photograph. '. . . can you say that your wife is as strong?'

Reed handed it to Simpson. The photo was of Mavis entering Trafalgar House that morning.

'You son of a—'

'Hey!' Reed backed off a step. 'I like you. And for Christ's sake, look at what I've given you over the past three years. I'm the good guy, the go-between, the deal-maker. You think I want this shit on my head? I want five minutes alone with a guy who is wanted for the most controversial murder this city has ever seen. Or, quite frankly, some things are going to slot into play which neither of us want.'

'We're done here.' Simpson put the photograph of his wife in his pocket.

Reed offered him a cheap mobile phone. 'There's one number in the call list. When you have Lucas, call me.'

Simpson snatched the phone. 'Show me out.'

'Do we have an understanding?' Reed asked.

'If your phone rings and it's me, then you can assume we do.'

'Don't make me go places I don't want to go, George.'

Simpson turned his back and walked out the room, his face darkening.

The cliff-edge Bradford teetered on was beginning to crack.

EIGHTEEN

'WHERE IS HE?' SAIMA asked.

'Outside. In the shed. Handcuffed to a wheelbarrow,' Harry replied.

Saima chewed her lip. She was sitting on a dining-room chair with her belly out, rubbing oil into her skin. 'You're telling me that we've got Bradford's most wanted in our shed?'

Harry nodded. 'I know. It's not ideal.'

'Ideal? No. It's far from ideal. I don't know what's worse: the fact my husband lied to me about being suspended or having a murderer in my shed?'

She was right. If he could go back . . . ?

But that was Harry all over. When the red mist set in, he couldn't disengage. 'Did I ever tell you about the time my dad beat me for stealing?'

She looked puzzled and shook her head.

'When I was eleven, my mum gave me five pounds a

month. Pocket money.' Harry pulled out a chair and sat down opposite his wife, close enough so their knees were touching. Saima continued smearing oil across her stomach.

'I never spent it,' Harry continued. 'I knew we didn't have much money and I always saved it, thinking one day maybe I'd save enough to get my parents away from the shop. Make things easier. Kids' dreams.'

'What happened?' Saima asked. She finished with the oil and pulled her top over her bump.

'I can't remember exactly what the crisis was, but we lost some money. I always remember my mum's voice. She was panicking about paying my and Ronnie's school fees and my dad was vexed about the loss.' Harry screwed his eyes shut.

'Go on,' Saima said, and leaned closer towards Harry.

'Anyway, the next day I snuck into my mum's room and put the money I'd been saving in her coat pocket. Fifty quid I think – nearly a year's worth.' Harry smiled ruefully. 'Just my bad luck that my dad came into the bedroom at the exact moment my hand was in my mum's coat pocket, stuffed with money. It looked . . .' His voice trailed away.

'Like you were thieving?' Saima whispered.

'My dad was so mad.'

'Why didn't you tell him?'

Harry shrugged. 'I looked guilty. I never thought he'd believe me. I'd dug my own grave.'

'What did he do?'

'Took off his belt.' Harry held up his hand to show her the story was over. 'When I saw Lucas today . . . I don't know, I just had that same feeling. That there's more to this. Can you understand that?'

Saima took his hands and squeezed them gently. 'I'll always trust you, Harry Virdee.'

Harry thanked her and got up.

'Before you bring him in,' she said.

'Yes?'

'Tell me about the case. About Lucas.'

'We don't discuss my work at home—'

'Technically' – she turned her head to the side to look at him – 'you're not at work. You're suspended, remember? So tell me.'

Harry retook his seat. 'First, I *am* sorry about what I did last week.' He sighed and put his hand on her face. 'It wasn't smart.'

She nodded. 'As long as we're in this city, knowing when and when not to defend your wife is going to be central to making our relationship work.'

'If I had more of your patience and less of my temper, we'd be formidable.'

'We *are* formidable,' she replied. 'That's the point. No matter what people say, no matter how racist they are or how much hate they throw at us, we, Harry and Saima Virdee, *are* formidable.' She removed his hand from her face and put it on her stomach. 'And when our daughter, Aliyah, arrives and is thrust into a world where her identity is questioned and poked fun at, she will also be

163

formidable. Because that's who *we* are. Who we *need* to be. Who we *have* to be.'

'This is why I married you. Exactly why.'

'So, tell me about this case. Let me see if I can help you.'

'OK, but firstly, I'm vetoing Aliyah.'

'Had to try.'

Harry told her. Her green eyes were flickering like the lights on a hard drive, absorbing data. When he had finished, she took a few moments, chewed her bottom lip again, and then spoke calmly and authoritatively.

'Pretending to convert to Islam might be the best alibi he could get. Like that movie where a woman writes about killing someone, then a guy ends up dead in exactly the fashion described in her novel.'

Harry nodded. 'The prayers looked and sounded authentic enough to me. I've seen you do it enough times.'

'What you see and what you feel are two different things.'

'Agreed. But he had more than one chance to escape. He *wants* my help and, to be fair, he had floored me with a killer punch to my liver. I was out. At his mercy. And he retreated.'

Saima took a few deep breaths.

'Baby?' asked Harry.

'Kicking. Somersaulting. Cartwheeling. The usual.'

'Don't give birth today.' Harry tried to sound jovial but he was deadly serious.

'It's Eid and Karva Chauth. That hasn't happened in centuries. She would be blessed to be born today. Fuses two worlds perfectly.'

Harry smiled. 'Even so, not helpful today. So, what do you think?'

'I think I need to speak with Mr Dwight.'

'About what?'

'His conversion to Islam. Whether it's authentic or not.'

Harry grinned. 'You're the best thing that ever happened to me, you know that?'

'You're going to tell me that I saved you again?'

'It was I who saved you. If I hadn't rescued you, you'd be married to some dude called Abdul, wearing a burka and tripping over your own feet whilst cooking for his seventeen family members.'

'Massaging oil into his balding scalp and combing his three strands of hair?'

'You got it. I saved you from that.'

'And me? What did I save you from?'

'Myself,' Harry replied. 'I was tired of dating all those nondescript Asian girls. All style and no substance.'

'How many were there again?'

'Less than three, more than one.'

'Liar. You are *such* a liar,' she said. Although Harry was Saima's first relationship, Harry left his colourful history open to speculation.

'We're getting off radar here. Shall I go and get Lucas or not?'

'First tell me, how many women there were? Or else I'm not helping.'

Harry stood up. 'Prince Charming had to kiss a few frogs before he found his princess.'

Saima nodded grimly. 'Go. Go and get him, but the cuffs stay on.'

Lucas Dwight was sitting at the dining table in Harry's living room. Lucas's hands were on the table, handcuffs glistening in the overhead light. He looked dishevelled and in need of a wash.

Harry was sitting next to him, watching him carefully as Saima entered the room carrying a large wooden box. She placed it in front of Lucas, who stared at it.

The box was a dark chestnut colour, with an elegant gold plaque inscribed with Arabic writing in the centre.

Saima took a seat opposite Lucas.

'Open it,' she said.

He smiled. Warmly. And then shook his head. 'You're Muslim?'

Saima nodded.

'Bismillah hir Rahman nir Raheem.'

'Subhan Allah,' Saima replied softly.

Lucas turned his attention to Harry. 'You married a Muslim woman?'

Harry nodded.

'But you're not Muslim?'

'No.'

Lucas nodded slowly. As though he understood something.

They shared a look. A silent acceptance that they had both perhaps walked a path others would never understand.

Lucas held up his hands. 'I won't touch the Koran with these hands.'

Saima smiled. And looked at Harry.

'However,' Lucas continued, 'if you allow me the briefest of washes, I'm happy to pray with you.' He looked at the clock on the mantelpiece. 'It's twenty past one. Shall I lead you in Friday prayers?'

'If my husband doesn't object,' Saima replied.

'Would he object to opening these?' Lucas said, waving the handcuffs in the air.

'Yes, he would,' replied Harry. 'You can pray with them on.'

'I'd rather he didn't,' Saima said.

'And I'd rather ensure my wife wasn't at risk.'

'I won't be,' replied Saima. 'You're going to be here, in the room. And I would like to see Lucas read Friday prayers with me.'

Lucas stared at Harry and raised his hands. 'I had my chance to cause you some harm. I'm not about to cross you. This is a test, no? See if I'm using faith as an alibi?'

'My wife likes playing detective. And whilst you might be able to fool me with your conversion, she's a different animal entirely.'

'Smart,' Lucas replied. 'Only somebody Islamic can really judge if I'm playing you. Very smart.'

Harry put his hand underneath Lucas's arm. 'Come on, you can wash upstairs. I'll chaperone.'

The day had started off bizarrely but nothing could have prepared Harry for what he was about to witness.

Saima had laid out two prayer mats on the floor in the living room. A brown one for Lucas and, behind it, a green one for her. Lucas picked up the wooden box, with clean hands, and kissed it before touching his forehead to it. He repeated this three times. Saima watched intently. Harry knew she loved this stuff. Tradition. Religion.

Harry was about as far detached from it as she was involved. He watched in amazement as the ex-leader of the BNP started to lead his wife in Friday prayers. Up the street, the local mosque started its call to prayer.

Only in Bradford.

Harry thought it unlikely he would ever find anything in life so strange again. He was listening to the rhythmic whispers of the prayers, the call from the mosque in the background, when there was a loud knocking on the door.

A complication he hadn't anticipated.

Harry, still standing in the living-room doorway, glanced nervously to his right.

Another knock.

And now the letter box creaked open. A pair of eyes

stared through it, fixing Harry with a look he'd seen hundreds of times before.

It was his boss, Detective Superintendent George Simpson.

NINETEEN

BASHIR IQBAL WAS PARKED in his taxi outside the Midland Hotel, a grand Victorian building which had played host to every prime minister up to Harold Wilson. It was, of course, where Martin Davis chose to stay. A place steeped in successful history. A place which in the sixties had welcomed the Beatles and the Rolling Stones. A hotel which now perfectly reflected its Bradford surroundings: living off old memories, unable to forge new ones.

The concierge at the hotel was a friend to Zain Ahmed and had told Bashir that Davis was due to check out the next day. They had formulated a hasty extraction plan but the sight of Martin Davis walking down the steps of the hotel, suitcase in hand and getting into a waiting grey Jaguar had not formed part of it. Davis got in the back, behind the driver.

Bashir started his car and moved quickly. He overtook

another taxi and swung in behind Davis. There would be the driver to contend with but Bashir wasn't panicked. He would have the element of surprise, worth far more than another pair of hands.

Traffic was light and they were out of the city centre, on Wakefield Road, within a few minutes.

The motorway.

That's where Davis was heading. If he made it, then he would be lost to Bashir.

The Jaguar was speeding, well over the forty limit. Bashir's options were few. He felt his blood pressure rising. He took one hand off the steering and quickly placed it inside his shirt collar, on the back of his neck; he picked at a fresh scab and felt the sudden wetness of blood.

The momentary sting was calming. Bashir put his foot down and tailed the Jag.

The dual carriageway was a straight road, a few miles long. There was no time to call in assistance. In roughly five minutes, Davis would reach the M606 and from there he would be out of reach.

Bashir accelerated wildly and overtook the Jaguar. He gained twenty metres and then moved back into the middle lane. There were several sets of traffic lights on Wakefield Road and Bashir stopped at the first one. He felt the slow trickle of blood seeping down his neck into the creases of his skin. Bashir stared in his rear-view mirror. The driver looked middle-aged, maybe early forties. Broad shoulders. Wearing a suit. Speaking with Davis.

The lights had changed to green. Bashir hurriedly put the car in gear and moved on.

He kept his speed just under forty; every second he could slow Davis was critical. But the Jaguar simply undercut him and tore past.

Bashir reached across and opened the glovebox, frantically searching for a weapon but there was nothing but an old takeaway wrapper.

His tools.

They were in the boot.

Bashir's car swerved in the middle lane as he took his eyes off the road. He caught up to Davis and stopped behind the Jag at the next set of lights. The pursuit was back on.

Bashir was leaving the country tomorrow. Of that he was certain, because irrespective of how *this* played out, he would visit the house tonight and pay off decades' worth of waiting. So he could afford to take more risks than he usually might. He just needed one opportunity.

They reached a roundabout at the top of Wakefield Road – and Bashir caught a break. The driver started to indicate right. And then paused.

A long pause. Normally Bashir would have hit his horn, but there was a discussion going on in the Jaguar. And then the indicator changed. The driver looked over his shoulder and manoeuvred into the left lane, forking away from the motorway.

A last-minute detour.

It was exactly what Bashir needed. *Sticker Lane's a*

good spot. A place where Bashir had friends. Ones who could help.

Bashir was betting that Davis would head back this way because they *had* intended to turn right at the roundabout, towards the motorway. Sticker Lane was popular with car showrooms. There were enormous VW, BMW, Mini and Suzuki dealerships, but there were also several smaller, independent garages.

He called a trusted friend, the manager of SL Motors, and gave some hurried instructions. Bashir hung up abruptly, knowing his orders would be followed. Nobody disobeyed him. The penalties were well known.

The Jaguar stopped at the crossroads with Leeds Road. The driver indicated right and Bashir followed him. Davis's car slowed down, then took a sharp left into Mother Hubbard's Fish & Chips restaurant. Bashir didn't follow. Instead he went on a little further, turned right into a disused car wash and parked facing the restaurant.

Martin Davis had been raised a Yorkshire lad. In the eighties, the best place for fish and chips in Bradford had been Mother Hubbard's. It had been opened by *Coronation Street* stars in 1972 at a staggering cost of £92,000. The restaurant had been unique, looking like an old fairy-tale cottage, something straight out of 'Hansel and Gretel'. People had travelled across the county to sample the food. But in the late nineties with the migration towards Indian food and cheap 'Asian fish and chips', Mother Hubbard's had gone out of business.

Now, a decade later, it had reopened right in the centre of Bradford's premier restaurant district. It was a bold building, commanding an entire corner, with enormous floor-to-ceiling windows and a large illuminating sign. It took Davis back to his youth: greasy chip-shop food, wrapped in newspapers, eaten on a park bench after kicking around a football. Martin Davis was an excited school kid again as he entered the shop. To think he'd nearly left town without visiting this place.

The inside was brightly lit with gleaming white tiles and simple wooden chairs with white tables. The left-hand wall had a huge article describing the history of the restaurant and there were pictures from its grand beginnings in Great Horton back in the seventies.

The restaurant was empty. Davis checked his watch. Before midday. He was pleased to see that all the workers, including the fish-fryer, were white.

Finally, an authentic fish-and-chip shop back in Bradford.

Davis ordered a deluxe portion with mushy peas. It was six quid, a world away from the forty-five pence he remembered paying as a child, but on seeing the size of the cod, Davis couldn't grumble at the price.

He took his food into the corner of the restaurant and sat down to enjoy his first Mother Hubbard's meal in over twenty years.

Bashir changed his mind. He had quickly put a haphazard plan together but now, looking around Leeds Road, he realized there would be no better time. Quarter to twelve. The lunch rush hour was fifteen minutes away.

Davis's car was parked to the side of the building, away from the front, almost in a blind spot. Davis had got out and left the driver inside. In all probability the back doors would be open. Unless the driver had locked them again, which seemed unlikely.

He was sitting absorbed in a newspaper, not expecting to be ambushed.

Bashir pulled his taxi out of the car park and drove across Leeds Road into Mother Hubbard's. He parked behind the Jaguar and got out of the car.

From the boot, Bashir took a large black sports holdall and rummaged through it until he located his stun gun. It fitted snugly in the palm of his hand.

Bashir headed towards the Jaguar. Without hesitating, he tried the back door, found it unlocked and slipped inside, behind the driver. He jolted electricity into the driver's neck and, before the man had a chance to react, rendered him comatose. The driver slumped to the side, held upright by his seatbelt so it looked like he was stealing forty winks. Perfect.

Bashir got out of the car. He had left his boot open so that from the street it was blocking the view of the Jaguar. He needed to move the driver's body into the boot. Bashir glanced towards the street. It was a risky play. For a few brief moments, Bashir was caught in no man's land. He reconsidered and left the driver at the wheel.

Bashir got back into his car and waited. If Davis was

longer than fifteen minutes, Bashir was going to have a problem.

Martin Davis unwrapped his meal and poured mushy peas over his chips. The fish was golden and crispy, and the chips were chunky and glistening with oil. For a few moments, Martin Davis forgot all about losing the by-election and his fraught meeting with Colin Reed.

He sprinkled a generous amount of salt over his food and then shovelled a huge chunk of fish into his mouth.

He opened the leaflet the woman at the counter had given him. It was information about the restaurant and a menu. The prices were certainly high, especially for that part of Bradford, but Davis assumed people would pay for authentically made fish and chips.

And then he stopped chewing and focused on the menu. At the bottom right-hand corner. It carried the word 'halal' in Arabic script. Davis recognized it immediately – it was on most Asian restaurant shopfronts in Bradford.

Davis looked suspiciously around the restaurant. It didn't feel Asian-owned. There was nothing to suggest it was anything other than an authentic British chippy.

Davis looked at the menu more closely. The sausage wasn't pork. It was chicken. This was not the Mother Hubbard's he had been hoping for.

Davis felt betrayed. He crumpled up the rest of his meal in its wrapper and forcefully squeezed it together. He left the mess on the table, stood up and stormed out of the restaurant, ignoring the polite goodbyes of the assistants.

Outside, the bitter cold was welcome. Sacrilege to have taken a Yorkshire institution like Mother Hubbard's and given it to the bloody Asians. Davis's mind was full of blind fury as he opened the Jaguar's back door and got in.

'Come on, let's go,' he growled. 'Place was a shit-hole.'

But his driver didn't reply. Instead Martin Davis's door was flung open. He had a brief glimpse of a scruffy-looking Asian man with thick greying stubble before an agonizing pulse tore into his neck.

Davis didn't even have time to scream.

TWENTY

HARRY WAS SURE SAIMA and Lucas had heard the door go, but neither reacted. They continued praying and Harry was caught in limbo. They wouldn't stop now they'd started. It was forbidden.

'Bloody religious people,' Harry muttered and closed the living-room door quickly.

Simpson knocked again and Harry knew it was more than just a social call. His boss never visited him at home.

Did he know?

Harry didn't like it. Cornered in his own home. As though he was under surveillance.

Harry could see the silhouette of Simpson through the frosted glass. Harry fidgeted with his keys, buying precious seconds. To do what with, he wasn't sure.

He glanced towards the living room and then looked at his watch. Prayers didn't last long. Maybe another few minutes. Lucas was alone with Saima. Harry felt confident she wouldn't come to any harm but he was taking chances.

Unnecessary ones.

'Sir,' Harry said, opening the door.

Simpson didn't hesitate. He pushed past Harry into the hallway.

Harry closed the door. Simpson took three long paces towards the living room. He hadn't been invited in, paused to remove his shoes or exchanged any conversation with Harry.

'You can't go in there, sir,' Harry said, louder and more forcefully than he intended.

Hoping that Lucas and Saima could hear.

Simpson paused but didn't turn around. 'Why not?'

'Sir, my wife is praying,' Harry replied loudly, thankful for once that he was able to play the race card. Simpson wouldn't disrespect it. 'Can't let you in there until she's finished her Friday prayers.' He pointed across the road towards where the mosque was still relaying a sermon.

Simpson hesitated and turned around slowly. 'I understand.' Something had changed since that morning. He was looking at Harry differently. Not quite suspicion but certainly *distrust*.

'What's going on, sir?' Harry asked. 'Why have you come storming into my house?'

'You tell me.'

'I don't know what you mean.'

'I think you do.'

'Sir, am I missing something?' Harry put on his best blank stare.

Simpson moved closer, away from the living room, and dropped his voice. 'Are you hiding something from me, Hardeep? Because I reached out to you this morning. I offered you a chance to put things right.'

'And I appreciate it, sir. I'm making inquiries like you asked.' Unlike Simpson, Harry didn't drop his voice.

'I have it on good authority that you found him. Lucas.'

Harry shook his head and took his boss's arm, leading him almost to the front door. 'Are you kidding me? My wife's a week overdue, I'm facing a disciplinary and *you think* I'm keeping him all to myself? Can you hear yourself?'

'Where were you this morning?' Simpson was suddenly less sure of himself.

Harry filled him in quickly, feeling more and more apprehensive that Lucas was alone in the living room with Saima. He could still hear Saima's voice, which had got louder.

Clever girl.

She was keeping Simpson out. Prayers hadn't finished. But they couldn't last much longer.

Harry wanted to tell Simpson, but there was something wrong. Simpson wasn't himself.

'I've had a report that Lucas was seen with you,' Simpson said.

'Where?'

Simpson put his hand in his pocket and handed Harry his wallet. 'Care to explain?' The living room had gone quiet. Simpson didn't wait. He pushed past Harry, ignoring his request for his boss to stop.

Simpson opened the living-room door and stormed inside.

Saima was on her knees, struggling to get up. She looked over her shoulder and smiled at both men. 'This is a surprise,' she said innocently and beamed Simpson her warmest smile. 'Come to wish me a happy Eid?'

Simpson forced a smile and nodded. 'Sorry to interrupt,' he said sheepishly. 'I . . . er . . . just had some urgent business with Harry.'

She nodded and held out her hand to Harry. 'Help me up, Jaan?'

Harry stepped forward, desperately scanning the room. There was no sign of Lucas. The second prayer mat had disappeared, as had the cuffs and the key.

He's gone, thought Harry.

Shit, he's gone.

You hid this from your boss. Now you can't tell him because it will land you in more trouble. You've lost the only man who could have saved you.

Harry helped Saima to her feet. He winked at her and she smiled.

A reassuring smile.

'Sir.' Harry turned to face Simpson. 'You want to come into the kitchen? Have a cuppa?'

181

Simpson shook his head. 'Just a word if I may. A few minutes and I'll be on my way.'

Both men were in the kitchen. Harry told Simpson that he had tried to locate Lucas that morning, leaned on a few leads but nothing had come of it. And then a drug addict had said he had information but wanted a 'score' as payment so Harry had taken him down to Lumb Lane to land a hit. They'd got into a little trouble with the junkies and Harry's wallet had been taken. It turned out the addict was using Harry and had nothing useful to offer.

'I got played,' said Harry. 'Now, you want to tell me what's going on?'

Simpson put his hands across his face and rubbed his chin. He looked drained. As if he'd aged ten years since that morning.

'I . . . I got some bad intel.' Simpson shook his head. 'I'm sorry. I didn't think it through.'

Saima was hovering next door in the living room, lighting incense sticks and humming merrily.

Where the fuck was Lucas?

Harry stared past his boss to the shed at the bottom of the garden. 'If I had Lucas Dwight in my possession, then you would have him in yours. This intel – where did it come from?'

Simpson shook his head. 'A source. Somebody I trust. Guess the pressure is on for everyone right now.'

'The scumbag I was helping this morning might have

182

been mistaken for Lucas. Thinking about it, they look kind of similar.'

Simpson stepped to the side and patted Harry on the shoulder. 'I'm sorry. You want to close the door for a minute?'

Harry exchanged a strained look with Saima before he closed it.

'Harry. I don't expect anything from you, but in the unlikely event that you do hear something – *anything at all* – I want that first call to be to me. *And only me.* My ears. Understand?'

'Is there something else going on that I don't know about?' Harry asked.

'No. I'm just under some pressure. You know?'

Harry nodded. 'Look, it's Eid today, sir, and I've got to look after Saima. I'm limited to what I can offer you, but I've got a couple of feelers out. If anything comes of them I'll be on the blower.'

Simpson thanked him and opened the kitchen door. He apologized to Saima for intruding and made his way hurriedly to the front door. Harry saw him out and then rushed back to the living room. Saima put her finger to her lips and he followed her into the kitchen.

'Where is he?' whispered Harry.

Saima shrugged. 'He finished praying and then scooped up his prayer mat and the cuffs and sneaked out of the back door.'

'Argh, crap,' hissed Harry. 'Lost him.'

'For what it's worth, his conversion isn't a ploy. He read

the *namaz* prayers perfectly. But more importantly he didn't break them to escape.'

'What's with that? He needed to put himself first.'

'He—' Saima corrected herself. 'We wouldn't. When you are praying, there is nothing more important.'

'I think you people need to check your priorities.'

She rolled her eyes. 'You wouldn't understand. You never do.'

'So he's legit?' Harry asked, ignoring the dig.

She nodded.

'I'm hoping that he's in that shed but I'm not feeling it. He's going to think I set him up.'

'He shouldn't – you were clearly trying to warn us. Go and check.'

'Not yet. Too quick. I don't trust George not to double round and have a nosy. He knows something.' Harry leaned back against the kitchen worktop, keeping his eyes firmly on the shed. 'Something's not right. I've not seen him like that before. He was . . . I don't know. Panicked.'

'He's got to be under some pressure. Shakeel Ahmed was a big fish. And a racist murder has to be stirring up trouble right now.'

'Dead right. Give me something to carry down to the shed. Something plausible.'

Saima hunted around the kitchen. 'You could take the rubbish out. On your way back, pop into the shed and bring me a sack of potatoes. I need to cook bhajis for tonight.'

Harry grabbed the bin bag and headed out. He glanced

casually around the garden, over the neighbours' fences, towards the road. He didn't see anything suspicious and doubled back up the path.

Harry opened the shed door and stepped inside.

TWENTY-ONE

'LUCAS HAS GONE,' SAID Harry. He put the prayer mat and cuffs he had found in the shed on the kitchen table.

'You don't think he'll come back?' asked Saima.

'Would you?' replied Harry. 'The boss turning up on my doorstep isn't exactly reassuring.'

'Lucas isn't guilty. Well, not of a racist murder. He put his faith first. That's dedication.'

Harry scratched his stubble anxiously. He closed his eyes and thought hard about his next move. 'I know where he'll be when it gets dark. He's going for the guy who tried to put him down. I need to get there first.' Harry checked his watch and then looked at Saima. A look she knew well.

She shook her head. 'You need to be here when the moon appears.'

Harry grimaced. Couldn't hide it. He didn't have time for superstitious nonsense. 'Saima—'

'You promised,' she snapped, 'and we are only here because of what *you* did last week. You can't put this on me.'

'Five o'clock? Is that what time we start?'

She nodded. 'You'll be free by half past. You promised.' She poked him in the chest.

'We can do it outside. We don't need to—'

'No, we can't. We need to go to your parents'.'

'Saima, they won't even know we are there—'

'That's not the point and you know it.' She was keeping her emotions in check. 'You might not hold anything about our culture close but *I do*. If we don't do this the right way, we'll have bad luck. And I'm about to give birth, or had you forgotten? I want to pray for you. I want to see my mother-in-law on the single most important day for married women, even if I can't talk to her. Why can't you understand and put *that* first?'

Harry shook his head. 'Lunacy,' he muttered.

'No!' she snapped, unable to contain her anger any longer. 'Lunacy is putting someone who means nothing to us, had no influence over us, in hospital for being an idiot.' She pushed Harry more firmly in the chest and let her tears flow. 'You dropped to *his* level – and what have you always told me? Rise above it. Love overcomes hate. But do you actually believe that any more? Did you ever believe it? Or are you so bitter about what has happened that you'll look for any opportunity to dish out your own version of justice?'

Harry remained stony-faced. 'You finished?'

She nodded and wiped the tears from her face.

'Saima—'

But she turned away from him. 'You do what you have to. Leave? Stay? We'll see just what *is* important to you.' She walked out of the kitchen and slammed the door.

Harry was sitting at the living-room table on his laptop. He had cancelled his credit cards, fearing they might have been compromised, and was now logged on to chat rooms and websites trying to see if Lucas's name was trending. He found several key references which confirmed what he had suspected: there was a bounty on Lucas's head. A big one.

Every dealer and snitch in the city had been told to keep their eyes peeled. Harry was looking desperately for the source of the bounty. The names he found were mostly known to him. Members of street gangs. Drug pushers. High up the chain of command.

If Harry had more time, he might have been able to get an audience with one of them – but time was something he didn't have.

Harry closed his eyes and tried to put the events into some sort of order.

Lucas's release from prison, Shakeel's murder, DNA at the scene, and a street bounty on Lucas's head, but not originating from Shakeel's army of followers. Harry expected a possible revenge bounty, which this was not.

It seemed to stem from the streets.

Simpson had been acting strangely. He had a huge case

on his hands – a massive headache – yet instead of manning the fort and ensuring all his detectives were working their bollocks off, he was turning up at Harry's place, obviously believing Harry had Lucas.

How did he find out?

Harry fished his wallet from his pocket and opened it. The drug addicts who had taken it were right at the bottom of the food chain. Harry's money, driving licence and credit cards were all missing but his gym, casino and national insurance cards were intact.

The wallet was handed in to Simpson.

But not by the low-life who stole it. They wouldn't have access to the boss.

Which meant his wallet had travelled quickly up the chain of command, until it hit somebody on the streets who *could* contact his boss.

Harry needed to know who – but would Simpson give the name up?

He dialled Simpson's number but it went unanswered. Harry redialled but got the same outcome. He sent a text asking his boss to call him immediately.

Harry wrote down everything he knew so far. He liked to put things down on paper; it made seeing patterns easier. He wrote in capitals, spacing each entry three lines apart.

When he was done, he stood up and stared at the solitary piece of paper from a bird's eye view. He crossed his arms, read and reread everything. For almost fifteen minutes.

Drugs.

The connection. He drew a line connecting the clues and then circled Shakeel's name.

Why was he murdered?

Because he was about to become powerful in Bradford.

To the detriment of the streets?

Maybe.

But why was Lucas framed?

Easy target.

And then he struck gold.

Misdirection.

Shit, this wasn't about race. But somebody was trying to make it look like it was.

Why?

Bradford would turn quickly on race. Lucas Dwight was an easy man to frame. The picture twisted quite easily to show he had motive.

But whoever was pulling the strings had lost control of Lucas, which meant the fall guy was now a loose cannon.

His boss had the clue. Because whoever handed him his wallet knew what was going on.

He needed that man.

Harry really wanted to leave – chase down this link – but he couldn't let Saima down. He flirted with the idea of calling some of his colleagues but didn't dial.

He heard his boss's voice in his ear.

. . . in the unlikely event that you do hear something – anything at all – I want that first call to be to me. And only me. My ears. Understand?

It was so strange. Out of character. At first Harry had thought it was because Simpson only had a few days left in the job. Now, he wasn't so sure.

Misdirection. Mistrust.

Harry put down his phone. Whom could he trust? There was another plan in play here. If apprehending Lucas was the priority for whoever was setting this up, then it meant there was another act yet to come. Otherwise containing him wouldn't be so important.

Lucas Dwight was the key. Not because he was guilty, but because he wasn't. Harry thought about what Saima had said. That Lucas hadn't broken his prayers when Simpson had arrived. That it was no act.

Harry checked his watch again. Four o'clock. He needed to get Saima out of the house quickly and complete the ritual which was important to her. Harry wasn't going to fight her. She was right. He had taken an opportunity last week to vent his anger at choices he had made. The responsibility was *his* to deal with.

So he was going to shower, put on his suit and put a smile on his wife's face so that when he hit the streets, he could do so with a clear mind.

He needed to get to Lucas. Who wasn't being hunted because he was guilty . . . Lucas was being hunted because he was already a dead man.

TWENTY-TWO

WHEN MARTIN DAVIS REGAINED consciousness, he was in unfamiliar surroundings. His head was pounding. The room came slowly into focus. There was a desk opposite. A grand mahogany desk.

His hands were tied behind his back and his legs secured to a chair. Each small movement of his neck felt as though it was pressing against barbed wire.

'Hello?' he called out in a shaky voice.

From behind, he heard the clink of ice cubes in a glass and even though the pain was excruciating, he turned his head but couldn't see far enough to make an ID.

'Who's there?' he called.

He heard liquid being poured into a glass and then nothing.

The room was dark, save for a brass lamp on the desk giving minimal illumination. Davis gave up trying to see who was behind him. He focused instead on the desk. He saw a fountain-pen holder with a pot of ink next to it, but aside from that, the enormous surface of the desk was bare.

Behind it hung a huge painting of Mecca. An oil canvas, crafted beautifully out of black and white.

I've been kidnapped by the Asians. Oh Christ.

'Mecca,' a voice said from behind as Davis's eyes lingered on the picture. 'Not a place you'll be familiar with.'

Davis turned his head again and caught a shadow out of the corner of his eye. As quick as it appeared, it was gone.

'Who are you?' Davis asked. 'Why have you brought me here?'

'To kill you.'

Broad Yorkshire accent. Softly spoken.

'What? Why?' Davis's voice rose with panic.

'I'm kidding. But I wouldn't rule out a little torture. Ripping off your toenails – shit like that.'

Bashir was sitting out of sight in a dark corner of the room watching Zain's attempt at intimidation. Zain had insisted he would break Davis and extract the information. Already, Bashir knew his tactics were wrong. He was talking too much, telling instead of showing. With his first contact, Zain should have instilled the fear of God. It was a skill Bashir was proficient in.

'Please—'

'There'll be plenty of time for pleading,' Zain replied.

Bashir grimaced. Did this kid only watch bad movies?

'Who are you?'

'I'm Shakeel Ahmed's son.'

Zain walked past the chair and took a seat at his father's desk. He placed his feet on it, darted his gaze momentarily towards Bashir and crossed his legs. Zain took a slow sip of bronze-coloured liquid from a crystal tumbler and stared blankly at Davis.

'It's quite a coup to have the leader of the BNP sitting in my office. Feels like when you get your first hooker and realize that even though it might be wrong, for the next sixty minutes you can fuck her brains out whether she wants it or not. Ever experienced that?'

Davis shook his head.

'I'd recommend it.' Zain chuckled. 'And depending on how we get on, you might still get the chance.' He took another sip of his drink.

'Look – I don't know what happened to your father—'

Zain smirked and raised his eyebrows dismissively. 'Standard opening line.'

'It's true.'

'I'm not buying.'

'Where's my driver?'

'Which part of him?'

Davis opened his mouth to reply, and then stopped.

'I'm kidding.' Zain smirked again. 'He's taken a vacation for a couple of days. I'd say someplace warm, but it's more likely to be cold and damp. Still, it's a couple of days off work.'

Bashir stood up to leave. He hated small talk. He worked

the old-fashioned way and only spoke at the end. He was going to give Zain an hour with Davis. After that, Zain would lose interest. He spoke softly in Urdu to tell Zain he would be outside and to call him when he was needed. He didn't give Zain a chance to reply.

'Who was that?' Davis asked, alarmed.

'The man who brought you here. The man I'm trying to keep from you. You've heard of good cop, bad cop, right?'

Davis nodded.

'I'm bad cop, and him? He's something else entirely. You want to know an interesting fact about my colleague?'

Davis shook his head. 'No, I don't want to know anything. I just want to leave.'

'And you can. As soon as you tell me who murdered my father.'

'I told you, I don't know—'

Zain wagged his finger, as if he was scolding a small child. 'Like I was saying, something interesting about my colleague. I don't know if it's true or not; he's not exactly the kind of guy you ask.'

'Look—'

'If you keep interrupting me I'll have to get started with you sooner than I intended,' snapped Zain.

Davis closed his mouth.

'So my friend outside . . .' Zain continued, regaining his previous calmness. 'Rumour has it he's obsessed with blood. Fucked up, right?' He laughed. 'I don't know: stuff people say? I've even heard that he sweats blood – now come on, you have to admit that sounds pretty messed up?'

Zain removed his feet from the desk and stood up. He raised his arms and performed a full-body stretch, cracking his spine. Then he made his way towards Davis and perched on the end of the desk. 'Thing is, Martin – you don't mind if I call you that?'

Davis shook his head.

'If you don't play nice with me, I won't be here when he comes back. So I guess you'll just have to let me know if it's true. Yeah?'

Davis shook his head vehemently. 'I didn't kill your father.'

'Rumour has it Lucas Dwight did. You remember him? Old pal of yours?'

'He's not my pal.'

Zain removed his jacket to reveal a thin, wiry frame. 'My father taught me one thing really well,' he said, folding the jacket neatly and placing it in the middle of the desk. 'He taught me the only way to get the truth from somebody is to beat it out of them. How do I know this? Because . . .' Zain removed a brass knuckle-duster from his pocket. '. . . this was my father's.'

Bashir was sitting outside the office. He could hear Zain beating Davis, who was groaning in pain. It was a dull, measured, repetitive noise.

Bashir knew little about Davis. He didn't need to.

He had a unique way of getting people to see reason.

The call would come. Zain would soon tire. He had the stamina of a child.

Bashir put his hand under his shirt. He always wore black to mask the bleeding. He removed it and was comforted to see his fingers were covered in fresh blood. He wiped them on his trousers and waited.

It was twenty minutes before Zain opened the door. He was sweating and looked furious. He threw the brass knuckle-duster on the floor. It clanged noisily on the concrete and came to rest by Bashir's feet.

'He doesn't know anything.'

Bashir nodded. He didn't get up.

Zain untucked his shirt from his trousers and fanned himself. 'You want to have fun? Be my guest, but he's a tough son of a bitch.'

This was why Zain couldn't succeed at the helm of the empire. He thought somebody taking a beating made them 'tough'. He thought a few punches with a knuckle-duster made him king.

The kid was pathetic.

'He knows something,' Bashir replied. 'It's in his voice.'

'Please—' Zain gestured towards the office door. 'Be my guest.'

'I have rules.'

'Such as?'

'You give me the key for the room. No matter what

you hear from inside, you are not allowed in.' In English, Bashir was unnerving because of his lack of words. When he spoke Urdu, it was *what* he said that worried Zain.

'Dramatic, aren't you?'

'You agree?'

Zain shrugged. 'I don't see how you making him bleed is any different to me doing it.'

Bashir stood up and stretched out his hand. 'The key.'

'It's in the door.'

Bashir moved past Zain and lifted a black holdall from the floor. There was a jangling of metal.

'What *is it* that you do?' asked Zain.

Bashir didn't reply.

'How long will it take?'

'Not long.' Bashir disappeared into the office. The door clicked shut behind him.

Bashir stood in the doorway and looked carefully around the room, taking in details he hadn't noticed before. Davis was slumped in the chair. There was a dome-shaped CCTV camera in the ceiling, far corner. Bashir walked towards it. Halfway across, he dropped his holdall on the floor. There was an audible clang of metal. Bashir could feel Davis's watchful eyes.

He pulled up a chair, grabbed the camera and turned it around. Away from Davis.

Now, he felt comfortable.

Now, it was time.

'Please . . .' Davis pleaded. 'I didn't kill Shakeel Ahmed.'

Bashir grabbed the back of Davis's chair and turned it 180 degrees. He stepped in front of him, ensuring his back was towards Davis. He didn't want to look at him. Not yet. Not until the anger overcame him. Bashir turned his face towards the painting of Mecca. He was fascinated by it. The details of the Kaaba were breathtaking.

'Fuck you!' Davis spat. He was becoming more and more agitated in the chair.

For Bashir, these moments were beautiful. It was the anticipation. The beautiful calm before it started.

Davis's behaviour was normal. Denial turned to anger. But only briefly. Once the mind was broken, information would flow quickly.

Bashir took a few moments to compose himself. He knelt down and slowly, almost reverentially, removed a chain from his holdall. Attached to it were five heavy steel knives. A zanjeer. An Islamic implement for religious self-flagellation.

Bashir placed it carefully on the table. He still hadn't turned around to look at Davis.

Bashir closed his eyes and started to unbutton his shirt. When it was open, he paused. He thought about the house he would visit tonight. About how he had ended up in England.

A slave to his past.

Anger started to build. Slowly at first.

And then he thought about the girl.

Ruksa.

He could still picture the scene. Her body thrashing to escape. Begging for it to stop.

Bashir dropped his shirt to the floor.

There was a sharp intake of breath from behind.

He lifted the zanjeer from the desk, cradling it like a child.

'Jesus Christ,' he heard Davis whisper. 'What the hell are you?'

Bashir didn't answer. Instead, he closed his eyes and took a deep breath.

Then, with sudden, devastating ferocity, Bashir threw the zanjeer over his shoulder and lashed the first of many blows against his back.

The blood splattered across Martin Davis's face.

TWENTY-THREE

SAIMA WAS IN THE kitchen. It was half past four and she was preparing a puja thali: a metal worship tray on which she placed a gold bell, a pot of water, incense candles, some butter, some sandalwood paste and a few petals of dried flowers.

The steel tray and water symbolized purity. The bell was used to alert the gods that worship was about to begin and the incense and flowers were to please the gods with offerings of simple beauty. When the moon showed itself tonight, Saima would pray for the long life of her husband. She rubbed her stomach as her daughter hammered out another kick. 'I know, I know,' Saima whispered, 'we'll be eating within the hour.'

Harry opened the door and whistled. Saima didn't turn around.

'When did you do that?' he asked, pointing at her outfit.

'It's traditional to wear your wedding dress. I got the tailor to put in some extra material so I could wear it.'

'I'm ready when you are. And I'm all in. I'm sorry about before.'

Saima didn't reply but focused on perfecting her thali.

'Tailor must have thought you were mental,' Harry continued. Saima's pink wedding sari was covered in hundreds of sparkling sequins. She had on matching bangles and a gold necklace Harry had given her for a wedding present.

'How do I look?' she asked, almost nervously.

'Like a big beautiful Christmas tree.'

She finally turned to look at Harry. 'I like the James Bond look.' Harry had known she would appreciate the suit and tie.

Harry stepped close to her and put his arms around her. 'I'm sorry. I know this is important to you, so that makes it important to me.'

Saima pulled away from him and smiled. 'Come on. We need to be on our way. Don't want to miss your mum.'

'Sure.' Harry tried to conceal the tension in his voice. 'I promise. For the next thirty minutes, all that matters is you.'

'We're early,' Harry said. They were in Laisterdyke, by the side of a park in front of Harry's parents' corner shop. Even though Ronnie was a millionaire and had tried to get their parents to retire, they insisted on keeping their store. It was all they knew.

'Doesn't matter.' Saima shifted uncomfortably in the passenger seat, adjusting her belt.

'Imagine if you went into labour now? You'd be the best dressed mum they've ever had in the delivery room.' Harry was trying to keep on point, but his mind was circling around the links between drug gangs and Lucas Dwight.

'Let's *not* imagine that. Little Zana will not be ruining my wedding outfit.'

'Zana?'

'I was going to text you earlier.'

Harry shrugged. 'It's not so bad, I guess.'

'I hate it.'

'Why do you keep doing that?'

'To see if you're paying attention.'

'I always pay attention.'

'Jaan, last week when I was asking you which soft toy to buy, Pooh or Tigger, which did we decide on?'

'Pooh,' he replied confidently.

How did Lucas's blood turn up at Shakeel Ahmed's residence?

'The choice was Minnie or Mickey. You see?'

'You ask a lot of questions. My brain has a screening process.'

Was this an inside job? Are Ahmed's family the ones to look at? Power. Influence. Wealth.

'Tell me the story of Karva Chauth while we wait,' Saima said.

Harry wasn't paying attention. A handful of teenagers stood smoking outside his parents' store. One of them was holding a bottle of cider. Harry hoped his parents hadn't sold it. When Ronnie and Harry had been there, his parents had been strict with the law, but they were elderly now and living alone. Harry wondered just how lenient they were with pushy teenagers.

'Jaan?'

'Hmmm?'

'It's not a bad evening. The rain has stopped. Even the fog has lifted. Do we have to hide in the car like criminals?'

'Huh?'

Saima shifted in her seat again. 'We've got at least fifteen minutes. Let's go to the park.' She pointed to the playground.

'No, Mum and Dad might—'

She held her hand up. 'This year, I don't care. This year I don't care about anything, other than showing my husband that I love him.'

'Come on then.' Harry opened his door and pushed thoughts of Lucas's whereabouts from his mind. 'Ten minutes in the park.'

The park was uncharacteristically quiet. The local hooligans must have been causing mischief someplace else.

Harry and Saima were sitting side by side on the swings. He was staring at the seesaw intensely.

'What is it?' asked Saima, putting her hand on his shoulder.

'Nothing.'

'I can see it in your face.'

He shook his head.

'Jaan—'

'I used to go on that thing with Mundeep. Best sister-in-law I could have asked for. You know. Before . . .'

'She'll come round. She—'

'No. She won't,' he said coldly and turned to face his wife. 'You represent the ultimate threat to her sanity. To her family. To her . . . children.' He looked away and dropped his voice to a whisper. 'Doesn't make me not miss her though. We were close. For a decade. Shit, I wish I hated her.'

'Tell me the story of Karva Chauth,' said Saima, grabbing his face and turning it back towards her.

'Why?'

'It's a nice story. And it will put your focus where it needs to be: *here*, not with Lucas Dwight.'

Harry looked at his watch.

'Please.'

'OK. Since we have time to kill.' It had just turned five. Almost time. 'I don't know why we bother. It's originally a Hindu tradition embraced by Sikhs over time.'

She nodded. 'Your lot stole it—'

'Adopted it,' he corrected. 'So, about a million years ago . . .'

'Don't take the piss. Tell it nicely. It's important.'

'Sorry,' he said, trying not to sound patronizing. 'OK, in the olden days an innocent village girl called . . . ?' He looked at Saima for an answer.

'Veervati,' she replied.

'Well done. Veervati married a king.'

'Innocent village girl like me,' Saima whispered.

'Exactly. So, after marriage, she went back to her parents' house and began observing a strict fast for her husband until the moon came out.'

'What's the importance of the moon?'

Harry shrugged. 'Something to do with the lunar calendar pre-empting everything that's good in the world.'

'You Indians are kind of weird, aren't you?'

'Says the Islamic girl who's observing my tradition.'

'Yours? You stole it—'

'You want the story or not?'

She nodded and blew him an air-kiss.

'Right, so Veervati was fasting but she was finding it hard. She had seven brothers who couldn't bear to see their sister in distress, so they deceived her by taking a mirror and a light and reflecting it through the trees.'

Saima gasped theatrically.

'Veervati thought it was the moon and ate something. The moment she did, she received news that her husband, the King, had died. She rushed to the palace and on the way met Lord Shiva and Goddess Parvati. They confirmed the King had died because she broke her fast. She begged forgiveness and Parvati granted her wish on the proviso she kept a Karva Chauth fast every year. The Gods revived the King, legend began, and everyone lived happily ever after.'

'That's a nice story. Didn't her brothers get into trouble?'

'I don't know. Lord Shiva probably made them stand on a naughty step for a few hundred years.'

'You shouldn't take the mick out of these things.'

'Myths and goblins are for kids. The same as fairy-tales.'

'We're living a fairy-tale.'

'We are? How so?'

'Over there is the castle.' She pointed to the store. 'At the moment, the Prince and the Princess are trying to get there to meet the King and the Queen. One day they will and everyone will live happily ever after. See?'

At exactly four minutes past five, Harry's father, Ranjit, limped out of the side door of the building. It provided a little privacy from the shop entrance. The overhead security light came on. Ranjit was wearing a dark turban and his shirt was too tight, forcing his stomach out over his waistline. Then Harry's brother, Ronnie, appeared.

Of course, it was a family day – they would all be together.

But not Harry.

A few moments later, Harry's mother and Ronnie's wife, Mundeep, appeared, both dressed in colourful saris. They were carrying silver trays, similar to Saima's.

'Look,' Saima whispered excitedly. This was as close to her mother-in-law as she'd ever been.

Harry watched his mother, taking in every detail: her hair pulled into a tight ponytail and a few gold bangles on each arm. She was ageing rapidly, the moon reflecting grey off her scalp. Perhaps it wasn't age. Perhaps it was trauma.

Losing a son.

Sitting on the park swing, Harry was invisible, hidden in the shadows. He had always been his mother's favourite. Now he was considered impure.

But she still loved him. He had seen it in her face the last time they had spoken, before Harry's father had disowned him.

Ranjit was standing awkwardly, hands in his pockets, with his usual emotionless face showing no empathy for his wife who had starved all day.

His mother walked away from Harry's father, keeping her back towards him. She raised the silver tray above her head, moving it in large circles, and worshipped the moon. She threw some rice, poured some water and then held out a mirror, looking at her husband's reflection in it. Then she turned, approached her husband and offered him some water before taking a sip herself. With the fast broken, Harry's parents waited for Ronnie and Mundeep to do the same.

With the ceremony complete they went back into the shop. Ronnie was last in line. He paused. Glanced towards the park. Stared into the darkness.

Just past the towering oak tree: two silhouettes.

Ronnie stood still. For almost a minute. Then he finally disappeared into the store.

Saima and Harry stood on the paved area next to the swings. The lamps in the park were broken so the only light came from the full moon. It shimmered on the cracked pavement slabs. Saima walked towards the moon, away from Harry, and began her ritual. She locked eyes with Harry's reflection in the mirror and gave him a look so loving it took his breath away. For the briefest of moments, Harry forgot about everything. Where he was. Lucas Dwight. His job.

Harry took a sip of water from the steel cup and handed it back to Saima. He pressed his index finger into some red dye on the tray called sindoor. Harry carefully transferred it to Saima's forehead and made a bindi. It was the final step – a show of their marriage.

With their ritual completed, Harry leaned forward and kissed her. Next year, when they did this, they would have a daughter.

'Made your wish?' Harry asked.

'Are you supposed to?'

Harry shrugged. 'Why not?'

'OK.' Saima closed her eyes. 'Done.'

Harry nodded. 'We're good?'

'Yes. It will get easier,' she whispered and squeezed his hand. 'Have faith.'

'I do. On Eid, the holiest day for Muslims, instead of going out, my wife is standing in a derelict park, after fasting all day, giving thanks for the life of her husband. I don't need any more faith than that.'

Saima turned away so he couldn't see her eyes well up.

'Here.' Harry put his hand in his pocket and removed a small red box.

Saima beamed him a smile. 'An Eid present?'

He nodded and placed it in her outstretched hand.

She opened it and a warm glow spread across her face. 'Diamond earrings?'

'It's a dual gift. An Eid *and* an advance push present,' he said, placing his hands on her tummy.

'One carat, easy,' she said enthusiastically.

'Most women drop the odd hint. You've told me every day since that test turned positive.'

She closed the box and wiped tears from her face. 'Bloody hormones,' she said and laughed.

Harry's phone beeped. He checked the message.

Why do you do it to yourself?

It was from Ronnie. Harry looked towards the store, at the upstairs window where he could see Ronnie's silhouette. He didn't reply and put the phone back in his pocket.

'The earrings are perfect,' Saima said. 'You can go and save the city now.'

'I'm just trying to save myself.'

Saima knew he wasn't only talking about his job.

'I'm sorry to cut short our evening, but I need this.'

'Just be careful.' She put his hand on her belly. 'Because

we need you. Promise me if I call you'll come running.'

'In spite of what's happening, you and her' – he rubbed her stomach – 'are my priority. Nothing will stop me.'

TWENTY-FOUR

A DENSE WHITE GHOST had suddenly descended across Bradford and it took double the normal twenty minutes for Harry to reach Undercliffe Cemetery.

He arrived after six, just as the moon had been swallowed by the mist. He had dropped Saima at home, ignored her request for him to change out of his best suit and promised he would call regularly.

It was an important day for Saima. Normally she would have been surrounded by family: feasting, celebrating and creating memories. All the things she wouldn't experience any more. Things Harry wouldn't. And instead of making sure she *never* felt alone, Harry was out tracking shadows.

It was the blueprint of his life. Doing penance for rash decisions.

Harry was on edge. On the way he had passed more patrol cars than he ever had seen. There was a large police presence circling the streets. Harry had tried calling several of his colleagues, none of whom had answered. Either they were ignoring him or they were busy.

The wrong kind of busy.

Harry parked the BMW across from the main entrance of the cemetery. He was in a blind spot, between two fused streetlights, with only the mist for company.

Undercliffe was predominantly an Asian neighbourhood, part of a twenty-five-acre estate, one of the largest English Heritage parks in England.

The cemetery had once been the resting place for wealthy wool merchants in Bradford. An exclusive burial ground. It had become run-down in the nineties, ending up a derelict ruin until Bradford Council took over its upkeep. Nowadays anybody could be buried there. It mirrored the fortunes of the city – wealth and exclusivity had been eroded.

Harry killed the engine and turned off the lights. A quiet, calming darkness surrounded him.

There was a sudden tap on the driver-side window. Harry nearly jumped out of his seat. He turned to see Lucas Dwight staring in at him, his knuckles pressed against the glass. Harry saw the familiar tattoo of 'Love' and, underneath it, 'Hate'. He hadn't fancied his chances of finding Lucas but he'd had no other place to start.

Harry released the locks and Lucas jumped in the back. The two men stared at each other in the rear-view mirror.

'Surprised?' Lucas said finally.

'Damn right.'

'At the house.' Lucas pointed a finger at the mirror. 'What the fuck happened?'

'Not sure.' Harry looked away, scanning the immediate area.

'I'm here to clear my name. All kind of places and things I could have gone and done. You need to level with me.'

Harry didn't reply.

'You know something and you're not sharing. Not how this works, Harry. You in or am I walking?'

'I got nothing concrete,' Harry said. 'My wallet – the one that was stolen on Lumb Lane – somehow ended up in my boss's hands. Only one way it got there.'

'No way those deadbeats got to your boss directly.'

'Exactly. Which means it went up the chain of command until someone – on a street level – had access to my boss.'

'He dirty?'

'Not a chance.' Harry put his eyes back on Lucas. 'Most stand-up guy I know. He's bled for this city and cleaned it up the hard way.'

'You saying he never got his hands dirty?'

'We all get our hands dirty. Just some more than others.'

'You trust him?'

'I did.'

'Meaning?'

'He wanted me to give you up. To him personally. Which . . . well, isn't his style.'

'He's dirty. The fact he came to your home when he's got bigger things to worry about?' Lucas's face creased in disbelief.

Harry nodded. 'Nothing's black and white. Of all people, you should know that.'

Lucas took a deep breath and slouched down into the seat. 'You and me? Are we good?'

Harry nodded. 'My wife vouched for you.'

'You didn't tell me she was Muslim.'

'Why would I?'

Lucas shrugged. 'Seems like we might have shared a few of the same struggles.'

'What do you know about it?' Harry replied, rather more bitterly than he intended.

'Plenty.' Lucas leaned forward suddenly so his breath was warm on Harry's neck. 'In prison, there were two camps of Asians: the Muslims and the rest. I know that divide. Can't say I understand it. I thought you were all the same.'

Harry turned his face so he had Lucas in the corner of his eye. 'I don't do divides. Neither does Saima.'

'Worked out well for me. She's a good woman. I could see it.'

'Your mate, is he in there?' Harry asked, changing the topic.

'I don't know. I've been waiting for you.'

'Let's hope so. Something's going down. There are patrols everywhere. This city's got more blue flashing than a strip club.'

'Any thoughts on why I'm being set up?'

'You're a decoy, but I'm not sure for what.'

'Come on then,' Lucas replied. 'Let's go and see what Daniel Levy knows about it.'

Harry scanned the street quickly, then followed Lucas towards the gates, keeping only a few steps behind.

Next to the gates was a low wall with iron railings barely five feet high. They climbed over.

The cemetery was built on top of a hill that overlooked the centre of Bradford. A road snaked its way to the summit and on a clear day gave a view which stretched miles across the city. But today was different.

It didn't feel like a burial ground. It was a barren land, long forgotten and left to decay. The grass was wiry and unkempt, trying almost treacherously to trap a stray ankle.

Harry kept Lucas at his shoulder. They didn't need to be covert – nobody would see them coming in the fog.

'This place is all wrong,' Harry whispered, coming to a stop.

Lucas was at his side and nodded. 'Not how I remember it. Not at all. Used to be owned by a private developer.'

'That deal ended a long time ago. Your mate – where's he likely to be?'

'He's not my mate. He'll be where the best tomb is; it gives the best shelter. At the top.'

The cemetery was full of elaborate gravestones, some with sculptures above. Harry paused at a dirty white statue of clasped hands.

'Means a husband and wife are buried together.' Lucas grabbed Harry's arm to lead him away, but Harry didn't move. He stared to his right, at a towering stone column which rose so far into the air it disappeared into the mist. He pointed to it, almost mesmerized by how elaborate some of the monuments were.

'And that one?'

'Size of the column reflects how long they lived,' Lucas whispered. 'This guy lived a full life. Pretty rare in them days. Folk didn't last long in the mills.'

Harry turned to face him. 'How do you know all this?'

Lucas shrugged. 'I used to sleep here. Got to know the caretaker, back in the days when this place was taken care of. You learn shit.' He pulled Harry's arm a little harder. 'We need to go.'

They walked quickly. Most of the shrines were detailed works of art – a phoenix representing resurrection and a serpent biting its own tail. The bigger they were, the more they put Harry on edge. It was a walk back in time, to when wealth and grandeur meant something in Bradford.

'Why on earth would anyone deal here?' he whispered.

'Last place the cops will look. When business is done and you're high and alone, there's no better place to sleep. Nobody fucks with you in a graveyard.' Lucas was breathing heavily and he slowed down to a crawl. 'It's just over there,' he said, pointing into the mist. 'There's a huge column about twenty metres high. Biggest grave in this place.'

'Whose is it?'

'I don't know. Some wool merchant's – back in the day. Get off the road – we're not far.'

Harry followed Lucas on to the grass, walking across graves. He didn't look at them, feeling uncomfortable at stepping on the dead.

These were newer, humbler gravestones with shimmering fresh flowers scattered across several of them. They broke up the grey dullness, colourful bursts in a black and white world.

Harry suddenly stopped. Lucas didn't notice and disappeared ahead. Harry stared at a tiny headstone. It was a baby's grave. Harry thought of the nightmares plaguing him.

Saima screaming wildly in the hospital. Harry with his arms around her. In front, an empty baby's cot.

Karma.

He'd taken a life and got away with it.

A life for a life.

The writing was a blur, but Harry saw the age.

Three days old.

His stomach turned over and Harry looked away, feeling short of breath.

The grass was wet and treacherous. Harry slipped and cursed silently, catching up to Lucas. At the top of the cemetery Bradford was invisible below them.

'Shame,' whispered Lucas, 'the view's the only thing which makes coming here worthwhile.'

Harry let Lucas have a moment, lost in some memory from the past. Then: 'Ready?' he asked, touching Lucas's shoulder.

He nodded. 'Let's see if Mr Levy is present.'

'If he's here, you make him think whatever you want. Fear is a great motivator. But you overstep the mark and I'll put a stop to it.'

'I'm not going to kill anyone. I know where to draw the line.'

'For your sake, I hope so.'

'A threat? Seriously?'

'I'm still a copper.'

'No, you're suspended. Remember? You can't make your own rules when it suits you. Just leave him to me. Levy knows what I'm capable of.' Lucas's eyes gleamed in the darkness. 'More to the point, so do you.'

Harry crept behind Lucas, keeping low and stepping where he did. They used the enormous gravestones as cover. Lucas pointed to a towering memorial which looked like a finger pointing to the heavens. It had a marble roof, supported by thick pillars.

'Bingo,' Lucas whispered.

'In there?'

Lucas nodded. 'Don't you see him?'

Harry focused where Lucas was pointing and made out the shape of a curled-up body.

Lucas moved silently, keeping on the grass. When they

were only a few feet away, he stepped on to the road and dragged his feet purposefully. 'Yo, Levy?'

The body didn't move. Harry and Lucas glanced at each other. They split up, one standing either side of the grave.

'Daniel? It's Lucas.'

Still no response.

'Fuck sake – you high, man?'

Lucas reached down and rolled Daniel from his side on to his back. He recoiled as if he'd been stung.

Harry's breath caught in his chest.

Dead at their feet, with his throat slit, was Daniel Levy.

Next to him lay a weapon which looked very much like Lucas Dwight's switchblade, still gleaming with blood.

TWENTY-FIVE

THE BLOOD WAS WARM and salty on Martin Davis's face. Each lashing of the zanjeer across Bashir's back splattered more.

Davis could feel Bashir becoming angrier with each blow. He wasn't yelling in pain or screaming. He was grunting. Welcoming the bitterness of the blades, taking himself to a place where he would be able to unleash fury without remorse.

Davis was too afraid to close his eyes, which compelled him to watch the macabre act.

The blades and the blood were bad enough, but the raw anger was truly horrifying. And still Bashir hadn't looked at Davis.

Finally he stopped.

Bashir's arm came to rest by his side, the zanjeer dangling impotently. Blood dripped steadily on to the floor.

There were deep lacerations across Bashir's back. Some were new, but most were old wounds which had easily reopened. He was breathing heavily. He stepped to the side, away from Davis, and then made his way behind him.

Bashir was close: Davis could feel his breath on the back of his neck.

And then the zanjeer was suddenly dumped into Davis's lap. It was cold and heavy and streaked with blood.

'No, please – I don't know what this is about.' Davis flinched away from the blades. 'I didn't kill Shakeel Ahmed!'

Bashir pushed forward Davis's head. Davis felt a blade on his neck but it didn't cut him.

Instead, Bashir sliced the back of Davis's clothes and pulled them open roughly, exposing his skin. For a moment, Davis felt Bashir's hands, warm and clammy, running down his back, stroking unblemished skin. It felt like the touch of a lover, yet was more sinister than anything Davis had experienced.

Another stroke of Bashir's palms. Massaging the skin.

And then Davis's hands were cut loose.

Bashir walked in front of him and for the first time the men came face to face.

Davis stared at an intense-looking Asian man. Easily late fifties, with emotionless eyes and sweat running down his brow. Bashir was heavy-set with a wildly hairy chest. His shoulders were powerful, broad with honed deltoids. With Zain, Bashir spoke his native language, but with Davis he was forced into English.

'You know something,' Bashir said dryly. He pointed to the zanjeer. 'You or me. Choose.'

Davis looked at him in disbelief. 'What?'

There was no response from Bashir.

Davis suddenly realized why Bashir had sliced open the clothes on his back. 'You want me to whip myself?'

Blood was dripping from Bashir's body on to the laminate flooring and pooling by his feet. 'Yes. It helps memory.'

Davis had witnessed how forcefully Bashir had whipped himself. He still had Bashir's blood splattered across his face. But the alternative, of beating himself with the blades, seemed unthinkable.

'Pick it up,' Bashir said, greater impatience in his voice.

Davis put his hand reluctantly around the handle of the zanjeer. It was slippery with Bashir's blood. The weight of it was considerable and Davis's hand was shaking.

Perhaps it was the terror of the zanjeer in his hand, but suddenly, Colin Reed's name came screaming to mind. In the chaos of the past hour, Davis hadn't had time to think about what had happened. And while he wasn't responsible and had no real knowledge of Shakeel Ahmed's murder, that morning's covert meeting almost certainly had something to do with it.

Give them Reed. Save your ass.

Bashir could tell that Davis was sizing up information. The weight of the zanjeer usually helped jog people's memories.

Martin Davis didn't want to die. Especially in these circumstances. At the hands of a barbaric psychopath.

He raised his head and looked at Bashir. 'What guarantee do I have that you'll let me go?'

'None.'

'Then why should I tell you anything?'

'You speak now or later. But you speak.'

Davis paused. Dropped his head. Gripped the zanjeer harder. He was trapped. If he told them what he knew, which wasn't a great deal, they were apt to beat him or murder him anyway. 'Call in the other guy.'

'First you are taking *one* hit.' Bashir pointed at the zanjeer.

'Please – just call in the other guy and I'll tell you—'

Bashir stepped forward to grab the zanjeer but Davis snatched it away.

'OK – OK. I'll do it!'

Bashir backed off. 'Hard,' he growled.

Davis lowered the zanjeer to his left side and heard the blades scrape along the floor. He was hyperventilating, trying desperately to muster some courage. His breathing became quicker and shorter until he saw Bashir's feet shifting impatiently towards him.

Davis yelled in fear and, with as much force as he dared, lashed the zanjeer over his shoulder and down against his back. There was a crash of metal and an immediate shock of pain as the knives tore open his skin, cutting into him like butter.

Davis dropped the zanjeer and started to cry.

Bashir's expression didn't change. Davis was broken. Co-operation would come freely. Bashir had demeaned him sufficiently that escaping would be Davis's only priority.

Bashir picked up his shirt and dressed. Then he lifted the bloodied zanjeer, cradled it carefully and placed it back in the holdall. He closed the bag and left Davis sobbing, cowering in the chair, his cuts exposed, and walked to the door.

Bashir unlocked it but didn't open it. He went back over to Davis and sat down on the edge of the desk in front of him.

After a brief pause, Zain entered the room. He had heard the sound of the zanjeer but hadn't been able to determine what it was. He had also heard Davis pleading and then yelling in pain, but when he saw the bizarre way Davis was doubled over in the chair with his clothes torn open and deep, angry wounds on his back, he couldn't understand what had taken place. 'He ready?' Zain asked uncertainly.

Bashir nodded.

Davis continued to weep in the chair. Bashir thought it was mostly because he'd been broken and not from the pain of the cuts.

Zain wheeled his father's leather chair from behind the desk to face Davis. He took a seat and clapped his hands to get Davis's attention. 'Less crying and more talking. What do you know?'

Davis kept his head bowed, unable to look at them. He

spoke slowly, through clenched teeth. 'I got a call this morning from somebody I do business with. Early call, six a.m.'

'Louder,' Zain said arrogantly, 'so I can fucking hear you. Give me a name.'

Davis hesitated, but only for a moment.

'Colin Reed.'

'Colin Reed? Never heard of him.'

'Neither had I until a few years ago.'

'Details?'

Davis's mind was racing. He'd given his word that his members would march through Bradford tonight and he wasn't certain of surviving his current predicament. 'He told me to get out of the city. Get somewhere public where I had an alibi.'

Davis was trying to buy some time. For what – he wasn't sure. But he wasn't about to let them in on the potential for a riot in the city. Bashir had humiliated him. It was more than politics now. If Davis died in this chair, he wanted to do so believing Bradford would fall. That some small measure of compensation might result from his death.

'Why?'

'I can't be sure. Plausible deniability maybe. I didn't need to know. But he spoke about Lucas Dwight and about your father's murder. He didn't say he was responsible, but he didn't say he wasn't either.' Davis raised his head and finally looked at Zain. 'On my life, I swear, that's all I know.'

'How long did you meet for and where?'

'Maybe twenty minutes. Top of Baildon Moor. In a discreet location.'

'Twenty minutes? What else happened at this meeting?'

'We spoke about my losing the election.'

'He a supporter of yours? This Colin Reed?'

Davis nodded.

'A donor?'

Another nod.

'How much we talking?'

Davis hesitated. 'Maybe ten grand. Twice a year.'

Zain smiled. 'Now that was a good, old-fashioned, poorly thought-out lie. In fact, scrap that, it was *complete* bullshit. How much did this guy give you? Or shall I have my friend here ask?'

Davis dipped his head again and then shook it. 'I'm sorry. OK, it was more. He's offloaded nearly two hundred thousand over the past year.'

'Cash?'

Davis nodded.

'So he's no small fish.'

Davis shrugged.

'Where can I find him?'

'I don't know. Honestly, he's always sought me out.'

'But you have a way of contacting him?'

'I have his mobile number. That's all.'

'Where is it?'

'On my phone.'

Zain spoke quickly to Bashir in a language Davis didn't understand. The big man nodded.

'I need something else – some other detail that you're overlooking. In all the times you've met this guy, he's never given you any idea about where he works or lives? I find that hard to believe.'

Davis looked at Zain angrily. 'Don't you think if I knew how to find him, I'd tell you? I'm in self-preservation mode here. Guys who hand you two hundred grand in cash are careful. Not stupid. I don't know where he lives or how to get hold of him.'

Bashir reached into his holdall and pulled out a large brown paper bag. Davis stared at it suspiciously.

'What . . . what's that? What's he doing?'

'Jogging your memory,' Zain replied.

Bashir moved behind Davis, who tried to turn his head to look but Bashir hit him forcefully. The blow thudded into Davis's jaw and sent his head back the other way.

Bashir opened the paper bag and dumped a fistful of salt into Davis's still-bleeding wounds.

Davis shrieked and Bashir grabbed his neck to keep him firmly in the chair. After a few seconds, just enough for the salt to dissolve, Bashir let Davis go, leaving him to thrash around with the pain.

Zain shook his head. 'I bet that hurt.'

Davis snarled at the men. Fury had replaced fear. He spat at Zain, lashing out with his hands but unable to get close.

'Come,' said Bashir, patting Zain on the shoulder. 'We finished.'

Bashir grabbed Davis's hands and secured them once more behind his back. 'When you remember something else, you just let us know,' Zain called out.

The men walked out of the room.

Martin Davis knew they'd be back.

The nightmare had just started.

TWENTY-SIX

HARRY STARED SUSPICIOUSLY AT Lucas. The last time he had seen the switchblade was at the gym. Where Harry had left it.

Lucas already got to him, Harry. You've been played.

'I didn't do this,' Lucas said, sensing what Harry was thinking. 'That knife was left at the gym – you know that. You saw that.'

Harry didn't reply. He was looking hard at Lucas. He couldn't remember seeing him pick up the blade. But he had no idea where he'd been for the last few hours.

Lucas grabbed Harry's arm and pointed behind him to the outline of a man who had slithered out from the shadows. He was stalking his way towards them, cutting through the mist like one of the undead.

Harry fumbled in his pocket for his phone.

'No time for that,' Lucas whispered. 'Let's get the fuck out of here.'

They turned around to run but were stopped by the silhouette of another man calmly sitting on a gravestone. He waved, almost comically, at them.

The first man approached slowly. He had a cigarette in his mouth. The end of it burned a vivid orange. He removed the cigarette from his lips. His other hand was in his pocket. 'Phones on the floor.' Smoke escaped his mouth, curling across his face.

Harry wasn't intimidated. He stood up and stepped forward. 'I'm Detective Inspector Harry Virdee. Stay right where you are.'

'I know exactly who you are, inspector,' the man replied. 'You're a man in the wrong place at the wrong time.'

The man's attitude surprised Harry. His rank should have had greater impact. 'I'm placing you under arrest . . .'

'You can't. Because you're not on official duty, are you, inspector?'

These guys had no right to know that.

'Don't be surprised. You weren't to know what you were getting suckered into,' the man said. He reached inside his pocket and removed a brown envelope. He threw it on the ground to land at Harry's feet. 'Ten grand. I would surmise that in your current predicament, that kind of cash would go a long way?'

'Fuck you.' Harry ignored the package. 'I don't do blood money.'

'Sure you do,' the man replied. Harry made out a few details. Heavy-set. Balding. Maybe six-three. A few hundred pounds. Strong Yorkshire accent. Gleaming rings on the hand holding the cigarette.

'Who are you?' Lucas asked, stepping past Harry. 'Why'd you kill Levy?'

'We have business with you, Lucas. We can do this the easy way or the hard way.'

Harry stole a glance behind him. The men had them boxed in the corner of the cemetery. The only escape was for Lucas and Harry to jump off the hill into the undergrowth below. The steep slope was at least fifty feet and although it was obscured by fog, Harry envisaged razor-sharp thorns and ankle-snapping potholes.

Both men were bulky. Sluggish on their feet. If Harry and Lucas ran, they wouldn't be caught. But two on two was a fair fight and Harry fancied his chances. Especially knowing that Lucas was more than capable with his fists.

'You didn't answer my question,' Lucas replied. 'Who the fuck are you? Man's got a right to know who's hunting him.'

'Oh,' the man replied with enough venom to ensure Lucas realized they were there to inflict damage, 'you'll find out. Of that you can be *damn* sure.'

Harry was assessing their location. If they could gain twenty metres on the men the mist would provide cover.

'Nobody wants to make this any messier.' The man took another drag on his cigarette.

'Murder makes this messy,' Harry replied. 'And I can still arrest you, irrespective of my current position.'

The man grunted. 'Turn around and walk away,

inspector,' he said, raising his voice. 'This case is beyond you.'

'Don't be stupid—'

'And I don't want to add any unnecessary bodies to this place.'

'You're threatening a cop?' Harry said, still trying to exert some authority.

'I'm in the disposal business. There'll be no one to hear your story if you don't leave.'

'I'm tired of your shit,' Lucas snapped and made as if to rush the man.

'I wouldn't try it,' he said and withdrew a pistol from his pocket, a silencer on its end. 'Not my preferred choice, but if you force my hand . . .'

'Who are you?' shouted Lucas. 'And what do you want?'

'You've a debt to repay.'

Harry raised his hands, trying to defuse the situation. He was fixated on the gun, trying to make out if it was genuine or not. 'I'm not leaving and if you shoot a policeman – there'll be no place you can hide.'

'I've got ten policemen in my phone,' the man boasted. 'You have no idea who you are up against or where we can reach. Now, I'm not going to ask again. Put your phone and car keys on the floor and walk away.'

Harry stepped in front of Lucas to shield him. Shooting Harry would be the last option these guys would take. He could hear it in the man's voice. He needed Harry to walk.

'I'll hand him over and leave if you tell me what this is

about.' Harry put his hands behind him and pointed to his left, inching slowly away from the man – towards the edge of the hill, trusting that Lucas would see what he was thinking.

The man shook his head. 'You're not in the driving seat.' He waved the gun to his left, beckoning Harry to step aside.

'OK . . . OK.' Harry raised his hands. He turned around to face Lucas. 'I'm sorry, Lucas,' he said loudly. 'Hit me, then jump,' he whispered.

Lucas hesitated but Harry glared at him and darted his eyes to the right.

Lucas snapped out a right jab and caught Harry on the side of the head, glancing his fist across his scalp. As Lucas turned and leapt down the slope, Harry pretended to crumple to the floor but no sooner had he landed, he rolled over the edge of the hill, scrambling away quickly and jumping to his feet in pursuit of Lucas.

The men didn't react in time, affording Harry and Lucas precious seconds. They crunched through thick spiky brambles, gaining speed with each metre. Harry tucked his chin into his chest and raised his elbows to shield his face. Even so, piercing scratches sliced across his cheeks.

At the bottom of the hill was a low brick wall which Harry and Lucas vaulted. Beyond it was a narrow cobbled street with back-to-back houses on either side. Harry felt an agonizing pulse in his liver where Lucas had struck him at the gym earlier. He grabbed his side and tried to slow down. The street was on a steep decline and his momentum was making him unsteady.

Lucas lost his balance and went sprawling to the ground, sliding five metres on his side. He was up quickly and Harry caught up, grabbed his arm and pulled him to the side of an alleyway, into a concealed snicket. They crouched to their knees and looked at the hill.

Nothing.

No pursuit.

Just a smokescreen of mist.

'You OK?' Harry asked, panting heavily.

Lucas nodded. 'You?' He pointed to where Harry was massaging his side.

Harry grimaced. 'Where you hit me at the gym,' he whispered. 'Caught it on a bastard branch on the way down.' Harry removed his hand. It was smeared with blood.

'Bad?'

'Flesh wound,' Harry said, but he was clearly struggling. 'We need to keep moving.'

'Who were those guys?'

Harry shook his head. 'I don't know. Let's get safe. Can't get back to the car. They'll have it covered.' He took out his phone.

'Who are you calling?' Lucas asked.

'Friends. Down the nick.'

'No!' Lucas snatched the phone. 'We don't have *any* friends. I don't trust the police – these guys have eyes everywhere. He just told us that.'

'Not my guys. Look—'

'You make that call and I walk.'

'I know you're not involved. I can vouch for that. We just—'

'Listen.' Lucas handed back the phone. 'It's me and you or I'm gone.'

Harry put away the phone begrudgingly. 'Come on.'

They walked hurriedly down from the road and followed it until they reached an adjoining street. The fog was dense enough to keep them hidden.

'Barkerend Road is just down there – we can get a taxi,' Lucas said.

They jogged to the bottom of the street and paused. Harry was breathing heavily. The pulse in his side was getting worse. They scanned the area for signs of hostility, and, satisfied they were clear, crept on to the main road.

'There.' Lucas pointed to the yellow glow of Barkerend Fisheries. There were three taxis loitering outside.

'Pull your hoodie tight.' Harry put his bloodstained hand in his pocket and approached the first taxi. The driver had a large container on his lap filled with kebab meat and chips. Harry tapped on the window but the man waved them away and pointed at the car behind.

The second driver was also eating but welcomed them into the cab.

'Where to?' he asked when Lucas and Harry were in the back. The car reeked of fish and chips. The Asian taxi driver licked oily fingers and scrunched up the white papers he was eating from.

Harry hesitated. He didn't want to take Lucas home. It was too dangerous.

'St Peter's Church. Top of Leeds Road,' Lucas replied quickly.

'Is only half-mile, other side of road,' the driver said disapprovingly. 'Minimum fare is four fifty.'

'Fine.' Harry turned to Lucas. 'Church?'

Lucas dropped his voice to barely a whisper. 'Can't go back to yours. They know who you are.'

Harry nodded. 'You got friends at this church?'

'One,' Lucas replied hesitantly. 'But we need to keep her out of this.' He grasped Harry's wrist. 'Understand?'

Harry nodded. 'Got it.' He removed his mobile. 'I need to tell Saima to get out of the house. She's not safe any more.'

'Where are you going to send her?'

'To A & E. She works there. No place safer, especially in her current state.'

'Do it.'

'Any idea who or what we're up against?' Harry asked as he heard a busy tone on the phone.

Lucas nodded slowly. He met Harry's eyes, his face burning brightly. 'What he said about me having a debt to repay? Found out about you? Police in their pocket? A reach that knows no boundaries? There is only one organization that gets intelligence that quickly and crosses so many agencies.'

'Who?' Harry redialled Saima.

'The BNP. But this is a big play.'

'What? You're not making any sense.'

'What time is it?'

Harry looked at his watch. 'Seven.'

'The Bradford Mela is about to start.' Lucas closed his eyes and took a moment. 'I don't understand all of this,' he whispered, 'but I reckon there's going to be a clash at the Mela tonight. I've been blamed for a racist murder of the most popular Asian man in Bradford.' He inched closer to Harry, who was dialling Saima for a third time.

'Damn it, pick up,' Harry whispered.

'A clash at the Mela means a repeat of two thousand and one. You remember two thousand and one, right?'

It was the year the Bradford riots had decimated the city. Harry recalled it vividly. He'd been on the streets and witnessed first-hand what a race riot looked like.

'Bradford's about to burn, Harry,' said Lucas. 'And I'm the fall guy.'

TWENTY-SEVEN

SAIMA VIRDEE WAS ALONE in the kitchen. She hated being alone. When Harry wasn't there, the natural creaks of their home sounded more sinister and the mirrors seemed to reflect untrustworthy shadows.

Outside, she could hear sirens from ambulances and police cars. Their house was en route to Bradford Royal Infirmary and even though sirens were commonplace, the volume of them tonight was unprecedented.

Putting away the items on her thali was strangely calming. Even more so was having made the sacrifice on Eid, a demonstration of how much she loved Harry. Karva Chauth wasn't an Islamic ritual but that's what made it special. Saima was determined to fuse their lives and make a success of their relationship. On both sides of their families, nobody believed they would last. Theirs was a union forged amongst bloodshed, mostly their own. It made the equity in their marriage bottomless.

She knew the birth of their daughter would strengthen their bond but it would also open unhealed wounds. Their daughter would have no cousins to play with. No grandparents to spoil her. No family outside of Mum and Dad. The absence of family would be a tough welcome into the world.

Saima tried to shake the thoughts from her mind, but today of all days she couldn't. It was the first time for centuries that Eid had fallen on the same day as Karva Chauth. Yet instead of celebrating, she was alone in the house while her husband battled to save his career.

A career she feared he wouldn't hold on to for much longer. Because of his rage.

Harry didn't deal with the rejection from his family half as well as he pretended to.

Saima touched the scar on the side of her face.

Was she any different?

It had been a painful separation.

She closed her eyes and saw her father's snarling face. Then the heavy gold ring on his index finger accelerating towards her face. Saima shuddered and almost dropped the thali as the memory overtook her. She opened her eyes and swallowed the lump in her throat.

'Sorry,' she whispered and rubbed her bump protectively. Her daughter didn't like her mother being tense. Saima's stomach knotted thinking of the past. There was so much Harry didn't know. So much she daren't tell him. So much her friends at A & E had covered.

Because when it came to Saima, Harry's need to

protect her outweighed his ability to see reason. To take a step back. To think first.

Saima lit an incense stick, her third of the day, and left the kitchen.

She picked up the Sky remote and muted the sound while she flicked through the channels. Saima was half-way through the list when she heard a noise from the back yard. It sounded like breaking glass. Saima's stomach tightened. Her daughter lashed out a kick and moved across her belly in protest. It momentarily took Saima's breath away and she doubled over, gasping at a powerful cramp. She glanced at the sliding doors which led out to the garden. The blinds were closed but she had definitely heard *something*.

Saima put down the remote. She whispered to her daughter to calm, and rubbed her bump soothingly. After several moments of intense listening, Saima shuffled reluctantly towards the kitchen. She was still wearing her pink wedding outfit and the tassels rattled rhythmically.

The smell of incense became stronger as she entered the kitchen. The window blinds were closed in there too. She listened carefully, holding her breath involuntarily. And waited.

The lights in the kitchen were off, which meant if somebody were outside she would be able to see their silhouette.

'You're being silly,' she whispered, slowly letting her breath out. In her stomach, her daughter agreed and jammed her heel into Saima's ribs. She winced and gently pushed it away. There was a shift in her daughter's position and another ripple across her waist.

Saima took a couple of deep breaths, then opened the blind quickly.

Nothing.

The garden was undisturbed.

Saima peered nervously to both sides and then towards the gate at the bottom. It was closed. No evidence anybody was there.

'Stupid,' she whispered and then suddenly let out a shrill cry as her mobile phone rang.

She swore in Urdu and hurried back to the living room.

It was Harry, but what he said didn't calm her. A few moments into the conversation, she was more frightened than she had been since her father dragged her by her hair and threw her into the street.

Harry was speaking quickly and though he was trying to sound calm, he was anything but. He told her to drive to A & E. *Immediately.*

To stay there, amongst colleagues, until he collected her.

'But why?' she asked. 'Harry, what's happened? What's going on?'

'Saima, I don't have time to explain. I'd just feel better if you were around people, especially given how close you are to giving birth. Please. Stay on the phone with me until you get to your car. Once you're moving, I'll hang up.'

Saima knew when not to press him. She grabbed her car keys and her hospital bag from the hallway and checked from the window that the front garden was clear.

She kept the phone to her ear, giving Harry a real-time update as she unlocked the door and stepped outside. She paused and nervously scanned right and then left. Satisfied there wasn't an ambush, she hurried down the path to her car.

Saima opened the door of her Yaris and threw the bag on to the passenger seat. She got inside, locked the doors and started the car.

'Jaan, I'm in,' she said. 'Leaving now. Are you OK?'

'I'm fine. I just want to focus on what I'm doing and not have my attention split worrying about you. Now go. Text me when you arrive.'

'OK,' she replied and hung up. Saima placed the phone on the passenger seat and put the car in gear. She stole a last glance at her house and was about to pull away when she remembered the incense burning in the kitchen. 'Shit,' she whispered. For a moment she convinced herself it would be fine. She had lit so many of them over the years, why would one cause the house to burn down now?

The distance to her front door seemed unfathomable. Her home suddenly felt hostile, a place to be wary of. Another pang of tension seized her stomach. She was gripping the steering wheel, wringing the rubber in frustration.

It would needle her. Increasingly. By the time Saima reached A & E she would be convinced her house was on fire.

She snatched the phone and started to redial Harry. But the call wouldn't connect. Saima tried several times but she couldn't get a signal. Suddenly the sirens sounding in the distance and her isolation in the car seemed overwhelming.

Saima hissed at her own dramatics and flung open the car door.

TWENTY-EIGHT

THE TAXI DRIVER WAS on Leeds Road, dubbed 'Curry Mile' or 'Neon Mile' because of its tacky strobing restaurant signs. Usually it was the busiest area in Bradford with over two hundred restaurants. But tonight, a lot of the shops were closed, shutters pulled tight, signs switched off. The few that were open looked deserted. Either everybody was at the Mela or they were keeping away.

Lucas shied away from the window, pulling his hoodie tight across his face as several police cars and ambulances tore down Leeds Road towards the city centre.

It took only a few minutes to reach the grounds of St Peter's. Harry paid the fare and hurried after Lucas towards the entrance to the church.

'Your wife safe?' Lucas asked.

'On her way to work.'

Harry was applying pressure to the wound in his side, which was still seeping blood. 'With all the ambulances flying around she'll probably get roped into working.'

Lucas paused outside the entrance. He hadn't been back here for decades. It used to be his regular Sunday-morning ritual – until the streets replaced the church and anger banished faith. But now he was returning with an altogether different view of the world. There was room for Christianity *and* Islam in his life.

'Want to tell me what we are doing here?' Harry asked.

Lucas didn't turn to face him. He was still staring at the front door.

Lucas sighed and spoke quietly, almost as if in a trance. 'Today is turning into my own fucked-up episode of *This is Your Life.*'

'You want me to do it?' Harry asked, removing a blood-stained hand from his side and raising it to knock on the door.

'Wait. Just need a minute.'

'Come on, Lucas. You hear that?'

More police sirens screamed down Leeds Road.

Lucas ignored them. 'She's inside.'

'Who? Somebody we can trust?'

Lucas knocked on the door, then took his fist away and cracked his knuckles.

'Hope so. Haven't seen her in . . . well . . . a long time.'

'How do you know "she" is still here?'

Lucas didn't reply instantly. He cracked his knuckles again. 'She wrote to me. One letter every six months for fourteen years. Last one a week ago. Told me she knew I was coming out and she'd be here every evening for the first week in case I needed help.'

'Mother?'

'Sister.'

'You have a sister?'

'No, she is a *Sister*.'

The door opened suddenly and Lucas took a step back, bumping Harry off the step. Harry concealed his wound with his bloody hand.

A nun dressed in a black habit appeared in the doorway. She stared at Lucas, who was shuffling uncomfortably. She was slightly built with rosy cheeks which contrasted with the white veil across her hair.

'I might not believe my eyes,' she said quietly.

'I . . . I . . . need . . . some help.'

She didn't mince her words. 'What kind of trouble this time?'

Lucas's face was burning and the awkward silence compelled Harry to interrupt.

'Lucas isn't in trouble.' He removed his badge and held it high. 'I'm Detective Inspector Virdee. Lucas is an important colleague of mine working undercover. He has been since he came out. Trying . . . to . . . right a few wrongs. We need a place we can talk – away from prying eyes.'

Her expression didn't change but her eyes darted between both men. 'Is this true?' she asked Lucas.

He nodded and uncomfortably dropped his eyes to the floor.

'Then you had better come in.' She pointed to the blood

on Harry's hands. 'Looks like you're in need of some assistance.'

The interior of the church was dimly lit. There were candles burning, and imposing stained-glass windows let in a little light from outside. All the window ledges held vases of white flowers.

Harry always found churches eerily unsettling and this one did nothing to change his opinion.

He was sitting on a pew, clutching his side, while Lucas and Sister Clarke spoke by the altar. Harry could hear their hushed voices but couldn't make out the words. Behind them was a towering silver crucifix. Harry couldn't look at it.

He was guilty of murder.

The cross felt hostile. Like a spy, intruding into his past. Judge. Jury. *Executioner.*

Harry tried to block images of what he'd done all those years before. Thinking them felt wrong here.

Harry avoided religious places, whatever the religion.

Murder was murder, even if it felt justified.

At the edge of his vision, he saw an embrace between Lucas and Sister Clarke before she disappeared behind the tabernacle. Lucas made his way over and sat next to Harry.

'My aunt.'

'Figured there might have been a family connection.'

'She was entrusted with my guidance after my parents died. She believes she failed because of what I . . . became.'

Lucas pointed to the baptismal font to the left of the altar. 'I was baptized there. How're you doing?'

'I'll live,' Harry replied but his breathing was more laboured than usual.

Lucas nodded towards Sister Clarke, who had reappeared with a tray. 'Let her look at it. She's good with stuff like this. Used to work as a missionary in war zones.'

'Over here,' the nun said, putting the tray down on a pew in front.

'In here?' Harry wobbled to his feet.

'Yes.'

'Isn't it . . . I don't know . . . improper?' he asked, nodding towards the cross.

'He's seen worse,' she replied abruptly.

Harry wasn't sure if it was an attempt at humour or not. She was hard to read.

'Take off your shirt.'

'Easy, Sister, I'm a married man,' he joked.

She wasn't amused.

Harry dismissed the awkward silence and struggled with his shirt. He dropped it by his feet. 'I did it while I was—'

'I didn't ask.'

Harry towered over her petite frame. Her eyes were momentarily drawn to the Maori tattoo wrapped around his arm. Then she placed cold hands on his skin and turned him so she could examine the injury.

'Need to take out those splinters. Clean the wound.'

'Appreciate it,' Harry replied.

'It'll hurt.'

'Do I get a lolly if I'm brave?'

This time, Sister Clarke did smile. Then told Harry to grit his teeth. 'I don't do screamers.'

Ten agonizing minutes later, Harry was sitting beside Lucas with a potent sharpness pulsating in his side. Sister Clarke had been efficient but far from subtle.

'Put your mind someplace else,' said Lucas. 'I can see it all over your face.'

'Antiseptic.' Harry grimaced. 'Didn't need that.'

'Some day you're having.'

'Tell me about it. What do you think is going on out there?'

'Let's start at the beginning. Shakeel Ahmed comes out of nowhere and takes a political seat.'

'Not nowhere.' Harry exhaled deeply. The cleaning of the wound had been more painful than the injury. 'Although from what I've heard, it was a short campaign for such a landslide victory.'

'I may not be part of the BNP machine,' replied Lucas, 'but I kept up with their progress. Didn't have much of a plan when I came out – thought I might need to piggy-back some favours. They were odds-on favourite to take Bradford West until Ahmed got the Asians to vote him in.'

'Whatever keeps the BNP from power.'

'Sure, but that must have pissed off a lot of people. I'm guessing that setting me up for his death – using the image of who I was fourteen years ago – will get the city rattled?'

'Race has always unsettled this city.'

'In two thousand and one, what caused the riot?'

'It was nothing. A smokescreen of police heavy-handing a few Asians in Manningham.'

'That's all it takes in Bradford. Tonight is the Mela. It's started?'

Harry checked his watch. 'Yes.'

'There'll be thousands of Asians at the Mela. They'll be giddy because it's Eid but there will also be those in the park who are outraged by Ahmed's death. The man must have had a following to get elected. He promised change. Regeneration. Ahmed was rich. Like silly-rich?'

'Multi-millionaire,' Harry replied. 'A poor immigrant who hit the big time but he did put the work in.'

'Not saying he didn't. You get a small BNP scuffle at the Mela tonight and it's going to spread like a virus. Imagine there's a full-scale riot in Bradford – let's say it's the worst we've ever seen. Tomorrow, when the fires stop burning and the city is ruined, who gets the headlines? A few white BNP thugs or the Asians who destroyed their own city?'

Harry shook his head. 'Lucas, that's—'

'Exactly what happened in two thousand and one. I was there, Harry. I helped. And I knew – we all knew – that we wouldn't get the main headlines. How many Asians were jailed for those riots?'

'Two hundred.' Harry recalled the riots vividly.

Hundreds of police officers had been injured. Three hundred people had been arrested, almost 90 per cent Asian. Jail sentences totalling 604 years had been handed out: unprecedented in English legal history.

'I get it,' Harry whispered. 'Shakeel Ahmed promised this city change. Infrastructure. Jobs. You take him out – a hate crime on your release from prison – and we've got mayhem. We need to stop it. Lucas, if I take you in – I've got a few people I can trust—'

'No chance. *We* fix this. *You* and *I*. There is *nobody* else.'

Harry sighed, checked his watch. 'Seven p.m. Mela just started. There are six hundred officers around the city. At least let me phone my boss and warn him—'

'No. You tell him you've got me and he'll force you to bring me in.'

'Lucas, you're the only person who can stop this. If you're in custody *nobody* can riot. Nobody can claim the police didn't do their job and bring in the prime suspect. Once you're in, the city has "justice".'

'That's why they want me so badly. That's why they've tapped their sources at the police. If you take me in, their plan is ruined, but so am I. Nobody will fight for me. Harry, you're no good. Your credibility is in question and your boss . . . well, we're not even sure about him.'

Lucas was right. Trust was a scarce commodity at the moment. 'We're missing something. There has to be another factor. We just haven't worked it out yet.'

Harry got up and moved away from the pews, towards the votive candles in front of the lectern. He kept massaging his side but in truth, the pain was now in his head. It seemed such a risky play for the BNP. And for what? A shit-hole like Bradford? Was that really what this was all about?

Harry returned to Lucas.

'Your blood?' he said. 'How was it found at Shakeel Ahmed's house?'

Lucas shrugged.

'That's what we need to establish. There must be someone else sticking their oar in. Start from when you were released. Who could have planted your blood?'

Blood, thought Lucas. An image came suddenly to him.

Four large sample bottles.

'My blood.' Lucas leaned forward and placed his head on the pew in front, the wood cold against his skin. 'Can't be,' he whispered. 'Can't be.'

'Tell me,' Harry said, quickly sitting next to him. 'It's always the smallest details which make the difference.'

'Before I was released, I had a medical. You know: thorough check-up before they enrolled me on a community detox programme. Made sure my HIV meds were organized. The nurse . . . she messed up my blood samples.'

'Meaning?' Harry put his hand on Lucas's shoulder and pulled him upright.

'Can't be.' Lucas shook his head. 'She filled a couple of bottles with my blood and then made a big show of getting it wrong. Filling the wrong containers without any heparin. It's an anticoagulant. Stops the blood from clotting, apparently, before it hits the lab. I nearly passed out with blood loss by the time she'd finished.'

'What did she do with the other bottles? The ones she said were dud?'

Lucas shrugged. 'Threw them away, I guess? I didn't notice. I'm only mentioning it because now I think back, she did over-dramatize it. Like she was trying too hard. Look, that's the only place where I've had blood taken recently.'

'You didn't think of telling me this before?'

'It's not exactly been a routine day.'

'That's the clue. That's where we need to focus. Her name? You remember it?'

'Sure. I saw her most days for my methadone. Karen. Karen Steele.'

'We need to find her.'

'Can you?'

'She worked at Armley?'

Lucas nodded.

'Won't take me long to track her. I can use the police database.' Harry took out his iPhone and stood up.

'Harry – it doesn't make sense, I mean . . .' Lucas stopped talking.

Harry was staring at the phone's screen. The expression on his face got Lucas to his feet.

'What is it?'

Harry's hands were shaking and his eyes glaring at a text message. It was from Saima.

It said just one word.

HELP.

TWENTY-NINE

HARRY WAS IN SISTER Clarke's Ford Focus racing down Leeds Road. The fog had temporarily lifted, allowing Harry to weave between cars at speed. Ignoring his protests, he'd left Lucas at the church. Lucas might be the only leverage Harry had. He wasn't about to throw that away.

HELP.

He had tried calling Saima but she hadn't answered. Harry had called A & E but Saima hadn't arrived.

HELP.

Harry swerved the car on to the wrong side and over-took three cars at once, red-lining the rev counter. Drivers blasted their horns and flashed their lights in outrage.

Harry accelerated to sixty. Neon signs blazed past and he triggered a speed camera at the bottom of Leeds Road. Harry nearly lost the car on a bend into the city centre and would surely have been pursued by a patrol car if there hadn't been more pressing issues at hand.

The squad cars with flashing lights, the ambulances, the gangs of youths tearing across the city centre – none of them concerned Harry.

He called her again, but she didn't answer.

Harry knew she was in trouble because Saima would never have sent a message like that unless it was critical.

HELP.

He couldn't remove the image of that single word from his mind.

'Please,' he whispered to himself. 'Let it be a mistake.'

Harry flew through more red lights. More flashes from traffic cameras. But he remained utterly invisible to squad cars coming urgently the other way.

Harry skidded on to Manningham Lane. He blindsided several parked cars and his wing mirror flew off into the night.

Then he was on Oak Lane.

His house was halfway down. Harry slammed the brakes on and was out of the car before it came to a stop. He jumped over the gate and sprinted to his front door.

It was open.

Harry's heart started to pound, the sound echoing through his mind. He scanned the immediate vicinity but despite sirens wailing, the street itself was peaceful.

Harry snatched an empty milk bottle lying on the ground. He turned it in his hand, raised it high and moved to the side of the door. He pushed it open.

Blood on the handle.

He felt the world swaying and a crippling fear seized his mind.

Blood spraying across his face.

Images flickered and he tried to block them out.

Karma. The word rang in his mind. *Karma, you son of a bitch. Karma.*

A life for a life.

Harry was scared to cross the threshold. He took a few deep breaths and forced himself inside.

The Islamic painting on the wall which said 'Welcome' was hanging clumsily, skewed from its usual position. The corridor was dark and untrustworthy – a foreign sensation for Harry. This was his home. His centre of peace. Harry opened his mouth to call Saima's name but his voice failed.

The ache in his side was more potent than ever, like a hot blade slicing through him.

Then he looked to his left and knew she was in trouble.

His mother's slippers were missing.

The table they rested on was lopsided. Saima must have put the slippers on – her message to him: *I'm in danger.*

Harry pushed open the living-room door and stepped inside.

The room's usual order had been destroyed. The red sindoor Harry had placed on Saima's forehead had been trodden messily into the carpet. Cushions were scattered and shiny golden sequins from Saima's wedding outfit showed a telling trail. Saima had been dragged from the kitchen. She'd struggled and they'd grabbed hold of her, tearing her heavily embroidered pink outfit. There was a scrap of torn cloth on the floor.

Harry checked the kitchen. It smelled strongly of incense but was unspoiled. He searched upstairs quickly and found nothing noteworthy. Whoever had taken her had ventured into the bedrooms; there were wet footprints on the landing. Frenzied footprints. Spaced wide; the perpetrator had been in a hurry.

Harry ran downstairs and closed the front door. He charged into the living room and picked up the phone. Just before he dialled 999, a mobile phone rang.

Saima's. He recognized the Bollywood ringtone.

It was on the floor under the dining table. Harry pulled his sleeve over his left hand, picked it up and answered. 'Saima?'

'First and foremost, she's fine,' the male voice said.

'You son of a bitch! What kind of sick fuck takes a heavily pregnant woman?'

'The kind who has no choice. I told you at the graveyard to leave this alone.'

'If you've hurt her—'

'She's fine.'

'There's blood on the front-door handle.'

'It's mine. Your wife's quite the firecracker.'

Flashes of Saima struggling with her captor made Harry squeeze the phone harder. 'I swear to God—'

'We don't have time for theatrics. You have something I want – something valuable. And in return, it appears now so do I. Bring me Lucas Dwight and take your wife. It's that simple.'

'Give her back to me – right now. You can take me instead – she is due to give birth any moment.'

'We realize. I'm a professional, Harry. I don't want this any more than you do. Give me Lucas Dwight and you have my word: this is over.'

'I . . . don't have him.' Harry realized that Lucas was his only bargaining chip. 'When we ran from the cemetery, he took off. I've been searching for him – but I don't know where he is.'

The man paused. Harry could hear his breathing, soft and shallow. 'Is that why you arrived back here alone?'

Harry opened his mouth to reply but was stunned into silence. He moved quickly out of sight of the curtains even though they were drawn. He dimmed the light in the living room and moved to the window, peering through the drapes. There was nothing untoward. Harry moved quickly into the hallway to his front door and stepped outside.

'We're not amateurs, Harry. Want to give me a wave? Towards your right.'

'Fuck you,' Harry spat, glancing that way. 'I swear before this day is over I'll—'

'You'll have your wife back and we'll have Lucas Dwight. You've got until midnight to bring him to me. No police, Harry. You know how many I have in my pocket. Keep this phone on you. Midnight. Or . . . she dies.'

'Hello? Hello?'

But the line was dead.

Harry ran out on to the street. He looked both ways: nothing. But now he knew they were watching.

Harry stood for a moment. Scanning the periphery of his street.

Then, slowly, he retreated, back to his house.

Harry was sitting in his living room. The pain in his head was far worse than the one in his side. He was shaking and poured a double shot of Jack Daniel's into a glass. The bourbon burned its way down his throat into his stomach.

Saima didn't approve of Harry drinking in the house. But for the first time in three years, she wasn't here.

Harry closed his eyes and let pain suffuse his body.

He had never been superstitious but the fact Saima was wearing his mother's slippers was comforting. If there was such a thing as karma, Harry hoped his wife's was better than his.

What had she ever done except love him?

'Saima,' he muttered and kept his eyes tightly shut. All day, his wife had fasted for the longevity of his life. She was the woman he had lost everything for – and now she was at risk.

Lucas? Shakeel Ahmed? Bradford? His job? Nothing mattered – except Saima.

Harry started his descent to a dark place. To memories which would bring the worst out of him.

He needed to ensure he was battle-ready.

Three years before, Harry's father, Ranjit, had beaten him. Drawn blood while his mother bowed her head and let tears drip quietly to the floor. Ronnie had tried to intervene but Harry had stopped him. With each blow from his father, Harry had felt superior. Because no matter how ferocious the beating, Harry hadn't caved in.

He took it.

Standing firm against the only man who could strike him and not expect any retaliation. Harry had looked his father in the eyes. And it had angered Ranjit. The rage Harry had inherited took over. His father lost control and in that instant, when he grabbed his kirpan, the sacred sword owned by devout Sikhs, his mother had finally stepped between them.

Harry wasn't sure what he would have done. He had thought about it in the three years since. Blocked the blow? Or called his bluff?

Harry's mother had led him out of the house but before he was banished, she had taken off her slippers and gifted them to him. It was her way of showing she loved him but that she couldn't walk this path with him any more. She had torn a piece of cloth from her Asian suit, wiped the blood from his face and handed him her shoes before closing the door for ever.

Harry opened his eyes and stared at the lopsided table in the hallway. It wasn't a bad omen. The slippers guarded his house. Saima had them on her feet – so she was protected. The thought was soothing and he clung to it fiercely because it was all he had.

Harry started planning. He wouldn't call his colleagues. He couldn't take the risk his enemy wasn't bluffing. Harry would do whatever it took to get Saima back. There were no laws any more.

It was eight o'clock. Harry had four hours before the deadline. He knew his next move. He was just trying to figure out the tactics. If he got it wrong, everything would go to hell.

Twenty frantic minutes later, Harry was ready.

It was time to release a fury which had blighted his life ever since he could remember.

This time, there were no shackles. No restraint.

This time when he shed blood, it wouldn't be something he would live to regret.

THIRTY

DETECTIVE SUPERINTENDENT GEORGE SIMPSON'S phone hadn't stopped ringing for the past hour. Intelligence reports were flooding into Trafalgar House from across the city about a rising BNP demonstration. There were claims it was a solidarity march to condemn the brutal murder of Shakeel Ahmed. Apparently the BNP were outraged their party was being defamed by accusations of responsibility.

Simpson knew better.

This was no peaceful march.

This was the lighting of a fuse. The dynamite was in Lister Park. The explosive effect would decimate the city.

Simpson didn't have concrete intel about where or how the gathering was taking place. The Mela was an obvious target and Simpson had every spare officer ring-fencing it.

He had experienced 2001.

But this felt different. In 2001 the riot had been unexpected. A sudden flash of deep-seated unrest. This was something else.

Shakeel Ahmed's crucified body came to mind. That was a real flashpoint: racial homicide of Bradford's finest. And now the march? Simply petrol on the fire. Simpson needed to contain it.

He thought of Colin. Of his desperation to get Lucas Dwight.

How were the two connected?

Simpson was missing something. He could feel it but had no time to investigate. He had informed Colin that Lucas was still loose and that his suspicions about Detective Inspector Virdee were unfounded. Colin hadn't spoken, just disconnected the call. It took all the power in their relationship from Simpson: not knowing Colin's intent – or his response.

There was a knock on his door and a detective sergeant called Howell burst into the room.

'Sir, we've received word that the football match at Elland Road has been cancelled. Fog's too severe.' He was panting heavily.

The room became silent, the tension palpable. The FA Cup replay had been specially arranged for the evening to maximize television revenue. Historically Leeds United vs Millwall was a bad-tempered affair. It brought out the anarchists.

'Millwall supporters?' Simpson wasn't really asking, more airing what he already knew. 'Dear God.'

The sergeant nodded glumly.

'How many?' Simpson croaked.

'Four – maybe five thousand?'

Simpson felt momentarily nauseous.

'There's more, sir.'

Simpson didn't respond. Howell pressed on.

'We've got wind of some troublemakers. The ones we know about – they're making a beeline for the Mela.'

'Where did you get this information?'

The DS hesitated. 'It's all over Twitter, sir. We've also got a Facebook post created by the EDL urging people towards Bradford. Something terrible is building online, sir. It's going viral. Could be a right shitstorm.'

Simpson looked at the DS, standing awkwardly in the doorway. The English Defence League had been organizing increasing noise in Bradford, claiming the BNP were no longer the primary voice of true patriots. 'Gather everyone in the briefing room now. I've a phone call to make.'

He took a deep breath, picked up the phone and dialled the on-call Assistant Chief Constable in Bishopsgate.

The battle to save Bradford had started.

The phone call didn't take long. The Assistant Chief Constable was already in the loop. He had assumed gold command for the operation and organized patrols from across Yorkshire, even as far as Humberside, to unite in the city and brace themselves for an epic onslaught.

Police dogs, horses, police support units and helicopters were all at Bradford's disposal.

Simpson, who'd assumed silver command in the operation, prayed he wouldn't need them.

But in this city, prayers were seldom heard. Tonight would be no different. Because tonight, hell had a new home.

THIRTY-ONE

HARRY WAS READY. HIS reflection in the mirror was startling.

A criminal.

That's what he looked like: dressed in black, a dark beanie tight over his head and reckless anger simmering in his eyes.

Outside, the fog had started to settle again. It was ideal because he didn't know who was still watching.

Harry put on his gloves and turned off the lights in the bedroom, plunging it into darkness. Finally, he took the piece of cloth his mother had used to wipe blood from his face before he left her home three years earlier. He wrapped it around his wrist and knotted it with his teeth. If he ever needed her blessings, it was tonight.

Harry took a moment. He closed his eyes and tried to feel for his wife's presence. He inhaled her scent: the mixed aroma of incense and perfume. He pictured her resting in bed, flicking through baby-name books, jotting down the ones she could claim as 'fusion'. Harry reached out his hand in the darkness.

He opened his eyes and exhaled his fears.

He would find them.

To do so, Harry was going to give himself to the streets and embrace the darker side of Bradford.

He slipped out of the back door and into the snicket running behind the terraced houses.

First, Harry needed a car.

He couldn't take Sister Clarke's Ford; he was too paranoid he would be followed.

Harry broke into a jog when he was free of the snicket and kept on the side of the road where the streetlights weren't working. He focused on his breathing, ignoring the pain from his wound. He thought about the last twelve hours. It seemed unfathomable how much had happened in such a short space of time. Like a virus invading its host. Quick, brutal and without mercy.

Harry quickened his run, darting between the main street and the gulleys in case anyone was following.

On Manningham Lane, the fog exploded into blue lights, helicopters and anarchy. Youths were running amok, towards Lister Park. Gangs of Asians were hunting like wolves.

Focus, Harry. Focus.

He kept his head down and merged into the many pounding the streets. Harry covered the mile and a half to Thornton Road in ten minutes. His lungs were screaming and the wound in his side felt as though it was splitting open.

Thornton Road was a red-light district. Several alley-ways leading off it were engulfed in darkness. A necessary darkness for the work done there.

He checked the time.

Eight thirty.

Half an hour gone.

At the end of an alley, Harry disappeared into the shadows and crouched behind a pile of scrap metal. In spite of what was raging in the city, the hookers still needed their cash and their punters still needed a fix.

It wasn't an easy wait.

Harry tensed his jaw and focused on the end of the street like a hawk stalking its prey.

It was the longest twelve minutes of Harry Virdee's life, each one painful to suffer.

Tick tock.

Just as he was about to choose a different alley, a Mercedes crawled along the cobbles. It lit up the alleyway for a moment but then killed its lights. Harry kept his head down, concealed in the shadows.

The car had its engine running. Harry waited a few minutes until the windows started to steam and then made his move. He walked urgently to the front passenger door.

Prostitutes always kept it unlocked in case they needed a quick exit.

Harry opened it and got inside.

The hooker was straddling the driver. She stopped fucking him and screamed as Harry took a seat. The driver, a balding middle-aged white man, was dumbfounded.

'What . . . what the hell are you doing?'

'Stealing your car,' Harry snapped. He looked at the young blonde, who had her blouse open. She looked about eighteen but her eyes were street-hardened. The man had his hand on one of her breasts.

'Get your shit together and leave. Punt's over.'

The girl slipped her hand to the side of her skirt and produced a knife, brandishing it towards Harry. He grabbed her hand mid-air, twisted her wrist and disarmed her.

'Don't be fucking stupid,' he said and threw the knife on the floor, by his feet. 'I'm not here for you.'

Her lower lip trembled as she nodded and hurriedly fastened her shirt.

'Wait,' Harry said before she got out. 'You been paid?'

'Yes.'

'On your way then.'

She snatched her underwear from the driver's hands and exited awkwardly, flashing Harry her arse.

Harry focused on the driver. Gave him a dead stare.

'Please—' the man begged.

'Shut up. You drive an E-Class Merc and need a crack-addicted street girl? Dickhead.'

'I . . . It's my first—'

'Save it.'

'Give me your wallet.'

'But I—'

Harry slapped him suddenly. A full palm-rich strike which caught him square. The man started to whimper.

'Wallet,' Harry repeated. 'And put your cock away.'

The man zipped up his trousers and struggled with his wallet.

'Reginald Wade?' Harry said, checking his identification. 'You married?'

The man nodded.

'I'm guessing if your wife found out about this, she'd be none too happy?'

'Look,' Reginald said, 'take the money, and take whatever you want, just don't hurt me.'

Harry nodded. 'That's the kind of co-operation I'm looking for, Reg. Let me tell you how this is going to work.' Harry fished his badge out of his pocket.

'Oh Jesus.'

Harry nodded. 'As it happens, today is your lucky day. Because I'm undercover and someone stole my ride. I'm taking your car to finish my work and tomorrow night, or maybe Sunday morning, I'm going to return this car to . . .' Harry checked the address on the driving licence: '624 Woodcroft Place. Agreed?'

Reginald started to protest.

Harry slapped him again. Harder. 'Reg, listen to your cock. Right now it's about as shrivelled as it's ever going to get. You need to follow suit. Get the fuck out of the car. You're not going to report this car stolen. You're not going to tell anyone. Because I'm deep undercover and I can't afford to be discovered. You do that and this ... *indiscretion* of yours is forgotten.'

Reginald wiped his face and nodded quickly. He feared another slap. The detective had fire raging behind his eyes. 'OK,' he said shakily.

'I'm going to keep this.' Harry waved the wallet and then removed the money from it. 'Here – I don't need your cash. Get out and find a taxi.'

Reginald looked suspiciously around the alleyway.

'Now!' Harry said, raising his voice. 'You got yourself into this mess – you can find your own way home.'

The punter opened the door and almost fell out. Harry grabbed his shoulder before he left. 'Remember, whether this story finds its way back to your wife is on you.'

'I ... won't say anything. Just please don't ruin my car.'

Harry waved him away and moved into the driver's seat.

'Nice ride,' he muttered and reversed the Mercedes out of the alleyway, skidding it across the road. He put his foot down, accelerating recklessly into the fog.

THIRTY-TWO

MARTIN DAVIS WAS ALONE. He'd been in Ahmed's office for five hours. Abandoned. Frightened. And now – *angry*.

He couldn't rest his back on the chair because the wounds from the zanjeer were still open.

Outside, Davis could hear sirens. Blue lights flashed by the windows, bouncing off the walls. There was drama going on near by.

His supporters were here. They must be. Which meant Davis was close to the action.

If he could just free himself of the restraints.

It had been some time since he tried. Davis mustered his courage and attempted to wriggle his hands free. But the restraints wouldn't give a millimetre.

Davis's legs were taped to the chair. He felt he had some leverage but the only way he might break free was by tipping the chair on its back, but that would bring the rear harshly into contact with his wounds.

He wasn't a supple man. He doubted his ability to turn his body ninety degrees and then get to his feet. But, with time passing agonizingly slowly, he was becoming more and more desperate.

They had left him: taken his mobile phone and done what? Triangulated Colin Reed's location? Davis knew it could be done. These guys weren't only in the restaurant business, that was for sure.

Was Zain just a bitter son, out for revenge? Or was he something else entirely? Was he somebody more like Colin Reed?

Davis thought about a television programme he'd seen where a guy in similar circumstances had freed himself by standing and running backwards until the chair legs hit a wall and the chair disintegrated on impact.

Davis's feet were tied but he could at least stand. And jump. Bring his full weight down on the legs. Sure, the force would make his back even more painful.

Outside, the darkness was banished by passing blue lights.

Davis stood up and felt the cold sensation of wood on his back. There was a fleeting pulse of pain. He steadied himself and took a few breaths. He was over ninety kilos and hoped the force of his body weight would be enough to fracture the seat.

One.

Two.

Three.

Davis jumped up and raised his knees as high as he could.

His weight was transferred through his body, down to his backside which hit the seat of the chair forcefully.

Ninety kilos of inertia thundered into the seat and there was a splintering crack. Davis gritted his teeth as the chair smashed into his back and his wounds oozed fresh blood.

He stifled a scream.

But the chair didn't break.

Davis was sweating and breathing heavily. He rocked the chair from side to side. Once more was all it would take; he didn't hesitate.

He was going to get out of this.

This time, as Davis's weight hit the seat, the chair disintegrated. The back split from the seat and Davis went careering to the floor. His head hit the laminate with a sickening crack. For a moment, the world became hazy and then disappeared.

Nothing but black.

But the sirens were still there on the periphery: Bradford's desperate cries for help. Davis fought the darkness and after a few moments the colour came back into his vision – long enough to see the office door opening and the hurried approach of Zain and Bashir. They looked blurry as they came up to him and, although he could hear their voices, he couldn't make out what they were saying.

Davis was lifted from the floor. Zain took his arms and

Bashir his feet and they moved him to a couch, throwing him carelessly on to it. Then they sat Davis upright.

'Oi,' said Bashir, slapping his face lightly.

Davis smelled marijuana on his breath.

More chatter in Urdu. And now water. Being thrown over Davis's face.

'Hey,' he protested and shook his head, which made the crippling pounding in his head worse.

'Get him focused,' Zain said. 'Quickly.'

Bashir grabbed Davis's face, squeezing his cheeks between rough fingers. 'Oi,' he said again.

'Get off,' moaned Davis weakly.

Bashir let him go and Zain waited.

Slowly, Davis regrouped and stared at them, puzzled at first and then the reality hit home. 'Let me go.'

'We will,' Zain said. 'But first, we need you to call your mate Colin Reed.'

'Why?'

'We know where he is. Top of Toller Lane. Not far from here. In a car garage.'

'How?'

'His mobile phone. Bastard's had it off all this time, but just as the shit in Bradford kicked off, he switched it on.'

'Who are you people?' Davis asked. 'Not just restaurant owners?'

Zain smirked. 'No. Much more than that.'

Bashir spoke quickly and harshly to Zain, who stopped talking. The smile disappeared off his face.

'You,' Bashir said, leaning forward and pushing a

finger into Davis's forehead. 'Phone friend. Tell him you need to see him. Alone.'

'And then you're free to go,' added Zain. 'You're the messenger and we don't shoot the messenger. We want the big dog. Putting down his poodle isn't our end game.'

'So . . . you're going to let me go?'

'Yes,' Zain said. 'But we need you to call Reed. Make it sound urgent. Figure out how many people he's got up there. Tell him you are coming, whether he likes it or not.'

'And how am I supposed to say I found him?'

'Tell him you're connected, just like he is. What? You don't have any loyal supporters working for the phone companies who can get you information? Keep it brief. It's not an exam. Get us how many men there are and you walk.'

Davis took his eyes from Zain and looked at Bashir. The big man was brooding. Silently. He had impatience etched across his face and was fidgeting with his shirt, pulling it from his body.

Blood. Sticking to his clothes.

Davis had never been so afraid of anybody. It was Bashir's aura. The man wanted to hurt Davis. It radiated from everything he did. The stare. The curling of his lip. Even the way he looked at Zain.

'OK,' Davis said. 'I'll do it.'

'You need to make it credible. Or, to be blunt,' Zain said, 'Bashir's itching to put somebody down.'

Davis nodded. 'Give me the phone.'

'Cut him loose.' Zain removed a pistol from his pocket.

'Seriously,' Davis said, 'who are you people?'

'Restaurant owners.' Zain turned away.

Davis flinched as Bashir came towards him and set him loose. He could smell the man's sweat.

'Here.' Zain threw Davis's mobile at him. 'You warn him? You die.'

Bashir sat down next to Davis, who flinched.

'Call,' Bashir mumbled and then put a hairy hand on Davis's knee.

'I am,' Davis replied. Bashir's hand on his leg felt like a cobra's head about to strike. 'I want out. I have your word you'll let me go?'

'Yes,' Zain said. 'Do it.'

Martin Davis took his time and thought about what he needed to say. There would be no coded message. Bashir's hand on his knee was more than enough to convince him that one wrong move would unleash a monster.

He made the call.

Reed answered immediately. Davis's phone was on hands free and they could all hear sirens in the background. Davis didn't need to fake the urgency. He was desperate and made sure Reed knew it.

'How the fuck do you know where I am?' Reed asked angrily.

'You're not the only one on a leash in this city,' Davis replied, equally angry. 'I'm coming to you. There are things you need to know. About today. *About Lucas Dwight.'*

'You have him?' Reed asked suddenly. His attention was immediate. The sirens, which had been noisy, now diminished. Davis assumed he had moved to a quieter spot.

'Not on the phone. You alone or with people? I *cannot* be seen,' Davis said as dramatically as possible. Zain had the pistol aimed not at his head, but at his testicles. It still wasn't as intimidating as Bashir's presence.

'Fuck's sake,' Reed said. 'It's not a good time.'

'How fucking many?' Davis asked. 'Are we secure or not? I have to see you.'

'Three,' Reed replied. 'All secure. Thirty minutes. Flash your lights on the front shutters three times.' He hung up.

Davis threw the phone at Zain, who caught it.

Bashir got up, pressing his hand against Davis's knee.

'I did what you said. Now let me—' He didn't finish his sentence.

Bashir turned suddenly and unleashed a vicious backhanded blow into Davis's jaw. It knocked him unconscious and his body rolled off the couch on to the floor.

Zain stepped back, momentarily startled.

Bashir was breathing heavily. 'I need to go.' He pointed to the window. 'Now – is *my* time.'

Zain nodded slowly. He could see Bashir was at breaking point. 'You don't want to come with me?' he asked, trying softly to engage Bashir's help.

'No. You must go alone. Make name for yourself. Three men is a good start, you can send a message. Shoot the first two quickly.' Bashir raised his hand and poked Zain hard in the chest. 'No talking – understand? No games. Then . . . with last one. Reed. Put bullets in his knees. Leave him blind. Deaf. Dumb. But leave him alive. Send a message. Make sure people remember. You cross Zain Ahmed? You cross the devil.'

'And you?'

'My money? Get it.'

Zain was still holding the gun, pointed at Bashir. For a moment they both stared at it but then Zain put it away. 'I'll honour my kasam. I wish you luck, my friend.'

'No luck,' Bashir replied. 'This my kismet. This is – *his* kismet,' he said, referring to the man he was going to kill.

'And him?' Zain nodded towards Davis.

'Send message. You decide how written.'

'You want to start your killing now? Be my guest.'

Bashir shook his head. 'You avenge your father.' He looked away, at the window, across a city under siege. 'I'll find my own vengeance.'

THIRTY-THREE

HARRY ARRIVED BACK AT the church in the stolen Mercedes. He told Sister Clarke her car had broken down and he would return it the following day. He didn't mention the broken wing mirror.

Outside, Lucas and Harry disappeared into the shadows by the side of the church.

'Your wife's been taken?' Lucas asked.

Harry looked at him solemnly. 'Yes.'

'Who the hell are these people? How did they know where to find you?'

Harry spoke quietly, his breath forming a white mist in the plummeting temperatures. The fog smothering the city was starting to freeze. 'I've been asking myself the same thing. Two ways. One, you were right and they have connections down the nick. But I don't think one of my own gave me up.'

'Which leaves?'

'My wallet. When it was stolen this morning. Had all my details. It found its way quickly from the street to my boss. I reckon somewhere along the way we have our main players. This isn't about race, Lucas. This is about drugs.'

'I don't follow.'

'All this time, I've been thinking about this the wrong way. The murder – the race riot? It's all a distraction. Something bigger is going down but it won't register amongst the madness.'

'This is all a decoy? That what you're saying?'

'Yes. From that low-life pusher this morning – this has unravelled. And the only connection is drugs. It's how they nearly killed you.'

'But to take your wife – it must mean—'

'That somebody has something on the line worth risking everything for. Because when they lost you, they lost control. They don't have someone to blame for Ahmed's murder. It's making them desperate – they want you at any cost so their plan isn't exposed.'

'What's the play?' Lucas asked. 'Can you even function with what's going on inside your head?'

'Have to. And it's forcing me to think clearly.'

'Fucked up – that's what this is,' said Lucas bitterly. 'Taking a pregnant woman hostage? There are rules in warfare: lines you don't cross.'

'Agreed, but they're not interested. And it also means neither am I.'

'What *do* they want?' Lucas's eyes were bloodshot and he looked shattered.

'You.'

The two men locked eyes, assessing each other.

'And you're here to deliver me?'

Harry shook his head. 'I'm here because now I need *your* help.'

'Go on.'

'I'm supposed to hand you over by midnight.' Harry checked his watch. 'That's three hours from now.'

Lucas sighed and cracked his knuckles.

Harry continued. 'The only clue I have – the only one that makes sense – is this nurse who I'm damn near certain lifted your blood a few days ago. It's too coincidental to be chance.'

'Nurse Steele?'

'Karen Steele. Lives on Brompton Road. Thornbury.'

'You found her?'

Harry nodded. 'I'm suspended from work – doesn't mean I can't use their facilities to track people.' He waved his mobile at Lucas. 'She's got a case file.'

'For what?'

'Suicide. Tried to kill herself in two thousand and four. Police had to break down her door.'

'Really?'

'Yeah.'

'Say why?'

Harry shook his head. 'Let's pay her a visit.'

'Now?'

'Right now.'

'How do we know she's in?'

'Already called her. Pretended I was British Gas. She told me she wasn't interested and hung up.'

Harry checked his phone. 'That was nineteen minutes ago. We need to move.'

Lucas stared at Harry, trying to read between the lines, cracking his knuckles and attempting to figure out how far Harry would go.

Harry knew what he was thinking.

Do I need this? Why shouldn't I just bolt? This isn't my fight.

'And if we can't find Saima before midnight?' Lucas asked.

It was a question Harry didn't want to contemplate. 'We'll find her.'

Harry made as if to leave.

'But . . .' said Lucas, grabbing his arm. 'If we don't find her, you're going to want to restrain me, Harry. Save your wife even if it means putting my life on the line?'

Harry's silence needed no explanation.

Lucas sighed. 'The last thing I want is to go up against you. But a man will defend his right to survive. I'm not anybody's bait.'

'Understood.' But deep down, Harry was thinking only one thing: *If I had to go up against you – could I take you down?*

He thought about the incident in the gym. The fluidity in Lucas's movement and the ease with which Harry had fallen. 'Lucas, we've got time. We need to crack this nurse. She's the key. Let's do one thing at a time.'

'And if she doesn't talk? How far are you willing to go? You've been lecturing me all day about crossing the line.'

Harry removed his police badge. 'This morning when I stumbled across you, this' – he spun the badge in his fingers – 'meant something.' Harry put it away. 'Not any more. I will do whatever it takes to get Saima back. You've no idea what we've been through and I'll be damned if some punk is going to take her from me. I'm prepared for the possibility that Karen Steele won't break easily. I'm a husband and a father first, a copper second.'

'Survival doesn't have any boundaries,' Lucas replied. 'Whether you're a lone man in the jungle or living in civilized society, when it comes to it: there are no rules.'

'Agreed.'

'I'm speaking for myself as well.' Lucas stepped closer. 'The first sign you try to fuck me over, I'm going to pop your liver till it bursts. We clear?'

'Clear. Now tell me, what's the best way to force somebody to do something?'

'Put someone they care about in danger. Humans can self-sacrifice but we don't like making those choices for others.'

'Exactly. In order to make sure we leave no stone unturned, I'm going to have to break her. If she lives alone, that means we only have her.'

'Fear is a better motivator than pain.'

'I can make her fear me.' An iciness came across Harry's face which Lucas hadn't seen before. 'There is a way – a sure-fire way – to break her.' Harry reached out and lifted Lucas's sleeve. 'I need something from you. And I'm in no mood for rejection.'

'What is it?' Lucas glanced at the bulging veins on his arm. They were dark blue against his pale skin.

'I need your blood.'

THIRTY-FOUR

SAIMA VIRDEE WAS IN a warehouse full of car parts and tyres. It was freezing cold. She was alone. In the corner there was a scuffling which might have been rats. She was too petrified to look.

She huddled into herself, arms wrapped protectively around her belly. There was a rickety stool nearby but when Saima examined it, she found one of the legs was rotten. It certainly wouldn't hold a pregnant woman.

Water dripped through a crack in the ceiling on to the floor. Out of desperation, Saima walked towards it and put her face underneath. Dirty rainwater dripped slowly into her mouth. Her tongue felt like cardboard, each single drop making it a little softer. She'd had only half a glass of water all day and hadn't had the chance to eat before she had been taken.

There was a locked door at the back of the room with a barred window next to it. Through it, she could see a gap of a few feet with stairs leading down into a darkness which was absolute.

Saima could hear sirens outside, ambulances mostly. She thought she might be close to Bradford Royal Infirmary. The car journey hadn't taken long. Saima had counted the seconds, from when the car had started moving until she arrived, to gain some perspective of the distance. Harry had told her about the technique. Once in the car, Saima had switched into survival mode, desperate for any clue she might be able to give Harry if she got the chance.

Six hundred seconds, give or take. Only ten minutes from home.

Still in Bradford.

Still close to Harry.

She was only six hundred seconds away. He could narrow down the search grid.

Saima had no idea who had taken her or why. But she was comforted by the thought of Harry. He would be turning Bradford upside down. She knew.

She touched the scar on the side of her face. Harry wouldn't let her down. He never did. Amidst the drama of her abduction, Saima felt comforted that the rage she knew blighted Harry's life would, today, be used to find her.

And he would find her. And protect her.

Because he always did.

Her captors had given her a choice. Come quietly and unharmed. Or struggle and risk brutality. She had fought them when they had entered her home but only briefly. They showed no mercy and a knife to her stomach had rendered her mute.

Her baby wasn't content either, sensing her mother's distress.

'Shhh,' Saima whispered and stroked her stomach.

With a few drops of grimy water in her mouth, Saima moved back towards the front door. She leaned against it and slumped to the ground. She could hear movement outside but couldn't make out the voices. More than one though.

She felt foolish in her wedding outfit and wished she'd changed out of it. A fat frump draped in yards of tassels and shiny pink material. She had made the effort for Harry. To remind him that she had once been beautiful.

She had fasted all day for him, prayed to the moon and done everything right.

Saima glanced at the slippers on her feet.

Harry's mother's.

Lucky slippers, Harry always said. Because his mother had thrown them at him in his teens, almost daily, and missed every time.

Magical slippers because nobody could miss that often.

Saima clicked them against each other three times and made a wish.

'Dorothy had red slippers, stupid,' she whispered. But with them on her feet, she felt comforted. And right now, any morsel of comfort would do.

Saima felt momentarily unsteady. The room seemed to elongate and then rush at her, as though she were dreaming.

A spasm, in her hips. The urgency to pass water.

There was a sudden burst of warm liquid down her thighs. It made Saima cry out.

'Oh God,' she whispered, 'please not now.'

Saima straightened her legs and put them together as if it might stop the inevitable.

Then it hit her.

Her baby hadn't been flipping somersaults in her stomach.

They had been contractions.

Fairly far apart, but she had been so distracted, she hadn't realized.

Saima struggled to her feet. She hit the door, hysterically, begging somebody to help. She banged on the metal until her hands were numb.

There was the sudden sound of two locks opening and then the door was ajar. An Asian man, unshaven, with bloodshot eyes, was standing there.

'What?' he asked.

'Please,' Saima said, smelling marijuana on his breath. 'I'm ... I'm ... in labour – my baby is coming! Please, you have to get me to a hospital.'

'You staying here,' he replied in broken English. 'No going anywhere.'

Saima lunged towards him, grabbing his shirt. 'I beg you!' she screamed. 'Please!'

The man twisted her hand and tried to prise himself away but Saima had latched on to him desperately. She had strength.

He cursed in Urdu; then he shoved her stomach aggressively. Saima fell backwards and tripped over her feet, sprawling to her right. She crashed heavily to the floor and cracked her head on the wooden stool, hard enough to flip it over. It somersaulted and landed clumsily a few feet away.

Saima was unconscious before her head hit the ground, blood seeping from her temple.

The man slammed the metal door closed, the din echoing around the room. When it passed, there was only one sound to be heard: a terrifying patter of feet.

It was the rats – scurrying towards the scent of blood.

THIRTY-FIVE

ON THE DRIVE TO Karen Steele's house, Lucas told Harry everything he knew about her. Which wasn't a great deal. She had been his nurse for several years and, aside from their last peculiar encounter, Lucas couldn't pin anything on Steele which suggested she was part of a larger conspiracy. Harry had asked about their final encounter several times and lifted anomalies he thought he could lean on. One in particular.

Karen Steele lived in Thornbury, the final suburb separating Bradford from Leeds. It was a busy area, home to the headquarters of Morrisons supermarkets and a large entertainment retail park.

Harry was on Leeds Road when he saw another example of Shakeel Ahmed's influence within the city. The former tram-sheds and old bus depot, dating back to when Bradford had its own tram and trolleybus service, had been converted into huge food-storage warehouses. Ahmed's logo dominated the buildings.

With such a visible presence across the city, Harry was now questioning just which circles Ahmed might have moved in.

Restaurants had long been associated with laundering money in Bradford. Usually it was the smaller, single outlets. Ahmed controlled a vast empire. Harry was starting to see a picture forming. Transport links, international imports and the manpower to pull it off.

The sudden shift into politics – was he purposefully moving higher up the scale of influence?

'Where'd you get the car?' Lucas asked, admiring the leather interior of the Mercedes.

'Borrowed it from a friend.'

'Good friend?'

'Owed a favour.' Harry checked his watch.

'Stop doing that. It won't go any slower.'

'Three hours.' Harry pulled into Brompton Avenue.

'Which number?' Lucas asked, cracking his knuckles.

'I'll quit looking at my watch if you stop doing that.' Harry pointed at Lucas's fists.

'Been doing it since I was a kid. My pre-fight ritual.'

'Over there.' Harry pointed to a faded green door. 'Number eleven.'

Steele's home was a Victorian terraced house. The old stonework was stained with black soot. A downstairs light lit up the badly neglected front yard. The grass was overgrown and the gate hung from its hinges.

'How do you want to play this?' Lucas asked. 'Shock and awe?'

Harry shook his head. Checked his watch again. 'I'm going to try and get her to confess. I can't torture an innocent woman. I need confirmation of her guilt.'

'If she's involved, she's not going to volunteer it.'

'I know. Look, you've given me enough to go on. I'm going to lead her into a trap. This is the one part of my job I usually get right.'

'What, cracking suspects?'

'Yes. Sixth sense.'

'Let's hope it's charged.'

'I'm going in alone,' Harry said. 'You head around the back. Keep out of sight. Once I've got her reeling, I'll let you in. Seeing you might scare her into talking.'

'And if she doesn't?'

Harry opened the car door. He paused and turned to Lucas. 'If you don't want to be a part of this, give me what I need and leave. But if you try and stop me – no amount of liver punches will put me down. We clear?'

Lucas nodded once, but then shook his head. 'Shit's not right, Harry,' he said. 'You want to beat her, mess up her face – hell, even decommission her: I get that. But this . . . It's fucked up.'

'This whole day is fucked up. We have an agreement. Yes?'

Lucas hesitated.

'Are we going to have to go through this again?' Harry snatched at Lucas's top; Lucas slapped his hand away. Both men grabbed each other. Harry had Lucas by the throat and squeezed his trachea. Trapped in his seat, Lucas couldn't react. He let go of Harry and raised his hands submissively. Harry released him.

'Are we really going to have this problem?' Harry snapped. 'Are you forgetting what is on the line here? Your life.' Harry jabbed him in the chest. 'My wife? My child?'

Lucas glared murderously at Harry. 'I don't like living with things that don't sit right. There are rules in torturing somebody. This is fucking barbaric.'

'Listen,' Harry snapped. 'I don't have time for this. I'm going to play nice with Steele. But if she turns out to be an obstinate bitch, I'm going to need help and you'd be wise not to cross me.' Harry slammed the door, composed himself, and hurried towards Karen Steele's front door.

The footpath leading to number eleven had a carpet of green moss. Blades of grass from the garden were flopping on to it, brushing Harry's legs.

Harry lifted the gold knocker and hammered it against the wooden door. It echoed loudly and he glanced through the bay window to his left. The curtains were drawn but there was a sliver of light leaking through the centre. It didn't give anything away except a cream wall and the corner of an oak mantelpiece.

A silhouette approached the door.

'Who is it?' came the startled voice.

'Bradford CID.' Harry pushed his badge through the letter box. 'Could you open the door please, Ms Steele.'

He saw her bend down to collect his identification. There was a delay as she looked at it.

'Police?' Shaky voice.

'Yes. Ms Steele, it's an urgent matter so I'd appreciate your co-operation.' Harry tried to hide the impatience in his voice. 'If it makes you feel more secure, you can phone Bradford Police Station and verify my identity.'

He hoped she wouldn't. It would waste time Harry couldn't spare and it probably wouldn't pay off. Steele was obviously thinking about it. A precious minute trickled away. Harry checked his watch: 21.09.

He was breathing heavily, using every morsel of patience he possessed not to smash down the door.

Finally Steele opened it. She had peroxide-blonde hair and looked older than Harry although he knew they were the same age. There was the hint of a tattoo escaping her low-cut top, licking towards her neck. Jogging bottoms completed her outfit. She looked like an ageing Barbie doll.

Harry's first impression was that she was frightened. And not because he was on her doorstep.

Harry followed her through the hallway into the lounge which doubled as a dining room. The room had magnolia walls, a cream carpet and an insanely pink couch.

'You're dressed kind of casual for CID, aren't you?' said Steele, trying to conceal the shakiness in her voice. 'Thought you guys always wore suits.'

'You watch too many TV shows. May I?' He pointed at a chair by a dining table.

'Of course. I'm . . . er, sorry about the mess. Wasn't expecting company.'

Harry continued to scan the living room. It looked like she lived alone. The photos on the mantelpiece were of her. There was a bottle of wine on the coffee table and only one glass. On his way in, Harry had noticed the shoes by the door were all women's and all the same size. He had paused by the coat rack and again saw nothing to suggest she had a boyfriend. 'It's fine. Could you ask your partner to join us?'

'Oh,' she said. 'No, I live alone.'

'Sorry, I was assuming—'

'Can I get you a drink?'

'I'd rather get down to why I'm here. Time is critical.'

'Really? What's this about?'

Harry didn't sit down. Instead he stepped closer towards her.

'Lucas Dwight.' He searched her face for a response.

Steele's expression gave her away. It was the way her eyes narrowed and her mouth dropped open. When she replied, her voice was uncertain. 'Lucas Dwight?'

'Why don't *you* sit down?' Harry pointed at a chair opposite. 'This won't take long.'

Steele sat down and put her hands in her lap.

'Could you place your palms on the table,' Harry said. 'Face down.'

'Why?'

'Gives me a better read of you.'

'I'm not really comfortable with this, inspector. I—'

'We can do this down the nick,' Harry snapped. 'Or you can set me straight and I'll be on my way.'

'Shouldn't I have a solicitor present, if you're questioning me?'

'You're not under arrest. Look, if you humour me, clear up a few trivial matters, I can be on my way and you can get back to your evening.' He waved in the direction of the television.

Steele placed her hands on the table. Palms down.

'So, Lucas Dwight. You know him?'

She paused, as if unable to decide whether to answer or not. It wasn't long, maybe a few seconds, but she was leaking emotion.

Fear.

'As well as I knew any inmate.'

'You saw him before he was released? Gave him his final medical?'

'Routine. Everyone gets one before we release them. Well, anyone who's an addict.'

'How come?'

'We give them a tox screen before enrolling them on a community programme.'

Harry nodded. 'Anything unusual about that appointment?'

'No. Why?'

'Lucas is wanted in connection with an important case. I'm chasing down the last few people who spoke with him.'

'It was a routine appointment.'

'You take blood from him?'

There was the faintest of hesitations. 'Yes. Standard practice.'

'Hmmm. Is it standard practice to get it wrong the first time?'

There was the faintest movement in her hands and her eyes looked away momentarily. 'Huh?'

'You messed it up. How do I put it? Filled the wrong sample bottles?'

'How do—' she started before quickly correcting herself. 'I don't think I did.'

Harry had her.

And she knew it.

It was all over her face and her hands had become fidgety on the table.

'You did,' replied Harry. 'You had to do it again. You don't remember?'

He was goading her.

She paused, an uncomfortable silence. Finally she smiled. Steele moved her hands from the table and ran them through her hair, revealing the narrow lines of her jaw. 'Of course,' she said, clearly trying her best to sound casual. 'That's right. I did. I was rushing – there's never enough time in that place.' She let out a forced laugh.

'Sounds like my job,' Harry replied, trying to reel her in. 'You've got a dozen patients and a dozen minutes, right?'

'Something like that. Public-sector pay but they expect a private-level service.'

'Isn't that the truth?' Harry smiled insincerely. 'The blood you took. The first time. What did you do with it?'

'I'm sorry?'

'The vials. What did you do with them?'

'Why?' Steele was becoming increasingly restless.

'I'm interested.'

'For what reason?'

'Ms Steele, we can swap seats if you want to play detective?'

'I . . . I put it in clinical waste.' Her cheeks flushed.

'Can you elaborate?'

'Yellow clinical-waste bins,' she said coldly, almost snapping.

'Is that protocol?'

'It is.'

'And this was just before he was released?'

She nodded.

'If I was to go down to Armley prison, go into the infirmary and examine the contents of those yellow clinical-waste bins, I would find two clotted vials of Lucas Dwight's blood?'

Karen Steele seemed to shrink into the chair. The muscles on the side of her face twitched. 'Yes,' she said with a faint quiver to her voice. 'You would.'

Harry exaggerated a nod. 'OK. There was a prison riot in . . . er . . . I can't quite call it to mind now – help me out?'

'Two thousand and four,' she replied quietly.

'You were caught up in it?'

She didn't reply. It was the year she had tried to commit suicide. Harry wondered if there was a link. He couldn't see it. Instead, he used the information he had got from

Lucas. 'When they rebuilt the prison, repaired all the damage, they installed some fairly decent CCTV cameras in the infirmary, right? I bet that made you feel a lot safer, especially considering you were caught up in the mess?'

Steele's face dropped; the colour drained instantly.

'I'm going to take a punt here and suggest, Ms Steele' – Harry leaned forward and placed his hands on the table – 'that if I were to look at that footage, I wouldn't see you putting those vials in the clinical-waste bins. In fact, if we went down there right now and examined them, we wouldn't find anything, would we?'

She remained placid. Didn't answer.

'Who did you give them to?'

Steele couldn't look at him. She blinked repeatedly.

Harry was breathing heavily. His heart was racing and the red mist descended.

Saima: starving all day to wish for his long life. Missing. Overdue with his child. Wearing his mother's slippers.

And this bitch is complicit.

Harry pursed his mouth and exhaled slowly. 'Ms Steele . . .'

'I have nothing more to say,' she said suddenly. 'Either arrest me or leave.'

'You really want to take this down the station?'

She shrugged and glared at him. 'If you insist. I want to call a solicitor. I know my rights.'

Harry got to his feet. 'Your rights', he hissed, 'ended when you opened your front door.'

She recoiled momentarily.

'You . . . you . . . need to leave . . .' she began and stood up on shaky legs. 'Or I'll . . . I'll call the police . . .'

'What good is a phone – if you are unable to speak?' said Harry, suddenly snapping out his hand and grabbing Steele by the throat. She was too stunned to fight back and Harry constricted his fist powerfully around her neck.

He turned Steele around and choked her in a sleeper-hold. Her resistance was futile and when she faded, Harry lowered her limp body to the ground. Then he walked to the back door, opened it and whistled.

Within a few seconds, Lucas Dwight appeared from the shadows. He looked at Harry's face and got the answers he needed.

'We're not going to have a problem, are we?' Harry asked as Lucas mounted the steps.

When the two men were close, Lucas paused. His breath was warm on Harry's face. 'Let's get her talking.'

Harry grabbed his arm and Lucas responded by clamping his hand across Harry's.

'Worst thing we can do is fall out right about now,' Lucas said. 'Let's see how deep this pile of shit is and then . . . we'll see.'

Harry let go of Lucas. 'She'd better talk. Because if I've got to go through you to crack her, I will.'

THIRTY-SIX

WHEN BASHIR LEFT ZAIN, he didn't go to the house he had been observing. If this was to be his last evening in Bradford, then Bashir wanted to say goodbye. Blood from the wounds on his back trickled down his skin.

Bleeding was a need he had developed.

First it had been the pain. He needed the blades to cut him. To dwarf the agony in his mind.

But lately, it hadn't been enough. Now, Bashir needed to bleed constantly. In a few hours, he would conquer that need. He would, once and for all, gain vengeance.

Bashir wasn't concerned about Zain. He had done the boy one favour – as agreed. Zain needed to forge his own reputation.

Bashir was doubtful the boy would succeed. He had seen him develop into a man; a needy one. A daddy's boy. Too much money, too much complaining. Not enough elbow grease.

Three men. One warehouse. The odds were favourable. Zain would have the element of surprise.

Did he have what it took to pull the trigger? Could he instil fear into the gangs he wanted to control? Could he manufacture a reputation in one night?

Bashir put his hand in his pocket. Felt for his passport.

It wasn't his fight any more. His allegiance had been to Zain's father.

Now, he had different priorities.

Bashir made his way to Lister Park. To the Mela.

There was an enormous police presence. Squad cars, vans, horses. In the distance, Bashir could hear the rotor blades of a helicopter.

But, for now, the Mela was peaceful. Bashir was at a stall, waiting in line for samosas. He was irritated at the racket on stage. It was too loud; there were too many disco lights. The introduction of an Indian dhol-drum and some bhangra dancers took the crowd's heartbeat to new heights. They pulsed along with the drums, hands in the air, moving to the rhythm.

The park was heaving. It was a dual celebration with Eid, an opportunity to celebrate the diversity of the city and one the council had seized. Muslims, Sikhs, Hindus: they all had stalls and ongoing events and, for the first time, there were English stalls selling beers and pies.

It didn't matter that it was raining through the fog. The crowds were oblivious to the downpour. The harder it fell, the quicker they danced. Bashir glanced towards the stage. The bhangra dancers in bright yellow turbans were spinning and twisting their bodies as if possessed. Their moves were perfectly synchronized with the pounding rhythm. Above them fireworks exploded. There would be no darkness tonight.

The crowd was a lot younger than in previous years. Ten years before it had been predominantly families. Now it was overwhelmingly teenagers, boisterous groups of boys and giggling girls. The second-largest gathering was the taxi drivers. This weekend, the restaurants they frequented would suffer. The Mela was the place to be. Eye candy and food in the same place.

There was a crack of thunder above his head. Bashir jumped. The crowd went wild, screaming excitedly. They bounced up and down, pounding the earth, absorbing the intoxicating atmosphere.

In the queue in front, two white girls were speaking a language Bashir didn't understand. Foreign students, he thought. They were pointing at the strange food on display.

Next to the van, a group of teenage girls skipped up and down, holding cans of lager. Their tops were low, breasts trying to escape.

Bashir's turn had come. He ordered a portion of samosas and some masala chicken. Bashir asked the chef for extra chilli. If he didn't sweat when eating a curry, Bashir felt as though he was eating a poor man's meal.

He wandered away from the van. The rain was

annoying. He walked quickly to an unpopulated area of the park and veered from the path, through an area of dense woodland. The towering oak trees were curling over, branches finally blocking out the rain. Bashir had parked on the main road and wanted to enjoy his food in relative quiet. He heard twigs snapping to his left. A young couple were fooling around. Bashir carried on.

At the end of his route, Bashir crouched down and jumped off a shallow wall. His car was ahead, parked in a row of vacant taxis.

Bashir removed his waterlogged raincoat and threw it on to the back seat.

Inside the car, Bashir switched on the heater. He put the masala chicken on the passenger seat and started to eat his food. Sunrise Radio was playing a classic Indian song from his youth. He hadn't heard it in decades. Bashir closed his eyes and thought about his farm back home.

The chicken was extra spicy. Bashir wiped sweat from his temple. But it was good. Almost like his mother used to make. He thought about her now. About the shame he had brought upon her.

About the injustice he had suffered.

His colleagues at the Mela would be wondering where he was. He looked around Manningham Lane. At the side streets where he had fucked so many whores. Cut so many women. Spent so many dark nights. He was tired. He wanted to go home.

Bashir wiped greasy hands on his trousers and removed his passport. A British national. That was who he had become. But his heart was always in Pakistan. A land he would soon walk again.

Alone.

Without his wife.

He thought about her momentarily. About her broken mind. Eyes which couldn't look at him. Not like a husband anyway. But like a fiend she had been forced to endure.

Bashir's appetite disappeared.

He wouldn't be held responsible for what happened to her. Bashir had suffered equally.

He lowered the window and threw the remains of his meal out of it. Then he made his way back to the Mela.

Bashir's friends were on the lookout for fares – but not the kind who'd pay cash. Tonight they were predators and it was easy pickings. Bashir didn't like to fuck his passengers. He'd had a few experiences, but they never gave him the pleasure he enjoyed. Without drawing blood, Bashir couldn't be satisfied.

But it was a spectacle to watch his colleagues competing to see who could pick up the easiest fuck. There was a direct correlation between alcohol, the desperation to get home, and the weather. Once the girls were soaking wet, penniless and drunk, it became so easy to barter with them.

The gales had become a little stronger, dictating the ferocity of the downpour. The crowd reacted as if a long-standing famine had come to an end.

People were laughing. Dancing. Falling over. The atmosphere was infectious; even Bashir cracked a smile at the absurdity of the dance moves. They came so easily for some, yet for others, co-ordinating bhangra moves was too skilled a task to emulate.

Some of his friends were chatting to a group of pissed-up girls, no doubt negotiating fares home.

And then something changed.

It happened over perhaps ten minutes. Mobile phones lit up. Large sections of the crowd became edgy, texting or speaking on their phones. Nervous chatter swept the park. To his left, a large section of the crowd began moving away, some walking, others running.

Bashir asked his friends what was happening. They shrugged, oblivious to the change, and kept talking to the girls.

Bashir saw swarms of police officers suddenly infiltrate the park. Some were wearing riot gear. On stage, the dancers became distracted and lost their synchronization.

Bashir tapped his friends on the shoulder and pointed in the distance. They were speechless as they realized the police had surrounded the park and sealed off the exits.

Some of the crowd rushed towards the police. Angry shouts and questions replaced the previous celebratory mood. A police officer appeared on the stage and took the microphone. He spoke clearly and slowly. There were disturbances in the city and, for their safety, everyone was being held for the time being. Ludicrously, he told the crowd to continue enjoying the Mela and let the police do their job.

The crowd booed and whistled. Some looked frightened, others furious. There was a sea of mobile phones in the air trying to catch updates on the web. Groups of boys ran away from the police barricades, wanting to see what was happening in the city.

Nervous whispers of the BNP spread. Like a drop of blood in the ocean attracting a great white, the BNP murmurs caused the predators amongst the crowd to disperse and go hunting.

The change was so sudden, Bashir didn't register the skirmishes already happening at the far side of the park. The police were forcefully trying to keep the Asians in and the BNP out. It was a foolish ploy. The fuse of anarchy had been lit. Painful lessons of the past hadn't been learned.

Bashir's friends ran quickly with the crowd. But he stayed where he was. Deep in thought, calm amongst the chaos, Bashir evaluated the situation. A group of boys tore past him, shouting about the BNP. He heard mutterings about football supporters.

Bashir remained very still as the world around him fractured. The police were trying desperately to regain control over a situation they had lost. As the crowd headed towards them, Bashir turned and walked the opposite way, a lone character, cutting through the masses with purposeful intent.

It was time.

As the rain tried to dampen the steam rising from the irate crowd, Bashir headed back towards his car.

It was all falling into place.

Although much blood would be shed on the streets of Bradford tonight, Bashir would be responsible for only one death.

The one he'd been planning for years.

THIRTY-SEVEN

KAREN STEELE CAME ROUND sitting on a chair in her upstairs back bedroom. Her hands and feet were tied. There was a click of fingers to her left. She was alarmed to see Lucas Dwight standing beside her. He was eating a Mars bar. From *her* fridge. And drinking one of *her* cans of Diet Coke. She closed her eyes in disbelief and then looked again.

'You've no regular downstairs?' he asked, waving it disapprovingly.

'Please, Lucas.'

'Shut up. Not interested. You know something, and to be honest, one way or another, you're going to tell us.' Lucas took another bite of the chocolate. 'You set me up.'

'I didn't—'

'Save it!' he snapped and shook his head. 'Do you have any idea what you are involved in? That detective – and he *is* a detective – his pregnant wife has been

311

taken by the same sons of bitches who want me dead.'

'What?'

Lucas nodded. 'Whoever wants me has no boundaries. Now, before I let him in here – before I *unleash* him – you've got one chance to save yourself a lot of pain.'

Lucas finished the Diet Coke, crumpled the can in his hand and threw it across the room. 'A man whose family is at risk? He is not going to follow any rules.'

'Honestly, Lucas, I really don't—'

He slapped her. Using the back of his hand where the rough skin across his knuckles would slice. Steele yelped. Lucas grabbed her face in his hand, squeezing her cheeks against her teeth. He crouched down so their eyes were level. 'You stupid bitch, I'm being the nice guy here. Don't you get that? When he comes in, he's going to kill you. Look at me! Look at me.' He forced her eyes to meet his. 'You're going to die. And it's going to be horrible unless you tell me what I need to hear.' He let go of her face roughly and she started to cry. 'Whoever you are protect-ing – are they worth dying for?'

Steele stifled her sobs and dropped her head on to her chest. Lucas let her be. He popped the remainder of the Mars bar in his mouth and dropped the wrapper on the floor.

'I can't help you,' she said, struggling with her words. 'Do what you will.'

Lucas let out a desperate sigh. He had hoped the threat of violence would break her. But something greater was at play here.

She had something to lose.

'Someone you love? Or do they have something on you?' he asked.

She didn't reply. Didn't move.

'I gave you a chance,' Lucas said. He turned and opened the door. He called Harry into the room. Steele didn't look at him. 'Nothing,' he said as Harry walked past. 'Not a damn thing.'

She felt his presence in the room. Saw his dark trainers out of the corner of her eye. She tensed her body, prepared for an assault.

'At least tell me why.' Harry's tone was soft. Deceptively so. 'You're not going to tell me who? You must have something to lose, or why else would you subject yourself to this? Is it a partner? If you're willing to die protecting someone you love – I can live with that. I'm here for the same reason. In return, I won't make you suffer. I promise.'

His offer lingered in silence. Harry closed the door.

'She won't talk, Harry—'

'Two thousand and four,' Steele replied suddenly. She didn't look at them. Her voice was shaky. Distant. Calling upon a memory she didn't want to relive.

'Go on,' Harry said.

'The Armley riots.'

'I remember them.'

'An Asian guy was murdered inside the prison. Racist attack, they called it. Whole place went to ruin. Inmates rioted. I was trapped inside the infirmary when these

313

two . . . bastards', she hissed, 'trapped me inside.'

Steele was stationary in the chair. Harry knew Lucas had hit her. Creeping through the blonde curls down the side of her face was the painful graze.

'Fucking rapists,' she mumbled.

That put Harry on edge: this wasn't on his script.

'First one tied me to a trolley. Cut off my uniform. Bit me when he did it.' She tried to stop her voice from cracking. 'Always remember the feel of the scissors against my skin. Cold and foreign but so much better than his skin.'

Scissors. Images of a bloodied pair in Harry's hand. A man's life leaking across them.

'The other one watched. They did rock, paper, scissors to decide who went first. They laughed about it.'

Lucas cracked his knuckles. Harry wouldn't look at him. Steele's voice was heavy with pain. It made what they had to do so much harder.

'I don't really remember the first one. I closed my eyes. But the second one. He was . . . he wanted me to open my eyes. He needed to see what I . . . was feeling.'

Harry wanted her to cut to the details that involved Lucas. But he was afraid interrupting would halt the story.

'He put the scissors in my mouth. Said he would cut out my tongue if I didn't open my eyes. So I did.'

Lucas was breathing heavily. Angrily.

Steele raised her head and looked at him. 'Uncomfortable?' she snapped. 'Don't want to hear the next part? How is what you're doing any fucking different?'

Her words stung them both, as though she had taken the higher ground.

'Keep going,' Harry said coldly. 'My wife? My unborn child? That's where my focus is.'

Steele looked away, towards the window. The blinds were open, streetlights revealing the mist.

'Before the second one started, another inmate arrived at the infirmary. He saw what was happening and took care of them. Knocked them both unconscious. This man – who I had never seen before – this *inmate* freed me, gave me back my clothes.' Steele shot Harry an angry scowl. 'Do you know what I did next?'

'No,' replied Harry.

'I picked up the scissors and I stuck them through the head of the second bastard. The one who wanted me to look at him. And I did it so quickly that nobody could stop me. You know the best part?' she spat.

Harry wanted her to stop. It was suddenly too similar to what he had done all those years ago.

An explosion of rage.

'I would do it again,' she said. 'The pleasure I got from seeing his blood all over the floor is the only memory which gets me through darker days.'

'I would have done the same thing,' Lucas told her. 'This inmate? The one who saved you. He the guy you're protecting?'

She nodded. 'He took the scissors from me. Told me the law wouldn't see it right. He murdered the first inmate but made it look like the men killed each other in a fight.

Did it right so that no one ever questioned it. I testified they had set upon each other.'

'How do you go from that? To this?' Harry asked, trying to steer the conversation.

'I took a lot of time off work.'

The suicide attempt in 2004.

'The man who helped me was released three years later. I sought him out. He was the only person I could speak to about what I'd done. He understood. He was nice. We became close.'

'What was he inside for?'

'Drugs.'

Harry and Lucas exchanged a knowing look.

Drugs.

It all fitted into place. Steele's motives for protecting this man were iron-clad.

'I . . . I . . . couldn't get into a relationship – not after what happened – but we became good friends. He helped me to become . . . whole again.'

'And this is the man who wanted Lucas Dwight's blood?'

She nodded. 'He came to me a few months ago – three maybe? Said Lucas had a debt to pay. Knew you were coming out. Asked me for a favour. Your blood,' she said, looking at Lucas. 'And I agreed. I owe him my life.' Then she added fiercely, 'Now, is that story acceptable enough for *why*?'

He nodded. 'Your reasons are solid.'

'Then let me go.'

Lucas touched Harry's arm. 'A word.' He beckoned Harry on to the landing before leading him to an adjacent bedroom. 'We can't do this. Not after what she just told us.'

'If it's the truth.'

'You know it is. You heard her voice.'

'Doesn't change the facts. You're being strung up and I'll do whatever I need for Saima.'

'Listen.' Lucas dropped his voice to a whisper. 'We cannot kill this woman.'

'We're not going to. She has a choice to make.'

'If we rough her up—'

'That won't work. There's only one option.'

'When you asked me before – I didn't know what I do now. If you want to take her life, Harry, be my guest, but not how we discussed.'

Harry stepped closer to Lucas, who didn't back away. 'Are you really going to put this between us now? Does it look like we have time to entertain this bullshit?'

'I'm not a sadist.'

'Neither am I. You trust me?'

'I trust you about as much as I'd trust anyone I'd known twelve hours.'

'Give me what I need.' Harry glared at Lucas. 'You're going to have to trust that I know what I'm doing.'

Lucas backed away. He moved to the other side of the room, by the window.

'She knows who set you up and who has my wife,' Harry said. 'And in a perfect fucking world, we wouldn't have to make this decision. But we do. And it's now. And the only thing you need to ask yourself is: your life or hers?'

'Threat?' Lucas asked, not turning to face Harry.

'Whoever wants you isn't going to stop. Only a sick, desperate man takes a pregnant woman. These . . . these people have spies within the police and are one step ahead of us. If you want your life back, then you better make a call. *Right now.*'

Lucas was angry at himself, disgusted by what Harry was going to do. 'I have one condition.'

'Name it.'

'If we do this. If we go through with it, we're done. Me and you: it's over. You go your way; I go mine. You'll have what you came for. You won't need me any more.'

'I can live with that.'

'Why like this? Why not just make her suffer? You'd be surprised what a hot iron pinned to somebody's skin can do. Why not go there?'

'Because she's damaged. Physical pain won't break her. She'll likely feed off it.'

'And *this* will work?'

'Yes. Let me ask you a question. When you get in the boxing ring – who wins? The man who is mentally stronger or physically?'

'Mentally.' Lucas turned the side of his face towards Harry.

'Exactly,' replied Harry. 'I'm going to break her mind.'

THIRTY-EIGHT

SAIMA OPENED HER EYES to the yellow-eyed stare of a rat. Its teeth were bared and it turned its head to one side, displaying dishevelled grey fur.

For the briefest of moments, time stopped.

Then she released a blood-curdling scream which forced the rats to scatter. And she kept screaming. Her insides were cramping and she only stopped when her breath ran out.

Saima raised her body and found blood on the floor, beneath where her face had been. She tried to calm down. She touched the side of her face and felt the stickiness of a cut.

'Help,' she panted, but it was no more than a whimper. She doubled over in pain as another contraction crippled her insides. 'Help,' she whispered again. 'Please.'

But there was no one to hear.

Saima started to cry.

This was all wrong.

She'd obeyed all the rules.

How was this nightmare possible?

Saima gritted her teeth and crawled towards the door. She could hear movement outside and tapped desperately on it. 'Please, my baby's coming. Please, I beg you.' She began crying hysterically. 'Don't punish my baby,' she sobbed. 'I beg you – show me some mercy.'

No response.

There was a crack between the edge of the door and the frame, no more than an inch. Saima put her eye to it and could see the back of a man, sitting on a chair.

Scuffed white trainers. Socks which didn't quite meet his jeans, revealing brown skin.

Saima spoke in Urdu, pleading for him to listen. She promised him money, told him God would reward him and that if he didn't help her, could he live with himself knowing he had killed a child?

But he remained motionless.

She heard another man's voice.

He told the man sitting watch that he was wanted downstairs and took his place on the stool.

A changing of the guard.

Saima started pleading with him but stopped as another contraction took her breath away. She groaned as the spasm sent a pulse of misery through her body.

Then the man on the stool turned around quickly. He stood up, came towards the door and put his eye to the gap. He spoke quickly in Urdu, real urgency to his words. 'Behind you,' he whispered. 'Now.'

Then he was gone. Back to his chair.

Saima turned around.

The door at the other end.

It was open.

She struggled to her feet and hurried towards it. Her legs felt shaky and there was cramping in her stomach but the adrenaline from the possibility of escape drowned out the pain.

Saima stepped through the doorway. She was on a landing with a metal staircase leading down. She lowered her foot on to the top step and slipped. She would have fallen down the stairs had she not grabbed the handrail in desperation.

She dropped painfully to one knee, cracking it on the steel. She suppressed a scream and cursed quietly in Urdu.

From somewhere deep inside, the need to get her baby to safety took over. She got to her feet and put both hands on the railings.

Outside she could hear sirens.

The steps were deceitful, as though they were covered in oil. Saima didn't trust the strength in her arms to take her weight if she fell. Instead, she sat on each step and lowered herself to the next one like a child.

At the bottom the floor was dry. She searched for the wall and used her hands to drag her body along it.

Until she hit a door – a metal one with a steel bar across it. A fire door.

Saima's spirits rose and she pushed it hard.

It didn't move.

Stupid, you've got to depress the bar.

Saima held it with both hands and tried again.

Still it didn't move.

A distressing sharpness in her womb took her breath away once more. Her legs crumpled and Saima collapsed, suppressing her natural instinct to cry out. She writhed, curling into the foetal position with her hands on her stomach. It felt as though she was drowning. She coughed and suddenly threw up. The retching continued for almost a minute before it subsided.

Saima lay still, trying to recover. 'Get up!' she hissed. 'Get up, Saima. Open the door.'

She put her hands on the floor and raised her upper body. Getting on all fours, she crawled towards the wall. She had a window before her next contraction and needed to utilize it. Saima whispered a prayer, gathered her courage and got to her feet. The tassels on her wedding outfit bounced against the silk, the only sound which might alert somebody to her presence.

Saima put both hands in the middle of the bar, then straightened her arms and applied her weight through them. With a sudden jolt, the bar retracted and the door flew open.

An alarm started beeping by the door. Not loud enough for anyone on the street to hear – it wasn't that type of alarm. It was an internal warning; the fire door was open.

They would know.

Saima placed her hands under her stomach, supporting her baby, and ran. She'd taken only a few paces before she heard them.

Footsteps on the metal stairs.

The alleyway was dark but there were streetlights at the end. The sound of sirens was deafening.

Ambulances close by. She just needed someone to see her.

Or hear her.

Saima called out for help but her voice was lost in the chaos around her. The darkness was everywhere: behind her, on the floor, invading her vision. 'No,' she whispered, and fought the blackness flirting with her consciousness.

They were coming for her.

Voices shouting close behind – more than one.

The streetlights were getting brighter. Forty metres. The sirens louder. She burst into a sprint, letting go of her bump and clenching her fists, swinging her arms by her sides.

Thirty metres.

She tried to shout but there was nothing. The footsteps behind were closing in.

She was only twenty metres from the street.

Another attempt at a scream.

Nothing.

A sudden rough hand on her elbow – and now she did scream and shrugged it away.

An iron grip on the back of her neck.

Pain.

Another hand on her arm. Grabbing. Pulling.

And now she was struggling. Being dragged to a halt. She felt a sudden kick at her legs. Saima was falling, face first. Everything seemed to slow down. The ground seemed to elongate and then it was rushing towards her. She closed her eyes and braced for impact as her face accelerated towards the concrete beneath.

And when she hit it she felt her insides explode.

THIRTY-NINE

'LAST CHANCE,' HARRY SAID, closing his eyes tightly and massaging his temple.

'After what he did for me – would you talk?' Steele replied.

'I'm not the one whose life is on the line.'

Steele stared at Harry. It looked as if she was deciding whether he was about to renege on his oath to uphold the law.

'I assure you this isn't a bluff. Frankly, I don't have time to waste while you decide where your loyalties lie.'

'I might have died in two thousand and four but I didn't, because of him. I can't give him to you.'

'Your loyalty is admirable, but you might want to put self-preservation to the top of your list.'

'If you're going to torture me, then you're just as bad as the men who raped me!' she spat.

'What I'm going to do is give you a choice.' Harry turned to Lucas. 'You're up.'

Reluctantly Lucas removed his hoodie and threw it on the bed, leaving him in a dirty white T-shirt. 'You remember what you used to treat me for? Those daily pills.' He rolled up his sleeve.

Steele nodded and watched him closely, apprehensive about what was happening. 'HIV.'

'You know the best things about community drug-treatment centres?'

She shook her head.

'They give you fresh needles and syringes. Reduces the spread of the disease.' Lucas removed some from his pocket. He unwrapped one of the needles and attached it to a new syringe. Slowly he inserted it into a vein on his arm. Steele kept her eyes rooted to it as dark-red blood started to fill the barrel.

Lucas withdrew the syringe and held it upright. He removed the used needle and placed it carefully on the bed. Then he unwrapped a new one and attached it. Lucas glanced nervously at Harry. There was a delay of no longer than a few seconds but Steele could sense the men were uneasy with each other. Finally Lucas handed Harry the syringe.

Before anyone could move, Harry came over to Steele and jammed the needle through her jogging bottoms into the fatty part of her thigh.

'No!' she screamed. 'Oh God, no!'

Harry placed his hand over her mouth and his elbow

across her body, pinning her to the chair. 'Don't move.' He put his face close to hers. 'You struggle and I'll inject.'

Harry let go but remained kneeling in front of her.

'Oh God,' she repeated. 'You . . . you . . . sick bastards. Take it out of me! Now!'

The needle was fully inserted. Blood was swaying in the barrel with a clear air-gap of a few millimetres. The plunger was retracted, waiting to be pushed.

'You wanted Lucas Dwight's blood and now you have it,' Harry said. 'Three minutes. That's what I am going to give you before I hand you a death sentence.'

'Jesus! Please! Take it out! I beg you, take it out!'

Lucas sat down on the bed, behind Steele, and clasped his hand over her mouth. 'Shh. I need you to listen very carefully,' he said, real urgency in his voice, 'because believe me, like you, I *don't* want this to happen.'

Steele didn't struggle, paranoid that a sudden movement would somehow force the infected blood inside of her.

Lucas whispered into her ear. 'You know the worst thing?'

Tears were dripping down Karen Steele's face, leaving pale streaks on her burning cheeks before hitting Lucas's hand.

'It's not knowing.' Lucas eased his grip across her mouth. 'Every time you get a cough? A cold? Shit, even a nick whilst shaving, you think, is this the start?' He removed his hand and placed it on her shoulder. 'This body of yours? It starts to betray you. Your blood starts to give way to something else. And it's always inside of you. Invading. Killing. A virus that breaks you down. And there is nothing you can do. No amount of praying or eating healthy or yoga. You *will* die. And it will be terrible.'

Steele's body trembled. Blood continued to swirl around the syringe with each quiver of her leg.

'People find out and they treat you differently,' Lucas continued, urging Steele to reconsider her silence. 'They say they won't but they can't help it. *You're infected.*'

Harry was motionless in front of her, staring into her eyes. He never wavered. Never glanced at the syringe. 'Two minutes.'

'You fulfilled your part of the deal when you gave this man my blood.' Lucas raised his voice, pleading because he knew Harry wouldn't hesitate. There was poison in his eyes, a terrible rage in his very essence. Behind a motionless façade, Harry was starting to crack.

'Give yourself a fifty-fifty,' Lucas said. 'Give him up and we'll stop. Until Harry hits that syringe, the only thing you have lost is a night's sleep. Ask yourself – one night or a thousand?'

Lucas got off the bed. 'Minute left. Choose carefully.'

He grabbed his hoodie and walked towards the door, pausing halfway there, by Harry's side. The two men didn't acknowledge each other but the message was clear.

Are you sure, Harry? Really sure about this?

Then Lucas left. And with him went Karen Steele's chance of reasoning.

Because no matter how unlikely, Lucas was the only one capable of mercy. In front of her, Harry got to his feet.

'Please—' she whispered.

'Thirty seconds.' Harry raised his hand in preparation.

Steele sobbed hysterically. She yelled for Lucas to help her, begging him. She felt sick; she needed some air. 'Please . . . I can't breathe.'

'Five seconds.' Harry moved quickly and wrapped his hand around the syringe. 'Damn you for making me do this!' he hissed. 'You have only yourself to blame. I *gave* you a choice.' He put his thumb on the plunger. 'Three . . . two . . . one—'

'No! Stop! I'll tell you! I'll tell you!'

'Give me a name!'

'Colin! Colin Reed!'

Lucas stormed into the room. 'Pull it out, Harry! Now!'

Harry retracted the syringe carefully. He waved it in front of her face. 'Blood never touched you.' He handed it to Lucas and then backed away. Behind him Steele was broken in the chair, wailing and rocking back and forth.

Harry turned to Lucas. 'It's done with.' He pointed at the needle. 'Get rid of it.'

Lucas resheathed it and placed it inside his pocket.

'I want to go to a hospital,' Steele sobbed.

'Where do we find Reed?' Harry asked.

'A hospital,' she repeated.

'You'll get what you need. The faster you talk, the quicker you get it.'

'I don't know where he lives.'

'Fuck sake,' Harry said, 'back to this?'

'I don't! He was really weird about stuff like that. He always came here to see me.'

'You better give me something. Lucas, give me back the syringe.'

'No!' said Steele. 'I . . . I . . . know where he works. He always works nights. I can tell you that.'

'Go on.'

'A warehouse – behind Toller Lane.'

'Warehouse?'

'Yes. It has big blue shutters across it. Some packaging company? Blade Packaging maybe? They sell spare car parts. Or something like that.'

'How do we know he still works there?'

'He does! I saw him there when I took him the blood.'

'What does he look like?' Harry asked.

'He's white, around six-five and bald. He has a tattoo of a British Bulldog on his neck.'

Lucas grabbed Harry's arm. 'We've got what we need.'

'Please untie me,' Steele begged.

'No,' Harry replied and then turned to Lucas. 'Make her comfortable. Can't have her calling this guy or the authorities. She stays here. Gag her. We'll send a patrol over later to pick her up.'

'What? But you said—' she began.

Lucas grabbed one of Steele's shirts from the floor and tore off a sleeve. He wrapped it around her mouth. She didn't even try to fight. 'You don't need a hospital. It never got near you and it was a clean needle.'

'Before we leave, I want to make a deal with you,' Harry said.

Steele mumbled through the gag.

'I know, I know, listen. I did what I had to because my wife and child's lives are on the line. *You* forced my hand. I'm going to make you an offer and leave. Give you time to think it through. If I were to report you for what you've done – gather the evidence, so to speak – you'd be looking at prison. Complicit in framing Lucas and ultimately playing a part in the death of Shakeel Ahmed and the abduction of a pregnant woman.'

Steele dropped her head on to her chest.

'I understand you had a debt to pay and, well, things haven't exactly been easy for you. But you keep your mouth shut about what happened here tonight and I'll forget everything you told me. But you burn me – and I'll fuck all over you. Believe me.'

Downstairs, Lucas was by the back door.

'Did what I had to,' Harry said unashamedly. 'You're free to go, Lucas. A deal is a deal.'

'Would you have gone through with it?'

Harry didn't answer. Truth was he didn't really know. 'Colin Reed – you heard of him?'

'No.'

'I'm going down to this warehouse. Sounds like the kind of place you might take a hostage. Drop you off someplace on the way?'

Lucas glanced at the clock on the kitchen wall: 22.00. 'Two hours. Then no matter what happens, I'm gone.'

'I'm not asking you to stay.'

'I don't want this to end badly, Harry. If we can't find your wife – you're going to want to trade me in.'

'I am, which is why you leaving removes that possibility. If it comes to a choice between you and my wife – there is no choice.'

It had the makings of a really complicated two hours. But Lucas wanted to be free. Not looking over his damn shoulder for ever. 'You weren't a match for me this morning, Harry, and nothing's changed. So, if and when we arrive someplace bad, I won't hesitate. You understand? I'm nobody's bait.'

'I get it.' Harry stepped past Lucas and opened the back door. 'Come on. Clock's ticking.'

FORTY

THERE WERE VOICES ARGUING. Saima could make out two. The pain in her womb had become one continuous throb: an unending spasm which was squeezing her insides. She could taste dirty water in her mouth and felt blood trickling down the side of her face.

'I didn't sign up for this!'

'Are you crazy? Colin will kill you. Get her out of the alley, back in the warehouse.'

Colin.

A name.

'Look at her? You think this is right? I'm not killing a baby.'

The men flicked from Urdu to English. Mixed accents. Saima imagined they might be immigrants who'd been in Yorkshire a few years.

And then a scuffle. Voices raised.

She turned her head and saw one of the men

approaching her with a knife, silver-bright in the darkness.

He was almost upon her when he was taken to ground.

They were struggling, right beside her. Two men thrashing on the floor. They careered into her and the impact sent another ripple of agony through her body.

'Run!' the man was screaming. He cursed at her in Urdu, urging her to get to the street. 'They're going to kill you!'

Saima scratched at the floor, desperately trying to find the energy to escape. She snatched at a large piece of jagged rock by her side and struggled to her feet, dragging her spoiled wedding dress. She could feel blood leaking down her thighs.

Behind her, the men continued to fight. There was a blood-curdling scream and then the men went silent. Saima turned to see their shadows – one on top of the other.

She couldn't make out who had won.

There was movement: a silhouette getting to his feet. Turning towards her. Starting to run.

Saima charged towards the street, ignoring every warning in her body not to do so. Her legs were leaden and her stomach felt detached.

She wasn't going to make it.

The street was agonizingly close.

Saima squeezed the rock in her hand tightly. It was the size of a cricket ball. She slowed down.

It was time to fight. As Harry would.

Saima doubled over and leaned to the left.

The footsteps came closer.

She didn't move. Gripped the rock firmly. Prayed, gathering her courage.

Then he was upon her. Rough hand on her shoulder.

She uncoiled quickly, like a snake attacking its prey, and smashed the rock into his temple. Saima hit him with everything she had.

There was a sickening crack of bone, a shocked yell of pain and the man crumpled to his knees.

Saima raised the rock high above her head, screamed in rage, and hit him again. Harder.

And again. Harder still.

She kept going, screaming all the while.

Saima could feel blood, warm and urgent, running across her hands, but still she didn't stop – there was such anger exploding through her body, as if her own blood were on fire.

And then the man was motionless. On the floor. The side of his face had caved inwards.

Saima dropped the rock. She turned around and limped to the street.

Towards the sirens.

She emerged from the side street like a ghoul. Covered in blood: some her own, most of it her captor's. Her hair was strewn chaotically across her face and blood was running down her thighs like water.

Saima walked brazenly into the middle of the road and

forced an approaching vehicle to stop. The headlights hit her like sunshine. She was on Toller Lane, only half a mile from the hospital.

The driver jumped out of the car and she could hear the voice, angry to start with, then horrified.

Another car pulled over.

Saima couldn't focus. Everything was becoming dark and hazy and she hadn't the energy to resist. She felt as if she were dying.

She thought the driver might have been a woman but it was too late. Saima was slumping towards the road.

FORTY-ONE

LISTER PARK COVERED MORE than a square mile. George Simpson was having a logistical nightmare trying to contain the anarchy.

Both entrances on Keighley Road and North Park Road had been blocked by officers. He stood outside a police van, looking up at a black sky. In his head, it seemed as if a dark cloak of evil had been thrown over Bradford. There was a zip of lightning and a booming crack of thunder. It felt like the end of the world.

Somehow the BNP had infiltrated the park. Most of the thousand-strong crowd were teenagers, roped into the adrenaline rush of a fracas. Simpson had received word that known fascists were running amok, orchestrating chaos. The speed of the pandemonium was startling.

It felt a long way from orderly.

The police had blocked off the events area in the park, trapping thousands of Asians inside. They were equally

337

as boisterous, venting their fury at being boxed in.

Three hundred officers, all decked out in riot gear, were trying to force the BNP back. Taking small, measured steps. Bottles were being hurled at them, stones, cans of beer, and metal ball-bearings fired from pellet guns.

And then the first petrol bomb sailed through the air.

A threat of intent, flame wavering in the gusts, sailing towards his officers. The bomb hit the floor and detonated. An electrical current of anger swept the park. It wasn't now a case of trying to hold anyone back, more how to stop the whole thing exploding.

Petrol bombs were now landing in threes and fours, pushing the crowd at the Mela into a grand-mal seizure. The Asians charged towards the activists.

Police lines fractured.

Hell erupted.

Bashir arrived in Baildon, and parked outside the residence he'd watched for many years. It was five miles from the city centre, a predominantly white, middle-class area of Bradford.

He dimmed his headlights and sat in almost complete darkness, tucked away at the side of the road. He'd seen the fierce battles raging in the town centre, and was stunned at the destruction which had already taken place.

Yet again the BNP had underestimated the unity existing in the cauldron of Bradford. Faces that had never met now united, the colour of their skin binding them closer than blood.

On a night when the moon was choked by the clouds, Bradford was bright orange with flames. Smoke bellowing from the infernos took the city back a hundred years to when the mills had been operating. And while Bradford was suffering its own nightmare, here a prominent figure was about to feel the force of his own karma.

Bashir looked at the bag on the passenger seat. He could almost feel the zanjeer. Alive. Waiting. This visit was a long time coming. Perhaps too long. Bashir reclined his seat, closed his eyes and started to build his anger.

From a place forty years in the making.

Simpson was on the phone to the Assistant Chief Constable, shouting that he needed more reinforcements. He didn't know where the rioters were coming from, but Lister Park was about to burst. Ripples of anarchy fluxed through the ground, resulting in fierce clashes to the east and west. The police dogs were having most success, causing offenders to run instead of charge.

Simpson was taking casualties. By the ten. He looked around the events area. The realization was stark and hit him like a sledgehammer.

This is being orchestrated.

'Sir! Sir! It looks like we might have quashed this. They're leaving the park in their hundreds!' one of his officers shouted.

Simpson knew it was fantasy.

This was a long way from over.

He picked up his radio and took stock of what was

happening around the park. Another ambulance pulled up near the makeshift police base. Simpson saw two of his officers, blood pouring down their faces, stumbling towards it.

A few minutes later, as the heavens reopened, George Simpson was shouting at his men to mobilize and head towards City Hall.

Bradford was under siege.

Colin Reed was in his office, watching the mayhem on CCTV monitors. He had got one of his hackers to tap into the city's mainframe.

Bradford was on fire. Riots were raging in Manningham, Lister Park and Centenary Square. It looked random.

Exactly as they'd planned it would.

Reed had placed sections of his men in the park. Some white. Some Asian. They had infiltrated the peaceful BNP march and engineered a clash. And the rest? The rest was Bradford.

And Bradford had fallen.

It was going as planned. They'd been plotting this for months. A chance to take one of the largest cities in the UK.

The riot was nothing more than a distraction. Reed was eliminating his competition. One location at a time. His men were burning them to the ground and it appeared to be part of the anarchy close by.

Now all he needed was Lucas Dwight.

Without him, his plan might fail. Word might leak

that this wasn't anything to do with race or the BNP. And people higher up the food chain – people he didn't want to awaken – might realize they had been played.

Three depots were caught up in a crazy night of violence.

There was a fourth location.

The most important.

He was looking at the location on-screen. Shakeel Ahmed's flagship restaurant, next to the iconic National Media Museum. Bang in the centre of Bradford. Reed watched eagerly as his men, dressed in black, disappeared into the building.

Reed tapped the desk nervously.

Five minutes later, his men reappeared. And then they were gone. Dispersed into the night.

Reed peered closely at the screen. He had to wait a few minutes before the windows of the restaurant blew out.

Colin Reed's work was done.

Almost.

He looked at his watch: 10 p.m. He sighed and switched off the monitor.

Saima Virdee.

Whether Harry arrived to rescue his wife or not, her fate had been sealed the moment Colin Reed had been forced to kidnap her.

Martin Davis couldn't breathe. The building was on fire. Escape was impossible. He had woken up on the floor, handcuffed to the desk, in Shakeel Ahmed's office.

Davis needed to do something. He was going to die otherwise.

He leaned back and put his weight into pulling the handcuffs against the leg of the desk. Smoke crept under the doorframe and stole towards him like an assassin.

Davis pulled with everything he had. He put his feet against the wood and applied as much force as he could, tearing skin clean from his wrist.

The urgency and sheer force cracked the leg. The handcuffs slipped away.

Davis went tumbling over, but was quickly on his feet. He rushed to the phone. Dead.

He could feel the intensity of the fire behind the door and he wasn't going to open it.

Smoke had now seized the room. Davis dropped to his knees and put his jacket – the part Bashir hadn't cut into – across his face.

Useless.

He keeled over, fighting to breathe. There was no air left and the heat was suddenly upon him. The office door wilted and the flames burst inside, eating up the floor and everything before it.

The last thing Martin Davis saw before he died was the canvas painting of Mecca, high above him on the wall, its corners starting to curl.

Simpson didn't know where to send his men. City Hall, one of the oldest buildings in Bradford, was on fire. A crowd more than a thousand strong was rampaging through the streets, looting, destroying and engaging in fierce battles. Two riderless police horses bolted past the van, charging north.

He'd received eight missed calls from his wife, no doubt terrified as she watched the mayhem on television.

There were too many rival groups in the city. The cancellation of the Leeds United – Millwall football match had added to the disorder. Football hooligans were treating the riot as an excuse to do what they did best.

The mob had broken through strategic barriers blocking access to Bradford. The mentality to destroy was infectious. Simpson had witnessed it in 2001.

The rain couldn't fall hard enough to wash the blood from the pavements. Batons smashed into skulls, bones were shattered, bodies dropped like bowling pins.

Simpson was on the phone, getting another update from across the city, when the National Media Museum went up in flames. The old, withered building which had withstood two world wars had succumbed to the madness.

It was a spectacular sight. For a moment everybody paused and looked at the inferno. George Simpson ended his call and jumped out of the van. One of his officers had become isolated. Instinct took over and he drew his baton.

'Oi!' Simpson shouted, running towards the officer who was being beaten. He stood side by side with him, baton out, CS gas at the ready.

'Fuckin' pig!' spat one of the skinheads. A mouthful of phlegm landed on Simpson's arm. Somehow, they'd got separated from the crowd who'd drifted some fifty yards up Centenary Square.

Simpson was set upon by several men.

The ageing superintendent fell to his knees and cowered into a foetal position, hands over his head, knees tucked into his chest. His hair was being pulled ferociously. A fist smashed into his face. His head cracked on to the concrete.

The world went hazy. He heard the barking of dogs getting louder; then feet hitting the ground, running desperately towards him.

'Sir? Sir! Are you OK?'

Panicked voices. Hands helping him to his feet. A trickle of blood down his face. Somewhere, a powerful flash went off.

Tomorrow's headlines.

An hour later, George Simpson hobbled out of a patrol car outside his home. He'd refused to go to hospital. His wife would tend to his wounds. The tight bandage around his head had been applied by the paramedics in Centenary Square. The phone lines were down and he had been unable to reply to his wife's earlier missed calls.

He had handed silver command on to one of the DCIs and unwillingly left the carnage.

Tomorrow morning, George Simpson would retire, four days earlier than planned. He couldn't stand the fallout from yet another riot, this one on a scale he'd never seen before.

Simpson unlocked his front door and stepped into his home. He placed his protective vest on the floor and threw his hat on the stairs. He kicked off his shoes and hung his jacket on an antique coat rack. Turning, he looked in the mirror and saw a ragged, patched-up face.

Simpson spotted light under the living-room door. Mavis would have been following developments on the news and would be furious he hadn't answered her calls.

He cautiously opened the door.

At first he couldn't take in the sight. Mavis was bound to a chair. Behind her stood a large, angry-looking Asian man.

He was standing bare-chested, blood dripping from his body, with a metal chain in his hand.

Simpson instinctively reached for his radio. It wasn't there; he'd tagged it on to his riot gear. With his mouth suddenly parched, he retreated a step. 'Who the hell are you? Let my wife go. Whatever your grievance, she has nothing to do with it.'

The intimidating figure filled the room. He looked unwashed with untidy stubble. His eyes were bloodshot. Simpson noticed it wasn't just a metal chain he held. There were knives hanging from it. The man had a thick accent when he finally spoke.

'It has everything to do with her, George. Look at me. Recognize me. You know me.'

Simpson stole a glance at Mavis and saw the panic in

her eyes. There was blood splattered across her face yet she looked unharmed.

'I say look at me, bastard! Look my eyes – remember!'

Simpson locked eyes with the man, wondering which of the many animals he'd put away had come back to haunt him.

Then, slowly, George Simpson recognized Bashir Iqbal.

It couldn't be.

Simpson recoiled.

It was impossible.

Standing in front of him was the man who had haunted his nightmares for decades.

A ghost from the past.

With the strength in his legs failing, Simpson realized that tonight, not even God would save him.

FORTY-TWO

HARRY AND LUCAS HEADED towards the city centre, towards Toller Lane.

Towards Colin Reed.

'Something's wrong,' Harry said, approaching Thornbury roundabout.

'You're telling me.' Lucas slouched into the passenger seat.

A procession of police cars screamed by, blue lights flashing. Harry pulled the car over, out of the way. He tuned the radio to BBC Leeds.

'We are in the heart of Bradford where fierce clashes between the police and gangs of Asian youths are becoming increasingly violent. Authorities have blockaded routes into the city to try to calm—' The reporter's mic suddenly went off air. The presenter tried to reconnect; it only showed how volatile the situation in the city had become.

'It's happening,' Harry said. 'We're too late.'

'To save the city, maybe,' Lucas replied. 'Let's focus on your wife.'

They both glanced at the clock: 22.22.

Harry took the car around Thornbury roundabout, away from the city centre.

'Where are you going?' Lucas asked.

'Avoiding the madness.' Harry pointed to the radio. 'We'll head towards Bowling Hall Road, take the back way towards Toller.'

Harry took the Mercedes past sixty, causing two speed cameras to flash. 'What the hell is going on here?' he asked quietly. Almost to himself.

Lucas sighed. 'Can't understand what I've got to do with it. This guy, Colin Reed? He's gone to a lot of trouble to put me at the centre. That's the part I'm struggling with. All this effort?'

Harry agreed. 'It's drugs. Some kind of power play. The riot is a distraction. Question is, by who?' he said. 'It has to be someone powerful or with a lot to lose. Ahmed wasn't a target without risks.'

At Dudley Hill roundabout, the traffic stopped as more police vans rushed past. The M606 was only a few hundred yards away; these looked like summoned re-inforcements.

Harry overtook stationary cars and moved on to Wakefield Road, descending towards the city centre. Halfway down, he took his foot off the accelerator.

The car slowed to a crawl and then stopped. Lucas swore

under his breath as they got out and stared in disbelief at the clouds of smoke rising over the city. The central library and museum were burning in an inferno that lit up the night. To the west of the city, where they needed to go, helicopters and blue sirens warned them away.

'We've got to go through that to get to the warehouse?' said Lucas.

'No. We can't. We'll never make it.'

It was the scale of the disorder which dismayed Harry. 'What are we missing?' he asked, pointing to the flames.

Lucas shook his head and then shrugged. 'Never seen anything like it. Two thousand and one was a walk in the park compared to this.'

A crack in the distance made them both jump. One of the helicopters rotated wildly. It looked as though it might have hit power lines.

Harry and Lucas held their breath, scarcely able to watch as it struggled to stabilize. There was a moment when the pilot looked to have it under control, but then, with flames from the museum illuminating its descent, the helicopter dipped critically before nosediving towards the ground.

For a moment the madness seemed to stop. Time paused.

But the pilot regained control. And as quickly as it had descended the helicopter was back in the air, circling high and then pulling away to safety.

Harry and Lucas let out their breath and got back in the car. They drove in a stunned silence away from the epicentre and headed to the ring road – subdued, trying to understand who Colin Reed was and why he had put himself at the centre of this.

There were so many different elements to decipher.

All of the clues led back to Lucas. But the carnage in the city was way beyond a BNP-motivated riot. The damage would be far-reaching and no one would come out unscathed.

Ambulances were hurtling past them, heading for the infirmary close by.

Harry had turned off the radio. By all accounts, the city was in the grip of a madness from which only daylight would save it. He checked the time: 22.40.

'There.' Lucas pointed towards a sign for Toller. It led on to Duckworth Lane, where Bradford Royal Infirmary was currently at breaking point. Ambulance sirens were all around them, blue lights bouncing off the houses.

Lister Park wasn't far from Toller Lane. Gangs of youths charged through the side streets, faces covered, mobiles to their ears. Harry took a sharp turn on to Toller and slammed on the brakes as a group of four Asian youths leapt into the road. They ran in front of the car, one of them slipping and putting a gloved hand on the bonnet. Then, as quickly as they appeared, they vanished across the dual carriageway, into the darkness of a snicket.

'Crazy that we're heading to the middle of this madness,' Harry said.

'I was thinking the same thing. What is all this for?'

'When you deliberately burn a building down, it's usually to hide something or to rebuild,' said Harry. He pointed into the distance, where flames were rising from the city. 'Question is, which one?'

Harry covered a few hundred yards on Toller Lane before they reached the warehouse. It was set in a barren area of land. The grass was wildly unkempt and there was a narrow dirt track full of potholes leading to it. There was a protective but badly rusted metal railing around the perimeter and a decaying sign on the front gates, which were open: 'Blade Packaging'.

Harry stopped the car and got out, hovering by the driver's door.

'Plan?' Lucas asked, rushing around to his side.

'Not sure.' Harry checked his watch.

'Look.' Lucas pointed to the building.

The main doors next to the shutters swung open and a man scurried out. He opened the back doors of a van and threw two bags inside. Harry trained his eyes on the van. A light inside showed it to be empty. The man slammed the doors shut and got into the driver's side.

No sign of Saima.

'Someone's in a hurry,' Lucas said.

The van screeched off the tarmac and came blazing down the dirt track. Harry turned his face, out of sight. The van slowed when it hit the kerb and then raced away.

Harry noted the licence plate and took out his phone. He tried to make a call but it wouldn't connect.

'Who are you calling?' Lucas asked.

'Only man I can trust.'

'Colleague?' Lucas asked suspiciously.

'Brother,' replied Harry. He shook his phone in frustration. 'Damn thing won't connect.'

'Phone masts are probably down.'

Harry typed a frantic text. He punched in the licence plate of the van and gave Ronnie a brief idea of what had happened and where he was going.

'Sounds fucking insane,' Harry said, sending it. The text struggled to transmit. Harry hit resend and put the phone in his pocket. 'Come on. We're going in.'

They hurried to the gates and sneaked inside. Harry was suspicious at the ease with which they were able to approach, but pressed on down the dirt track, taking care to avoid potholes. The wind picked up as they ran, cutting at their faces – warning them to retreat. A chill crept up Harry's spine and he couldn't shake the notion they were being watched. But even on this hostile terrain, the need to get to Saima drew him magnetically towards the warehouse.

The ground disintegrated into a bog. Lucas slipped and Harry grabbed his arm, keeping him upright. Harry kept glancing at the building but it was too dark to spot any cameras. They reached the front of the warehouse and both men dropped to their knees – silhouettes camouflaged in the night.

There was an enormous blue shutter across the main entrance and a side door which was open. Harry glanced at Lucas, who nodded for him to enter.

Harry was alarmed at not having a weapon. It seemed foolhardy to charge in unprepared. But he was here now, with no time to delay. He needed to get to Saima. Being unarmed was irrelevant.

The iron door creaked heavily. Harry slipped inside, holding his breath. There was a lamp directly above the door. Its light petered out a few feet in front, leaving a corridor of impenetrable darkness. It was all too similar to that morning at the boxing gym. Unfathomable how much had happened in the few hours since then.

Harry pulled Lucas to the floor and pointed to a faint glow in the distance. They headed towards it, keeping low.

Suddenly the door behind them slammed closed. The morsel of light disappeared. In front, the glow they had been focusing on eclipsed and then vanished too. The corridor shrank into blackness.

Harry and Lucas were motionless on the floor, only their laboured breathing breaking the silence.

And then there was the sound of a gunshot.

FORTY-THREE

'TELL HER!' BASHIR SCREAMED.

Simpson was speechless.

Bashir raised the zanjeer as if to strike Mavis. Simpson leapt forward to intervene.

'No!' he screamed. 'Please, don't hurt her – I'll do whatever you want.'

'Give me back the last forty years of my life, bastard!' Bashir shouted. 'Tell her!'

'It . . . it was so long ago, Bashir. I'll make it up to you, I promise, just let my wife go.'

How was it that after four decades, mistakes from his past were standing in his living room?

'I say, tell her!' Bashir bellowed. He brought the zanjeer down and smashed it into Mavis's legs. Although she was gagged, Mavis released a muted cry and started to shake. Simpson threw himself at Bashir.

Bashir stepped aside and shoved him easily into the

marble mantelpiece. Simpson crashed into it, banging his head, and fell to the floor.

Grabbing him by his clothes, Bashir pulled Simpson to his feet and threw him on the sofa.

'Please . . .' Simpson mumbled, 'don't hurt her. It's me you want.'

'Start talking.' Bashir raised the zanjeer again, this time aiming it towards Simpson. Sweat trickled down Bashir's bare chest, then on to the floor.

Simpson looked ashamedly at his wife, who was crying hysterically. 'Mavis . . . I did something terrible to this man many years ago.' His voice was trembling with fear; he paused, uncertain how to proceed. Bashir backed off a beat and lowered the zanjeer, his eyes burning fiercely.

This was a tale which had stolen his life.

Simpson continued. 'I . . . did something which I have never been able to forget, Mavis. You know I spent the first twenty years of my life in India and Pakistan? My father was stationed in Bashir's village to help the local police after the partition of India. He was one of the last working guards at that time . . .' His voice was shaky. Blood escaped from his bandaged head and his cheek was swelling with speed.

'Bashir and I were friends – we . . . we lived near each other.' His words slowed as Simpson focused on the past. His eyes dropped to the floor and his voice cracked. 'One day, a Pakistani girl was walking back from the well. She stumbled and fell. I'd been drinking – I didn't know what I was doing. I . . . I . . . was only young. She . . . she came over to us for help and I was drunk, Mavis. I didn't mean it, I didn't think.'

Mavis made as if to speak and Bashir removed her gag. She was grimacing at the flesh wounds on her legs and stuttered her words. 'What d-did you d-do, George?'

He paused. He couldn't look at her. 'I was only fifteen,' he said again, as if it were a defence.

Another pause.

'I knew the girl. I'd been . . . chasing her for a few weeks. I wasn't in my senses, Mavis, and I . . . I . . .' Simpson couldn't bring the words to his lips.

'He raped her,' Bashir whispered, pointing at Simpson. 'I was there. Then people came – from my village. I never put finger on her.' Bashir raised his voice and waved the bloody zanjeer at Simpson. 'Tell her what you did, bastard!'

Simpson's head was weighted to the floor. 'I . . . I . . . did rape her,' he said quietly, finally acknowledging his sin after all those years. 'And . . . I blamed Bashir. But please . . .' Simpson turned to Bashir, away from his wife's shocked expression. *He couldn't face her.* 'Let my wife go. She doesn't deserve this.'

Bashir twisted the chain ominously in his hands.

'What do you want from me?' Simpson pleaded. He had started to sob.

'You know what happened to this woman? She is cast away from her village. An untouchable. Like me.'

'I'm sorry. I'll do anything you want. Money – I have money! My retirement fund—'

Bashir stepped forward and smashed his elbow into Simpson's face. The crack of his nose breaking jolted Mavis into action.

'George? George? Are you OK? Leave him alone, you monster!'

'Even in *my* country you could beat the system,' Bashir said icily. 'Because you are white and your family had money and power.' He struck Simpson again. 'Your family paid this girl to blame me – and I was easy to sacrifice. Poor man. No future. No hope. And then your family moved back to England. Left me ruined.'

Bashir was breathing heavily, almost panting. He was struggling to decide what to do with the woman. What use was life without her husband? He knelt in front of her, keeping Simpson in his line of sight. 'This girl – you know what happened to her?' he asked Mavis softly.

She shook her head and Bashir wiped tears from her face. She jerked her head away.

'In my village in Pakistan, no police then. No court. Only "panchayats". Village elders. Wise people.'

'I beg you,' Mavis whispered, 'forgive him and leave us alone.'

Bashir grunted. 'Forgive?' He shook his head. 'No forgiving.'

He was speaking to Mavis but his eyes were fixed solidly on Simpson, who was teetering on the brink of consciousness.

'Panchayats make decision. Remove my family land. Bring shame on my family. Shame in my community is very serious.' Bashir panted, almost growled, as he spoke. His face darkened and he wrapped the chain across his hands. 'The girl – the one you raped – she is here. In Bradford.'

Now Simpson finally raised his head and looked at the fury raging in Bashir's eyes. 'What?'

'Panchayats make decision. Make right what happened. My family? My mother died of shame. My father few months later. You know why?'

Simpson was lost for words.

'Ruksa.' Bashir almost hissed her name. 'The woman you spoiled. She is here. In my home.' He stood up, towering above Simpson, with his end game in sight. He raised the zanjeer high above his head and looked more terrifying than anybody Simpson had ever seen.

'She became my wife.'

FORTY-FOUR

GLASS ABOVE HARRY'S HEAD shattered and fell like sand to the floor. The piercing crack from the gunshot was deafening, as though someone had punched him in the head.

The world became mute. In the darkness, Harry experienced an overwhelming sensation of helplessness.

They were trapped in the corridor, with no way of knowing where the gunshot had come from. Lucas grabbed Harry and was pulling him back when the lights suddenly came on. In front of them, filling the doorway, was a six-foot-five, three-hundred-pound hulk. His arms were crossed, his sleeves rolled up. Even his forearms were enormous. The light above the doorway bounced off his shaven head.

Harry spotted the tattoo of the British bulldog on Reed's neck.

Colin Reed.

Reed stared at them with narrow, emotionless eyes, and then spoke, but the ringing was still echoing in Harry's head. Harry massaged his ears urgently and spotted the pistol in Reed's hand.

Reed walked slowly towards them, massive Doc Martens crunching on glass. Harry's hearing started to return, the whine from the bullet still in the background.

'Move,' said Reed coldly. Lucas made as if to charge him. Harry saw the move and grabbed his arm.

'Try it,' Reed said. 'It'll make it quick.'

'Come on,' Harry whispered into Lucas's ear. 'This isn't the time.'

They backed away down the corridor towards a door at the far end. It opened as they approached and they walked into a makeshift office. There was an old table in the corner with a desktop fan moving humid air around. Several laptops were receiving harrowing images from the rioting in the city.

There were two men in the room, both armed. They trained their pistols on Harry and Lucas.

'Over there,' Reed said, pushing Lucas roughly towards the back wall. Lucas turned and swiftly cracked a vicious right hook into Reed's jaw. It was so quick Reed didn't have time to react. But the strike had no impact. Reed's neck was as thick as a python: layers of muscle simply absorbed the blow. His expression never changed. 'You want to try that again, Junior?'

Lucas dipped his left shoulder and threw his trademark

liver punch. This time Reed caught the blow in his oversized hand. He pulled Lucas towards him and brutally head-butted his face, shattering Lucas's nose.

Lucas was thrown like a matchstick and collapsed three feet away, clutching his face and writhing on the floor in agony.

Reed turned to Harry. 'How about you?'

'Where's my wife?' Harry replied, holding his ground.

'No idea.' Reed pointed the gun at him. 'Over there – next to Sleeping Beauty.'

Harry didn't move. 'What kind of sick fuck takes a pregnant woman?'

'What kind of arsehole puts his wife in harm's way when he's been told to back off?'

Harry pointed towards Lucas. 'I brought you what you asked. Now give me back my wife.'

'This wasn't our arrangement.' Reed nodded to the men standing behind Harry. 'Keep packing it up. We're done.'

The men moved swiftly, powering down their laptops and unplugging hard drives.

'Car's out front,' Reed continued. 'I'll finish up here.'

Harry turned his face to get a good look at the men. As soon as his focus was removed from Reed, he suffered the consequences. Reed lashed out a thunderous blow and hit Harry in the chest. He collapsed to the floor, gasping for air.

Reed's accomplices grabbed their equipment and hurried out of the room, closing the door.

Harry rolled on to his side. He tried to calm the panic in his chest and take shorter breaths but Reed had struck him hard enough to crack ribs.

Saima. She's here. She has to be.

Get up, Harry. Find a way.

Lucas was on his knees, clutching his nose, which was still haemorrhaging blood.

Reed took out his phone and made a call, ordering two more graves to be dug.

Two more.

More.

Was he talking about Saima?

Harry got on to his hands and knees and found his breath. He searched the room desperately for a weapon but it was useless. 'Why?' he asked finally. 'Why the obsession with Lucas? Why this . . . this destruction in the city?'

'None of your damn business,' Reed replied.

'None of my business? None of my business? You turned my whole fucking world upside down.'

'That makes two of us.' Reed turned, took a huge stride forward, and kicked Lucas. The Doc Marten shattered the side of Lucas's face. There was a nauseating crunch of bone and his head smashed into the wall, hard enough to crack the plaster. His limp body crumpled to the floor. 'This prick', Reed said, pointing to Lucas, 'was all I needed. Not you fucking things up. Involving your wife. Complicating my night.'

Harry stared at Lucas's body. Blood pooled from his head around his neck.

Then, without warning, Reed fired two shots into the back of Lucas's skull. Bone and brain fragments splattered across the wall.

More ringing in Harry's ears. Visions of twenty years ago.

You're next.

Don't die easily, Harry. Go down fighting. At least make him earn it.

With the echo from the bullets still resounding in the room, Harry lunged forward from his knees and threw his arms around Reed's legs in a forceful rugby tackle.

Reed was too muscular to be brought down and instead cracked the pistol down into Harry's neck.

The pain was intense but Harry couldn't relent. If he lost this tussle, it was over. He removed his right hand from Reed's legs and grabbed his testicles.

Reed yelled, first in surprise, and then in pain. He pointed the gun towards Harry, who raised his other hand to grab it.

Harry, still on his knees, was at a huge disadvantage as Reed bore the weapon down whilst trying to fire. But Harry had wedged his finger behind the trigger so Reed couldn't pull it. Instead Reed hammered the gun into Harry's face.

Harry responded by using a trick he'd learned on the rugby pitch: a move any second row would have been proud of. He yanked Reed's testicles and twisted.

Reed groaned and collapsed to one knee but didn't let go of the gun. Harry got quickly to his feet and punched

Reed repeatedly in the face but the blows weren't enough. He daren't let go of the gun with his other hand and Reed's mammoth neck was like rubber, absorbing everything Harry threw at it.

Reed recoiled, preparing another head-butt. Harry saw it coming and was forced to let go of the pistol to move out of the way as Reed brought his head forward with everything he had. Harry scrambled out of the way, moving behind Reed and wrapping his arm around Reed's neck. He trapped him in a powerful sleeper-hold, choking the bastard.

Reed had an energy Harry had never encountered before. He got to his feet, lifting Harry off the floor. Harry hung on to Reed's back. Now his feet were off the floor, he transferred his weight to the sleeper-hold, squeezing, trying to bring the big man down. Harry clasped his left hand to his right wrist, locking the choke-hold.

Reed was like a man possessed. He dropped the gun and grabbed Harry's wrists.

Harry closed his eyes and didn't wilt but Reed was so much stronger.

Saima.

You have to win this fight.

Harry resisted Reed's urgent attempts to prise his hands apart. Reed thundered backwards, smashing Harry's body into the wall. Still Harry didn't let go. He kept squeezing, constricting the oxygen, and it was working. Harry heard the welcome sound of Reed gasping.

Another charge at the wall and again Harry was slammed forcefully into it.

And now Reed was on his knees.

Fading.

Harry felt the ground beneath him and used it to strengthen his grip, bending his legs and using his weight to apply further pressure. 'Where's my wife, you bastard?'

It would do no good to kill Reed – he needed Saima's location.

Reed stopped struggling. He leaned forward, taking Harry with him.

'That's right – give in, you sick fuck,' Harry hissed.

But Reed had removed a knife from his inside pocket. Harry didn't see it – he just felt the sharp stab of it pierce his left shoulder.

Harry cried out and let go of Reed, who twisted the knife further into his flesh. Harry collapsed to the floor.

Reed was up quickly. In three enormous strides he made it to the gun, picked it up and pointed it towards Harry. His eyes were raging with an anger Harry didn't understand.

'Why?' Harry croaked again as he pulled the knife out of his shoulder. He pointed the blood-soaked blade towards Reed. 'Why?'

Reed massaged his neck. 'Power!' he spat. 'Power.'

Harry shook his head. 'Please . . . my wife . . .'

Reed cocked the pistol. 'Fuck your wife. You were warned to leave this alone. You should have listened.'

Harry put his hands in the air, ignoring the agony in his shoulder. 'Just . . . tell me she'll be OK,' he said, closing his eyes. 'Give me that much at least.'

I know I have to pay for what I did twenty years ago, but spare her – her karma isn't mine.

But there was no reply.

Just the ear-splitting crack of another bullet.

FORTY-FIVE

'IN OUR VILLAGE – in our traditions – if you spoil woman's decency, you are forced to return it,' Bashir said bitterly. He still had the zanjeer poised and was aiming it at Simpson's head.

'Please – I had no idea, I was young and foolish,' Simpson pleaded.

Bashir swore in Urdu and kicked Simpson again. 'All my life I am suffering what you did. Her face. Her body. Knowing you ruined her. I lost everything. We moved. Many times. Until I found you.'

'You've been in Bradford all this time?' Simpson asked incredulously.

Bashir nodded. He lowered the zanjeer but kept it pointed at Simpson. 'My honour is linked to your death. I wait many years for tonight.' Bashir was struggling to carry out his revenge. He looked at Mavis out of the corner of his eyes. They were both at his mercy.

He twisted the chain anxiously in his hands.

It was the woman he was having problems with.

He couldn't leave her alive.

Simpson continued begging for forgiveness.

'You can be the better man,' Mavis said, trying to get Bashir's attention. She had either resigned herself to her fate or wasn't afraid. 'It was a long time ago and he was wrong,' she continued quickly, 'but he's done so much good since then. Find it in your heart, Bashir, forgive him. *Please.*'

Bashir's face was blank. He continued to twist the zanjeer.

One blow was all it would take.

'Look at me, Bashir, please,' she continued.

Bashir struggled with the urge to break down. I can't go through with it, he thought. After all these years – the waiting, the watching – he felt . . . empty.

What's wrong with me? I've waited my whole life for this.

He'd never killed anyone innocent before, and it was hard.

What was the woman's crime? Her marriage to Simpson? Wasn't she in fact just like Bashir? An innocent party, now forced to endure a darkness she wasn't responsible for?

'I know you don't believe me, but he's lived with the guilt of that day since it happened. I know it, Bashir. George has spent years talking to me about forgiveness and how to absolve sins. Why do you think we ended up in Bradford? In the largest Asian community in England?

It's atonement, Bashir – that's what my husband has been doing since he arrived here.'

'I have to . . .' Bashir looked away from her. 'No turning back now.' But his voice was suddenly unsure.

Empty.

The rage had gone.

'Yes, you can,' she said urgently. 'Please, untie me. I can't hurt you, can I?'

Bashir didn't feel in control of his actions. He grabbed a knife from the chain and cut Mavis's arms free.

It was her face: full of compassion – something alien to Bashir. He had spent his life working for Shakeel, torturing scumbags. Bashir had never taken an innocent life, nor dished out any injustice without reason.

Now she knew the truth about her husband, was there any greater pain he could inflict?

The wounds on Mavis's legs were still bleeding, but instead of tending to them, she stood up and reached out, taking Bashir's face in her hands.

Bashir started to shake. He was still clutching the zanjeer.

I can't do it.

'It takes far more strength to forgive somebody and walk away,' she said, almost reading his thoughts. 'You're not weak. Neither you nor George are the same person you were forty years ago.'

Bashir dropped the zanjeer.

Mavis inched forward, amazed at her own nerve, and put her arms around Bashir.

* * *

369

He sat alone in his car.

Bashir had left them clutching each other, grateful they were still alive. The empty feeling in the pit of his stomach was painful. He'd been preoccupied with revenge for so long, he didn't know what to do. He wasn't even sure that he would leave Bradford. There seemed little need to escape now.

Bashir had dreamed of returning to Pakistan and farming the land he was raised upon. Restoring some balance to his life. For the first time since he could remember, Bashir thought about his wife, about her mental frailty, and wondered if tonight was a chance for them both. Whether he might take her with him.

He had focused on his hate for so long, he hadn't considered Ruksa. He thought of her now: alone, depressed. Broken.

All the anger and malice Bashir had carried was suddenly absent.

Above, helicopters continued to swirl across the city and there was a potent smell of burning in the air.

This city is doomed, Bashir thought.

Also, for the first time since he could remember, his back was *painful*. He could feel the sores and the dried blood.

He removed his passport from his pocket, flipped to page twenty-one and stared at the Pakistani visa. It was time to go home. But he wouldn't go alone.

Bashir started the car and drove away from Simpson's house, relieved that he'd never return.

FORTY-SIX

HARRY DIDN'T FEEL THE pain of a bullet. Didn't feel anything at all.

Must be dead.

Ronnie Virdee was standing behind Colin Reed, having fired a shot into the ground. 'Put down the gun, Colin.'

Reed turned his face but remained unmoved. 'Not going to happen.'

'Colin—'

'No, Ronnie, just turn around and leave this alone.'

'Are you crazy? What the fuck has come over you? I told you—'

'I know what you told me,' Reed spat. 'I was there when you said it, remember?'

Harry was perplexed. 'What the fuck are you doing here, Ronnie?'

Reed sneered. 'We're business partners.'

Harry thought he'd heard it wrong. He searched Ronnie's face for confusion. He found none.

'Colin, I need you to put the gun down,' Ronnie said calmly. 'Let's work this through.'

'There is no way to work it through,' Reed replied. 'Tough decisions had to be made and I made them. Like you taught me.'

'Jesus. My brother? His wife?' Ronnie waved the phone at Harry, who realized he must have received his text.

'Ronnie,' Reed said slowly, 'look around you. Bradford is on fire. We planned this for over a year and you think I'm going to let your brother get in the way? I warned him. Jesus, even *you* warned him to stay away. He's got only himself to blame.'

'Colin . . . he's my brother—'

'And that's the problem. You can't see what needs to be done. You're weak when it comes to him – always have been.'

'Hey!' Harry snapped. 'You mind telling me what the fuck is going on? Where's my wife? Ronnie, you knew about this?'

Ronnie shook his head. 'Don't be stupid. Where's Saima, Colin? You lifted a pregnant woman? Have you lost your goddamn mind?'

Reed still had the gun trained on Harry. His finger on the trigger. He kept his eyes on Harry but turned his head, hissing at Ronnie: 'What were the stakes tonight? Huh? You remember? If we got made – if this shit didn't go down exactly as planned? You know what would happen. You? Me? Our families? Hell, anyone we ever cared about? Cut into dog food. And you think I'm going to give a flying fuck about one man who put us at risk?'

'You should have told me! Jesus, Colin.'

'Plausible deniability – isn't that what you said? Make it happen and—'

'This wasn't on the blueprint!'

'Always your problem. Blueprints and theory. Maybe you want to get your hands dirty once in a while?'

'Fuck you, Colin, I built this empire – I made you what you are—'

'No, *fuck you*, Ronnie. We both made this. There is expertise you don't have that I do.' He pointed towards Lucas's body.

Harry got to his feet. 'My wife. You better tell me right now, or I swear to God I'll swallow every bullet in that gun but I'll get to you.' Harry waved the bloodstained knife he'd pulled from his shoulder at Reed.

'Your wife escaped,' Reed replied. 'It's why we're packing up. One of my men betrayed me – cut her loose about an hour ago.'

'Bullshit.'

'I don't do bullshit. She got to the alley behind here. Gone.'

'This true?' Ronnie asked, taking a couple of steps closer.

'Yes.'

'She OK?'

'How the fuck would I know?' Reed replied. 'Educated guess? She's at the hospital.'

The revelation buoyed Harry. He was getting out of here. To his wife. To his baby.

'Put down the gun, Colin. We can work this through,' Ronnie repeated. 'Come on now, we've been through too much—'

'To let this son of a bitch end it,' Reed snapped. 'You've got a choice to make, Ronnie, because I'm not putting down the gun. You pick – him or me?'

'Doesn't need to be this way,' Ronnie said calmly, trying to get Reed back on-side. 'This isn't black or white.'

'Yes,' Reed replied, 'it is. He's a cop with a grudge to settle. We didn't come this far, risk this much, to let one man – whoever that might be – end it for us.'

'Harry can be reasoned with.'

'No!' Harry hissed. 'I fucking well can't.' He had turned the knife in his hand and wiped the blood from the blade. He was contemplating throwing it at Reed. It was his only chance to end this on his terms.

'You see?' Reed said. 'It's over.'

Ronnie put his gun to Reed's temple. 'Put. It. Down.'

Reed shook his head. 'Only one way it's going to happen. One way.'

'Don't put this on me, Colin.' Ronnie's voice was shaking as well as the gun. 'Don't make me do this.'

'If you don't pull that trigger,' Colin said, 'I'll pull mine. We're as good as dead if he walks.'

'Why don't you tell me what the hell this is about?' Harry turned the knife. He was running through the motions in his mind.

Raise it high. Throw it straight. Step quickly to the side. But it would take too long. Harry didn't have three moves to save himself.

'Tell him, Ronnie,' Reed said. 'Tell him who you really are. Why you can always get your hands on details Harry wants.'

Ronnie looked uncomfortably at Harry. 'Jesus, kid, why didn't you stay away?'

'Who are you?' Harry asked. 'Really?'

Ronnie remained quiet.

'He's the boss of the second largest drug cartel in Bradford,' Reed explained. 'After tonight, we're the sole suppliers of drugs in this city.'

'What?'

Ronnie nodded. Not ashamedly.

Harry felt the energy slipping from him.

'It's true,' Reed continued. 'Your brother and I are partners. And tonight, we took out our competition. Hit their locations. This morning – their boss – the guy who bankrolls them – the guy who yesterday won the Bradford West seat.'

'Shakeel Ahmed?'

'Yes,' Ronnie replied. 'The guy was almost as difficult to catch as I was. But he wasn't nearly as smart. Got lazy and we made him. You want a guy like that in political office? He was becoming too powerful. This riot was orchestrated so that when we hit his locations in the city, it looked like part of the riot. It can't be traced back to us because tonight the whole of Bradford is burning – on a scale so massive, there will be no evidence to trace.'

'That is,' Reed said, 'until you got involved.'

'Why Lucas?' said Harry. 'Why now?'

'Misdirection,' Ronnie replied. 'All those card tricks I showed you when we were younger? Remember?'

Harry nodded.

'Misdirection. It's plausible that the ex-leader comes out of jail and loses his head. Maybe he wants to go straight back inside? Maybe he's still a fucked-up racist? Who gives a shit?' Ronnie said. 'We needed someone to blame for Shakeel's murder – a name who would get Bradford reeling. Lucas Dwight was perfect. That's why.'

'The man was innocent,' Harry said, getting angry.

'No one's innocent in this world,' Ronnie replied. 'Not even the guy who did time for his little brother.'

It was a shitty thing to say but perfectly weighted to force Harry on to the back foot.

'If I put a bullet in him now,' Reed said, 'it's even. You did time for him – he owes you.'

Harry stared at Ronnie, trying to find the brother he once knew. 'What the hell happened to you?'

'Life.' Ronnie lowered the gun from Reed's temple. 'I don't regret going to jail for you, Harry. Truth be told, it made me. Opened my eyes to the fact that living by the rules – this stuff you believe in – it's bullshit. There is no equality in this country. You either have power or you get fucked over.'

'Ronnie, this isn't you . . .' But it was all becoming clear in Harry's mind.

Sixteen corner shops to distribute and wash the money. Cash and Carries to import and export drugs. Ronnie's 198 IQ one step ahead, *all the time.*

'This *is* me,' said Ronnie. 'That day, when you . . . killed that man? He deserved it. Bastard came into our parents' shop, stabbed Mum and would have done the same to us if you hadn't stopped him. He deserved to die.' Ronnie pointed the gun at Harry. 'And I did what any decent big brother would do. I stepped forward and they locked me away. For what? Excessive force? Bullshit.' He spat bitterly on the floor.

'If I'd known this is what you would become . . .'

'You need to open your eyes, Harry. How long has the law been clamping down on drugs in this city? Twenty? Thirty fucking years? And it's more widespread than ever? I've got half of law enforcement in my pocket. Customs officers on my Christmas card list. Judges who love my product. I supply something people want. No more. No less. You call that a fucking crime?'

Harry shook his head. 'You deluded son of a bitch.'

'No!' Ronnie snapped. 'It is *you* who is deluded. You and I were supposed to run this city. You from the top and me from the bottom. Your boss – soon to retire? Everyone moves up the chain of command including you, then one day? It's you who lands the top job and, finally' – Ronnie waved the gun towards the city – 'we could have brought *real* change to Bradford. Tonight there aren't two dons in Bradford any more. There will be no more clashes between gangs. There's only us. Only one don. Tomorrow the rebuilding begins. You don't want to be a part of that?'

'Ronnie, what the hell are you talking about?'

'Just for once,' Ronnie shouted, 'can you not try to see past your own narrow-mindedness?' He stepped in front of Reed suddenly, square on with Harry, and prodded him in the chest. 'You owe me,' he said. 'I'm the brother who always took the pain for you. Always!'

Harry stared at his brother. Ronnie was barely recognizable.

'Look around you,' Ronnie continued. 'You got arse-holes in Whitehall pilfering millions for their damn expense accounts – politicians who earn millions taking money from people like you and me to do up their damn second homes – but that . . . that's not theft? Because it's written in black and white somewhere?'

Ronnie glared at Harry, who lowered the knife to his side. 'The banks play roulette and lose trillions of pounds and what do we do? Lend them more money. Can't you see that everything in this world is about money and power and greed, and I don't want to play the game, Harry. I want to run it so I can change it!'

'Robin Hood? Is that who you're striving to be?'

'Yes,' Ronnie replied. 'You're damn fucking right it is. Tonight I got rid of the bastards who flood this city with impure product that kills. I obliterated their depots, eliminated the boss and burned down all of his restaurants. Tomorrow I'll be the most powerful man in Bradford, and yes, I will rebuild this city. No fucking jerking around with empty promises. You give me five years, and Colin and I, with your help, can reform Bradford.'

'Step aside, brother,' Reed said quietly to Ronnie. 'He's not one of us. He won't turn. Doesn't understand the rules.'

'There are no rules.' Ronnie retreated from his brother. 'Tomorrow we write our own.' He pointed at Harry. 'You got yourself caught up in this. Was never meant to be like this. Can we work this out? No one needs to die here.'

Harry pointed the knife at Reed. 'My wife? She really get away?'

Reed nodded. 'Feisty piece of work.'

'You put down that gun,' Harry said, 'and we'll settle this man to man. That's the only way this is going to end.' He pointed at Lucas's body. 'There's no way I can let this lie or the fact you took my wife.'

Reed didn't lower the weapon.

'You shoot me,' Harry said, 'and he'll have to watch.' He pointed to Ronnie. 'But we settle this as men and there's nothing fairer.'

Reed didn't take his eyes off Harry as he spoke to Ronnie. 'You hearing this? You can live with it?'

Ronnie sighed and looked at Harry, alarmed. He pointed to the wound on his shoulder. 'You won't last two minutes. Don't listen to your ego.'

'Are you game for this or not?' Harry asked. 'Only one of us is leaving this room, Colin. Ronnie, the son of a bitch would have killed Saima if she hadn't escaped. He's murdered Lucas and if you hadn't walked in here, he would have put me down. Whatever he is to you, he's a liability.'

'Drop the knife,' Reed said, 'and I'll surrender the gun.'

Harry dropped the knife and kicked it towards Reed.

'Here.' Reed handed the gun to Ronnie. 'This is the only way to settle this without you making a choice.'

'I know.' Ronnie shook his head. He took the gun. 'Thing is,' he said reluctantly, 'it's already made.' He stepped in front of Reed and unloaded a bullet into his massive chest, right through his heart. Their eyes connected for the briefest of moments.

Ronnie dropped the gun and threw his arms around Reed, supporting his massive body as it fell to the floor.

The bullet had punctured his chest, spraying blood across Ronnie's face. Harry remained motionless, dumbfounded. Reed tried to speak but instead pooled a mouthful of blood. Ronnie held him close in a terminal embrace.

And then there was silence.

For the second time in their lives, Harry and Ronnie Virdee were alone in a room with murder defiling their karma.

Neither had noticed the door open. Or the shadow of Zain Ahmed slipping into the room.

Until Zain stepped forward, gun pointed at Harry and smiled. 'I thought I'd have to waste three bullets. Turns out I'm only going to need two.'

FORTY-SEVEN

RONNIE TURNED TO FACE Zain. 'Who the fuck are you?'

'Your competition. Looks like you forgot about one thing in all your scheming. Me. The son. Zain Ahmed.'

Ronnie looked closely at the boy. Because that's all he was. A boy with an unsteady hand in a man's world.

'You better put that thing down before you hurt yourself,' Ronnie said.

Zain smiled. 'You sound like my father,' he replied and then fired the pistol.

Harry was frozen and watched in horror as the bullet tore into Ronnie's arm and spun him round a full 360 degrees. Harry caught hold of his brother and together they fell to the floor.

'No!' Harry shouted. 'No!'

Harry turned Ronnie on to his back and saw blood staining his shirt. He grabbed Ronnie's hand and put it over his arm where he'd been shot. 'Press here,' he said urgently and then looked towards Zain, who was still pointing the gun towards them.

'You hurt yourself by opening your mouth,' Zain said to Ronnie. 'That was for my father. But truth be told – you did me a favour. So that bullet won't be the one which kills you. The next one will.'

'Hold on,' Harry said, and put his hand over Ronnie's arm, applying more pressure to the wound. 'Think carefully. Think about what I can give you!'

'Nothing,' replied Zain. 'You are worth precisely nothing to me.'

Harry needed a little leverage. He needed to get close to Zain, so he had a chance of disarming him.

'Think like a businessman – like your father would have done,' Harry said, desperately trying to buy some time. 'If we play this right, I can take credit for nailing Lucas Dwight and bringing your father's killer to justice. I can become the most respected officer in this city! And *you* will have my allegiance. That is power. *Real power.*'

Zain sniggered and waved the gun at Harry. 'You must think I'm a fool. You're trying to save your brother's life.'

'How long have you been waiting over there?' Harry asked. 'Long enough to hear what these two fucks did to my wife today?'

Harry applied more pressure and Ronnie gritted his teeth and turned his head away from Zain.

'What I want is for you to put that gun down and walk away,' Harry continued. 'Let me deal with this. You think

I'm going to forgive my brother after what he's just told me?'

'By that measure, why should I believe that I have your allegiance?'

'Because' – Harry took his hand away from Ronnie's wound – 'it's pretty bloody simple. You're waving a gun at me. You have my allegiance.' He slowly got to his feet and put out his hands. 'Honestly? My brother was a dead man the moment he revealed what he was. He kidnapped my wife. He might not have been the one who took her, but he was in charge here. He's culpable. I need you to let me finish this. It's between me and my brother. This is *our* business.'

'He killed my father,' Zain replied.

'And did you a favour. You said so yourself. Think better, Zain. Think higher. Like you're in a game of chess. You can buy my partnership here. I want out of this. I want to find my wife. Have my child and earn some decent fucking money. Like my brother. Fuck if I'm trusting him after what he's done. But you and me, we can make this work to our advantage. Jesus,' Harry said, desperate now. 'Think about what we could achieve.'

He had Zain's attention because the kid was no longer holding the gun with intent. His arm had become limp and the gun wasn't pointing at Harry's head. It was aimed at his hip.

'You want to partner me?' Zain asked.

Harry nodded.

'Prove it.' Zain kicked Colin Reed's knife towards

Harry. 'Pick it up, finish off your brother, and you live.'
The knife landed by Ronnie's body. 'Show me.'

Harry nodded. 'You're on. I . . . I need to say a few
things to him. Before—'

'Get on with it. I'll give you two minutes before I make
the decision for you.'

Zain backed off. Harry picked up the knife and got on
his knees. Ronnie was breathing heavily and looking at
him.

'Do it,' he said, nodding at Harry. 'Karma.'

Harry nodded. 'You stupid fuck,' he whispered.

Ronnie closed his eyes. 'One year in the planning and
my little brother makes it all go to hell.'

'Story of your life,' Harry replied. 'You never could
just let me sink.'

'I don't know what's worse,' Ronnie replied. 'The fact I
had to end Colin, or' – he turned his face towards Zain –
'the fact that prick wins.'

'You sow what you reap.' Harry twisted the knife in
his hands. He turned it upside down, covertly holding it
by the blade. Ronnie watched the move and shook his
head slightly.

'Thing is about life, Harry. You never know when it's
your last chance. When one miss might be your last one.
You get me?'

'Yes.' Harry turned the knife again, holding it by the
handle. 'But like you said, brother, it's about misdirection?
Right?'

Harry raised the knife high. His hand disappeared

behind his head and he called out to Zain. 'Hey, you want to watch me do this?'

Zain took three steps towards them, gun primed, pointing it at Ronnie. He was close enough that Harry couldn't miss. The question was where would Zain be hit?

Behind his head, Harry slipped his hand down the knife until he was holding it by the blade again.

'Do it,' Zain said.

Harry closed his eyes and paused. 'Let's call us even now.' He opened his eyes and threw the knife as hard as he could at Zain. Harry had aimed for his chest, but the blade jammed into Zain's throat. It didn't strike clean, instead lodging to the left of his trachea.

No sooner had Harry thrown it, he rolled across Ronnie's body and kicked out furiously, jamming his foot into Zain's knee, sending it back on itself until it cracked. Zain screamed and started to fall. He dropped the gun.

Harry grabbed the pistol, scrambled to his feet and pointed the gun at Zain, who had hit the floor hard.

But Zain wasn't beaten. He tore the knife from his throat and made to throw it.

Harry pulled the trigger.

With the deafening sound of the bullet, Zain's face exploded, sending flesh and bone splattering across the room. His body flew backwards and came to rest next to Lucas Dwight.

The echo temporarily dominated the room. Harry slumped to his knees and let out a deep sigh. He put the gun on the floor and stared at Zain, absorbing the enormity of what he'd done.

Another murder.

The echo died away.

Ronnie propped his body up and hissed in pain. 'You OK?' he finally said.

Harry didn't reply. He couldn't look at him.

'Look, you had no choice—'

'I did. I could have let him kill you.'

'So it's lose-lose no matter what you did.'

'You want to know the reason why I didn't?' Harry asked.

'Cos you're a good brother. That's why.'

'No,' Harry said. He took his eyes from Zain. Looked towards Ronnie. 'I did it for Mum. She's already lost one son.'

Ronnie struggled to his feet. He let out a muted cry and kept his hand over the bullet wound in his arm. 'We both sacrificed something today.'

'You talking about your pit bull?'

'Blood is thicker than water. And I'm telling you, what he did to Saima? To you? I would never have cleared that. And he knew it. Which is why I didn't know.'

'I need to be on my feet now. I should be out there, looking for my wife. Heading to the hospital where I hope she'll be. You want to know why I'm not?'

'Why?'

'Because I'm afraid,' replied Harry. 'Because ever since I killed that robber in Dad's shop and you took the fall,

I've had this feeling that one day, like today, karma was going to get me. And I felt it all day. From the moment I went running this morning and found Shakeel Ahmed's body to the moment I put a bullet in his son.'

'Life doesn't work that way.' Ronnie put out his hand. 'Come on, get up. Go see that Saima is safe. I'll take care of . . . this.'

Harry ignored Ronnie's hand. But he did get up.

'Hey, Harry, look, I'm not the monster you think I am. There are rules to what I do – there are ethics involved.'

'Ethics? Ethics? Jesus, can you even hear yourself?'

'You need to—'

'There are three dead bodies here, Ronnie. Do you even see them?'

'Of course I do,' Ronnie snapped. 'I met Colin when I was inside. He was like my brother.' He raised his hand to stop Harry from interrupting. 'There are things about me you don't know, but when you give me a chance, when you see what I was trying to achieve, trying to build here – you might understand.'

'We're polar opposites, you and I,' Harry replied.

'No. We're not. You try and clean the streets up from one end and me the other. This is about change, Harry, about Bradford and the streets. You've spent all this time running through them without ever realizing what the end game is.'

'I need to see about my wife. You put her in danger. God help you if—'

'No. Don't you put that shit on me. You had enough

warnings today to back the fuck off. You had the one thing in your possession which could have stopped this a long time ago but instead you chose to do shit your way. Like always.' Ronnie stepped closer to Harry, aggressively. 'It's about time *you* took some responsibility for your actions.'

His breath was warm on Harry's face and the brothers were eye to eye.

'I judged the man who dared lay a finger on you, brother,' Ronnie whispered. He cocked his head to one side. 'You know the wars me and him have been through? How many times he had my back?' Ronnie looked painfully at Reed. 'I judged him. In an instant. Because he crossed a line. I'd hate for you to do the same thing.'

'A threat? Really?' Harry asked. '*Now* you want to threaten me? If I'm not mistaken, I just saved *your* life.'

'Then we're even. There's no debts here any more. When I took the fall for what you did all those years ago? This? Here? Is the slate wiped clean.' Ronnie stepped away. Took a few deep breaths.

'Which slate are you looking at? There are still three dead bodies in this room.'

'I'll take care of that. You need to go.'

'How are you going to clean this up?'

'Those aren't details you need to concern yourself with.'

Harry nodded sarcastically. 'Bradford's own Al Capone, huh?'

They moved away from each other, Harry to the

door while Ronnie remained in the middle of the room.

'Harry?'

Harry stopped.

'You know I would never have put you or Saima in the middle of this, right? Tell me you believe that.'

'I do.' Harry didn't turn around but pointed towards Reed's body. 'I do.'

'One last thing.'

'Go on.'

'Something to think about, some other time . . . Jesus, Harry, would you just look at me?'

'No.'

'The case against you – with Pardeep. It'll be dropped – you're in the clear.'

'How?'

'He had a change of heart.'

Harry visualized Ronnie's influence.

'Once you're ready to work again, I want you to work with me. Take Reed's place.'

'I'm leaving. You're full of shit.'

'Hey!' Ronnie snapped. 'Just give me another minute, Harry. You owe me at least that much.'

'You have thirty seconds.'

'Tomorrow this city will be put back two decades. But the rebuilding will start. We can change Bradford together. You clean the streets from the top and me from the bottom. We can be a force in this city, Harry. I do far more good than you realize. Give me the chance to show you. That's all I'm asking. Tell me that when the dust settles you'll hear me out? There is more to this than you realize. A lot more.'

'You finished?'

'Yes.'

'One thing. Before I leave.'

'What?'

Harry pointed at Lucas's body. 'There's a church, top of Leeds Road. St Peter's. Speak to Sister Clarke. Give Lucas the rites he deserves.'

Ronnie didn't reply.

'I'm not leaving till you give me your word.'

'OK. I'll make it happen.'

'Kasam?'

'Kasam.'

Harry walked out and slammed the door.

FORTY-EIGHT

HARRY HURRIED DOWN TOLLER until he got to Duck-worth Lane. Police cars and ambulances were still hurtling to and from the hospital. The wound in his shoulder had stopped bleeding, but the pain was intensifying.

The drama unfolding in Bradford was obscene. Fumes strangled the air and a crescendo of sirens was constantly echoing. The shops on Duckworth Lane were closed and gangs of youths continued to run through the streets.

Harry arrived at Bradford Royal Infirmary and hurried past the police vans parked outside A & E. Ambulances were arriving in their threes and fours.

Approaching the entrance, Harry was stopped by uniformed officers dressed in riot gear. He struggled with his back pocket and removed his ID.

An officer looked at his wounds and asked if he was OK. Harry told him he'd been caught up in the rioting and pushed past into A & E reception.

The main desk was inundated with people clamouring to get information. There was also a hastily organized triage area where new arrivals were being assessed.

Harry hurried to the end of the corridor. This was Saima's department; she had only finished work a fortnight before, working almost to her due date. He pushed past several injured patients, some with bandages around their heads, others with blood-splattered clothes.

He made it to the staff room and tried to hammer on the door. But the first time he hit it, pain pulsed through his shoulder. Harry kicked the door, shaking it from its hinges, but there was no answer. Everyone was on the shop floor.

Harry headed towards the minor injuries department, clutching his shoulder. He saw one of the consultants Saima worked with. He was dressed casually and the only thing which revealed his position was the name badge hanging around his neck. He'd obviously been called into the crisis at short notice. 'Hey! Chris!'

Chris looked towards Harry and gasped at his blood-stained clothing. 'Harry?'

'Saima? Is she here?'

Chris hurried towards Harry and chaperoned him away from the nursing station. 'Harry, what the hell happened to you?' he asked, noting the wound in his shoulder.

'Nothing,' said Harry, 'just a few scratches from the rioting. Saima, is she here?'

'Yes.'

Harry grabbed hold of Chris, digging his fingers into his arms. 'Thank Christ.'

Chris removed Harry's hands and led him back towards the staff room.

'Where is she? Is she OK?' Harry was silently running through every prayer he could remember.

They entered the staff room and Chris closed the door. 'Harry, what happened tonight?'

'Never mind that. Saima, is she OK?'

Chris's expression changed. He nodded at first and then told Harry to sit down.

'Chris, don't treat me like an idiot. I want clean, fast answers. Is my wife all right? The baby?'

'She was brought here about an hour ago. She . . . was in a bad way, Harry. We're not sure what happened, whether she fell or was assaulted but she'd suffered some internal bleeding.'

'Where is she? I need to see her.'

'She was in labour, Harry, and I mean well on the way. But she wasn't conscious so we had to arrange an emergency C-section.'

'Where?'

'Fifth floor.'

Harry moved past him.

'No, wait—'

But Harry had already opened the door and was running towards the lift.

'Harry? Harry?' Chris shouted but it was no use.

* * *

The lift was out of order so Harry took the stairs. By the time he made it to the fifth floor, he was starting to feel faint and black dots were flickering across his eyes.

He paused and leaned against the handrail. The world was shifting, walls moving from side to side.

Harry made it to the maternity ward and pressed the buzzer. A female voice asked who he was and then released the electronic door.

Harry was slow getting to the counter, each step increasingly difficult. The ward felt intensely stuffy and the lights were dimmed. Another bout of dizziness swept through his head.

'Saima Virdee.' Harry put his bloody hands on the counter and struggled to calm his breathing. 'My wife?'

The nurse was shocked at his appearance and asked him for ID.

Harry handed it over and asked about Saima again.

'This way,' she said and asked him if he was all right.

Harry nodded and followed her, struggling to keep up. She led him to a family room, telling him a doctor would be with him shortly.

'Is she all right?' Harry snapped. 'Tell me that much at least.'

'I've only just come on shift, Mr Virdee,' she replied and left him alone.

There was a water cooler in the corner and Harry poured himself a cup. He wiped sweat from his temple, downed the water and poured some more.

'Mr Virdee?'

He turned around to see a short balding doctor in blue scrubs by the doorway.

'Doctor.' Harry hurried towards him. 'Please, just tell me what's going on. Is my wife OK?'

The doctor stepped back apprehensively as he took in Harry's appearance, but Harry dismissed his concern, urging him for details about Saima.

'She's asleep. You can't disturb her. Please, Mr Virdee, I need you to sit down.'

Harry took a seat, positioning himself on the edge so he could lean closer to the medic.

'Are you sure you are all right, Mr Virdee?' He looked pointedly at Harry's bloodstained clothing.

'Yes, yes, yes, I'm fine,' Harry snapped. 'Please—'

'My name is Mr Woollard. I'm the on-call surgeon. Your wife was admitted an hour ago. We're not sure what happened but she had suffered some trauma, either a fall or an assault.'

Harry nodded, keenly focused on the doctor's every word. 'That's what the consultant told me.'

'She was in the late stages of labour and we were forced to do a C-section.'

'I know. The baby?'

'Fine. Healthy baby boy. Seven pounds.'

'A boy? We were having a girl.'

The doctor smiled. 'Scans are never one hundred per cent accurate.'

Harry put his hands on the doctor's arms. 'A son.'

The doctor nodded and reluctantly continued. 'I'm

afraid the prognosis for your wife isn't as clear-cut, Harry.'

'What do you mean?'

'There's no easy way to say this, but I'm afraid Saima is in an induced coma at the moment and until we feel she is safe, we are going to keep her that way.'

'Coma? Why? What happened?'

'We're not sure. She was in a bad state when we found her. She had lost a lot of blood and the C-section was complicated. She became distressed in surgery and her vital signs became critical.'

'Is she going to be all right?'

'We don't know, Mr Virdee. I'm afraid that's really up to her now. Saima's survival is in her own hands.'

FORTY-NINE

IT TOOK TWO FULL days for the fires to stop burning in Bradford. The city was again under the scrutiny of the world's media and, once again, for all the wrong reasons.

An investigation was under way – how had lessons of 2001 not been learned? George Simpson had taken immediate retirement. Harry didn't blame him.

This was a mess which would take years to unravel.

There was no mention of Lucas Dwight, Colin Reed or Zain Ahmed in the papers.

Soon enough, Zain's disappearance would be probed. The other two? Harry didn't know.

Harry thought about Ronnie. About the crematorium he owned. How bodies disappeared without investigation.

Harry wondered if Sister Clarke had buried Lucas.

Would she raise the condition of his body with the media? He didn't think so. She had been protective of Lucas and one thing was for certain: Harry's last meeting with her had ensured she knew Lucas was not culpable. He had returned her car, given her money for the wing mirror and simply told her that Lucas had passed away. That his body would be returned to her, to do with as she pleased.

The destruction of Shakeel Ahmed's businesses had been seen as a hate crime.

Strangely, Martin Davis's body had been found at one of Ahmed's restaurants, cementing the theory that the BNP were behind the anarchy. Harry wondered how Ronnie had pulled that off.

Bradford's destruction was being treated as a race riot, similar to those in 1995 and 2001.

Misdirection.

The story of Ronnie Virdee's life.

Harry was at the hospital, visiting intensive care. He had received an early-morning phone call that Saima was improving.

There were twelve patients on the ward, all with bleeping monitors by their beds. The windows were sealed and the humidity was uncomfortable. The sister in charge smiled warmly and led him to Saima's side room. Harry held his son in his right arm. His left was in a sling.

Saima was hooked up to three different monitors. The tube in her mouth had been removed and she was breathing on her own. Harry had been handed a bag with Saima's belongings when he'd first visited. Now, he removed his mother's slippers from it and placed them at the foot of the bed.

Saima was all about superstitions. Maybe it was finally getting to Harry.

He sat down by the bed. The monitors continued beeping in synchrony with her breathing. Saima's face looked anaemically pale.

'Hey,' he whispered.

She didn't respond.

'You know,' he said, 'the last time we spoke, we were standing underneath the moon. I should have sacrificed that day, not you.' Her eyelids were fluttering and she looked as though she would open them at any moment.

Harry leaned across and kissed her clammy forehead. He manoeuvred their son on to the bed, placing him by Saima's body. Harry lifted her hand and rested it on their son's skin.

'Typical for us. Nothing is ever simple. We've got a gorgeous healthy little Virdee. He's got your green eyes, Saima. If you don't wake up, I'm going to name him Harrydeeppreet-Singh the twenty-fifth.'

Saima's hand moved at the touch of her baby. He let out a whimper and her hand moved a little more.

Then, after forty-eight hours of medically-induced coma, Saima Virdee opened her eyes.

Harry was in the family room while the nurses gave Saima a bed-bath. He had left their son asleep in a cot by her side. Saima hadn't been able to take her eyes off him.

She was weak and the extent of her injuries wasn't yet known. Harry had started to breathe again. He had spent two dark nights terrified that he would lose her. That his life would fracture and he would be left alone.

There was a gentle knock on the door.

'Harry?'

He didn't need to look to know who it was. Harry turned around, away from the window. His brother was standing in the doorway.

'Not allowed flowers in intensive care,' Harry said. 'Infection control.'

Ronnie stepped inside and put the bunch of yellow and white roses on the table. 'I heard she's awake?'

'Is there anywhere you don't have snitches?'

Ronnie shook his head. 'I called, Harry. Have done every day.'

'You're not welcome.'

'I know.'

Ronnie's right arm was hanging deadweight by his side. Harry pointed at it.

'Fine,' Ronnie replied. 'No lasting damage. Will take a while.'

Harry turned away. Back towards the window.

Ronnie closed the door. 'Listen—'

'You're not welcome. Didn't you hear me?'

'I've some things I need to say.'

'Want to lighten your conscience?'

'Yes.'

'Figures.'

Ronnie moved closer. 'Give me five minutes? Then I'm gone. For ever if you want.'

'Get on with it.'

Ronnie reached his side. They looked out across the city. The rioting was no more but the darkness somehow remained.

'Was it worth it?' Harry asked.

Ronnie didn't answer.

'Lucas?'

'As you requested.'

'Zain?'

'Gone.'

'Same place as Reed?'

'Similar.'

Harry sighed. 'Fucked if I know where we go from here.'

'That's why I've come.'

'Penance?'

'I prefer rehabilitation. How's . . . the kid?' Ronnie asked.

'Strong.'

'And—'

'Too early to tell. Damn you, Ronnie. Damn you for doing this.'

More silence.

Harry thought of his mother. The only reason he couldn't ruin Ronnie.

She can't lose both sons.

He thought of her face, of the heartbreak she'd endured

when Harry had left. 'What is it you want, Ronnie?'

'To know what you plan to do. Break me? Or—'

'Damned if I do. Damned if I don't.'

'You're not looking at this the right way.'

'And how should I look at it?'

'A new start. For both of us.'

'Redemption? That what you're looking for?' Harry said bitterly.

'Yes. It is.'

'Say what you've come here to say. You're dancing around it and it's pissing me off.'

Ronnie pointed down towards the city. 'It's broken. This place.'

'It was starting to rise up again. Until you fucked it over.'

'I'm going to be blunt. Then it's up to you.'

Harry turned to face him.

Ronnie looked the same. Even smelled the same. But it was all a façade.

'I want you to work with me.'

Harry scowled. 'You keep saying that, but a partnership? Really?'

'Yes. Really. There will always be some criminal you're chasing in this city. Drugs have always been in Bradford. Always will be. You remove me and what do you get? Another arsehole to replace me. Crime is eternal. It will always be here. So play the game smarter, Harry.'

'Sounds like your idea of paradise. Getting me to turn.'

Ronnie sniggered. 'I don't need to "get you" to turn. It's already there. Within you. That rage. That anger. That need to hand out justice. Your way. The street way.'

Harry looked back out of the window. Across Bradford.

'Crime isn't about right and wrong. It's a business. And I can hand you this city. My network has a stranglehold. We're everywhere and – at the same time – we are nowhere. Ghosts in the night. Myths you can't authenticate.'

'I can,' Harry said. 'I could burn you right now.'

'But you won't. Because of Mum. Because of what we've done.'

Murder.

Deceit.

'You obsess about your karma,' Ronnie continued. 'About shit coming back to bite you on the arse.'

'We all do. Even you.'

'Agreed. Which is why you leave the drugs to me. And in return, I'll hand you every scumbag you can handle. On the books? Off them? Up to you.'

'Who do you think I am?'

'I know who you want to be. Play the game. I can give you fuckers you don't even know exist. You can't clean a city from behind a desk. You've got to get into the sewers. We are uniquely placed to change Bradford. This time – the right way. No Shakeel Ahmed. No distractions. Let's build an empire. Let's become—'

'Gods.'

Ronnie nodded. 'Give that kid of yours everything you want. Keep your job – hell, go for your boss's. Every Gotham needs a Dark Knight.'

'You finished?'

'Yes.'

'You can leave.'

'Promise me you'll think it over.' Ronnie paused a beat. And then turned and left.

Harry remained impassive. He was looking at the darkening clouds in the sky.

Gotham City, once again reduced to nothing but broken dreams.

If he refused to join Ronnie, then there would only be one outcome. Sooner or later they were destined to collide. A fight that would ruin them both.

Or Harry could entertain his brother: try to control the monster. Curtail the virus.

But whichever decision he made, one thing was certain: Harry Virdee's future was forever intertwined with Ronnie.

Alone or together, the battle for Bradford had begun.

ACKNOWLEDGEMENTS

Thank you to my friend Vinod Lalji – for always believing in my writing and sharing in monumental plotting sessions. You never let me quit (many times) and I am so grateful. You remain the most twisted co-creator of plots I've had the pleasure of working with.

To my agent, Simon Trewin, the 'game-changer', and the amazing team at WME for their awesomeness.

My editor at Transworld, Bill Scott-Kerr, for his passion, vision and good old Yorkshire charm, and the extraordinary team at Transworld.

'The Crimeandpublishment family': to Graham Smith and Michael Malone for rescuing a manuscript and ultimately opening so many doors; to my incredible editor Morgen Bailey for polishing a rough draft of *Streets of Darkness* and making it shine; to the formidable writing team who are 'Crimeandpublishment', for inspiring, assisting and making difficult writing weeks more bearable.

A. A. Dhand

To my staff at the pharmacy for putting up with me whenever I was writing/plotting/editing/procrastinating/moody/elated/subdued, etc., etc., etc.

To my parents, for demonstrating what hard work and single-mindedness can achieve. You arrived in this country in 'negative equity' yet proved dreams could be realized. Never easily, never without grafting, *never without believing*.

To my sister – quite simply for bringing the sunshine whenever I brought the rain.

Finally, thank you to my wife. For daring to fail with me. This is in many ways a joint effort. We *are* 'team A. A. Dhand' and without your patience, inspiration, constructive criticism and encouragement we would not have arrived here.

Ten years ago you told me we would win.

You were right.

Keep being right.

Keep doing what you do – it makes me do what I do.

Turn the page to read
the opening pages of

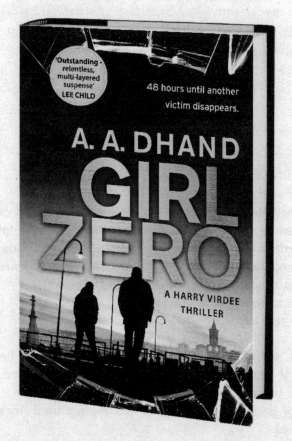

The next DI Harry Virdee book

COMING SOON

PROLOGUE

THORNY BRAMBLES TORE AT the little girl's face as she ran desperately away.

She wiped blood from her temple and sprinted faster, shredding the skin from her bare feet on bristly under-growth on the forest floor. The ground was solid, baked by an overwhelming heat that swirled around her face and felt like it might burn her skin right off her bones. She had never experienced anything like it.

Where am I?

Where's Mum? I was with her yesterday?

He was gaining on her, this man who'd told her he owned her. She could hear twigs snapping behind, her name being called; a deceiving concern to the voice.

She cried out, shrieking for her mother until her voice cracked.

There must be someone who can hear?

She wasn't certain there was.

The smells were different here: exhaust fumes, manure and sweat.

The van had finally stopped and when the back doors

had been flung open, she had taken her chance, surprising them; lashing out and breaking free.

Her pursuer was relentless. She had glimpsed sight of him as she'd fled. Heavy-set, balding and tanned with gleaming golden rings on his left hand.

She burst out of the forest, the darkness disappearing, and was confronted by a sight which snatched any morsel of hope.

Open fields.

Stretching far into the distance; green, brown and yellow. Nowhere to hide.

The realization hit her like the heat had.

It was over. No escape. *Oh God, he's close.*

She had learned how to fight on the toughest estate in Bradford and turned aggressively, determined not to be taken, but before she'd locked eyes with her captor her legs were kicked from underneath. A sack was thrown over her tiny body, overwhelming her with the familiar smell of potatoes, rough fibres scratching her skin.

She hit out at him, screaming wildly, but was easily dragged back into the forest and thrown on the ground.

She felt him straddle her, knees digging into her sides, his bulk pinning her to the abrasive forest floor until jagged splinters pierced her skin, drawing blood.

Strong hands seized her neck through the sacking.

A sudden sharp scratch in her arm and it all came flooding back; she had felt this before.

A blackness invaded her vision and the world began to spin as the sound of her attacker panting became fainter, his words, in a language she didn't understand, floated away.

The grip around her neck relaxed, the coarse sensation

of the sack across her face faded and a sudden warmth enveloped her tiny body.

A nightmare.

That was all.

She opened her eyes, her head heavy and spinning.

The darkness was absolute, the atmosphere thick, the air rancid and damp. She called out, her voice echoed alien and frightened.

Not a nightmare.

She moved to stand but it made her feel more vulnerable, like she might somehow be seen, so she cowered, huddling her arms around her knees even though it was far from cold.

The heat was unbearable; sweat bleeding into her clothes.

She tried to scan the room – to make anything out in the dark. There was nothing, escape seemed impossible.

The dark had always terrorized her, at night her mother had left a bedroom lamp on so she wouldn't be afraid.

Where am I?

A pernicious, crippling fear was making her breathless.

I'm going to die here.

She clamped her eyes shut and imagined she was at home, in the darkness under the cupboard below the staircase where her mother sometimes sent her when she was bad.

She started to cry – slowly at first, before hysterical sobs took over.

Then, everything changed.

A voice to her left. Young, like hers.

'Don't worry,' it whispered, 'you're not alone.'

ONE

Eleven Years Later

ANOTHER MURDER IN BRADFORD.

Another.

Detective Inspector Harry Virdee had taken the call an hour before.

Damn city was killing itself; killing him.

Why today?

Bad karma. No, the worst karma. Like disturbing a minute's silence for the dead.

Shit, he was getting more and more superstitious every day. He knew this would happen when he married Saima.

What's next, Harry, avoiding walking under ladders, fearing the number thirteen?

Bradford didn't appear to care for karma, Harry's or its own.

Gotham. That's *still* what the papers were calling it, a year on from the original article. It hadn't helped that it had gone viral.

Pissed Harry right off.

He checked the time on the dashboard.

03:50.

He had left home shortly after receiving the call, but

wasn't at the murder scene. Instead he was parked outside a house four miles away in Ravenscliffe; one of the most deprived areas of the city. Residents here were a third more likely to receive government benefits and crime was out of control. Harry's team were regulars around here.

The occupants of number 19 Belle Avenue, the Kings, had never been interested in benefits. Not until they'd had no choice.

Barry King had been a postman. His wife, Sheila, a dinner lady and they had both been signed off work. First Sheila. Then a few years later, Barry.

It was depression – after losing their only son, Michael, nineteen at the time, who had attempted to rob Harry's father's corner shop. The robbery had gone badly.

Wild arterial spray.

Michael's eyes, horrified at first, then fading until they were lifeless.

Harry had defended his mother and stabbed a pair of scissors into Michael's throat. Worse still, he had gotten away with it and the guilt continued to suffocate him. One way or another it needed dealing with, and he knew it started with the short journey up the footpath, through a rusted gate, past a dishevelled garden to a green door.

To tell Mr and Mrs King what? That he was sorry?

For which part?

That their son had joined a bad crowd?

Or that he had allowed someone else to take the blame for a murder he had committed?

Harry switched off the engine of his ageing BMW and removed the keys, his eyes lingered on the keyring his wife had given him, a picture of his one year old son, Aaron. He smiled at the image, then at two unopened presents on the passenger seat.

Today was Diwali, the Indian new year where gifts were exchanged and candles lit as a reminder that light would always overcome dark. Harry was no longer a practising Sikh but he entertained the tradition as his wife was determined to fuse their different backgrounds, as much for their son as to prove their families wrong about their marriage.

Harry glanced at the house.

You put the lights out in there forever.

What if Aaron got caught up with a bad crowd? Made a rash decision to rob a convenience store – and it cost him his life?

Is that fair? Is that reasonable?

'Fuck,' he whispered and ran his hand over his face, scratching at thick stubble. 'Argh,' he said and clamped his eyes shut. 'Why do you keep doing this? Let it go. Let it fucking go.'

It was no coincidence Harry had ended up working in HMET, the Homicide Major Enquiry Team, in Bradford.

Trying to correct his karma.

His colleagues thought he was just obsessive. They didn't know.

Only one person knew the truth; his brother Ronnie who had taken the blame and gone to prison – a decision which had shaped the rest of his life. Two decades on, Ronnie Virdee was the most powerful criminal in Bradford.

He focused back on the front door.

Not today. Maybe tomorrow?

Diwali; new beginnings.

New choices.

Harry started the car and pulled away from the house, stealing a final look at the drawn curtains, and headed towards the murder scene.

*

Wapping School had been built in 1877, right on the fringes of the city centre.

And like much of the city, the school had decayed and was now a ruin.

Harry parked beside two patrol cars and got out. He glanced towards the night sky, black like the soot soiling the once-impressive Victorian building.

A dead body in a place once lauded for protecting its young. Such esteemed history. Such dramatic collapse.

Harry opened the trunk and pushed aside a fifty-shot firework. Bonfire night was two days' away but he'd planned to surprise his wife and light the mammoth firecracker tonight; a celebration of their first Diwali with Aaron.

He slipped on a raincoat, grabbed his SOCO suit and a torch. Beside them was a large black holdall. Inside; a bulletproof vest, an illegal stun-gun and a second iPhone, all from Harry's brother and permanent reminders that he was walking a glass tightrope, one apt to break at any moment.

You get him to stop or bring him down – there is no other choice.

Harry closed the boot and leaned against the car. He saw the outline of a uniformed officer coming his way. A patrol bobby – first responder.

'Morning Detective Inspector.'

Harry acknowledged him with a nod and got the headlines. DS Gemma Eccles was inside. She'd been the one to call him in.

He walked behind the PC, shining his torch onto a building in woeful condition, large metal fencing around its perimeter, breached in many places. The school had been derelict for years. Like so many heritage sites in Bradford, it had fallen into disarray and simply been left to rot.

Harry focused on a white plaque by the entrance.

'Wapping First School'.

A vandal had spray-painted a red line through it, instead scrawling, 'Pakis First School.'

Harry stepped through a gaping hole where the entrance had once been, into a graveyard of broken dreams. The roof was missing, moonlight shining into the room, high-lighting dark, unsettling graffiti across the walls of a veiled Islamic woman crying whilst fascists surrounded her cowering body. The school might once have been a refuge for the vulnerable, now, however, the place was infected by a familiar misery.

The men walked carefully across a floor missing wooden beams, past old needles, used condoms and pornographic magazines. There were dead rats and the carcass of what appeared to be a cat. Dust swirled, forcing the taste of abandonment down the men's throats.

With deep unease, Harry arrived at the far end of the building, at a disused swimming pool, now simply a pit in the ground, twenty metres by ten, one end full of rubble from a partially collapsed ceiling.

In the centre, laying awkwardly across the bottom, was a body.

A murder case on the morning of Diwali.

Harry was briefed by his DS, listening loosely as the ghoulish aura of the room continued to creep into his mind. An anonymous tip had called the body in but hadn't stuck around. Harry moved away and lowered himself carefully into the pit while Eccles finished her speech.

He walked over, shining his torch on the floor, placing his steps carefully.

Harry had been involuntarily holding his breath and let

it out now slowly, watching it form a white mist in the chill as he squatted low beside the body.

He glanced once again around the room before his eyes settled on her and made a familiar silent promise.

I'll find out who did this.

For you.

And for me, to balance my karma.

Harry focused on the victim; Asian female, five-six, petite, maybe size eight with long black hair, chaotically strewn across her face.

She was on her back with a large kitchen knife crudely sticking out of her chest.

Harry reached forward and shone his torch directly on the body.

Deep red stains on her white top.

A gold bangle on her left wrist; a Kara; a religious symbol of Sikhism.

Still there. Not stolen.

Harry had worn one for many years before he'd opted out of religion.

He crouched beside the body, pulling a pen from his jacket pocket and used it to carefully move the girl's hair aside.

The blood drained from Harry's face and he felt unstable, like the pool had suddenly begun to fill with water.

He knew that face.

A pain detonated hot and deep in his chest. He looked away, releasing a wounded, harrowing cry. The victim was Harry's niece; daughter of the city's most dangerous man.

Bradford had been in perilous situations before but none would compare to the storm about to hit the city. Bradford was about to feel the wrath from two brothers.

One who enforced the rules.

The other who made his own.